MU01064415

Published by Scrivenings Press LLC
15 Lucky Lane
Morrilton, Arkansas 72110
https://ScriveningsPress.com

Printed in the United States of America

Paperback ISBN 978-1-64917-238-9

eBook ISBN 978-1-64917-239-6

Editors: Shannon Taylor Vannatter, Susan Page Davis, and Linda Fulkerson

Cover design by Linda Fulkerson - www.bookmarketinggraphics.com

~ A NOVELLA COLLECTION ~

IN ANY SEASON

REGINA RUDD MERRICK
AMY R. ANGUISH
SARAH ANNE CROUCH
HEATHER GREER

Scrivenings
PRESS
Quench your thirst for story.
www.ScriveningsPress.com

Spring Has Sprung

Regina Rudd Merrick

To my little sister, Andrea Rudd Peak, born seven years and ten days after my spring birthday. For this child I prayed with all the fervor of a first grader!

Acknowledgments

Special thanks to Linda at Scrivenings Press for the opportunity to collaborate on this novella collection, and to Amy, Heather, and Sarah for the wonderful time I've had running things by you, comparing notes, and just having fun together.

Thanks be to God for giving me a wonderful family and friends, and for their prayers as I go through what has been the craziest year of my life!

Jesus said to him, "No one who puts his hand to the plow and looks back is fit for the kingdom of God."
—Luke 9:62 CSB

"Spring has sprung, the grass is riz,
Wonder where the flowers is?
They are nowhere to be found,
'Cause they're underground."
—Unknown

Chapter One

"Spring is the time of plans and projects"
—Leo Tolstoy

Late January

T he meeting room door stood in front of her—large, in charge, and ominous.

Dread, not in the form of butterflies, but large, wild moths in the pit of Maia's stomach elevated into downright cold sweats and shallow breathing.

From experience, she knew the enthusiasm of the Chamber of Commerce's Daffodil Festival committee would be enough to make her sick.

Maia Pascal, focus ...

She stretched her spine and cracked her neck, preparing for the fight of her life. Most people saw the season as a time to celebrate new beginnings, new life, but Maia had the misfortune to live in Spring, Kentucky. Yes, her town celebrated all things spring. The Daffodil Festival gave everyone *carte blanche* to go over the top, and it drove her crazy. Pushing the door open, enthusiastic spring-lovers bombarded her before she could greet them.

"Mia …"

"It's Maia—like the Mayan temples in Mexico, but without the *n*." Why couldn't this woman, who was particular about everything else, pronounce Maia's name correctly? She'd literally known her all her life.

"I'm sorry. I don't know why I have a problem with that." Mrs. Cotton, the county homemakers' president, exuded excitement as she handed everyone a sheet of paper with a long and varied list of entertainment, games, food vendors, ideas for décor, and much, much more. "Anyway, after we spoke the other day, I made a list of activities we've done in the past."

As the county's most-organized person, why wasn't Mrs. Cotton in charge?

Because Mrs. Cotton isn't a city employee. That's why. Unfortunately, Maia's position as Assistant City Manager was to make this the biggest, best Daffodil Festival in the books. She'd have to suck it up and put on a happy face, even though, for her, all she could think about on the first pleasant day of the season were headaches, runny noses, bad hair days, and never knowing what to wear.

Why? Because springtime in Kentucky means thirty degrees in the morning and seventy by lunchtime.

She raised an eyebrow. "Good morning, everyone. It looks like the Daffodil Festival is well on its way." Glancing toward Mrs. Cotton, she voiced her query. "One of these days, I suggest you be in charge of the festival."

The older lady turned red, and waved her hands, flustered. "Oh, no. I work much better in an advisory capacity." She laughed nervously. "I'm just here to make sure every festival is better than the last, and that our love for all things spring is upheld."

Is something wrong with me, inherently, that I dislike this season so much?

Her naturally curly hair staged a rebellion when the weather warmed up and rained.

It happened. Every year of her life that she remembered.

People in Arizona or California didn't know how good they had it. Kentucky, on the other hand? Louisville ranked in the top five worst cities for seasonal allergies in the United States.

She'd looked it up. It was Internet-official.

The room had gone silent after Mrs. Cotton's comment, waiting for Maia.

"Thank you." Maia came to herself. She schooled her expression, but she worried it didn't quite reach her eyes. Glancing across the table at her best friend, Jasmine Carter, who she may or may not have placed on the committee to keep herself on an even keel, Maia inwardly cringed at the smirk on her friend's face. Having Jasmine on the committee meant nothing to anyone else at the table, but for Maia, Jasmine represented sanity in a crazy world.

Claudia Clay, on the other hand, looked utterly bored. At least that would be the first impression of her. Always.

Why was Maia here again? Oh yeah. She worked here. The co-op program had provided their office with a mixed bag of enthusiasm each year. Was it just last year that high school senior Brenden Behr volunteered to man the dunking booth, even in forty-degree weather? *I wonder if he still has that cough?*

"Could I just say, as a newcomer in town, how happy I am to be able to help with the festival?" Doctor Owen Roswell, hired at Spring Community Hospital late last summer, broke the silence.

With that last name, she so wanted to ask him if he'd seen any aliens lately, but she held back.

Cute in an eager-beaver sort of way, the well-cultivated ginger five-o'clock shadow gave Owen Roswell a slight *bad boy* vibe that was totally trashed as soon as he smiled or opened his mouth. She'd noticed him on the platform at church, playing drums or guitar with the praise band. He was a versatile musician. One of those *hand-lifters*. As a non-hand-raiser, it always made her feel not quite holy enough. But that was her problem, not his.

Yeah, that was Dr. Owen Roswell.

Insecure much, Maia?

Who was she to question the validity of his outward expression of worship? Who knew? Perhaps working on this project together would allow her to get to know him better. He wasn't too obnoxious. His eyes were nice. Kind of a draw-you-in color of blue, which made no sense. But it did. And he was cute if a little over-enthusiastic.

"Good to have you, Dr. Roswell."

"Please. Call me Owen."

"And you may call me Maia."

"Ah, the Roman goddess of spring." The brilliant smile he turned her way threatened to blind her this early in the morning.

She bit her lip, trying to hold back the sarcastic laugh that wanted to burst forth. "Unfortunately, yes." Maia glanced at him with a slight grin, then surveyed the committee. "I think we've got a good start on the festival. Mrs. Cotton, as usual, you're in charge of the food vendors. Mr. Simmons, traffic. Jasmine and Claudia, games." Maybe hanging around with Jasmine would improve Claudia's outlook.

She looked around. One person left, two positions to fill. "I need someone to be my assistant and someone to contact and hire an amusement ride company. Bounce-n-More?"

Curt Simmons, a local insurance agent wearing a polo sporting the company logo embroidered on the front, crossed his arms across his chest, nodding. "I'll be glad to manage that one in addition to parking. I've been contacted by a new carnival company up in Indiana, as well as Bounce-n-More, so I'll check out both places. I'd need to see if the equipment is up to liability standards, anyway."

Exactly who she wanted for that job. She nodded as she printed his name on her list. "Great. And that leaves ..." Maia looked up to see Owen Roswell beaming. "Dr. Roswell for my assistant." Her voice, and her smile, faltered in the face of his exuberance.

He tilted his head and quirked up one side of his mouth. "Ah. Call me Owen."

For some weird reason, his expression reached in and tugged at something inside her, but she slapped it away like an early mosquito, figuratively speaking. No matter what Jasmine said, the Daffodil Festival would not turn into a city-government version of speed-dating.

NOT ONLY HAD Owen secured a position on the Daffodil Festival planning committee, but he'd also agreed to be assistant to the chair. What a fantastic way to get to know people in the small town he'd adopted six months ago.

The January day promised to be brisk, but sunny. He walked out into the sunshine, glad he had his jacket with him today.

Perfect. Born and raised in Phoenix, Arizona, Owen understood summer well, but he hadn't experienced a true four-season climate until he attended medical school at the University of Kentucky in Lexington. He was hooked.

He closed his eyes and took a deep breath. Even in January, there were warm days sprinkled in that made the grass a little greener and fooled the trees and flowers into budding before the next cold snap. Those were the days that brought out that slightly damp, winter-turning-to-spring aroma present this time of year in Kentucky. It was what brought him back after he finished med school.

When the board of the Spring Community Hospital approached him at a job fair as he finished up his residency, it was just too good to be true. A chance to live in a town that lived and breathed all things spring. The small flags hanging from the decorative streetlights and fluttering in the breeze had the town logo on them—a bouquet of Daffodils. It didn't matter what time of year. Here, it was always *spring*.

On the way to his car, he smiled and greeted people on the sidewalk. In this first meeting, he'd watched as Maia Pascal organized the committee, and he wondered at a note of irritation. A difficult day in city government? No, it seemed like more. He also noticed she always kept a tissue handy. Allergies? Probably. Western Kentucky was known for being the allergy capital of the U.S.

"Dr. Roswell?"

Owen turned to see Maia walking briskly toward him, holding out a folder. "You forgot this."

"Thanks. Sorry about that." He smiled as he took it. "I don't know where my head was."

She scoffed. "Mine is one big ache this time of year in anticipation of allergy season, so I don't even pretend to know what I'm doing half the time."

"I wouldn't say that. I thought you ran the meeting well." He grinned. "I take it this isn't your favorite season?"

"Uh, no. Maybe because this town is spring on steroids?" She snorted quietly.

Owen laughed out loud. "I know what you mean, but I suppose it would be wrong to have a fall festival in Spring, Kentucky."

"Possibly."

He shrugged. "Fortunately for me, I love this time of year. Especially now. Never had it growing up, so it's all new to me. In the southwest, we have fall and summer. Mostly summer." He smiled gently. "And please, call me Owen. Who knows? Maybe we'll become friends?"

Her face held a skeptical, but open, expression. "Maybe we will." Maia glanced at her phone. "Gotta go. See you soon." She fluttered her fingers in a wave and was gone.

She was tall and reasonably attractive. No. Scratch that, calling Maia *reasonably attractive* was ridiculous. Her dark hair and eyes were as beautiful as was the rest of her. But that frown line between her eyebrows? That needed to go.

By the time the festival was over, he predicted that not only would he and Maia be friends, but she would love spring as much as he did.

Owen had been looking for a hobby. This could be it.

Chapter Two

"You can cut all the flowers, but you cannot keep spring from coming." —Pablo Neruda

Maia opened the front door of the café and breathed in the familiar smells of comfort food. Jasmine waved and then patted the space next to her on the scarred wooden bench in the café's foyer.

"I hope the waffle iron is still hot." Jasmine spoke quietly, biting her lip.

"Isn't it getting a little late for waffles?" Maia glanced at the clock. Eleven-thirty in the morning. After the committee meeting, Jasmine had to leave in a hurry for a hair-dye appointment, but she made Maia promise they'd have lunch together so they could rehash the meeting.

Jasmine had a look of utter seriousness on her face. "Maia, bite your tongue." She shook her head. "Breakfast is not only the most important meal of the day, but you can eat it any time you want to. You wouldn't want roast beef and mashed potatoes for breakfast, but waffles for lunch?" She nodded and leaned back against the faux 1970s wood paneling behind the bench, satisfaction on her face. "Oh, yeah."

"Y'all ready to be seated?" The server, middle-aged and bleached-blond Connie Evans, pointed to a table for two against the far wall. "I'll be with you girls in a minute."

"Thanks, Connie." Jasmine sat down and leaned toward Maia on her elbows. "So ..."

"So, what?"

Jasmine glanced around and lowered her voice. "What did you think about Dr. Roswell?" She quirked a brow at her friend. "Pretty cute, don't you think?"

Shrugging, Maia feigned disinterest. "If you like over-the-top enthusiasm." Maia, unsmiling, crossed her arms in a classic defensive move and leaned back in her chair, shaking her head. "I mean, I get it. He's glad to be here."

The laugh that burst from Jasmine made her clap her hand over her mouth when the diners looked their way. When they saw where the explosion came from, they smiled and resumed eating. She took a deep breath and shook her head in irritation. "Oh, Maia."

Maia slumped a little. "I just wish we celebrated something besides general-all-purpose spring, ya know?"

"That's the allergies talking."

"Anticipated allergies. Pre-allergies? Probably. That, and I've never been great at delegating."

"Don't I know it? Remember senior prom?" Jasmine huffed.

"How could I forget? You bring it up every time you have the opportunity." Maia twisted her lips and hoped her face wasn't turning all shades of red.

"And why do I do that?" Jasmine sat up straight in her chair.

Maia sighed. "Because I don't tend to play well with others."

"Exactly."

"If you recall, prom is yet another event that happens in spring."

"Are you building a case for eliminating an entire season?"

"Do you think I could?" Maia raised her eyebrows, considering.

Connie brought them each a glass of ice water and a menu. "Can I get you girls anything else to drink before I take your order?"

"I'm good with water." Maia glanced over the menu that hadn't changed in her twenty-nine years, she figured, except for the addition of exotic foods like avocado and kale to appease the health nuts in town. "I'll have a chef's salad."

"Ranch dressing?" Connie's pen poised on her order pad as she peered over her reading glasses.

"I think I'll live a little and go with French." Maia gave Jasmine a dirty look.

"Is the waffle iron still hot?" Jasmine asked softly.

Very few people within earshot agreed with Jasmine's obsession with waffles and all things breakfast.

"As soon as Juanita saw you, she plugged it back in."

Hand to her heart, Jasmine's mouth hung open. "That's just about the sweetest thing anyone's ever done for me."

Connie laughed. "Want anything with those waffles?"

"A cup of coffee, because, what else can you drink with waffles? Oh, and a side of bacon." She handed her menu to Connie. "And tell Juanita I appreciate it."

"Will do. Extra Maple syrup?"

Jasmine sighed. "You read my mind."

The server chuckled, then bustled away, and Maia took a long drink of her ice water.

"The sweetest thing anyone has ever done for you?

Seriously?" Maia shook her head in disgust. "I'm thinking you should go after Mr. Positive."

Jasmine held up one finger. "Ah, that's Doctor Positive, to you."

"Fine." Maia sighed.

Jasmine smoothed her napkin in her lap in anticipation of her breakfast/lunch. "You need to get over this negative attitude you have against a season, of all things." She pursed her lips as she made her point. "I mean it. Nobody's going to ask out a Negative Nellie."

Maia laughed. "What are you, eighty?"

"You know what I mean, and don't try to change the subject. Some perfectly nice guys have tried to ask you out, and you scare them off."

"I know." Maia slumped and leaned her elbow on the table, chin in hand. "I went out with one of them if you recall."

Jasmine sent a compassionate look her way. "I know, but you've got to ..."

"Get over it?" Maia snorted gently. "Eventually. But spring is its own problem. It's just so ..."

"Happy? Exciting? Easter-y?"

"I don't think that's a word."

"Probably not, but you must like Easter. It's like the main holiday of Christendom. Right up there with Christmas."

"Yeah. Christmas, where you get to sit inside and stay warm, there's no pollen to speak of, and it snows." Maia sighed. "Can't help it. Why couldn't my family have helped found a Scandinavian-themed town called 'Winter'?"

Connie brought out her salad and Jasmine's waffles and a steaming pot of coffee. "Can I bring you a cup, too, Maia?"

"That would be good. Anything to help this headache." She smiled up at Connie. "Thanks."

"No problem." She winked at her and put a thick coffee

mug on the red-speckled Formica table. "I had a feeling, so I came prepared."

"You're the best. I wish you were on the Daffodil Festival committee."

"Not me. It's our busiest day of the year, and the best tippers come out." Connie laughed. "Can I get y'all anything else?"

"We're good." Jasmine had her butter spread and her syrup poured. When Connie walked away, she spoke up. "Can we bless this already? I'm starving."

They both bowed their heads and Jasmine reeled off a quick prayer. "Thank you, God, for the food, and Maia, and this amazing café. Amen."

They ate in silence for a few moments, and then Jasmine spoke up. "You know you could go to an allergist and nip the allergies in the bud— no pun intended—before they start."

"Pun accepted and perfectly placed." Maia pointed at her with her fork. "I've thought about it. I guess I don't want to know how bad it is. Plus, they stick you with all kinds of things to test you." She shivered a little, just thinking about the needles involved. "You know how I feel about needles."

"It might be worth it."

"We'll see." She hoped Jasmine would leave it alone. She'd lived this long babying and medicating herself through the season. Why should this year be any different?

OWEN LOVED COMING DOWNTOWN. The buildings on the square surrounding the one-hundred-year-old courthouse were a mishmash of old, new, and badly restored, but as he saw last year when he came for his interview, in summer flowers were everywhere.

Similarly, in winter the Christmas decorations could rival a big city, and fall had the pumpkin farmers selling their wares on the vacant lot between the bank and an accountant's office. Plus corn stalks and chrysanthemums brightened every place not sporting a gloriously hued Maple tree.

But spring. This is what he was waiting for. When he'd seen that the city logo was a bunch of Daffodils, he had a feeling they would do it up right for this time of year.

After parking his Jeep down the one-way street adjacent to the café, he got out and rounded the corner, almost wiping out Maia Pascal and Jasmine Carter. "Whoa, ladies. Sorry about that." He'd seen the unspoken understanding between Maia and Jasmine at the meeting. So they were friends.

Jasmine burst out laughing. "No worries, Dr. Roswell."

"Call me Owen, please." He smiled, casting furtive glances at Maia, who hadn't said anything. He got a distinct impression that she didn't like him, and he couldn't for the life of him figure out why. "What do you recommend here?"

"Waffles," Jasmine spoke immediately.

Maia shook her head. "She's an indefatigable breakfast junky."

"Don't listen to her." Jasmine put her hands on her hips and tilted her head. "What is your stand on breakfast food?"

What does one say to this? "I'm ... for it?"

As he struggled to give an answer that would keep him in the good graces of both young ladies, his friend and associate pastor, Nathan Comer, walked up, smiling. Saved by the preacher.

"Hey, Nate."

"Hey. How are you ladies today?" The tall, thin man chuckled. "Did I interrupt something?"

Owen noticed Nate's gaze followed Jasmine. Interesting. Jasmine was cute, in a more flamboyant, expect-the-unexpected sort of way. He'd met her at band practice—she was one of the singers on the praise team—and had gone to her shop, Cut-It-Out, for a haircut a few times since moving here.

"Breakfast food. Yea or nay?" Jasmine stood straighter as if trying to make herself taller.

The young pastor tilted his head, considering. "I'm a fan of anything that includes syrup."

"Oh ..." Jasmine put her hand to her mouth as if she could cry.

Maia laughed.

It was nice when she laughed. He was surprised at how happy the sound made him.

"Thank you, Pastor Nate." Jasmine held her hand out. He shook it, lingering just a hair longer than necessary.

Maia shook her head. "I've got to get going. City work, you know."

"Party-pooper." Jasmine pulled her hand back, her color much warmer than before.

"The wheels of government, and all that." Maia grinned. "Have a great lunch, guys."

As Maia walked away, Jasmine sighed with a little wave. "I need to go too. Hair doesn't cut itself, you know."

She was a whiz at her job. The salon was hopping when he was there, and it was easy to see if he wanted to know anything about the town, he simply needed to make an appointment. Between Jasmine, the other two operators, and the clientele, a person could stay abreast of all the news in the county.

"If it did, you'd be out of business." Nate smiled broadly, his eyes never leaving Jasmine's.

If Owen couldn't manage to win Maia over to the spring season, a little matchmaking for Nate wouldn't be amiss.

Somehow, he didn't think it would be a hard sell.

Chapter Three

"The first day of spring is one thing, and the first spring day is another. The difference between them is sometimes as great as a month." —Henry Van Dyke

"I don't know ..." Maia propped her chin on her fist and slumped at the large granite kitchen island. When in doubt, go ask Mom.

Mom took off her readers—the kind that came in a six-pack at the local big-box store—and gave Maia her full attention. She hadn't yet succumbed to bifocals, but Maia knew it wouldn't be long.

"About what, sweetheart?"

It wasn't a good time to divide Mom's attention. She had tried for years to perfect the recipe for chicken pot pie. They'd made it once, perfectly, and ever since it had been trial and error.

"This whole Daffodil Festival thing." Maia put her head down on the cool countertop, speaking from that position. "Am I an insufferable pessimist?"

"Well ... who told you that?"

Maia jerked her head up, her mouth hanging open. "You think so, too, don't you?" Weren't moms supposed to be encouraging? Make their babies more confident? "Wait. Is this your version of *tough love*?"

"Hardly. I wouldn't call you a pessimist, but you do lean more toward Eeyore than Tigger, that's for sure." She rolled out the pastry dotted with herbs. "I'm hoping I finally found the right crust recipe. Does it look right to you?"

Maia took a deep breath. "It looks amazing." Twisting her lips, she tried to broach the subject again. "But really. How is it I'm the only person in all of Spring who has a perverse dislike of the season?"

"It is a little overkill, I'll admit." Mom took her glasses off and set them on the counter, focusing on her firstborn. "You've always had a thing about the obvious. Maybe you haven't been surprised enough in your life?"

She's been watching Dr. Phil again.

Maia thought a minute, then looked up at her mom. "You may have something there. It's like I'm on a treadmill, but I can imagine all the pitfalls involved if I jump off."

"When was the last time you felt good about things?"

"I guess when I got the job at city hall. I had so many ideas about how to bring Spring back to its former glory." She snorted gently. "But all I get is over-zealous city council members and a boss who gives me all the paperwork he can scrounge up."

Mom chuckled. "Bruce is like that. Ever the politician."

"It's not even a political position."

"Everything is politics, dear." Mom leaned on the counter facing Maia, putting them eye-to-eye. "Do you think it's the time of year?"

It wasn't as if a tragedy or traumatic occurrence had happened during those brief months. Well, her sister was born in March, but she liked Frannie well enough. *Hmmm.* Now that she thought about it, Frannie, as a music teacher, played right into the community consciousness when it came to all things *Spring.*

Hive mentality.

"Could be. It's dark all the time with these warm days sprinkled in with the chances of snow. Unfortunately, it's the warm days I dread, and the snow that makes me feel better." She quirked a brow. "Is there a place where the days are longer in winter, and shorter in summer?"

"I don't think so." Mom's eyes held hers. "It might have more to do with what happened in spring than the season itself. When you were little, you loved it."

Ugh. Why did Mom have to be so perceptive? Couldn't she just sympathize and go along? Did she have to bring up old hurts?

Maia had a tough time meeting her mom's eyes. "That has nothing to do with anything."

"Really?" She settled her glasses back on her nose and began chopping onions for the pot-pie filling. "Nothing to do with the breakup with Henry?"

"It's been three years, Mom. I'm over it. Over him." She refused to let loose the tears she felt gathering.

"Hmmm ..." Mom continued her prep. "Sometimes I think the best thing that could happen would be for you to meet someone who completely takes you by surprise."

A certain over-enthusiastic doctor flashed in her mind.

That's irritating ...

Owen whacked the guitar case on his Jeep as he hurried to practice. *Great. Another ding.* He couldn't help but smile. The case had bumped around in his vehicle for ages, and finally, a few months ago, when his friendship with Associate Pastor Nate was established, he got up the nerve to tell Nate that he played.

When he was introduced to the praise band coordinator, Owen was placed on the schedule for the next practice. No tryouts, just instructions to 'show up and be ready to play.'

The first practice was nerve-wracking, but he soon found the group easy to work with. Their style and rhythm matched his. A God-thing? Probably. He was good like that.

"Hey, Owen, we're getting ready to pray. Hustle up here." Brian Johnson, the leader of the band, turned and stood, smiling.

"Sorry I'm late. Last-minute walk-in."

Jasmine laughed. "I guess your 'last-minute walk-ins' are a little more serious than mine."

"Yeah. Ear infection, not bang-trim." He laughed.

Jasmine smiled broadly but had a speculative gleam in her eye. "Exactly."

The group circled to pray, asking God to settle their hearts and minds on Him, and to help them have a worship experience even as they practiced. Silently, Owen sent up a prayer for Maia.

God, help me be an encouragement.

They took their places, and he tuned his acoustic guitar. Jasmine wandered from her spot and faced him. "How do you like being on the Daffodil Festival committee?"

There was the curious look again. "I think it'll be fun."

"Yeah, if Maia doesn't suck the fun out of it."

That was surprising. "How do you mean?"

She waved her hand in dismissal. "Maia is my best, dearest friend, but she has her issues. I'll leave it at that."

Hmmm ...

"So, you're saying she's always like this?"

"A Negative Nellie?"

"I was thinking 'Debbie Downer,' but that works too." He chuckled.

"Exactly." She shook her head and glanced around.

He did the same. As the new guy, Owen didn't want to be the one holding up practice to have a private conversation and was happy to see that the others still weren't ready to start.

"Not always. Fall and winter are her times to shine. Spring has brought her some blows she can't seem to get over." She paused and arched a brow. "Maybe you can help."

"Okay, everybody. Let's look back at the final song we practiced last week—the new one." Brian's voice called everyone to attention, leaving Owen's concentration divided. Maia? Or a song he'd only played three times?

Better concentrate on the song.

"Any prayer requests before we leave?" The guitars were silent, and the group was back in a circle to finish up the rehearsal time.

Owen looked around. Folks shared issues, illnesses, and heartaches. The issue he had on the forefront of his mind seemed mundane and unimportant compared to theirs. But when he thought about what Jasmine said—about the 'blows' Maia had suffered—it was worth a mention. He raised his hand.

"Owen?" Brian nodded with encouragement.

"This may be out of the scope of this prayer-time ..."

"Hey, brother, nothing is too big or too small for our Lord." The lead guitarist had gray hair, loved metal bands and Jesus, and had a prayer life out of this world. A great source of encouragement.

"You're right." His lips tugged in a smile. "Sorry. I'm on the committee to organize the Spring Daffodil Festival." He nodded at Jasmine. "Jasmine and I both are."

"How can we help?"

Owen hesitated. He didn't want to get personal. "Pray for me, that I'll be an encouragement, and a good helper, for the committee chair. I'm her assistant."

A bogus coughing fit seized Jasmine as she tried to stifle a smile. The members of the group glanced with amusement from one to the other. *Curious.*

"Gotcha, Owen." Brian nodded, then shrugged. "It's a small town. We know who's in charge this year." He glanced around at the rest of the group. "It's for sure we'll pray for you and your role, and for Maia too."

Chapter Four

"In springtime, love is carried on the breeze.
Watch out for flying passion and kisses whizzing by your head."
—*Emma Racine Defleur*

I t was quiet in the office when Maia got to work. Bruce Becker, the city manager, hadn't arrived yet, which wasn't unusual, and she was glad to have a moment of quiet to get her head together before everyone started trickling in.

Walking straight to the coffee maker, she measured the beans and water carefully and hit the button that started the "grind" feature of the "grind and brew" machine. Some people in the office said it was her greatest accomplishment—getting good coffee in city hall.

Great. I'd like to be known for more than improving the quality of beverages in the building.

While the java brewed, she walked to her office and flipped the switch on her computer. Spring was a small town, and up-to-date computer equipment was about as far down on the list of necessities as possible. At least it was on the list. The only thing below it?

Write grant for a new building.

Yeah, that far down.

She flipped through mail on her desk that she'd set aside yesterday. The usual—a sale on bulk products at Winsome Paper, a catalog of random items and decorations for any season or topic imaginable, and a ballpoint pen sample with the office name and address on it.

The last gasp of the coffee maker, and the aroma of quality, legal stimulant, drew her attention. She could set her watch on when her officemates would arrive, so she poured her coffee and sat at her desk, waiting. She arrived ten minutes earlier than usual, so she'd have uninterrupted quiet.

Thank you, Lord.

She opened the left top desk drawer. It held staples, photo paper, random rubber bands, and a *read the Bible in a year* Old/New Testament devotional. As she pulled it out and opened it to today's date—evergreen in this volume—a slip of paper fell out.

An appointment card.

No, not just any card. It was a scheduled date to try on wedding dresses, pre-engagement. She and Henry had talked about marriage, and she'd considered it a given. She'd used the bit of card stock for a placeholder three years ago and had missed this date in her Bible reading for the last two years.

Why did I keep it? Is there a part of me that hangs on to hurt?

Of course, there was. Maia clung to the past as if it were a protective garment.

The scripture at the top of the page was the last part of Luke 9, verse 62. "*Jesus said to him, 'No one who puts his hand to the plow and looks back is fit for the Kingdom of God.'*"

Wow. No wonder she'd skipped it.

The door slammed behind Craig Holsapple, head of Cultural and Media Services. Somehow, she'd ended up sharing an office with him because Bruce didn't share with anyone.

"Howdy-doody, Maia. How's tricks?" Craig was one of those people who had an inflated idea of his brilliance and danced through life. He thought he was supposed to be the office entertainer, and lucky Maia got to share an office with him. Their desks were four feet apart.

After a deep breath, she smiled gently. "Good, Craig. How are you today?"

Wait for it ...

"If I were any better, I'd be illegal."

At least he's not the police chief.

"You win."

Maia settled into the salon chair and gazed into the mirror at her best friend. Next to Jasmine, the picture of health and vitality, her own eyes appeared extra puffy and nose red, raw from blowing it.

"At?" Jasmine grinned. "It could be any number of things, I know."

"I'll go see an allergist. I can't keep on like this."

"Finally. What made you change your mind?" Jasmine tilted her head curiously, all the while clipping away snippets of hair.

Maia raised her voice to be heard over the hair dryer in the next booth. "I strongly considered killing Craig this morning."

"Unclench your teeth, sweetie. It forms wrinkles." Jasmine

laughed when their eyes met again in the mirror. "What brought on the urge to commit murder?"

"Craig being Craig. Isn't that enough?"

Jasmine laughed again, and Maia took in a deep, audible breath. "Okay, I'll ask you what I asked Mom."

"Here we go," Jasmine muttered under her breath.

"Am I an Eeyore?"

The burst of laughter startled her. "Hey, watch out! There are scissors in your hand."

"Oh, I'm just reveling in validation." Jasmine stopped and tilted her head. "Are YOU an Eeyore?"

"That's what I asked. Mom said I tended to be more like Eeyore than Tigger." *Is it hot in here, or is it me?*

Jasmine turned the spinning chair to face Maia face to face. "Can I be honest?"

Maia had a difficult time meeting her eyes, so she settled for picking at the cape protecting her from stray hairs.

"Maia."

She looked up to see her friend gazing at her, a sympathetic smile on her face.

"I'm listening." *Don't want to, but I am.*

"Until spring allergies hit, I would consider you—hmmm …" Jasmine pressed her lips together.

"What? Irritable? Grouchy? Negative?"

"You forgot crabby, testy, and pessimistic."

"Cute." Maia gave her a fake smile.

"You tend to see the dark side. Before Henry—"

"Here we go …"

"Don't interrupt if you want my opinion," Jasmine said.

"Fine. Before Henry …"

"Before Henry-the-indecisive broke up with you, you loved Spring."

"No, I didn't. The allergies were just as bad, then."

"Yes, but you took them all in stride, took your meds, and just rode it out. Now?"

"Now, I am angry at the world because I don't feel well. Thanks for the diagnosis, doctor." Maia rolled her eyes and shook her head. "I know." Was her irritation that transparent?

"I think this is going to require a longer conversation than you have time for during a last-minute trim." Jasmine swept the cape off Maia and laid it aside, turning her chair back toward the mirror and admiring her work. "You are beautiful."

Maia turned her head from side to side and looked at the back using a hand-held mirror. "Thank you. If I am, it's all due to you."

"What can I say? I not only make you beautiful, but I'm also a whiz at counseling."

"Is that part of beauty school curriculum?" Maia smiled as she took a twenty from her wallet.

"No, but it should be." Jasmine took the bill and stuffed it back into Maia's purse. "Free for supper?"

"You know it." Maia sighed and hugged Jasmine. "Thanks, friend."

"Make that appointment, and text me when you get ready to leave work."

"Yes, ma'am."

OWEN SAT in his small living room and picked at the guitar, segueing from one worship song to another. Thursday was his day off, and no plans for the evening. It was a long day.

He set the guitar aside and pulled out the folder he'd started with the information for the upcoming festival. The event had gradually lost steam over the years. Made sense. Some years they'd had to cancel due to harsh weather, which made the next year harder. He'd make a list of things he thought would bring it back to life.

1. Hire a band for live music. *I wonder if Brian would be interested in our band playing.*
2. Host *A Taste of Spring* at the high school multipurpose room. Local restaurants and caterers supply bite-sized versions of their specialties. The public could attend for a fee, benefiting a local charity?
3. Beauty pageant? *Hmmm ... looks like they've done that in the past.* Maybe resurrect it?
4. Talent show? Charge admission, entry fee.
5. Tractor pull? He grimaced at that one.

Surely there were activities beyond bouncy attractions and funnel cakes. He pulled out his phone and scrolled to Maia's contact information. He'd run his ideas by her. Would that be too pushy? The committee was meeting next Monday, but wouldn't it be a good idea to have a few ideas to pass on?

Call or text? The clock on his phone said 6:35 pm. Not too late to call. What if she's busy? He had no clue about her personal life. She might have a boyfriend. For all he knew, she might be married.

But she didn't have any rings on her left hand.

He'd looked.

Text it is.

Hi, Maia. Owen here. Are you busy?

He waited for what seemed like an eternity, but finally, the dots indicated her answering.

Owen? I'm at dinner with a friend. What's up? Already bailing on the committee? ;)

No, had the day off and started thinking about ideas for the festival. Want me to send them to you, or save them for the meeting?

Why did he start this?

Sorry to bother you.

No bother. I'm here with Jasmine, so fire away.

She asked for it. All at once, or one at a time? Owen paused. One at a time. He didn't have a problem with her running his ideas by Jasmine.

He settled in on the sofa and put the notebook next to him.

Here's the first one: hire a live band.

Crickets.

Chapter Five

"Winter is on my head, but eternal spring is in my heart."
—Victor Hugo

February

W
hy did it take two weeks to schedule an allergy test?

Maia waited in the reception area, avoiding the *sniffling, sneezing, stuffy head, fever, coughing* crew that would like nothing more than to spread their juvenile school-related germs. She did not have time for that. She'd missed the flu this year, so yay for that, but there was a new wave coming through, and if she caught something just sitting here, she'd be pretty upset.

"Maia Pascal?" The nurse, one of her former Sunday School teachers, stood at the door to the examining area, looking around. She smiled when Maia stood.

"Here." She fluttered her fingers, then trudged behind the

nurse, stopping only for a quick step up on the scale and a blood-pressure check. A sneeze came to the surface and had to come out. Multiple times.

"You're here for allergen testing, right?" Nurse Angie Conrad checked Maia's temperature and oxygen level, then scribbled on the file after handing her a tissue.

"I am."

"'Bout time, don't you think?" Angie chuckled. "There's not been a spring I can remember that you didn't end up in here for a sinus infection or some other respiratory ailment."

"I decided I didn't want to hit thirty without looking into the luxury of breathing in the springtime. Hopefully, I've come early enough to do something about it this year." Maia gave her a wan smile.

Angie showed her to the examining room and stuck the folder in the pocket outside the door. "The doctor will be with you in a minute."

"Thanks, Ms. Angie."

"I think you're old enough to call me 'Angie,' now. You do realize I'm not even ten years older than you." She winked and closed the door softly.

Huh. Time flew. She knew Ms. Angie—scratch that, Angie —was young when she taught in the church's youth department but didn't realize she was that young. Now she remembered. Angie had been a college student at the time. Wow.

She pulled out her phone and noticed she had yet more text messages from Owen. It had been on silent since bedtime last night when she got tired of hearing enthusiastic ideas about the upcoming Daffodil Festival. *I should have given him Jasmine's number ...*

∼

OWEN WITHDREW the folder from the slot next to the door. He smiled when he saw Maia's name.

Just as Angie came by. "You take care of Maia. We go way back."

The look she gave him relayed not only was the nurse interested in Maia's well-being, but other people loved and cared for her, as well. For some reason, that made him happy. "I'll do my best."

The nurse winked and walked by to escort another patient to an examining room. "You just might be the one to change her life." She swept away, leaving Owen frozen by the door.

Life-changing? Oh. The allergies. He relaxed a bit.

Focus, Owen. Just because you've been thinking about the woman non-stop doesn't mean you have a future with her. She's just a patient.

He took a deep breath, adjusted his collar, and opened the door. "How are you, Ms. Pascal?"

"If I were well, I wouldn't be here, would I?" Her look of surprise schooled into a raised eyebrow implied he had his work cut out for him to gain traction with her. "Considering I've been without any over-the-counter allergy meds for a week, I think I'm about as positive as I can be."

"Sorry. That's rough. Completely understandable. Dr. Charles had an emergency at the hospital. I'm here as a General Practitioner, but my specialty track was allergies. He asked me to step in."

"I wondered. I've gone to Dr. Charles all my life, but if you know allergies, I'm glad you're here." She twisted her lips. "There are shots involved, aren't there?"

"Not necessarily." He perched on the edge of the examining table across from the chair where she sat in the windowless room. "We'll draw a few vials of blood, then use what we call a skin prick test. Sometimes it will tell us at once if it's something you're allergic to. The blood test is a way to double-check."

"So, no shots?"

The hopeful expression on her face almost made him laugh, but he held it in and smiled, instead.

"Only if we don't get any results from the skin prick or blood tests." He paused. "Are you ready to get started?"

Biting her lip, she nodded. "I've put this off for a long time."

"That's what I hear." He stood and opened the door, looking out toward the nurses' desk. "Angie, would you bring me the allergy kit?"

Owen turned back to his patient. "Don't worry. It won't take long, and hopefully, we'll get you fixed up before the Daffodil Festival."

"Wouldn't it be funny if we found out I'm allergic to daffodils, of all things?" Her relief at not having multiple shots showed in her ability to make a joke.

"If you are, we'll put together a plan to help you manage the symptoms through it." He smiled gently. "Relax. Angie will come in and draw the blood, then I'll come back in to help with the skin prick tests. Are you okay?"

She nodded and gave him a slow smile that did things to his insides.

"ARE YOU KIDDING ME?"

Jasmine's voice over the phone was a cross between disbelief and amusement.

Maia sat at her desk trying to stop herself from scratching one of the many red, itchy blotches from the skin pricks that had affirmed she was allergic to almost every kind of plant and tree pollen available. It wouldn't matter where she lived or what the weather was like. She couldn't believe when Owen shared the news she was, indeed, highly allergic to trees.

All kinds.

Everything but plants in the Narcissus family—daffodils.

"I can't believe it, either. I thought Owen—er, Dr. Roswell —was going to fall on the floor laughing." She paused. "You don't think he skewed the results, do you?"

"No, crazy girl." Maia could hear her stifling another giggle. "What are you supposed to do with this information? In other words, what will bring you back to your love of spring?"

Maia heaved a sigh. "Shots. I think he's talked me into it. They won't start until we get the results of the blood tests in case there are others we don't know about."

"I know you don't look forward to it, but if it helps ..."

An idea came to her. "I wonder if this could get me out of the Daffodil Festival?"

"Maia ..."

"I know. It was just a thought." She frowned. Maia knew Jasmine couldn't see her, but she had a feeling her friend's radar worked even through her cell phone's data plan.

"Are we still having our meeting tonight?"

"Ugh, yes. Are you going to make it?"

"It's at six?"

"Yep. I'm hoping to finish by seven."

Jasmine was quiet on the other end of the line, and when she did speak, her voice rose. "Will Owen be there?"

"He assured me he would."

"Good. I think it's high time you discussed the forty-eleven suggestions he sent you." Jasmine laughed as she ended the call.

Forty-eleven was right. It seemed that after the first day he sent suggestions for the festival, he'd sent at least one each day. Some were promising ideas. Others bordered on silly. She had to admit, though, that he'd made her laugh more than she'd laughed during spring in a long time.

She pulled out the thick folder of "Daffodil Festival" information and opened it. Her phone dinged with a text, and she shook her head. Owen.

Tractor Pull?

It could be the blood loss from earlier that day, but she had to laugh out loud.

Been there, done that, got the T-shirt.

Was it camo?

Owen included a string of farming and hunting-related emojis after the question mark.

Another burst of laughter bubbled out of her. Movement caught her attention through the window into the outer office. Every eye was on her. Craig, her officemate, was pointing at her with a look of wonder on his face. Dineen, the secretary-receptionist sat with her mouth hanging open. Bruce, her boss, simply looked at her like she'd lost her mind.

On the positive side, at least the mayor wasn't there.

Chapter Six

"In the spring a young man's fancy lightly turns to thoughts of love." —Alfred Lord Tennyson

Owen slowed as he reached the entrance to City Hall. There was a warmish breeze in the air, so he'd left his jacket in the Jeep. He was enjoying the beautiful spring-like day, but that wasn't why he slowed.

A blur came out of his peripheral vision and beat him to the door.

Jasmine. She stopped, eyes filled with curiosity.

"Hey, Owen." Her brows met. "You okay?"

"Yeah. Sure." He didn't even convince himself.

He hadn't been interested in many girls. There were the requisite girlfriends in high school and college, but once he hit medical school, he didn't have the time or the energy to put toward a commitment. Now, he was ready, but there was only one young woman who caught his eye.

And she's allergic to everything and every activity I enjoy.

The hairdresser paused, her hand on the door. "So ... are we going in?"

He came to himself. "Uh, yeah. You go ahead. I'll be there in a minute."

The frown on her face deepened. "You sure?"

He hesitated. His to-do list did not include talking to Maia's best friend—about Maia. How did this happen? He was interested in one girl, and she didn't like any of the things he did. Camping, hiking, swimming, general-all-purpose outdoor lifestyle stuff.

"Has Maia always disliked spring?"

Her hand fell away from the door as she turned toward him. "No, but it's never been her favorite." Jasmine sighed. "Naturally curly hair and spring weather aren't compatible."

"My hair curls, and the weather doesn't bother me."

"That's because you have a *Y* chromosome." She chuckled, then sobered. "It didn't used to be so bad. She's just so irritable this time of year, ever since ..." Jasmine waved both hands. "Let's just leave it at that."

Maia was irritated, and irritable because of her allergies. And if he was to glean anything from Jasmine's pause, there was something else.

In the meantime, so was he—irritated—because of Maia's allergies.

One of the reasons he moved to Kentucky was to experience the seasons. So far, he'd observed the end of summer, fall, winter, and the beginning of spring. He couldn't wait for summer to get here. Everyone complained about the humidity, but really? How bad could it be? A temperature of 110 wasn't unusual where he came from.

And then there was Maia.

He raked his hand through his hair, realizing he needed to schedule a haircut for his day off. His reflection in the glass door told him he was passable—but was he passable to Maia? And was he sure he wanted to go there?

"Speaking of curls ..." Jasmine eyed him thoughtfully.

"Are you a mind-reader, as well?"

"All part of barber school. It's kinda like bartending school, but in the midst of working, we focus on beauty, not booze." She laughed.

Why couldn't he have a crush on this woman instead of Maia?

Someone once asked him what he considered his 'perfect date.' After teasing with the 'April 25th' line from the movie, *Miss Congeniality*, he thought about it. It was a picnic, a hike, and stargazing. What was Maia's perfect date?

His phone buzzed with the reminder he'd set for the meeting, just in case. As if he would forget. He shut off the notification and opened the door, holding it for Jasmine. He was committed to the Daffodil Festival.

But did he want to commit to Maia?

THE COMMITTEE MEMBERS sat around the long conference table. Maia had asked Dineen to stay and take notes. She almost asked Jasmine, but Jasmine was an idea person, not a detail person—except when it came to hair. In that arena, she was persnickety.

Everyone was here. No. Not everyone. Owen wasn't here, and neither was Jasmine. Why did she have a sinking feeling, a little sadness clouding her already cloudy outlook?

Truth be told, she'd started looking forward to their exchanges. He was funny, and he was the most positive person she knew. He wasn't obnoxiously funny like Craig. Just cute-funny.

There. She admitted it. *He's cute.* She'd always secretly liked guys with red hair. Henry had blonde hair, and honestly? It was something she was ambivalent about. If you're ambivalent about your boyfriend, are they cut out to be your intended?

Her mind was running in circles. *Buck up, Maia.*

"Okay, gang, let's get this show on the road." Maia started the meeting, and everyone prepared to get down to business. "Anyone have a report since our last meeting?"

A hand went up.

"What do you have for us, Mrs. Cotton?"

The elegantly appointed lady wriggled in her chair. Outwardly, it seemed out of character for her to be so excited, but it wasn't. If there was something to organize, she was the person to do it. "Maia, I've spoken to the restaurants in town and the surrounding area, and they're all very excited about participating in a *Taste of Spring* event. All we need to do is clear it with the health department and secure the spot, and they're good to go."

The door opened. Jasmine and Owen entered quietly, the latter sliding into his chair as if trying to fool everyone into thinking he'd been there all the time. She smiled at him, then drew her eyebrows together when he didn't meet her gaze. Something was wrong, but she had a meeting to conduct.

When she glanced at Jasmine, next to her, her friend simply shrugged her shoulders.

The report was done, and silence became slightly awkward. Maia tried to interject some good will in word and facial expression. "That's great, Mrs. Cotton." She smiled warmly, then turned toward Owen. "Sounds like your idea for the *Taste of Spring* event is going to be well-attended. Now we just have to plan who will be where, what we'll need—and get tickets put together."

He nodded, glancing around the table at the other members. Still nothing.

Curt Simmons, the insurance agent, spoke up. "I checked with Bounce-n-More and the Hoosier Carnivals, and suggest we try the carnival company this year. If we approve it, that part of the festival is secure. We may be able to get extra kiddie rides thrown in if we pay in advance, and, if it's available, a portable putt-putt green."

Interesting. That would be something different. Maia thought a minute. "What do you all think?"

There was murmuring amongst themselves. She turned to Jasmine. "What do you think?"

Her friend shrugged her shoulders and nodded. "Sounds like fun to me."

"Owen? I mean, Dr. Roswell?" She looked pointedly at him.

The group turned toward him, and he cleared his throat. "I'm sure it would be popular with the kids." He frowned, looking down as he tapped his pen on his notebook—a notebook, she saw, with no notes whatsoever. "What is the cost we're talking about, and what is the cancellation policy? We don't want to get stuck with a big bill if the weather turns on us."

Did anyone else notice the shift in the wind hitting the building?

Maia's mouth hung open just as her office staff's had the other day when she chortled at Owen's text messages. She stared at him. Where was Dr. Positive? Was he using reverse psychology on her?

And was that thunder?

"I—I'm sure we could arrange for that. Curt?"

"Well, that's the kicker. They want the money up front, and if they get the stuff set up, no refund. If we cancel less than a week ahead of time, we'd get fifty percent back." He looked a little sheepish. His great idea had a few holes in it.

"Something to think about." Owen's face did not show what was going on in his head.

The rush of optimism that had accompanied her since finding out she could, indeed, find a way through her allergies was waning. Was it that, or that she'd anticipated seeing Owen outside of blood draws and skin pricks?

Owen winced as he watched Maia put on her raincoat and sling the strap of her purse over her head. The force used to cram her notes into the tote bag revealed impatience and irritation. When he walked in earlier, he'd seen the smile on her face. And he killed it.

Stupid, stupid, stupid.

Too many differences.

Oil and water.

Orange juice and toothpaste.

He stood, finally, and walked toward her. "How are you feeling?"

Maia looked up, surprised. "He speaks."

Did he? Speak, that is? His throat was dry.

"I'm sorry I was late for the meeting."

As she put her things in her bag, she avoided his eyes. "No problem. I'm sure it was an emergency." She gave him a frozen smile before frowning at the rainy sleet coming down outside. "You might be right. The weather is always a factor."

Was he using the elements to get out of collaborating closely with her?

She zipped her coat and let out a stifled sigh—he could hear it—then looked him in the eye. "Thank you for coming. I'll send out an email with updates and the time of the next meeting."

"Maia." He stood still as she turned and walked out the door without a backward glance.

What was wrong with him? He wasn't thinking about finding a girlfriend when he decided to volunteer to be Maia's assistant. He'd felt led to help, and, just maybe, encourage the anti-Spring girl to get in the spirit of new beginnings and rebirth. Who knew his feelings would go deeper so suddenly?

Personal relationship aside, he had ground to recover if he was going to meet his goal of changing Maia's attitude about their town's namesake. He would have to make celebrating spring enough and help her make it the best festival they'd ever seen.

Somehow.

If it killed him.

With the wind howling, the door to the street resisted his effort to open it. Owen frowned, pushed harder, surprised when he found that his beautiful, spring-like day was turning on him—just like everything else in his life.

Chapter Seven

*"In the spring I have counted one hundred thirty-six different
kinds of weather inside thirty-six hours."*
—Mark Twain

Mid-February: Six weeks until DF-Day
(AKA Daffodil Festival Day)

After the meeting that had shown promise up until the
time Owen arrived, Maia had gone to bed thinking
about all the things that could go wrong with their
plans.

She'd lost enough sleep, she was groggy. On the positive
side, today couldn't be as horrible as yesterday. It just couldn't.

It was strangely quiet for this time of the morning, and on a
weekday, at that. And was it just her, or was it excessively
bright outside? Pushing herself up, she saw what would
normally be a welcome sight in mid-allergy season.

Snow.

"No, no, no, no, no!" She rushed to her bedroom window when she heard the snowplow clearing the streets. She checked the local news app on her phone. No school today, and the list of office and organizational closings was growing by the minute.

The phone on the nightstand next to her buzzed with a group text. Bruce. Everyone was supposed to stay off the roads until the snowplows finished. The snow had come out of nowhere. What had started as an unexpected spate of freezing rain and a thirty-percent chance of flurries had already dumped four inches on the ground.

Welcome to Kentucky in February. Better snow than ice. She heard farmers talking just the other day about planting potatoes and sweet peas. Now they were treated to snow, also known as "poor man's fertilizer," due to the high nitrogen content found in snow and rain.

Another buzz. This time it was Jasmine, and Maia answered without the usual pleasant preamble.

"What is going on?"

Her friend's laughter on the other end wasn't matching up with her mood. "I figured you'd already be outside making snow angels."

Maia grimaced. "Not this time. Can I tell you something and not suffer the consequences?"

"Depends. Is it scandalous?"

It was, a little. For her. "Not really."

"Then shoot."

She took a deep breath and gazed out the window again. "I do not need this snow right now."

"For you, that is an admission of the utmost importance. Is the snow queen melting just a little bit?"

Maia could almost hear Jasmine's smile. Silly, she knew, but the telemarketers are right—you can hear a smile over the phone. She wanted to join in, but she couldn't.

"What happens when we get snow late in the season, especially when it follows the river?"

Jasmine heaved a sigh. "It melts to the north and east, and all that runoff ends up flooding our area."

"It could be a major mess." Maia bit her lip. Flooding. Roads cut off. Their citizens would be sandbagging their properties against flooding, not wandering from booth to booth at a celebration of spring.

She was getting more involved in the festival than she'd planned.

"At least it's still six weeks until the festival. It could clear up." Jasmine paused. "What's the backup plan?"

"What backup plan?" Maia pressed her fingers into her right temple, feeling the headache that had been absent since beginning allergy treatments.

This time plant life had nothing to do with it. This time it was stress, pure and simple.

OWEN TOOK advantage of the snow-induced delayed start to his day and decided to make the trek into town on foot. He hoped it would clear his head. It was sunny and already warming to the point that the main sound he heard was water dripping off buildings and running into storm drains.

He'd tossed and turned all night. Why had he decided to play 'Devil's advocate' at that moment? Was he letting his personal feelings get in the way of the task at hand, which was putting together a festival? His negativity had cast a pall on the group, causing a complete split in the vote.

After the meeting last night, he'd heard one of the committee members mention the words 'snow' and 'flooding.' Two things that could squash the festival completely with increasing temperatures and melting. Was this just the beginning of a series of events that festival planners had to deal with every year?

No wonder Maia wasn't completely sold on the yearly celebration. There were years it simply couldn't happen. She had begun to see the merits of the festival, and he quashed it.

Rounding the corner of City Hall, three blocks shy of the clinic, he stopped a moment to take in his surroundings. The Daffodil flags were stiff and frozen but would begin dripping at any time. Did someone mention flooding? From an arid part of the U.S., he couldn't imagine what a little snow could do to create that type of disaster.

Maia's Honda SUV pulled into the side lot next to City Hall, close to where he stood. She hadn't seen him. Good.

She got out, bundled for the weather, and immediately dropped her bag. "Ugh!"

"Let me help." He walked over to where she scrambled in the snow.

Surprise softened her features, then something shuttered in her eyes. It was obvious she hadn't forgiven him for last night. "I'm fine. I don't need your help."

He knelt and pulled her keys out of a section of mounded snow where the snowplow had cleared the lot, then stood there, facing her. He held on to the keys as she reached for them, tugged a moment, then gave up.

"I'm sorry, Maia."

"Whatever for?" She gritted out, resting her hands on her hips, probably irritated that he hadn't given her the keys.

Was that sarcasm? He narrowed his eyes, trying to figure her out. Yep. It was definitely sarcasm.

He tilted his head, trying to force her to look at him. "I was out of line last night. I'd had a bad day and took it out on you and the committee."

She didn't smile but instead twisted her lips. "How could you know at that very moment the weather was turning on us? Of course, if you had lived here as long as I have, you'd know that this time of year, you may as well go by smoke signals as to watch a weather report." Her hands dropped them to her sides.

"Was that a joke?" Owen began to breathe again.

"Perhaps." She raised her eyebrows and held out her hand for the keys.

He placed them gently in her outstretched palm. She was so pretty. There was just something about her that pulled at him. She met his gaze full-on.

"Thank you for risking life and limb digging for my keys."

"Let's start over." Owen held out his hand, still warm from his pocket. "Good morning, I'm Owen Roswell, and I'm the guy who promised to help you make this thing come to life."

With hesitation, she reciprocated. "I'm Maia Pascal, and I'm the girl who's supposed to make it come to life ... although it's looking more like you were closer to the reality of the situation last night than I was. I've got to remember that flashes of spontaneity and positivity can get me in trouble."

He didn't know what to say to that. Spontaneity. Positivity. Things he considered he had, in spades, and that Maia had to pull from deep within. No way could he leave their conversation at that. The idea sparked when Maia glanced up at the clock on the tower of the courthouse.

Owen gently gripped her arm as she turned away. "Do you have to report on time?"

"No, in fact, Craig called and told me not to come in until 11, but I have too much to do for that." She shrugged." I knew I could make it in. It'll be halfway melted by two."

"I'm on a delayed schedule as well." He looked away for a moment, then focused on her. "What would you think about getting a little breakfast? Talk this through?"

The timid smile was all he needed. Was it him, or had the sun suddenly brightened?

Chapter Eight

"Spring is when you feel like whistling even with a shoe full of slush." —Doug Larson

Maia slid into the booth while Owen hung her coat on the hook by the door. Was this a mistake? What was up yesterday? What would Jasmine tell her to do? Stop questioning everything and go with the flow.

Problem was, Jasmine was so in the flow that her life looked seamless. It wasn't, but to people who didn't know the insecurities lurking inside the brash, over-confident young woman, she was invincible. Inside, she was a melty marshmallow who cried at the latest Chevy commercial and could never pass up a Salvation Army bell-ringer without contributing.

Steepling her fingers, she waited while Owen stopped to speak to a few diners. Probably patients. Did he know them from church? He was more outgoing than she was, for sure. Mr. Positivity.

Until yesterday.

She was staring into space, thinking, when he appeared across the table from her.

"Earth to Maia." He waved a hand in front of her face.

"Ha." Maia was trying to dredge up her earlier anger, but it had dissipated. Owen was a nice man, whether she liked it or not.

That was the moment Connie chose to approach the table. "Good mornin.' Griddle and waffle maker are still going. Can I interest you in pancakes or waffles?"

Dare she go for another round of breakfast? Did toast even count? "Could I get the short stack of pancakes? And coffee?"

"Yes, ma'am." She wrote it down. "Maple syrup?"

"Is there any other kind?"

Owen chuckled at that, still looking at the menu. He put it down and looked up at the server. "I built up an appetite walking over. I think I'll have waffles, extra butter and syrup, and coffee."

"Comin' right up. I'll get your order in and get you that coffee." Connie peered from one to the other over her reading glasses.

"Thanks, Connie." She bugged her eyes a little bit, hoping to get the idea across that she'd appreciate no questions or speculation. Maia could see the wheels turning in the lady's mind.

Thank goodness she got the message. Connie winked at Maia and made her way behind the counter to the kitchen.

"Are you a *Lord of the Rings* fan?" Owen asked, chin in hand.

For a moment she avoided his gaze.. "The movies—couldn't get through the books, unfortunately. If you're asking if I know what 'second breakfast' is, then yes, I am. Shall we come back for 'elevensies?'"

Owen burst into laughter. "Touché."

It was a defensive move, she knew, but she couldn't help it. She crossed her arms and leaned back.

"So ..."

"So ... ladies first." Owen gestured to her to take the lead.

"Okay. I admit, I was trying hard to throw caution to the wind yesterday. I never do that. Apparently, I'm not meant to." She looked down at the table before lifting her eyes to his.

"And I was attempting to be a responsible adult."

Maia laughed. "What is wrong with us?"

"Nothing." He shrugged. "Everybody has a little bit of both in them—part of you wants to let go and enjoy life, and part of me craves peace and stability. It doesn't have to be an either-or situation."

The ire began to rise within. "I wouldn't say I don't enjoy life."

"That was a poor choice of words. The main idea is 'letting go' of control."

Was she controlling? In this situation, wasn't that the role of a manager? It had come up with Henry, as well. He said he never felt like he could measure up to her ideal, but she didn't know what that meant. That's why it hurt when he broke up with her.

After a deep breath, she nodded. "I get it. I've heard that I tend to be more of an Eeyore than a Tigger."

Owen chuckled. "That's a new one."

"That was from my mother."

He laughed out loud. "I feel vindicated."

"Why am I submitting to being psychoanalyzed by an allergy specialist?" She relaxed a little and shook her head in disbelief.

Connie brought their coffee. "Your order will be up in a few minutes. Cream or sugar?"

Both answered, "no," and Connie grinned. "I'll be back in a minute."

"Truce?" Owen was looking at her as if her approval meant the world to him.

Maia chewed her bottom lip, considering. "Truce. We've got to figure this out before the next meeting."

"When is that?"

"Monday. I called an emergency meeting after the weather event. You'll be getting an email."

"Sounds good." He took a swig of his coffee. "We need to come up with some ideas that would allow us to have the festival rain or shine."

Maia shook her head. "That's the problem. We have very few venues to hold an event like this. Carnival rides aside, the high school gym can only hold so many vendors."

"So, we're back to either-or?" Owen pressed his lips in a thin line.

Connie appeared, suddenly, with their plates. Maia was pleasant and grateful to the server, but she could feel the heat on her cheeks.

"Can I get you anything else?" Connie checked over their order on the table carefully.

"I think we're good." Maia saw Owen glance her way, obviously as irritated as she.

How dare he? Did he think the simple act of buying her breakfast would make everything work out to his expectations?

She was prepared to give a little. If he could convince her there was a place to have the event in case of another weather event like this one, she'd consider it. There had been a time when she loved the Daffodil Festival. Back in the day, when her main goal was to find the funnel cake vendor and win a Teddy bear at the ring-toss booth, life was much simpler.

But then, she'd been a child, and she never noticed the

adults scurrying around with walkie-talkies and concerned looks on their faces.

Now she was that adult. She had the T-shirts and walkie-talkies to prove it. It wasn't her idea of fun. When she took the assistant city manager job, she envisioned bringing well-organized events to her town, running a committee to keep the streets clean and the curbs painted, and other fun things that simply made life better for her favorite place on earth.

What she got was a boss who put all his paperwork on her desk and a committee of over-enthusiastic volunteers who could walk away.

Why didn't I take that job offer in Indiana?

"What's the capacity of the high school gym?" His voice startled her, interrupting her thoughts.

"Seated? About two thousand. Milling around, I have no idea."

His shoulders went down. "That's not a lot."

Maia raised an eyebrow. "Exactly. We have two churches with community centers and gyms, but they are smaller."

Finishing his waffles, Owen sipped his coffee and pushed his plate toward the center of the table. He leaned back and looked her in the eye. "Maybe the festival needs to be different this year."

Here we go. "Different? How?" Her anger built again. Wasn't it enough that she was even listening?

"Does it have to be the same every year?" His gaze turned curious.

She closed her eyes. He didn't understand. "There are certain expectations of the Daffodil Festival."

"It would seem so. Perhaps it's time to change the expectations."

"You just don't get it." She put a ten-dollar bill on the table and gathered her purse and bag.

When she got up to leave, Owen pushed out of the booth and stood next to her, touching her elbow.

"Maia." His voice was soft.

That was her undoing. A tear she absolutely dared to roll down her cheek did so, which only made her angrier.

"I need to go." She pulled her arm away from him and strode out the door before he could say anything else.

Please, God, don't let him follow me.

Chapter Nine

"Spring will come and so will happiness. Hold on. Life will get warmer." —Anita Krizzan

The morning after the late-season snowstorm, the sun came out, and the temperatures promised to soar into the sixties. Perfect day for a run. It was Saturday, so Owen was off. He wasn't even on call at the ER.

He put his air buds in his ears, selected his running playlist on his phone, and started on the route he had walked yesterday in the snow. Mud puddles had replaced the icy patches he dodged the day before.

When he got to the spot where he'd met Maia, he paused to take a drink of water. He felt bad about the way their conversation ended. When a tear made its way down her cheek before she could swipe it away, he was stunned. He never knew a woman's tears could affect him in such a way.

Not all women's tears. Just Maia's.

He stood there, thinking. Praying. *You're shining a light on me, Lord, that I'm not liking very much. Am I trying too hard to do what only You can do? I can't make Maia love a season—or me, for that matter. All that is in Your hands. Help me to keep mine off.*

The 'or me' in his prayer came out of nowhere. He'd have to tread softly if he had any chance at a relationship with her.

Whoa. Where did that come from? Did he want a relationship?

He shook his head and started back on his run. The plan was to run as far as the high school and then back. About three miles. The trees were just starting to bud, and the early magnolia trees, called *tulip trees* locally, were beginning to show off their blooms before any other variety. Beautiful.

As he rounded a corner heading toward the school, he heard a *beep-beep* in his ear. He stopped and pulled out his phone. Nate. He grinned. Maybe he wanted to get lunch or something.

"Hey, Nate, what's going on?"

"I wondered if you'd like to go on an errand of mercy with me?"

"Sure."

Nate laughed on the other end of the call. "You didn't even ask what it was."

"I figure you won't get me into too much trouble."

"I'd hope not." He paused. "I got a call from Mrs. Bentley."

"Isn't she the old lady who hugs everybody?"

Nate chuckled. "The same. Her husband was in an accident and landed himself in the hospital about an hour away. She can't drive that far, and the closest relative they have is a granddaughter in St. Louis, who can't get here until tomorrow."

"Wow. Do you need me to take her to the hospital?"

"No, just ride along. I think you'd enjoy talking to her. After, we could grab pizza and watch the basketball game."

"You're plying me with pizza and basketball?" Owen couldn't help but laugh. "I was planning on watching the game, anyway."

"I had a feeling. You UK grads are all the same."

"Hey, it's not just the ones who claim it as alma mater—seems like when it comes to the NCAA tournament, everybody is a Kentucky fan." They both chuckled. "I'd be glad to go with you. What time?" Owen checked the time on his phone, then at his surroundings, calculating how much time it would take to get back home and change.

"It's nine-thirty now. How about eleven?"

"Perfect. Gives me time to get home from my run and clean up."

Nate snorted. "I think we'd all be glad for you to do that."

THE HOUR and a half ride to Evansville, Indiana, just across the Ohio River from Kentucky, was the most fun Owen had experienced in a long time.

Mrs. Alice Bentley was in her late eighties, a tiny slip of a woman, and sharp as a tack.

"When did you and Mr. Bentley meet?" Owen was curious. He'd lost all his grandparents and enjoyed talking to someone who would have been their contemporary.

Ms. Alice chuckled warmly. "Oh, my. Well, I grew up in Spring, but Bill hailed from a farm in the next county. For him, coming to Spring was 'goin' to town.'" She smiled. "When I was a senior in high school, our Glee Club performed at the Daffodil Festival ..."

"Wait. How long has the festival been going on?" Owen was fascinated.

"That's right. You're on the committee, aren't you?" Nate glanced into the rearview mirror and met Owen's eyes.

"I am, and we're struggling with whether or not to cancel this year because of the possibility of flooding."

"Bless you. I wouldn't want to make that decision. Every time it's been canceled, the poor folks running the show have ended up with cranky citizens. It might not be the draw it once was when there wasn't anything else to do, but it's always been a big deal." Ms. Alice sighed. "Good times."

"You were talking about when you met your husband." Owen didn't want to distract her. Especially now. He could pick her brain a little. Maybe bring the festival back to its former glory?

"Oh, yes. Well, the Glee Club took center stage for the opening National Anthem, then at lunchtime, we were the entertainment while our folks ate barbecue and potato salad." She grinned. "Bill always says that year he zeroed in on me first thing in the morning and kept me in his sights the rest of the day. I don't know if that's completely true, but it makes for a nice story."

Nate reached over and patted Ms. Alice on the hand. "I've never known Bill Bentley to tell a falsehood, have you?"

The elderly lady put her other hand on his. "No, he hasn't." She arched a brow at him. "He may have stretched the truth on occasion."

"Maybe, but I have a feeling he took one look at you and was done for." Nate chuckled.

"How long have you been married, Ms. Alice?" asked Owen.

"Well, we started dating right after that—once my parents figured out who his parents were, and that they were good people." She turned to look back at Owen. "Back then everybody knew everybody, so there wasn't any mystery. Turns out, Bill's mother went to school with my mother, and they'd lost touch but renewed their friendship through us. We got married in April of '52, before I graduated from high school in May."

"Tell him which anniversary you're getting ready to celebrate." Nate urged her on.

"Seventy years this coming April." She beamed. "Of course, back then we didn't have big church weddings and such. A couple just invited their best friends to stand up with them and went to the preacher's house."

"Sounds a lot simpler than now."

"Oh, it was. Bill was the sentimental one. He wanted to get married during the Daffodil Festival since that's when he met me. Our anniversary is coming up right during this year's festival. That is if we still have it. It's a terrible time of year to plan a celebration." She looked down at her veined hands. "I just want to be able to celebrate, with or without any shindigs—I just want my Bill home with me." Worry tinged her voice.

"I understand." What would it be like to be part of a love story that spanned more than seventy years?

Chapter Ten

"Despite the forecast, live like it's spring."
—Lilly Pulitzer

Late February

The road trip to the hospital with Nate and Ms. Alice had been a joy. Just what Owen needed—a welcome break from his apprehension about the festival and his part in it. On the trip home, he'd picked Ms. Alice's brain to get ideas for this year's celebration of all things Spring.

He hesitated at the door to City Hall. This meeting would make or break this year's festival. Perhaps his ideas would kindle the imagination of his fellow committee members.

Entering the conference room, he glanced at each face. He saw excitement, apprehension, and boredom—but that was just Claudia. Bored, as usual. What he wouldn't give to see a spark of excitement on that face.

Maia slipped in the back door of the room and put her

notebook on the table as she sat. "Good afternoon, everyone. I hope you had a good weekend and came ready to make decisions about this year's festival."

As soon as comments about the weekend and the weather shift they'd experienced recently subsided, and the familiar, 'if you don't like the weather in Kentucky, just wait until tomorrow. It'll change'—an oldie but a goodie—Owen waited for a pause.

Before Maia could begin, he raised his hand. "I'd like to share something, if I could, about a lady I spent some time with this weekend."

Eyebrows went up all around the table, including Maia's.

"Her name is Ms. Alice Bentley."

Chuckles went around the table. Not the woman or the age bracket they were likely thinking.

"I'm sure you all know her better than I do, but in talking to her about her husband, I learned that they met at the Daffodil Festival, in 1951."

"How did I miss that?" Mrs. Cotton berated herself. "I usually know those kinds of facts."

Claudia spoke up. "How old were they?"

"In the spring of 1951, Ms. Alice was a junior in high school. Her glee club performed, and that's when she caught Mr. Bentley's eye." He paused, smiling at Claudia. She was hanging on to every word. Was she a romantic at heart? A history lover? Both?

"A year later, a few weeks before she graduated from high school, they married."

Maia's eyes widened, as if she were calculating in her head. "Is this their seventieth anniversary?"

Owen nodded. "It is."

Was she thinking what he was thinking?

"This could change everything."

"Good meeting, Maia."

Maia turned to see Owen at her elbow. She felt the heat on her face. Why was she blushing? Was it regret over their last encounter? She'd avoided him at church on Sunday, skipping the singles' Bible study class and scooting out the back door of the worship center before the band scattered after the second service. Jasmine had already fussed at her.

"Thanks." She held her notebook across her chest. "I thought it went well. Of course, if you hadn't brought up the Bentleys' anniversary, we might still be bogged down in minutiae."

"I think celebrating 'fifties style' will be fun."

"Time to dust off my poodle skirt." She couldn't help but grin at the thought of Owen in a black leather jacket, a la *Grease*.

"I'm not sure what the nerdy boys wore in the fifties, but you can be sure I'll find out."

"Would you like to go with me to interview Ms. Alice about the festival? I'd like to get some more ideas about the activities they had back then."

He smiled. "I'd love to. She told me that in the fifties and before, the festival was a big deal. It drew people from all the surrounding counties."

"That's the goal." She hesitated. "Owen ..."

"Yeah?" He turned to face her squarely.

"I'm sorry. And thank you." She tore her gaze from his.

He didn't say anything but waited until she got up the nerve to look at him again.

When she lifted her eyes to his, he was smiling. She frowned. "What are you smiling about?"

"Positivity wins the day."

"Oh, brother." She closed her eyes to keep herself from rolling them.

Chapter Eleven

"Some old-fashioned things like fresh air and sunshine are hard to beat." —Laura Ingalls Wilder

"I'm so excited you're going to celebrate my grandparents' anniversary. They deserve it."

The young woman ushered them inside Ms. Alice's home. "I'm Rebecca, one of their nine grandchildren."

Maia was taken aback when the young woman answered the door. To say she was beautiful was an understatement.

She waved them to the sofa in the front room and went to tell her grandmother she had company. Looking around the room, two pictures caught her attention. One was of the very same Rebecca, from high school, in a crown and sash.

Of course, she was a beauty queen.

The other picture was of a young couple, all dressed up. The Bentleys on their wedding day, perhaps? Looking at it more closely, she saw the strong resemblance between Ms. Alice and her granddaughter.

"Penny for your thoughts?" Owen nudged her with his elbow.

"Looking at the pictures, wondering if we can borrow some for the anniversary party." Her gaze turned wide-eyed. He was nodding.

"Good idea."

Had he not noticed what she had about Rebecca? One, she was beautiful. Two? She wasn't wearing a ring of any kind—engagement *or* wedding. And last, she was approximately their age.

Ms. Alice came into the room with her granddaughter. "I'm so sorry I didn't hear the door. I guess when the young'uns are here, I let go and let them take care of things like rushing to the door." She took Rebecca's hand and squeezed it.

"I'm glad I can be here, Grandma." Rebecca kissed her grandmother's wrinkled cheek, then turned at Maia. "Do you need me?"

"I don't think so, but you're welcome to stay."

"I'll be in and out." The young woman stood and smiled. "If you need me, holler."

"Count on it."

"I understand you're interested in my upcoming wedding anniversary." Ms. Alice tilted her head, glancing from Maia to Owen, and back again. "When I told you my story, I had no idea it might become part of this year's festival."

The encouraging smile gave Maia the confidence to continue. "When Owen told me about your anniversary, and how the Daffodil Festival tied into it, ideas started popping into my head. We were talking about making changes to the festival, trying to liven it up, and that it might be nice to celebrate the history of the Daffodil Festival in Spring. What do you think?"

"Well, that's nice, but what do you need from me? I'm an old woman, you know."

Owen laughed, then coughed to cover it up. "Ms. Alice, you're the youngest octogenarian I've ever met."

"That's sweet of you to say, Owen." She leaned forward and whispered. "I'll pay you later."

This time, he didn't try to hide his laughter, and Maia joined in as Rebecca returned and sat next to her grandmother.

"Would you and Mr. Bentley be interested in being the Grand Marshals at this year's Daffodil Festival parade?" Owen asked. "Only if he's able, of course. At the very least, we want to host a reception in your honor at our church activity center. We would also like to recreate the Daffodil Festival of the early 1950s as much as possible. Do you think you could help us out with ideas for that?"

"Oh, my." Worry creased her brow. "We're hopeful Bill will be home from the hospital in time for our anniversary. But at our age, you never know."

Maia nodded. "We will do everything in our power to make this as easy on both of you as we can." She paused, hopeful. "What do you think?"

Ms. Alice glanced at her granddaughter and smiled. "I think it's a splendid idea." Finger to her chin, she tilted her head at Rebecca. "You know, I think you could fit into my wedding dress."

At that, Rebecca laughed. "I doubt very much if I could, but if it fits, I'll be more than happy to wear it. I've been told I'm the most like you of all your grandkids."

Ms. Alice put her arm around her granddaughter and arched a brow at Maia and Owen. "I suppose you noticed a slight resemblance."

∼

Maia was quiet on the ride back to City Hall. Owen shot quick glances at her. Was she upset about something? Or was she concerned about organization and activities?

Maia's statement startled him with its seamless entry into his thoughts. "Just thinking about how many people get married in the springtime."

Owen's brows shot up. "That was random."

"Not really. I mean, we're celebrating a couple who married that weekend seventy years ago." She turned to stare at him. "Seventy!"

"That's a long time, I agree." He pulled into an empty parking spot on the street, turned the car off, and shifted to face her. "What's going on in that creative brain of yours?"

The slight blush on her face thrilled him. "It wouldn't help anyone marrying that soon, but what if part of our festival were a wedding showcase? It wouldn't have to be big, but could be something, along with the Bentley's story, which would draw brides from all around. There are a couple of wedding venues out in the county, caterers, nearby wedding shops—a one-day event."

"In addition to the *Taste of Spring* dinner and the historical aspect of the festival?" He wanted to make sure he was on the same page.

"Definitely." She stared ahead, chewing her bottom lip.

He'd noticed she did that when she thought deeply.

"The parade and downtown festival, including the carnival rides, on Saturday, *Taste of Spring* on Saturday evening, and then the anniversary celebration and wedding expo on Sunday afternoon." She turned toward him. "What do you think? Could we put together something like this in a month?"

Her expression told him she wanted to know his opinion.

"I think it's doable. What about the other members of the committee?"

"We'll find out." She pulled out her phone and started tapping. "I'm sending a text to all the members inviting them to an emergency meeting today, at six." Widening her eyes, she turned to him. "Can you come today? I need your support."

When this girl got excited, she was all in.

"Where is the lady who was convinced this event couldn't happen?" He grinned.

"That lady finally heard a great idea." She paused, thinking. "She also is feeling much better having had allergy shots. My head's not as fuzzy."

"So, it's not my cheerful outlook rubbing off on you, but my doctoring skills?"

She grinned, her cheeks still an adorable shade of pink. "Maybe a little bit of both."

Chapter Twelve

"An optimist is the human personification of spring." —Susan J. Bissonette

March—Three weeks, five days until DF-Day (Daffodil Festival)

The always-put-together Mrs. Cotton was close to having an apoplectic fit. "Maia, honey, there's no way we can put together a Bridal Expo in less than a month."

"She's right. Screening all the vendors, finding a location ..." Curt Simmons agreed.

Maia held her hand up. "I know it's a stretch, but I think we can do it."

Dineen brought in a sheaf of paper. "Here are the possible wedding vendors within a hundred miles of here." She saw the crossed arms of the dissenting part of the committee and crossed her own, daring anyone to nay-say Maia's plan. "I'll leave you to it ..." She quickly scurried out the door.

Even Jasmine's face bore a slight frown. Was her friend

another dissenting vote, or was she worried about the logistics of coordinating three separate events? "I'm not sure what kind of scale we can promise, but I think a small group of vendors adjacent to the anniversary reception could work."

Bless you, my BFF.

Owen spoke up. "I'm with Jasmine. It might be something that can grow in time. This can be a test run. Who knows? Maybe this can be a yearly event? If it flops, we'll know it won't work." He raised his eyebrows as if trying to bring the rest of the committee along, by sheer force of will, to be positive about the only decent idea they'd had. Maia grinned.

When everyone started talking at once, Maia held up her hand. "Please." When their attention returned to her, she spoke quietly. "Let's pretend, for a moment, that this *can* work. We've put together events before, all of us. What are the steps to creating a new event?"

Tensions began to relax. Mrs. Cotton looked a little sheepish. She was not one to admit defeat, so this was a good exercise for her. "If we're spit-balling ideas based on the concept that this can be done, I guess the first thing is to find a venue and some interested vendors, keeping in mind that some of the restaurants in town are already committed to the *Taste of Spring* event Friday evening."

Maia nodded and held up the list the receptionist had handed her. She glanced at the names of the businesses, and noted some were highlighted, and some were crossed out. Dineen had done the legwork for her already. What a blessing.

Usually completely silent in these meetings, Claudia timidly raised her hand. "This is probably stupid—I mean, maybe the whole idea is stupid—but my sister is a cosmetologist. She could do makeovers." As soon as she spoke, she slumped back into her chair.

"That's what I'm talking about." Maia beamed. "We all

know people who could be involved. Claudia's sister is trying to build her clientele. Curt, doesn't your brother own the rental place where everybody gets their tents, tables, and chairs? Would they like a booth?"

He pondered, nodding. "It's short notice, but I could ask."

"That's all I need."

"My sister got married a few years ago. They started planning their wedding more than a year in advance." Owen narrowed his eyes. "If we targeted newly engaged couples, it could be a huge asset to the vendors. It might be a way of pitching it to them."

Bless you, Owen.

Maia turned a grateful look his way. "So, we've come up with several ideas. What do you think?"

Silence. Since she was usually the dissenting vote, it troubled her that her committee was squeamish with the one idea she'd had that she wanted to see come to fruition.

Glancing from one to the other, her spirits dropped when no one would meet her gaze. Except for Claudia. She might just have an ally, but she'd have to be subtle about it.

When he finished scribbling on his notepad, Curt looked up. "I've made a shortlist of possible venues and their liability and parking issues."

Mrs. Cotton raised her hand, excitement displayed on her face. "I have a younger homemaker group that would be great hostesses, and the older ladies could help us come up with DIY wedding craft booths and snacks."

"Now we're talking." Maia smiled. "Dineen has already contacted different vendors on the list, and about half of them are available for the date of the reception."

Owen's smile seemed meant for her. It started something in the region of her heart she wasn't expecting. He was on her side, not against her. And she was beginning to think the world wasn't against her, either.

Three weeks from DF-Day (Daffodil Festival)

OWEN WASN'T SURE, these days, if he was a doctor or a city employee. The Daffodil Festival plans were moving along, and one of his tasks was to partner with Nate on the logistics of using the church's fellowship hall for the Bentley's reception and the gymnasium for the Bridal Expo.

It wasn't a huge facility, so they'd mapped out thirty spots for various vendors and a stage area for local wedding shops to feature a fashion show.

At three weeks before the event, they had twenty-three participants and three wedding shops for the culminating fashion show, which included Ms. Alice's granddaughter wearing her grandmother's wedding dress.

Who knew that he, a bachelor, would be excited about a bridal fashion show?

Entering through the glass double doors, he glanced around, noting where they'd discussed different tables and decorations. Mrs. Cotton and her friends had taken on the task of making it look good for both the reception and the expo. They'd have only two days before the event to set up, and only a few hours to tear down and get the rooms ready for Sunday services.

"Hey, Owen!" Nate Comer walked toward him with a clipboard and a notebook. "How's it going?"

"A lot of details to put together."

"I get that. When an event like this happens, it means a lot of other things have to slide." Nate narrowed his eyes. "Anything in particular?"

"Just a few things on Maia's end—her boss isn't liking her concentrating on the festival." Owen arched a brow. "It would seem that his work is piling up. You know, the stuff that has his signature on it, but comes from Maia?"

"Yeah." Nate paused. "I hear you volunteered for a few extra duties."

Owen rubbed the back of his neck. "I want to make it as easy for her as possible."

The grin on Nate's face let Owen know that he wasn't hiding anything.

"Headed to the meeting?" Owen juggled his bag and binder.

"Yes. Maia and Mrs. Cotton are in the fellowship hall figuring out where to put what. Shall we join them?" Nate seemed to hesitate

"Something wrong?"

Nate looked around, his lips pressed slightly. "No, nothing's wrong." He averted his gaze.

Owen narrowed his eyes. His friend had seemed a little quiet lately, which was not like him. "Something is bothering you. I haven't known you that long, but I can tell when something isn't right."

"I guess I was hoping Jasmine would be on the wedding expo committee." Nate rubbed the back of his neck.

"Hmmm." Owen lifted a brow, feeling very smug. "Sorry, buddy. You're stuck with me and the other ladies, but I'd be glad to pass Jasmine a note in study hall later."

"You're hilarious." Nate tried to glare, but his expression was so comical Owen laughed, and then Nate joined in.

"Have you considered asking her out?"

"It's tricky, being an associate pastor." He avoided eye

contact. "Anyway, that's not the mission for this meeting, is it? Shall we join the ladies?"

Nate turned away, but Owen stopped him. "Hey, if I were Jasmine's brother, I'd be relieved if you asked her out."

"So, you have no interest in dating her?"

"Nope." Owen bounced on his toes, grinning. He'd admit it. He was excited, but not because of Jasmine Carter. There was another person who filled his thoughts, and while both ladies were brunettes, only one of them had eyes the color of dark chocolate.

Chapter Thirteen

"Always it's spring and everyone's in love and flowers pick themselves." —e e cummings

Mid-March—Two weeks from DF-Day
(Daffodil Festival)

T he weather forecast was not cooperating.

Maia woke to the same sound she'd fallen asleep to—a pounding thunderstorm.

"Ugh." She opened the blinds and stared out. Flash flooding, the sounds of emergency services rushing down the road to something—fire? Was someone hurt? She'd never been able to discern the different sirens.

If someone's in trouble, help them, Lord.

She paused. *And help me know what to do about this Daffodil Festival.*

The text-message notification on her phone gave a soft *ding,* and she picked it up from her bedside table.

Owen. She couldn't help it. A smile slipped out. Who

knows? Maybe God sent Owen there at such a time as this to bring her some encouragement. When she read the text, she giggled.

Good morning. Extra activity for the Daffodil Festival. White-water Rafting down Main Street.

And here was me, thinking we won't need to fill up the dunking booth. Just push people off a stool.

;)

She sighed and gathered her things to get ready for the day, her brain buzzing with details. The carnival vendor was considering backing out if it didn't stop raining in the next few days. If flooding became a problem, they'd have to come up with an alternative for all the activities. She had this image in her head of models in wedding gowns sandbagging the church instead of chatting it up with the expo-goers.

THIS WAS TOO much for texting. He'd have to call her.

Owen ended the call with Nate, and found Maia's number.

"Owen?" Maia sounded a little flustered.

"Hey, bad time?" He didn't want to start with bad news.

"Just got in City Hall through the monsoon. I cannot believe it out there."

"Yeah, I'm at the clinic, still in the car and dreading getting out." He paused. "I just talked to Nate."

"What's wrong?"

Owen could visualize her stiffening. Ordinarily, he'd tease

her out of her immediate negative response, but this time? She might be right.

"Mr. Bentley had to go back to the hospital by ambulance last night. We're not sure we'll be celebrating an anniversary. They're worried about a small brain bleed."

"Oh, no. That's serious." She took a deep breath.

"Are you okay?"

"I'm fine. Just thinking about Ms. Alice."

"And the reception?"

"No, I wasn't even going there yet. I'm not heartless."

Great. She sounded a little huffy, now.

"I know that. I supposed the Bridal Expo could go on without the reception."

"I suppose." She paused on the other end of the line. "Are you available for a lunch meeting? We need to make decisions based on the weather report I just saw."

"You think we might have to cancel?"

"I didn't say that."

What do you know? Now Maia's encouraging me?

"I can get down there around twelve-thirty. Will that be okay?"

"I'll try to have as much information as I can before you get here. Better go—I have some more phone calls to make."

"Sorry, Maia."

"Don't apologize. Any time you plan something this time of year—or around people—there's always a chance of calamity."

He winced. Ouch.

Chapter Fourteen

"Springtime is the land awakening. The March winds are the morning yawn." —Lewis Grizzard

Mid-March—One week before DF Day
(Daffodil Festival)

One week. It still wasn't too late to cancel the whole thing, but they were running close. Maia slumped in her chair and gave in to a huge sigh. It was too much.

There was a light rap on the door, and her officemate, Craig, stuck his head in. "Wanted to see if it was safe to come in my office."

"Come in, Craig." She straightened her shoulders and pasted a smile on her face. "How are you this morning?"

He grinned as he plopped down in his chair. "Nice and dandy, like cotton candy."

"Ugh, don't mention cotton candy." She covered her face with her hands.

He had the grace to look genuinely sorry. "Poor choice of words."

"It's okay. I've got an entire committee encouraging me to cancel everything. Today's the last day to safely call it off."

"Even Dr. Roswell wants to cancel?" Craig looked surprised.

"Even him." She swung around, facing him. "Am I crazy to think we can still pull this off?"

He thought a minute, serious. "Not crazy. Just uncharacteristically positive."

"I guess Owen's prayers were answered, then." She shook her head and snorted. "Now I just have to convince the rest of the committee that we can do this. It won't be easy."

"What does Bruce say?"

"Mr. 'Hands-off?" She twisted her lips. "Said it was all on me."

"Typical." Craig hesitated.

"What?"

"I was Bruce's assistant before I took the Cultural and Media Services job."

Not new information. "And?"

"And I can say from experience that Bruce would be perfectly happy to let the Daffodil Festival die."

Maia stood up, suddenly more determined than ever. "Okay, that's it. This festival is going to happen if it kills me."

Owen almost flinched when he saw Maia sweep into the conference room and take her place, standing at the head of the table.

"Good morning, folks. Just wanted to let you know that we *will* be having a Daffodil Festival. It might be a bust, but I genuinely believe if we put our heads together and work hard, we will have a successful event. It might not be to the level of our most successful festivals, but we're trying something new.

"I've been seeing buzz all over social media about the Bridal Expo—thanks to Craig—and I think it's something we can build on in coming years. We're here to celebrate spring, y'all." She glanced around at the surprised faces. "Besides, we've got five hundred pots of forced-bloomed Daffodils coming in three days. Does anyone have anything to say?"

Each member of the committee sat there.

Was this the same girl who, on day one of the committee, would have just as soon ditched the whole idea of a Daffodil Festival? Oddly, he felt a smile tug at his lips.

You did it, God. It wasn't anything I could do, but You could. Thanks.

After several uncomfortable seconds of silence, Owen got up the nerve to raise his hand. "I have something to say."

"Good." She sat down and gestured for him to continue.

"I spoke to Pastor Nate a little while ago. Mr. Bentley is home from the hospital. They've given him an almost-clean bill of health and told him that if he didn't push it, he could be in the parade, weather allowing, and attend the reception."

Maia's eyes filled with moisture. "Oh, Owen. That is amazing." She dashed a tear that threatened to fall. "I was so worried about that. Not for the festival, but I haven't been able to get Ms. Alice out of my mind, thinking how bad it would be to lose her husband so close to a milestone like this."

A throat cleared, and Curt Simmons raised his hand. A bit timid, for him. "I spoke to the carnival company. Since the rain has stopped, and we're not expected to get any more until after the event, they're willing to keep us on their list if we can move it to a parking lot."

"That's good news. Do you have any ideas about that?" Maia looked almost giddy.

He nodded. "My insurance office is in the shopping center next to the public parking lot, and it's never full on Saturday since we and other businesses are closed that day. We're proposing marking off part of our lot for the rides, and then the public lot will be available for just that—parking. We may have to reduce the number of rides to fit the space, but still ..."

Mrs. Cotton spoke up. "My homemaker clubs are excited about the Bridal Expo. When I mentioned we might have to cancel, they were distraught. They had already planned their schedule, put together crafts, and enlisted models from the service clubs at the high school to populate the fashion show." She smiled happily. "They'll be thrilled."

"Claudia and I have secured businesses to run some 1950s-style games and provide prizes." Jasmine linked her arm through Claudia's, squeezing.

The younger girl rolled her eyes. "My sister's salon is giving away five makeovers and haircuts at the Bridal Expo. They're talking about doing 'ambush' makeovers — you know, where they pick people out of the crowd and do the makeover and reveal it in front of everyone? It sounds horrible."

"Splendid!" Maia bounced a little on her toes and then clasped her hands together. "I think this is going to be the best Daffodil Festival in the history of Daffodil Festivals."

Owen almost laughed, but didn't when he saw an involuntary smile on young Claudia's face.

Chapter Fifteen

"Spring is nature's way of saying, 'Let's Party!'"
—Robin Williams

DF-Day (Daffodil Festival)

Maia stood in the gazebo on the court square, looking out over the vendors, the volunteers in matching T-shirts and jeans or circle skirts to keep with the 1950s theme, and the citizens of their small town, and county, lining the streets to watch the opening parade.

She was happy they hadn't decided to ditch the modern tech for historical accuracy because the walkie-talkie system was invaluable. The parade float lineup started three blocks down, and the participation was higher than it had been in ten years. At the beginning of the lineup, Mr. and Mrs. Bentley, wrapped in blankets, were ensconced in an antique 1955 Ford convertible.

"Hey, isn't it about time for the parade to start?" Jasmine was at her elbow.

She was a dynamo, and Maia knew there was no way she could have pulled this together without her. And Owen, of course. Her cheeks heated. She credited it to the sunshine pouring across the flower-bedecked bandstand.

"Just taking one more look before we start. Have you seen Nate?"

"He's on his way." Jasmine pointed at the lanky young man making his way through the crowd.

Maia signaled the director of the high school chorus—her sister, Frannie—that it was almost time for the National Anthem, then picked up the microphone.

"Good morning, Spring!" Her voice echoed across the town square. "Thank you for coming today, and we hope you enjoy all the activities we have planned. Ask a volunteer for a brochure that lists all the fun things you can do this weekend. I hope everyone enjoyed the sold-out *Taste of Spring* dinner—I may not eat for a week! And you can see anyone in the daffodil-yellow shirts for tickets to the Bridal Expo, if you haven't already got one.

"Before the parade starts, I'd like to ask Spring Church's Associate Pastor Nathan Comer to lead us in a prayer of thanksgiving. Then the Spring High School chorus will sing the National Anthem, led by Mrs. Frannie Brown. Pastor?"

"Bow with me, please. Lord, we are so thankful to be here on this beautiful day that only You can make. We praise You for blessing our people with sunshine and receding floodwaters, and for the leaders who made this celebration possible. Thank You, Lord, for Your gift of salvation. In Jesus' name we pray, Amen."

Nate handed the microphone back to Maia, but his eyes were on Jasmine. She reddened, and he winked.

Looked like more had been going on than planning a festival.

The chorus wrapped up the National Anthem to rousing applause. Maia was proud of her sister and the talent she shared with the community.

"Thank you, Frannie and Nate. And now, let the parade begin!"

Her heart was full.

As he passed the post office for the tenth time during the festival, Owen ducked in to check his mail. Then wished he'd never stopped in. It could have waited until Monday.

The envelope had no distinguishing marks to indicate it could be a life-changing opportunity.

Owen stared at the letter in his hand and shook his head. Now? Why *now*, of all times?

Pushing his way through the exit, he looked around to see happy citizens of Spring all around him, visiting booths, playing games ... all the things he'd helped pull together.

He turned to head back to the town square, and immediately ran into Nate.

"Hey, bro, does God have you on speed-dial or something?" Owen chuckled, and it sounded nervous, even to himself.

"I'd like to think so, but that's not why I'm here." Nate peered at him, a familiar, searching gaze. "Something wrong?"

Owen couldn't help but think about the blessings of friendship. He shook his head to clear it. "First, tell me what you need."

"Just wanted to let you know I may be late getting to the church to set up tomorrow's reception. The youth minister is sick, so I was tagged to supervise a group of teenagers volunteering at the dunking booth. I'll get there as soon as possible."

Doing his best to take deep breaths to relax himself, Owen realized Nate had stopped talking. He pulled his attention back to the conversation at hand.

"Sorry. I'm a little preoccupied." Owen cleared his throat. "No problem. Hey, if any of your stronger teens want to help out, bring them along."

"I will." Nate paused. "Now, what's goin' on with you? The look on your face is different than it was this morning." He scrutinized him more closely. "If I didn't know better, I'd think you were pale."

"Now you sound like my mother." Owen chuckled.

"I can only imagine how bright and intelligent she must be. But in the meantime, how's about you and I hold this bench down for a minute, and you tell me what's going on in that thick head of yours."

The sounds of the festival—music, laughter, the clanking sound of rides, animal noises from the petting zoo—all receded into the background as the problem at hand returned full-force.

Owen glanced around to see who was within earshot. No one he knew. "I received an offer I can't refuse."

"Is the Mafia involved?" Nate chuckled, then stopped at the serious look on Owen's face. "No Mafia?"

"I've been offered a job at a large allergy clinic in Nashville."

"Whoa."

"Yeah. Whoa." He shook his head, looking down. "It's a really good job."

"Like, dream job, good?"

Owen nodded. "Career-maker-good. I applied for it while I was still in med school. For me, that ship had sailed. No turning back. Until now." He was incredulous. "The director himself contacted me." He handed Nate the letter.

Nate read it, then looked up, eyes wide. "You'd have to be crazy to pass this up."

Chapter Sixteen

"Spring's greatest joy beyond a doubt is when it brings the children out." —Edgar Guest

DF-Day (Daffodil Festival)

While Owen was busy supervising a group of volunteers in the church's fellowship hall, Maia was overseeing the Bridal Expo. In a stroke of good fortune, he'd enlisted a few youth at the dunking booth to put their backs into setting up tables and enough chairs for two hundred people, including the large Bentley family.

He hadn't seen Maia since the parade that morning, and they'd been working in the same building most of the day.

It was amazing. The Bridal Expo showed no signs of winding down, even though it was almost time for it to end. Brides flocked to the volunteer models to get a closer look at the featured wedding gowns and stylish tuxedos. There was no way they could have predicted the success of the festival.

When Maia emerged from the gymnasium-turned-ballroom, Owen approached her, shaking his head in amazement. "Is it just me, or are people so ready to get out of the house that they're turning out for every activity they can attend?"

She smiled. "Including a bridal show. I'm thinking those middle-school-aged girls aren't planning a wedding very soon." Her laugh made him smile even while he dreaded the conversation he needed to have.

"I think we've hit on things our people care about—honoring the Bentleys brought family into the spotlight, celebrating our local restaurants, honoring our town's history, and celebrating marriage through the expo. Something for everyone."

Nodding, he concentrated on the happy crowd leaving the building, gift bags in tow. "I just came from downtown. There's still a crowd."

"How did the praise band do at the lunchtime entertainment?"

He grinned. "Great. I think folks are surprised we can have good 'church music.'"

"To be fair, it's not like our grandparents' church music." Maia stopped and tapped her chin with her finger. "Hmmm. We should have had fifties praise music—hymns—instead of modern-day praise music. In keeping with the theme, of course."

"I think the crowd enjoyed our music more." He laughed down at her with a wink, then paused. Was he leading her on? Or was he reading more into their recent compatibility than was there?

The woman by his side had taught him much during the past six weeks. He started out thinking he needed to teach her how to be positive and learn to like the spring season. But in the end, she'd taught him that when bad things happen—and they will, because life isn't just a series of good things—deal with them head on and not brush them aside. It would be so much easier to brush them aside ... Owen pulled his phone from his pocket to check the time. "Things will start breaking up soon."

She knew something was up. He could tell by her expression.

"Can we talk after things break up downtown?"

"That sounds serious."

Owen took a deep breath and averted his gaze.

"Is something wrong?"

He tilted his head and stared blankly out the double glass doors. "Depends on how you look at it." Shaking his head to clear it, he smiled at her. "Better head downtown and see if Curt needs any help."

"See you there, as soon as this is over." She smiled and walked to the clutch of expo-attendees, future brides and grooms, greeting different ones, and exclaiming over the wedding gowns.

He knew every last wedding dress would look better on Maia than anyone there, including the models.

"HE DIDN'T GIVE you any idea what was going on?" Jasmine frowned. "That doesn't sound like Owen."

"How much do we really know about him? I mean, he's lived here less than a year." Maia shook her head as she continued sweeping up trash after the Bridal Expo breakdown. "We don't really know him."

"It just surprises me. That's all. We may not have known

him long, but what we do know tells us he's pretty much an open book. Hmmm. Maybe Nate knows something."

"Looking for a reason to talk to Nate?"

"And what is wrong with that?"

"You just want an excuse to engage in conversation with our esteemed associate pastor. Get it? 'Engage?' I mean, we are at a bridal show." Maia giggled.

"That is one of your more terrible jokes." Jasmine looked her dead in the eye. "And if you jinx it, I'll never forgive you."

She was serious. It was obvious there was an attraction between the two, but it had been a slow-burn romance. Seeing the frown line between her BFF's brows, Maia couldn't help but laugh, then made the motions of locking her lips and throwing away the key.

Preoccupied, Maia's mind wandered. What to wear for the reception tomorrow? Dressy, but not too. Maybe a swingy skirt and heels? Was it too late in the season for boots?

"Earth to Maia." Jasmine's flat tone got her attention.

"Sorry. Wardrobe contemplation." Maia twisted her lips.

"Important stuff. I think I need to buy a new outfit after that meal last night." Jasmine patted her stomach. "Nothing's going to fit."

The petite beauty didn't have a spare ounce that Maia could see. "Please. You look amazing in whatever you wear. Even a flour sack, to pull in the 1950s vibe, would look good on you."

"I agree." Nate walked up behind Jasmine, who promptly turned all shades of red.

"You shouldn't sneak up on a person like that." Jasmine frowned, but her voice was anything but gruff.

"Downtown is calling my name." Maia sighed.

"It'll be okay." Jasmine put a reassuring hand on her arm.

Nate glanced from one to the other. "What's wrong? Is everything okay with the Bentleys?"

"They're fine." Maia squared her shoulders, her insides beginning to tremble in frustration. Everything was going great, and then Owen ... Don't go there. Not until this is over. "They're fine. I'm fine. Everything is fine. Right, Jasmine?"

The arched eyebrow didn't go unnoticed. "If you say so."

Chapter Seventeen

It was one of those March days when the sun shines hot and the wind blows cold, when it is summer in the light and winter in the shade."
—Charles Dickens

Owen's heart wasn't in the cleanup effort downtown. He knew what he had to do. Nothing had started between him and Maia, so it shouldn't be a big deal to end things. Right? How do you end something that hadn't started?

Maybe, deep down, it had.

Out of the corner of his eye, he saw her drive up. She was close enough he could see she wasn't happy.

This might be easier than he thought.

"Owen." She walked up to him, hands in her jacket pockets. Daffodil yellow, just like her official festival T-shirt.

"Hey." He turned toward her. "Bridal Expo done?"

"We have the first one in the books. I think the vendors were very pleased."

He nodded, then turned back to take in the flower-bedecked stage. "Folks had a good time today."

The silence was deafening. He'd never had problems stringing words together—and usually, he was the one handing out positivity tied up in a bow.

"What's wrong, Owen?"

No beating around the bush with this woman.

Taking a deep breath, he shook his head. He was a doctor. He knew all about ripping off the Band-Aid to get the pain over with. "I'm considering taking a job in Nashville."

Hazarding a glance her way, he saw utter surprise and ... pain in her expression.

"But ... When?"

"I got a letter this morning from an allergy specialist practice I'd applied to a year ago." He shrugged. "I never thought it was a possibility after this long."

"Good offer?"

He nodded. "It would be hard to refuse."

Nodding, she looked away, saying nothing for a few moments. She turned, her eyes a little overly bright—but maybe it was the lengthening shadows of the late afternoon playing with his vision. Facing him, she smiled, but it didn't quite meet her eyes.

Why was there a pressure in his chest that made him feel as if he were making the biggest mistake of his life?

MAIA WALKED AWAY. She didn't have time for this. When Henry broke it off with her, she'd buried herself in work to the point that she'd started hating her job, her life, and everything else she came into contact with—except Jasmine and her family.

Hate was too strong a word. She'd simply had a jaded view of life in general since the day she'd thought her heart was broken.

Turns out, it wasn't broken after all. If Henry had truly been 'the one,' would she have been so attracted to Owen? Was she so shallow she'd fall for the first guy who paid attention to her?

Shaking her head furiously, she turned off her vehicle and got out, dragging her bag with her.

When her phone buzzed with a text, she let out a loud "Grrr," and picked it up. Jasmine.

Hey. What's up with Owen?

Did she really want to get into this right now?

He's moving.

Whoa.

Jasmine's surprise was evident even via text.

You didn't know? I figured Nate told you.

Nary a word.

A stray thought came to her. It was good to know her associate pastor was a good confidant, because she knew Owen must have told him. It would explain the sorrowful looks she'd been getting from Nate for the last few hours.

Running a hot tub and soaking as long as I can.

Maybe that would cut the conversation.

I thought we were going to dinner?

I can't.

She hesitated. She didn't want to lash out at her best friend.

I don't think I'd be good company.

Nothing. Then the little dots began to dance around. She was texting back.

Girl, I understand. Really I do. But you've got to eat. Nate was going to meet me at the diner, and I originally planned to see if you and Owen wanted to join us, but if you need me, I'm there.

Bless her. She really would be too.

Go. Eat. I'm still not hungry from last night.

She really wasn't, but it wasn't just the amount of amazing food she'd eaten at the dinner.

Nate said Owen hasn't accepted the job yet.

So she's talked to Nate. At least someone is having a good day. The sigh that emanated from her could have knocked the house down.

But he will.

As much as she'd tried to tell herself that there was nothing between her and Owen, her heart told her otherwise.

Chapter Eighteen

"'Is the spring coming?' he said. 'What is it like?' ... 'It is the sun shining on the rain and the rain falling on the sunshine ...'"
—Frances Hodgson Burnett, The Secret Garden

So, this is spring. In Spring.

Owen glanced at the homes and beautiful yards as he drove to his house a few blocks away. A profusion of azaleas and dogwood trees, along with the ever-present daffodils usually made him happy. He'd done it. He'd experienced spring.

That was his goal, wasn't it? To experience all four seasons in a four-season climate. Then what was the matter with him?

Apparently, the job in Nashville came open recently when someone decided to move closer to home.

Home. He'd begun to think of Spring as home.

It annoyed him—no, it made him angry—that this unknown person had to wait until *now* to decide he didn't like living in Nashville. Now, when Owen had started thinking of this place as home, and of Maia as someone he could possibly have a future with ...

Was he crazy? The salary amount on the letter was exorbitant. He never expected to make that much money until later in his career. It would help knock out student loans in just a few years, while most of his friends had refinanced everything they owned and would still be paying on their education for twenty-plus years.

He sat in his car. If he went in, he'd start thinking about moving, start looking at places to live in the Green Hills neighborhood of Nashville, and start a downward spiral of regret at the thought of losing Maia.

But had he ever *had* Maia?

"This is crazy." He got out of the car and slammed the door. Stupid car. "Where's Dr. Positive, now?" He laughed at his own joke, but it wasn't a pleasant laugh.

His phone buzzed with a notification. He'd set his Bible app to send a notification by 6 p.m. if he hadn't already read his passage of the day. Usually, he beat it, but today, it was the last thing on his mind. Unfortunately.

Here it was. Luke 9, verses fifty-seven through sixty-two, about following Jesus. This wasn't long before His death and resurrection, but the people around Him didn't understand that.

As they were traveling on the road someone said to Him, "I will follow you wherever you go.

Jesus told him, "Foxes have dens, and birds of the sky have nests, but the Son of Man has no place to lay His head." Then He said to another, "Follow me."

Owen couldn't help but feel guilty. Here he was, bemoaning the fact that he'd been offered an amazing job.

"Lord,' he said, "first let me go bury my father."

But He told him, "Let the dead bury their own dead, but you go and spread the news of the kingdom of God."

Okay, spread the Good News. Owen knew he could do that anywhere he found himself, Right?

"Another said, "I will follow you, Lord, but first let me go and say goodbye to those at my house."

But Jesus said to him, "No one who puts his hand to the plow and looks back is fit for the kingdom of God."

So, which was it? Was he wrong to look back at the job he'd given up on and abandon his current situation? Was he wrong to *not* accept the new job? Which one constituted 'looking back?'

He stared at the ceiling, even knowing that wasn't where God was located. It just helped, sometimes, to have a direction. Something he sorely needed right now.

"Okay, God. You've got me where You want me. Could You share, please?"

Maia had finally dropped off to sleep around midnight. She'd read. Watched television. Scrolled through Facebook and Instagram. Played Solitaire on her phone.

Nothing helped. As tired as she was, she'd thought sleeping would be the least of her worries. Eventually, it was.

She'd fallen asleep praying.

The sounds of night filtered through her sleepy brain, and finally, she woke with a start to hear pounding on her door. She grabbed a sweatshirt lying on the floor next to the bed and shrugged it over her T-shirt and pajama pants.

"Dad?" She rubbed sleep from her eyes, surprised to see her father standing in the doorway, a panicked look on his face.

"Honey, you've got to get out of the house."

The beating of her heart was threatening to send it outward. "Why?"

Somehow, the smell of smoke and the sound of vehicles made it through her sensibilities. There was a fire. "Is my house on fire?" Smoke was already starting to irritate her widening eyes.

"No, next door, but your house is close." He swallowed, and she could see his Adam's apple rise and lower. "When I got the volunteer fire department call and saw the address, I was afraid it was your house."

She leaned in to hug her dad, dressed in his turnout gear. It was hard to get to him past three layers of protective clothing, but she was glad to have her dad. "Go. Take care of Mrs. Albertson." A sudden thought stopped her. "What about her cat?"

"As soon as we drove up, we saw her in the front yard with a large fluffy cat in tow."

"That's Mr. Whiskers." She gazed heavenward. "Thank you, Lord." I'll go see if she needs anything." She pulled a couple of jackets from the pegboard next to her front door.

Jogging across the yard to her elderly neighbor, she stopped short when she ran into another firefighter. "Sorry."

"No problem." He stopped. "Maia?"

"Owen?" Her heart felt a jolt just about as real as the one that woke her minutes ago. "I need to see if Mrs. Albertson needs a jacket." The lady sat on the firetruck's bumper, a blanket around her and holding an oxygen mask to her face.

"Looks like she's being taken care of." Owen gestured with his head, his fire hat bobbling before he straightened it.

"Yeah." Awkward. He was a volunteer firefighter? Since when?

"I gotta ..."

"Yeah, go."

He touched her arm with his gloved hand, pausing just a few seconds before running to his station.

So, he's one of the good ones.

With her luck, that was exactly why a relationship wouldn't work.

Wait. What relationship?

Owen turned to look back at Maia as she made her way through the soaked yard to get to her neighbor. One of the EMTs handed her the cat he'd been holding while its owner held the oxygen to her face. He seemed happy to hand off the huge feline.

At least she wasn't allergic to cats.

She cuddled the cat, swaying automatically as if holding a baby.

"Focus, man. First, you think of her in a wedding dress, and now with a baby?" His internal conversation would sound crazy if anyone else heard it. Maybe he was. Crazy, that is.

That thought came out of nowhere, and he grinned behind his oversized helmet visor. When he realized he was looking back, the verse he'd read earlier came back to him.

"No one who puts his hand to the plow and looks back is fit for the kingdom of God."

With a shake of his head, he put on his breathing apparatus and grabbed the ax that he'd been assigned, then entered the house with smoke billowing out the front door.

Inside, the only light came from his headlamp and the beams of the other firefighters. The captain, Maia's co-worker Craig, motioned for Owen to follow him. Usually spouting a joke-a-minute, Craig was dead serious when it came to fire.

The roar in the next room grew louder. Craig yelled over

the flames and the sound of the firehose dousing the house. "Started in the kitchen. Door's stuck – must have something in the way."

When Owen tried the door, he confirmed. That door wasn't going anywhere. That's where the ax came in. Finally, a use for the training he'd completed a few months ago.

If anyone had seen him practicing in the backyard, they'd have thought he was crazy or an ax murderer. Neither. He didn't want to embarrass himself in front of his colleagues, who were of every age, gender, shape, and size. Besides the women, he was one of the smaller guys.

Whacking at the stubborn door, he felt it give.

"Careful, Owen ..." Craig had his back.

Using the head of the ax, he shoved it into the door close to the knob. Maybe that would break it. When he finally went through, it pitched him forward, into the flames. The room was fully engulfed, and he'd landed face-first into it.

MAIA WAS STARTLED when she heard shouting.

"Man down! Man down!"

Mesmerized, she watched as the trained men and women—regular people—pulled together and got the man out quickly and efficiently.

Who was it?

The EMTs rushed to the body the firefighters had pulled out of the fire. In turnout gear, all of them looked alike. She saw her dad take off his helmet, though, and was relieved.

"Oh, I do hope no one is hurt." Tears ran down Mrs. Albertson's face, making tracks on her soot-stained cheeks.

"Me too." She sat next to the older lady, feeling helpless

and on the verge of tears, herself. Why did she know nothing about how to help in an emergency like this?

Rushing the gurney to the ambulance and rescue truck, one of the EMTs pulled the helmet off to reveal the victim.

It was Owen.

He was breathing.

"Thank you, God."

Chapter Nineteen

"Where flowers bloom, so does hope."
—Lady Bird Johnson

"Mom, I promise. I'm okay."

Though he'd face-planted into a fire, he was fine. A few scorched places, but the equipment he wore had kept him safe. Glad they were on a two-hour time difference, he'd waited until the next morning to fill her in. The last thing he wanted was for her to read it online before he had time to reassure her.

When he finally ended the call, he shook his head. Mom would never understand why he became a volunteer firefighter, why he lived in a small town in Kentucky. She couldn't understand most of his decisions, to be honest. To her, his current path was a bad use of his skills.

For him? It was a way to give back. He'd been blessed and wanted to stay in the background. The last thing he wanted was attention.

Last night, once he was up, sitting on the ground next to the ambulance, the call came across the lawn the fire had been contained. Relief. His fear that rescuing *him* would hold up the process of extinguishing the fire, thereby putting more people at risk, eased. Owen looked back at Maia and her neighbor to see her eyes on him with an expression he'd never forget.

That's when he made the decision.

Maia couldn't stand the smell of smoke on her clothes, so she took a long, hot shower at 2 a.m. Not her usual grooming time.

Tomorrow—scratch that, make it today—was the anniversary reception for the Bentleys. She had to get some sleep if she wanted to be present for the festivities. It was her baby.

Sleep? What a grand idea. The events of the late-night, early-morning fire kept coming over her in waves. Too much excitement. From the time her dad woke her from a deep sleep to seeing Owen being pulled from the fire, Maia was geared up in a way she'd never been before.

Was this what love felt like?

The sick feeling in the pit of her stomach, along with the acrid smell of soot in her sinuses no matter how steamy the shower, kept her keyed up.

But that sick feeling had nothing to do with the fire. It had everything to do with realizing Owen had been the 'man down.' Did she want to feel that kind of fear? Was it worth it?

Her phone buzzed with a text. Not many people knew she would be up at this hour. But Owen would.

Hey. You okay?

She shook her head.

I should be the one asking YOU that question.

I'm fine. Beard got a little singed, but the helmet did its job.

I'm glad.

Crickets. Nothing. Finally, she saw he was either reading her text, or writing one. And it seemed to take forever.

Our conversation didn't go the way I hoped it would.

Hmph. What did he expect? *Be nice, Maia. Be nice.*

Congratulations on your new job.

There. Couldn't complain about that, now could he? Again, the blank screen underneath her statement. Maybe he'd fallen asleep?

I'll see you at the reception tomorrow.

I'll be there.

Goodnight, Maia.

Goodnight, Owen.

Then, nothing. Mercifully, she finally felt her eyelids droop.

HE'D SWAPPED duties with Nate to be closer to her. He had to find time to talk to her. Tell her how he felt.

As he nearly found out last night, life's too short.

When Maia realized what he and Nate had done, she used every excuse in the book to stay clear of him.

Two could play at that game.

For every time she finagled a way to distance herself, he came up with a way to get closer to her. She was pleasant, but there was an edge.

And she looked tired. He wanted, somehow, to lighten her load. He should have waited until after this weekend to tell her about the job, but that was water under the bridge. Or rather, in the case of Spring, Kentucky, sometimes it was water *over* the bridge.

Rebecca Bentley had been radiant in Mrs. Alice's 1952 wedding gown. It fit her perfectly. Owen was sure she was a pretty girl, but all he could see was Maia.

Both Mr. and Mrs. Bentley had a good time greeting friends and family and cutting a seventieth-anniversary cake replica, much like the conservative three-tiered confection of so many years ago.

Seventy years. At the rate he was going he'd have to get married within the next year to make that by the time he turned 100.

Chapter Twenty

"Spring drew on ... and a greenness grew over those brown beds, which, freshening daily, suggested the thought that hope traversed them at night and left each morning brighter traces of her steps."
—*Charlotte Brontë*

The Bentleys had left for a private celebration of their own at their daughter's house, but the look of happiness and contentment on their faces touched Maia. Her heart was full to overflowing.

There was only one thing that could spoil her mood now, and he was walking toward her, carrying a large trash bag.

"Thanks, Owen. You've been a big help." She had a hard time making eye contact. "I think I'll swing by the court square and make sure everything is in place for a normal workday on Monday.

"I'll drive you."

"It's not ..."

"I'll drive you. I'm your assistant, after all." He gave her a whimsical smile and continued toward the door. Turning and walking backward, he gave her an order. "Don't leave without me." Watching him go through the shining glass door, she wondered why he was determined to drag this out.

Stop it Maia.

Wasn't talking to yourself in an empty room a little troubling? After this weekend, she figured she could get by with it.

Owen had been a Godsend. Not only had he helped her come around to the idea of celebrating the season, but he'd encouraged her to step out of her comfort zone. It's easy to focus on the negative, but focusing on the positive is what got things done. With Owen's help, she pulled herself up by her bootstraps, and he'd been right there beside her.

Assistant? No, he was her partner. The thought sent a slight shiver through her body.

And he was leaving. Par for the course. Negative Nellie still threatened to rear her ugly head. She'd have to work on that.

When they got downtown, she saw that the risers had been picked up, and all the carnival rides had been removed as quickly as they'd arrived.

Volunteers from the school came earlier in the afternoon to pick up trash and sweep up. It was Sunday afternoon, so it was quiet, and the sun was dipping into the horizon.

"Penny for them?"

The fight within, between being angry and being hurt, decided to lay low. She was tired. She'd go with positive this time. Maybe it would last. Lips twisting in some form of an exhausted grin, she finally got up the nerve to face him. "Just a penny? For *my* thoughts? I'm insulted."

"Okay, then, a dollar?"

"Make it a dollar-fifty, and we might have a deal."

"Done."

His hands were stuffed in his pockets. She did the same, glad she'd put an extra jacket in the car. Temperatures were still cool in the evenings.

"I think I'm glad I met you." She tilted her head. "You didn't expect that, did you?"

"No." He looked away, then down at his toes. "I'm glad I met you too." He squinted a little in the bright low-lying sun. "I didn't come here expecting to make good friends so quickly."

Good friends.

Maybe it wouldn't be so hard to see him leave. If he stayed after placing her in the friend-zone, she would have to get over him slowly. It's probably best this way.

"What I meant to say was that I didn't expect to meet *you*."

"So, I fall into the 'good friend' category? That's nice."

Okay, she was getting irritated. It happened when she was really tired. And really emotional. Crying would be the last straw.

"No, you're not in the 'good friend' category." He narrowed his eyes. "You're ..." He closed his mouth and looked miserable. "I don't want to go to Nashville."

Her heart leaped, but she remained calm. Better to be cautious. "Are you sure?"

"Positive." He stepped closer to her. "Let's walk a little."

She shivered. Not from the cold, so much, as from her warring emotions. Falling into step with him, she said nothing when he reached for her hand.

That was new.

The deep breath seemed to relax him. "You still haven't told me what you're thinking."

Thoughts? She couldn't formulate a sentence right now if her life depended on it. At least she wasn't facing him, and it was starting to get dark, so he couldn't see her red face. Could she be honest? Could she trust him with her heart?

"You, first. Thoughts from the man of the hour."

Groaning, he relaxed and shook his head. "All I did was fall into the fire."

"Small town. It doesn't take a lot to make news." She was beginning to enjoy herself, to relax, to feel at home with him again. But she couldn't be too easy on him. "Tell me what you're thinking?"

"My thoughts are so good I may have to save them for a bigger audience."

"Ah. I'm not enough, eh?" she teased.

Turning to face her, he focused on her hand in his. "You want to know what's on my mind?"

Maia nodded solemnly.

"Remember, you asked for it. What's on my mind is I'm amazed at your ability to take what could have been a dismal experience and made it incredible. There, you have it. I think you're incredible, and I want to know everything about you."

There was a lump in her throat she couldn't get past, and tears threatened. They weren't tears of frustration or sadness, but relief.

"Come on." Owen caught a stray tear and smiled, tugging her along.

She could have walked hand-in-hand with Owen forever, occasionally glancing at him to see if this was real. That was how happy she was at this moment. Sure, there would be times when his positivity might rub her the wrong way, or that her negativity would discourage him, but she didn't want to think about that.

The focus was now.

ONCE THE CITY police removed the traffic barriers, the downtown area of Spring would be as if nothing had happened. As if it were just a regular Sunday evening in April. Only the Daffodils remained.

Maia had a feeling nothing would feel *regular* again since she'd met Owen.

"I just realized something." Owen stopped and turned toward her.

"What?" She chuckled, seeing the look of utter surprise on his face.

"We've never been out on a date." He paused, staring at her. "We've been working on this festival nonstop for over six weeks, and I've never asked you out on a date."

Her stomach fluttered, and her skin tingled where he still held her hand. She tipped her head to one side. "And?"

"Stay here. I'll be right back." He released her hand and walked to the other side of the square. When he came back into view, he held out a Daffodil, the official flower of Spring. "Starting today, we look forward, not back."

"Is that another one of your 'positivity' statements?" Maia chuckled. "I'm learning a few things from you about looking forward."

"Whatever works." The smile on his face bloomed.

"For me?"

He stood there, offering the flower to her, until she took it, then pulled her gently toward him.

The dainty yellow flower smelled like spring, and as he pulled her closer, she felt it begin. There was no way to stop it. She was paralyzed in a maze of feelings and involuntary movement. The only thing she could do was turn away. She didn't want to, but she knew it was no way to start a relationship.

She pulled away, and suddenly had to let go. The sneeze

she tried desperately to stifle came out in not one ... not three ... but seven sneezes.

As she began to breathe normally, she realized that he was shaking with laughter. He pulled her closer for a few moments, enveloping her in a hug that she wished never had to end. Safe. Content in his arms.

Pulling back to look at her, he grinned. "Maia Pascal, will you go out on a date with me?"

"Just a minute." He kept her in the circle of his arms as she reached into her jacket pocket for the small packet of tissues she always kept with her. After blowing her nose, she rested her hands on his chest and looked deeply into his eyes. "On one condition."

He pulled her closer, his eyes shining. "Anything."

"Please don't bring me flowers." She began to giggle.

Owen threw back his head in laughter, then pulled her even closer, if possible. "I promise never to bring you flowers, trees, grass, or any kind of plant life." He frowned. "Wait a minute. You're allergic to everything *but* daffodils."

"Do you think I need to get a second opinion?" She chuckled as he pulled her closer. "No flowers, but chocolate is always welcome." Her voice shook and her knees weakened. She couldn't keep her gaze off his lips, wondering what it would be like to kiss them.

"Noted." His gaze was intense.

When he leaned in to capture her lips, she realized she'd stopped breathing in anticipation. It didn't matter. He was breathing for her.

He raised his head, caressed her cheek with his fingers, his eyes never leaving hers, a silly grin on his face. "I've wanted to do that for a long time."

"I may have thought about it a few times myself." Maia's mind and heart were racing. She almost forgot where they were. When she met Owen Roswell at City Hall, she didn't understand him. She would have never thought she would fall for someone like him. What must he think of her? They were so different, and yet ...

"Maia ...?"

It confused her when she heard her name, but it wasn't coming out of Owen's mouth. Then it dawned on her.

"Jasmine."

"What?" Owen looked confused.

Maia closed her eyes. She was supposed to meet her friend for supper at The Diner.

Biting her lip, she gave him her best *sorry* look and turned toward the laughing figure of her best friend. "I forgot we had a date."

"Looks like I've been stood up." Jasmine laughed out loud, then glanced at the young man at her side. "Maybe we could double?"

"Sounds good to me." Nate smiled. "First dates all around?"

Maia was glad it was nearly dark as her face heated to scarlet. "Owen?"

He shrugged. "Sure."

All she could see, now, was his silhouette. If she could have seen him more clearly, she knew he would look slightly disappointed, as was she. At this point, she hadn't experienced enough of his kisses, but they had plenty of time. The rest of their lives?

A voice, this time definitely Jasmine, interrupted her thoughts. "Do you think I can get them to turn on the waffle iron?" Jasmine bit her lip, frowning.

Maia tucked her fingers around Owen's, and they began the block-long walk to The Diner. Four friends, two couples.

Of this, Maia was positive.

About Regina Merrick

Regina Rudd Merrick is a multi-published writer, church musician, wife, mother, former librarian, lover of all things beachy and chocolate, and grateful follower of Jesus Christ. Married nearly 40 years to her husband, she has two beautiful daughters and a delightful son-in-law, and lives in the small town of Marion, Kentucky. Her books include the Southern Breeze Series set in South Carolina, her favorite beachy state, and the RenoVations series set in Kentucky.

Find her books on Amazon or other retailers, and connect with Regina on Facebook, Twitter, Instagram, or on her website at https://www.reginaruddmerrick.com.

THE

Missing

PIECE

AMY R. ANGUISH

From one quilt-lover
to another, may all
your seams line up
Love,
Amy Anguish

This one is dedicated to my Mom and grandmothers for teaching me the joy of sewing—even if that means mastering the art of using a seam ripper first. The patience and love you put in every stitch through the years hopefully comes through in this story too.

Acknowledgments

Thanks to my fellow authors, Heather, Sarah, and Regina, who agreed to do a collection of novellas with me and put up with my self-imposed stress about planning things and preparing months ahead of when things are due.

Thanks to my family who puts up with me disappearing into my stories for hours at a time.

Thanks to the quilt shops, who bring so much happiness to lives like mine. Especially to the Stitcher's Playhouse and Thread Lightly, who have served myself and my mom the last few years.

Thanks to my editors who continue to help me grow and stretch and become better with each story I put out.

And thanks to my readers. Without you, there would be no point in me writing these stories!

Chapter One

"What's that sigh about?" Beth Norton glanced over at her mom on the other side of the desk.

"I've been able to determine some of these scribblings Laura left behind. But not enough. And I'm pretty sure we missed a payment or two."

Beth's heart sank to her stomach. "Any idea how much?"

"Not sure, but bills add up fast." Mom pulled her brown hair away from her face. "Laura was the financial and business-minded one—my expertise is more the customers."

"Mine too." Beth sighed. "But the Watermelon Festival is in just a few weeks."

"I heard that somewhere." Mom shot her a wink. "Maybe every time you found a new pattern to try out. You've only been sewing for our booth for months."

"Our booth is going to be the best ever this year. I've already completed three full-sized quilts, two twin, and several baby-sized too. Down to pillows, table runners, potholders, and other small items."

"If you kill yourself doing this, is it really going to be worth it?"

"If we win the Best Watermelon Festival Spirit award, the prize money would give us a tiny cushion, more notice, and honor Mama Laura's memory—she adored all things watermelon." Beth had been researching other ways to draw in more customers, too. The festival would be the perfect time to take advantage, as people flocked to their small town from all over the state.

"I know, I know." Mom glanced around at the piles of paperwork covering the desk. "But I'm working on a few other ideas too."

"You aren't going to need any other ideas. This is going to work." Beth gave a sharp nod. "Speaking of which, I'd better get back to it. I only came in here to print out this pattern piece I lost somewhere. That table runner isn't going to sew itself."

Back through the quilt shop and into the front room, set up with sewing machines and a cutting table, Beth cranked her radio up and sat at the machine which had been her near-constant companion these last few months. But it would be worth it. Soon, she found her rhythm and had the machine humming along at a good clip.

"Since when do you listen to pop rock?"

Beth jerked as her hand pushed the fabric under the sewing machine's needle. Air hissed through her lips as pain shot through her thumb, and the machine's hum groaned then stopped. Lifting the presser foot, she jerked her throbbing thumb out and stuck it in her mouth then turned to see who had snuck in.

"Sorry. You okay?" He stood in the doorway, about six feet even, a ball cap shading his eyes and a short brown beard covering his face. Despite the familiar voice, nothing about him looked recognizable, and his identity remained just out of her mind's reach.

"Fine." She faked a smile that she hoped looked hospitable, then stood and strode toward the store's small kitchen. Cold water had her cringing, even with the hot July sun coming through the window. But she needed to wash the needle wound before she could fully assess the damage.

"How can I help?"

There he was again. Hadn't he caused enough trouble? And how had she not heard the front doorbell?

She turned the faucet off and wrapped her hand in a paper towel. Blood seeped through the white material, spreading into a flowery blob. "Look in that drawer over there and see if there are any bandages left. I can't get the bleeding to stop." She bobbed her head toward the other counter's far end.

Darting to the drawer she indicated, he dug through its mess as if he belonged there. Who was this guy? And what was he doing in a quilt store in Sassafras, Arkansas, of all places?

"Ta da!" He lifted a mostly empty box stashed behind several old pairs of scissors and at least a dozen twist ties. "Let's see if we can get you patched up. I didn't see any antiseptic in there."

"I haven't died from pricking my finger yet." She lifted the soaked towel away and huffed as more red seeped out. Apparently, the needle had gone all the way through her thumb nail—a clean puncture. The nail side was bleeding more than the other, though.

"Here we go." He peeled the backing off a medium sized bandage and carefully wrapped it around her thumb. As his hand cradled hers, a new awareness of him seeped in. That, and the familiar scent of sandalwood and something else outdoorsy.

Before she could formulate a thought, he lifted her hand

and pressed a kiss to her sore digit. Shock and something else zinged through her. What in the world? Her gaze darted up to his face.

From this vantage point, she had a better view up under the brim of his hat. Two familiar brown eyes focused on her bandaged thumb. *Tommy?* Her rebellious heart skipped a beat before remembering how he'd betrayed and abandoned her all those years ago.

"Tommy." His name breathed from her mouth.

"How's that? Too tight?" His focus moved to her face.

She blinked and jerked away. Much too tight, but she was thinking about her heart more than her finger.

"Fine. Thanks." Never in a million years would she admit the dressing needed to be loosened before she lost circulation. She could fix it after he left.

"I didn't mean to startle you. I thought you heard the door." Tommy hooked a thumb over his shoulder, motioning toward the store front. His voice was deeper now, just different enough it hadn't completely registered earlier.

"No. I guess the machine drowned it out." She slid past him and pulled out the piece she'd been working on. No blood stains marred the white background or bright pink appliqué. But she'd have to replace the needle.

"Or maybe this music." He turned down the radio. "I don't remember you listening to this genre before."

"It's not like you've been around the last seven years." She loosened the screw so she could slide the old needle out and insert a new one. "You don't know a lot about me."

He rubbed a hand over the back of his neck. "Yeah. I know. When I left for college, I had no idea I'd get a job offer somewhere else right out of school. Trust me. I wish I'd been back more."

At the break in his voice, regret stirred in her chest. His

mom, who Beth lovingly referred to as Mama Laura, had been gone three months now. He had to be thinking about how little he'd seen her, not realizing cancer would steal her away before any of them were ready.

"So, you work here now?" The sadness lingered in his voice.

"For the last several years. Mom needs me more than ever. Especially with the Watermelon Festival coming up."

"She's actually the reason I'm here. She called and said she needed help." He glanced around as if expecting to see Mom over his shoulder.

He was Mom's Plan B? Surely not!

"She's in the office. Feel free to go on back. She's been trying to decipher your mom's notes and plans and organization strategy but isn't having much luck. That's probably why she called." Though Beth wished her mom had at least warned her Tommy was in town and might be coming by.

Then, maybe she could've prepared her heart to see him again. Braced herself for how good he looked with that beard and more muscles—details she hadn't noticed at Mama Laura's funeral when she'd been busy avoiding him. Or at least given her time to find an excuse to hide. When had he returned to town anyway?

"Right. Thanks." He paused in the doorway. "We should catch up sometime."

She refused to meet his eye. "I don't know. I'm pretty swamped right now, working on things to sell at the festival."

"Is something wrong, Bethie?" He lingered.

Seriously?

"I haven't been called Bethie in over seven years." Her voice came out more bitter than she intended, but so be it.

If he had to ask that question, he didn't deserve an answer. In years past, he could read her mind better than anyone other than Paige. But that ended years ago, back when they were seniors in high school.

"There you are." Mom's voice rang through the now quiet store. "You wouldn't believe how much trouble I'm having with these notes your mom left about the business's financial side."

Tommy shot Beth one more look before grinning and turning toward Mom. He wrapped her up in a hug like he'd done his whole life. After all, Beth and Tommy had been raised together, playing under the quilt frame in the back room, hiding and seeking between the fabric shelves. How could they be so estranged now?

"Hey, Mama Marsha. I make no promises, but I'm willing to take a look." He rested his arm across her shoulders as they walked down a row of green cotton prints toward the office.

"I miss your mom every day, Tommy. How are you and your dad holding up?" Mom's voice drifted away.

Beth laid her head down on the table for a moment before lifting it and loosening her bandage. Moisture gathered at the edges of her eyes, but she refused to let it fall. Not now. She'd told herself she'd moved on, and she planned to live up to that.

Beth glanced at the clock and then to the half-sewn watermelon table runner. Would it be ridiculous to go to lunch this early? She eyed the clock again, shot her mom a quick text, and slipped out the back door before she changed her mind. Perhaps Tommy would be gone when she returned. Hopefully for good.

"Hey, Beth. The usual?" Dawn grinned over her shoulder as Beth entered the sandwich shop.

"Please and thank you." Beth studied the menu to see what all Dawn had added, though she rarely varied in her order.

"Want to help taste test my new watermelon smoothie? I'm trying to come up with several recipes for the festival." Dawn pointed to a blender full of bright pink slush.

"No, thanks. But I'm sure whatever you make will be great." Beth paid for her order, but all the tables in the small deli were full. So much for staying here longer. In the July heat, even in the shade, it would be too uncomfortable to stay out long, so a picnic was out. Nothing to do, but head back to The Missing Piece.

The door jangled as she neared the corner the shop occupied. She paused, peeking around the brick. Tommy stepped out, pulled his baseball cap back on over his brown waves, and headed in the opposite direction. His shoulders were broader than she remembered, but also held what looked like the weight of five men instead of just one.

A twinge of guilt tempted her to call out and take him up on that offer to catch up, but she held back. Much as their history had her wanting to comfort him in Mama Laura's loss, the rest of their past got in the way. No need to set herself up to fall into the same temptation once more. She knew from experience that only led to heartache.

Chapter Two

Tommy London sighed as he opened his mom's sewing room closet. Just when he thought he had all the fabric sorted, four more big rubber tubs sat there mocking him. Why did a woman who co-owned a quilt store need this much of a stash at home?

When his father mentioned wanting to go through his mom's things this summer, Tommy couldn't let him do it alone. He'd finally reached a point in his career where he felt he could branch out on his own and work his website business from anywhere, without his mentor at the next desk. Between that and having yet another relationship go belly up, he packed up his few things and moved back to Sassafras.

Dad stepped into the doorway. "Is that what I think it is?" His voice held a touch of groan.

"Of course." Tommy hefted a box out and peeled off the lid. "Looks like heavier weight stuff. Denim and corduroy and whatnot."

"You can tell you grew up around a seamstress." His dad

perched on the upholstered chair in the corner. "Not many guys your age could list different kinds of fabric."

"Well, it helps that I also wear those kinds." Tommy smirked over his shoulder. "What are we going to do with all of this?"

"I was thinking about asking Marsha. If anyone in town knows where to get rid of a lifetime's worth of fabric, she will." Dad ran a hand through thinning hair. "Who knows what your mother had planned for it."

"A lot of it is probably leftover from various projects. Remember how she used to make me outfits when I was little? And she always had some craft or activity going."

"She was a Tabitha, through and through."

The mention of the woman in the Bible who sewed clothes for the needy pinched Tommy's heart. He'd been raised in a home where Christ shone in every corner, but had he continued the tradition and faith when he moved out? Had his mom died disappointed in him?

Not that Tommy was interested in God right now, either. What could he find in a god who would allow a woman, not even fifty, to die before seeing her son marry and have his own children? Who'd let someone who worked so hard to sew and take care of others succumb to cancer? Where were the apostles now to raise her from the dead?

"You all right?" Dad leaned forward and rested a hand on Tommy's shoulder.

"Right as can be." Tommy sealed that tub and grabbed the next. Flimsier pieces filled it, everything from tulle to satin. The next held all floral prints. He set those aside.

"What else is left in here?" Dad stretched as he stood.

"Just what's in the closet, unless she hid another stash behind a secret panel in the wall or something." Tommy lifted the last box out and opened it.

He paused. The material was sewn already. He picked up a small pair of plaid overalls he'd worn as a child. The cotton had held up well through the years, and a good wash would show this outfit wearable by someone else. Beneath that were a few other outfits, a couple baby blankets, and some dinosaur pajamas he'd worn in elementary school. All lovingly stitched by his mother. He had no idea she saved them.

An arm came around his shoulders, and Tommy leaned into the comfort Dad offered. At times, the grief crept up his throat, threatening to choke him, squeezing moisture out of his eyes he hadn't even known was there. Neither of them knew exactly what to do without Mom's presence in this house. Last night, he'd set three plates on the table because he'd always done that ... except for the nights Beth had been over for dinner.

Speaking of Beth. Wasn't that material from a dress she'd worn in their middle school play? Tommy leaned out of the embrace and lifted a much larger project. A quilt? Tiny rectangles curved into rings, intersecting each other on a white background. It was intricate and lovely.

But it wasn't finished. One corner lacked being pieced. And there was no batting or back. Most of the quilts his mom made had been smaller, lap-sized for elderly women or tiny for babies. This would cover a queen-sized bed easily.

Who had Mom been making this for? She must've started years before. Several pieces were from baby outfits. He recognized the tiny elephants from pictures.

"What's that?" Dad reached out to touch the unfinished blanket.

"Looks like a quilt. Though it's not finished."

"Huh." Dad flipped it over to the back and then right side up again. "I remember her working on it some through the years, but had no idea it was this big. I always figured it was pieces for other projects."

"Too bad she didn't complete it."

"I'm sure Marsha could help. She probably knew the final plan for it, too, considering how close those two were." Dad pushed back up off the floor and lifted a tub. "Since you were running these over there anyway, why not take that and see if she can finish it for you?"

Tommy didn't remember actually agreeing to take the extra material to The Missing Piece. But it sounded like his plans had been made for him. He'd promised Mama Marsha he'd come back by to help sort out more of his mom's notes and scribbles, anyway. Might as well knock all the birds out in one fell swoop.

Though he might try to avoid Beth next time. She was more than a little prickly earlier today, especially when he used her nickname. Was she simply upset about the needle puncturing her thumb or was it something else? Guilt tried to harass him about the wound, but he pushed it back. How could he have known she'd startle that much when he called out?

Besides, there was more to it. He might not have spent much time—okay, really any time—with her in the last seven years, but he still knew her well enough to read her expressions. She was hurt over something, though he couldn't fathom what. It didn't look like grief over losing his mom.

And if he had to guess, he'd say she hadn't recognized him at first. How was that possible? They'd spent more time together, growing up, than with their own families. He hadn't changed that much.

"Got that tub?" Dad huffed as he returned to the room. "I'll grab this other one."

Tommy smothered a sigh and bent his knees to pick up the heaviest box. Something which seemed so light when made into an outfit or curtains or whatever shouldn't weigh this much in its raw form. His breath came in pants by the time he'd schlepped it through the house and out to the garage.

Dad glanced at his watch. "Guess it's too late to head over there this afternoon."

"I've already been over once today to help Mama Marsha with some of the books." Tommy shut the back hatch of his SUV. "I'll go by again tomorrow. It's a mess, and Mama Marsha asked me to come back. Apparently, Mom learned her bookkeeping system from you."

"I don't know what you mean by that." Dad grabbed a water bottle from the fridge as they walked back through the kitchen. "I know exactly where everything is and when all the bills are due. What more does a bookkeeping system need?"

"How about the ability to let others understand it if you're not around?" Tommy leaned on the doorframe. "She spoke her own language or something. I'm trying to interpret all the symbols and shorthand she used. But I have a bad feeling a few bills have fallen through the cracks since she's been gone."

Dad cringed. "I may just hitch a ride in with you tomorrow and see if I can help. I know some of her shorthand."

"I'm sure Mama Marsha would appreciate it."

"What did she say about you inheriting Laura's part of the ownership?"

"I didn't bring it up. Just assumed she knew. Though I'm still confused as to why Mom only had a forty-percent share instead of fifty."

"You didn't know?"

Lifting an eyebrow, Tommy waited for Dad to enlighten him. "Know what?"

"Laura and Marsha each sold ten percent to Beth a few years back."

Evidently, he'd missed more than he thought. "I guess that makes sense."

"Of course it does. She's been a great help to both of them the last few years."

Tommy straightened and clapped Dad on the shoulder. "If you're okay with it, I'm going to check my work emails now."

"I'll let you know when dinner's ready."

Tommy didn't ask what dinner might be. One of them needed to learn a few more recipes soon or all their income would end up going to the local restaurants. Not that the few dishes they each knew how to make were bad. Macaroni and spaghetti just got monotonous after a while.

When he'd lived in Memphis, his boss's wife had helped feed him. As had his few girlfriends through the years. So, he'd never had to fend for himself much before now.

Mama Marsha would probably be willing to teach him a few things or share recipes. Had she taught Bethie all her tricks? More than likely. Beth had been baking cookies and cupcakes before they reached high school. On test days, she'd often bring a mini loaf of banana bread to help him have the brain power to get through. His mouth watered at the memory.

Of course, if today were any indicator, she wouldn't want to bring him banana bread or anything else. He rubbed a spot in the middle of his forehead. What had set her against him so?

Powering up his laptop, he told his brain to focus. Work now. Thoughts and worries over Beth later. Maybe Mama Marsha could shed some light on it when he took the fabric tomorrow. He made a note to check their website too. Something told him it needed an overhaul. Good thing websites were his job.

He didn't seem to be good at anything else. Relationship or otherwise.

Chapter Three

"What in the world?" Beth took three steps back as a big plastic tub came through the door.

The chime echoed, proving she'd had her music up too loud the day before. Too bad it was the same guy entering now. She couldn't exactly run and hide without him noticing.

"Mama Marsha around?" Tommy set the container on the floor and brushed his hands together.

"Somewhere." Beth pointed to his load. "But you can't just leave this here. What if a customer comes in?"

"She in the office?" He walked by her without even responding to what she said.

"Well, of all the—" Using her foot, she tried to push the tub out of the way, but it didn't scoot far. What was in that thing? Now the ache in her thumb had a matching pain in her toes.

"More where that came from." Tommy breezed past again, headed out the door.

"What is going on?" Beth asked Mom, who had followed him back out.

Mom leaned over and scooted the container toward a cutting table near the front window. "Fabric Laura had stashed away at the house. He wants to see if I have any ideas about what to do with it."

Three tubs later, Tommy leaned against the table while Mom lifted various pieces out. "Well?"

"I mean, I'm sure we can find something to do with them. There's some red in that bin that would work well for your watermelon projects, Beth." Mom pointed to the one nearest Tommy.

"But would that technically make it not from our shop?" The excuse was thinner than the piece of rayon her mother held, but Beth wanted a few more seconds before getting closer to him.

"Since Laura was part owner, and this was her stash, I think we're fine." If the tone of Mom's voice didn't tell her how she felt about Beth's ridiculous question, her eye roll did.

"And you know Mom would've been pleased to see her stash go to y'all's booth." Tommy nudged the tub closer to Beth, as if he knew why she hadn't started looking through it.

She swallowed, then knelt and pulled out the top piece. But it wasn't what she'd expected, because it kept coming and coming. And it wasn't only one piece of fabric, either. On closer examination, it was a quilt—a double wedding ring.

"Um ..."

"Oh, I forgot I stuck that in there." Tommy took it, his fingers brushing hers and sending heat to her cheeks. Though, once again, he didn't seem to notice.

"I didn't realize she had so much of it done." Mom ran her hands over the pattern as it settled over the table. "She must've been working on it all the way up—"

She didn't need to say the words. They all knew. Until she

hadn't been able to work on it anymore, when the cancer stole her strength and energy. Beth blinked back a few tears.

"It's not quite done." Tommy pointed to the corner nearest Beth.

Sure enough, a whole circle was missing from the pattern. Beth scanned the rest. "Doesn't look like Mama Laura had a particular color palette in mind."

"No. She was using—" Mom's lips clamped tight, as if she'd been about to say something she shouldn't.

Beth met Tommy's eyes for the first time since the day before, but he didn't seem to understand any more than she did.

"I know she used several fabrics from clothes I wore as a child." His long finger tapped several tiny rectangles.

Leaning over, Beth fingered a few others. "Are these from my old dresses, too?"

"Yes." Mom's reply was so quiet, Beth almost missed it.

"But why—?"

"Laura and I—" Mom twisted her hands, then gathered the piecework up and folded it away. "Never mind. It doesn't matter right now."

As if that didn't make Beth have four hundred more questions.

"I can finish that bottom corner for you, Tommy. If you want." Mom squeezed his arm.

"That would be great, Mama Marsha. Thanks."

She nodded. "Now, where can we store these until we have more time to deal with them? Beth's swamped with sewing, and I'm hopping between deciphering your mom's notes and helping customers."

"Oh, speaking of those notes. Dad said he'd come by this morning too. He thought he might be able to help understand her shorthand."

"Perfect. I don't know why I didn't think to ask him sooner."

And just like that, the mystery was shoved aside. But as Beth dug out some of the red pieces to use later that day, her curiosity lingered. What had Mama Laura planned for that blanket? And why use pieces from both Tommy's past as well as hers?

Mom's secrecy left a niggling suspicion of some matchmaking schemes that hadn't come to fruition. Just what Beth didn't need in addition to Tommy returning.

SUNDAY MORNING DAWNED EARLIER than Tommy was used to. Or at least, he was awakened before he'd planned. Because living in Dad's house again meant attending worship services. Something he hadn't done in a while. Definitely not since the sickness started winning and stealing his mom away.

A cup of coffee and a couple toaster pastries wasn't the breakfast of champions, but neither man was brave enough to try the waffle iron. Or half the other appliances collecting dust around the kitchen. He could almost hear Mom's tutting as he pulled the door closed behind them when they left.

The small auditorium was filling fast as they arrived. Tommy scanned for a place near the back, but Dad took off down a side aisle and worked his way up much closer to the front than Tommy preferred. So much for making an easy getaway afterward.

"Hey Doug." Beth's dad, Eric, shook Dad's hand as he motioned toward the end of their pew.

Even though Tommy had gotten along fine with Marsha, Beth still seemed distant and cold. So, of course, Dad chose to sit with them this morning. Apparently, none of the parents noticed the walls Beth had built between the two 'kids.' At least she wasn't here right now—maybe teaching a children's Bible class. She'd been volunteering since before she graduated high school.

Tommy tried to squeeze past his dad and sit on the end instead of closer to the Nortons.

"I'm supposed to help with the Lord's Supper later." Dad tapped the bulletin. "Mind sitting on this side, instead?"

"Right."

Through Bible class, Tommy pretended to follow along. But his mind wandered more toward what would happen if and when Beth joined their pew. This wasn't one of the longer seats. Not much room between him and her if she sat on this side of her parents. Would she be comfortable with that?

He didn't have long to find out. Class dismissed, and people filed into the auditorium for worship. Out of the corner of his eye, Tommy watched for Beth. She greeted her parents warmly, started to slip past them, and then froze for a split second before moving the rest of the way in.

"Good morning." Something in him couldn't resist goading her a bit further.

"Good morning." She leaned forward and set down a bag of what looked like visual aides on the floor. Then, she carefully leaned back, Bible in lap, stiff posture. But their arms were still only millimeters apart. And her slightly musky perfume filled his senses, overpowering someone else's cologne that bothered him all through class.

The service wasn't quite as uncomfortable as he'd expected. He still remembered most of the hymns. And the sermon on some verses in Romans kept his attention. Except for when someone's arm brushed against his while she turned her Bible pages. Or when she dropped her pen and they both reached for it, bumping together even more.

So maybe he didn't get as much out of the service as he figured Dad had hoped. But he couldn't complain about it, either.

"You guys want to grab lunch, for old times' sake?" Dad leaned past him and aimed the question at Marsha and Eric.

Beth's eyes widened. Was she afraid of spending even more time with him? A shard of pain ripped through him. Where had this wall come from? And how did he get over it to find the girl he'd been friends with forever?

"Can't today, brother." Eric motioned toward the door. "Meeting my sister's family for the afternoon. Rain check?"

"Of course." Dad waved.

Beth's eyes met Tommy's for one moment, and something in the expression made his chest tighten. She didn't want to be estranged, either. At least, that's what he thought it said. It was enough to give him hope. Now, he just needed a plan to make her talk to him.

The Nortons filed out into the exodus, and Tommy and his dad followed behind. At the back of the auditorium, an older lady stopped Beth, gushing about something. As they neared, she grabbed Tommy too.

"I was just telling Beth here that I was so glad to look over and see you two together again. You know all of us around here just figured you'd grow up and get married and carry on the lovely relationship your mamas started so long ago." She shook her head. "So sad about Laura. I know she'd be tickled pink to see her fondest wishes coming true."

Beth's cheeks were about as red as the watermelons she'd been sewing. And he was pretty sure his weren't far behind.

"Um ..."

"I've gotta go, Mrs. Peabody." Beth slipped away from the older woman's grasp.

How did she do that? Had Mrs. Peabody not been holding

her as tightly as she was him? Tommy shifted under the pinch to his bicep.

"Now you treat that girl right, young man. We expect to see good things come from you two." Mrs. Peabody left him to go corner someone else.

Tommy blinked a few times. Had that really just happened? And what did it mean?

Marry Beth?

But Beth was ... Beth. They'd grown up together. Like sister and brother.

Married?

Yet, the idea didn't seem off-putting the more it swirled through his thoughts. Beth had always been pretty. Had been the one he talked to about everything before they went their separate ways in college. And he'd always expected her to be a part of his life in some way.

Married.

A rightness settled in his middle as he followed Dad out to the parking lot. Not that it did him any good.

Beth wasn't even talking to him.

Chapter Four

"Oh, good. You're here." Mom's voice carried from the back of the store immediately after the bell jangled.

Beth looked up from laying out pieces for a few more bowl cozies, all watermelon inspired, of course. Seriously? Why was he back again? Shouldn't he be leaving town already?

Tommy gave Mom a side hug. "You said you needed more help today."

"And I do. But first, I wanted you to see something." She led the way back toward the room where they'd stored Mama Laura's fabric the other day.

Curiosity got the better of Beth, and she followed.

"Did you look through all of this before bringing it?" Mom lifted the lid off a container.

"No. Once we figured out it was fabric, we basically just loaded it up to bring in. The only container I really dug through was the one the quilt was in. It had some of my baby clothes and stuff too."

"Well, you should've dug further in this one." Mom lifted

out a few stacks of what she called 'fancy' fabric—satins and sheers and lacy edged materials. Then, she carefully unfolded a garment bag.

"What is that?" Tommy stepped closer.

"Come see." Unzipping the plastic, Mom spread it wide and revealed something creamy white and covered in embroidered lace.

"Is that—?" Tommy reached out a hand and then stopped before touching anything.

"Laura's wedding dress." Mom's voice was laced with emotion as she pulled it the rest of the way from the bag. "Didn't think you wanted to get rid of this."

"I don't even know what to do with it."

Stepping into the room, Beth caressed one of the cap sleeves. "It's beautiful."

"Prettiest one I ever saw." Mom nodded and then held the dress up to Beth. "And looks like it's in really good condition."

Beth brushed the skirt down in front of her, imagining wearing something so gorgeous. Then, her gaze lifted and met the wide-eyed stare of Tommy, and she quickly thrust the gown back at her mom. She had no right to even think of wearing that dress. Even if she had someone to wear it for.

"You can set it back in case your future wife wants to wear it." Mom wiggled it back into the garment bag.

"I don't even know who I might marry." Tommy ran a hand over the back of his neck. "Or when."

So, he was single. Beth tried to push down the elation that gave her heart. It didn't mean anything to her. Couldn't.

"Maybe Beth wants it." He wouldn't meet her eyes. "It almost looks made for her."

"I couldn't take your mom's wedding dress. Maybe I'll just wear my mom's if and when the time comes." Beth stepped closer to the door again.

Mom shook her head. "Silly girl. You're built much more like your dad's side of the family than mine. We'd have to completely alter my gown for it to fit you. And Laura did look at you like the daughter she never had."

"Not like I need to figure out a wedding dress right now anyway. No chance of me getting married anytime soon." Beth pointed out toward the store. "I better get back to work. Just another week and a half to get all this done for the festival."

"Before you get busy, I think you both need to see what I discovered in Laura's scribbles." Mom's voice held a more serious note than it had when showing them the gown.

Bracing herself, Beth followed Mom and Tommy into the office. Papers lay stacked all over the desk, labeled with sticky notes in at least three different handwritings. How could her mom find anything in here?

"The good news is, Doug's notes helped interpret quite a bit of these scribbles I couldn't make out." Marsha pointed to several different piles. "The bad news is, we're at least three months behind on several bills I had no idea even existed."

Beth sank into a chair. "Do we have the money to pay them?"

Mom's lips pinched together for a second before she answered. "Not all of it."

Why was it so hard to get a full breath? Had someone turned the air off? Was that one of the unpaid bills?

"How much do you need?" Tommy leaned over to take a closer look at the papers. "My website work has done well this last year, and I have a bit extra set aside."

"No."

"What?" Mom and Tommy both spoke at the same time.

"No. We don't need your money. We'll find a way to make this work. Maybe pay part of it now and then this booth at the festival will bring in the extra we need." Beth jumped to her feet. "I need to be sewing."

"Beth."

She didn't stay around to hear whatever her mom would say. She didn't want someone who hadn't even been around the last seven years to swoop in and act like a knight in shining armor. Couldn't let herself have a reason to be grateful to him. This mess was hers and Mom's, and Tommy London needed to butt out.

"Beth." Tommy's fingers covered hers before she could pick up the shears where she'd left them.

She jerked her hand away. "You don't get to do this. Don't get to come in and act like you suddenly care again. You've been gone for a long time—not even so much as a text message came my way. You didn't even greet me at the funeral lunch. So, you're not allowed to be here for this, either."

"You think I don't care?" His brow wrinkled, and she noticed his hair still curled in the middle of his forehead like it had when he was younger.

"You've pretty much proven it."

"Look, I'm sorry I didn't come back more. I already said that. But I'm here now. And I want to help."

Beth crossed her arms. "Why?"

"Why?"

"Yes. Why do you care anything at all about your mom's quilt shop?"

He mirrored her stance. "Well, at least partly because her shares are mine now."

A jiggle went through Beth's knees and she ordered them to stay straight and not give out. "They are?"

"Yes." He leaned forward, his nose just inches from hers. "And because I care about you and Mama Marsha. I don't want you to lose this place."

No words. She had absolutely no response to any of that. Part of her wanted to protest again that he wasn't allowed to care. Wasn't worthy to have a share in this store that was such a joy to the woman he'd abandoned seven years ago. And by that she meant his mom, obviously.

Because she was not allowed to think about anyone else that way—especially not herself.

"So, may I help you?"

His question pulled her from her head again.

"Like you know how to sew."

"I mean, I did make a few pillowcases back in the day. And one slightly lopsided pair of pajama pants."

A giggle burst out without her permission. "I remember those."

"I can cut pieces. Or iron. Let me do something."

"If we make too much inventory for the booth, we'll have a ton leftover and end up losing more money than we make. I don't know that it's a great idea to have you helping with stuff like that."

"You're just going to kill yourself doing it all?"

"You might be more helpful back in the office with Mom." Beth tugged at a loose thread on the fabric's edge she'd been cutting earlier.

"Would you be amenable to letting me help around the store?" Tommy rested a hip against her cutting table and she had to tear her gaze from how it emphasized his athletic frame.

"Like with customers?" She focused on her pattern, although none of the pieces looked like they fit together at this moment.

"More like with improving the website and social media presence. And a few other things I observed around here that would make them more noticeable."

Her back straightened again. "You mean to tell me you've

been here maybe three times in the last seven years and you think you know what we need to do to make this place better?"

"Relax, Beth." He held his hands out, palms down. "This is what I do. I look for ways to help people find businesses, be it online or in person."

"Don't you first have to get to know those businesses? Because I'm not sure three quick trips in here are enough for you to know what we need."

He raised an eyebrow, then grabbed her arm and tugged. "Come here."

"What?" She dug in her heels. "No."

"Seriously. I just want to show you something."

"I don't trust you."

They both stopped simultaneously, her words seeming to echo in the quiet space. There was the real problem. Hurt, then pride, and then stubbornness all chased each other across his face before he wrapped a hand around her arm and pulled again.

"Well, consider me a business partner with more marketing experience, even if you can no longer think of me as a friend." He pushed through the front door, looked both ways and then started them across the street. "I've already apologized for seeming to drop off the face of the earth the last few years."

"Seven."

Just when she began to think he was kidnapping her, he turned and pointed back toward the shop's front. "Tell me what the sign in the bottom right of the left-hand window says."

"It says 'Ask us about our classes.'" She finally freed herself from his grip.

"Would you know that if you hadn't seen it before?"

She glanced at the small rectangle again. Squinted. Pinched her lips together.

"Can you read it from here?"

"Seriously? Like someone is going to want to read a sign almost two blocks away from a store?"

He turned her to the right and pointed toward the diner. "What does that sign say?"

Letting out a huff, she growled out the answer. "Best apple pie in the state."

"Aren't we about the same distance from there as we are from The Missing Piece?"

"Point made. You can fix the sign." She hurried back across the street and to her corner, not caring if he followed or not.

"What's going on?" Mom poked her head out of the office. "I keep hearing the door."

"Ask *him*." Beth motioned toward Tommy with her scissors before gathering her pieces and heading to the sewing room.

He acted like he was going to stay a while this time. But that couldn't be right. It wasn't the way he did things. He came for a day or two and then left.

And her heart couldn't handle him changing things up.

Chapter Five

It was a risk, and Tommy knew it. But he had to do something. Being around Beth without their former relationship was killing him.

He rang the Nortons' doorbell and waited, shifting his weight from foot to foot. Would she slam the door in his face? Would she give him a chance to talk?

"Well, hi, Tommy." Eric grinned. "That for me?"

Tommy shifted the plastic bag in his hands. "Actually, uh. I was hoping Beth was around."

"Sure, sure." Eric chuckled. "Let me see if I can find her. Want to come in out of the heat?"

Tommy stepped into the entryway. Nothing much had changed from when they were in high school. Same pictures of Beth growing up through the years lined the staircase. Same framed quilt squares hung over the fireplace in the living room, which held the same country-style comfy furniture. What had changed was Beth, who now stood stiffly before him, arms crossed.

"Was there something you needed?" Her voice was pitched soft, as if she didn't want her parents to overhear.

"I was hoping I could talk you into a picnic." He lifted the bag. "I brought your favorite."

"How do you know my favorite?"

Lowering the bag, he ducked his head. "Dawn might have helped me figure it out."

"I'm gonna kill her."

"Will you at least sit with me and eat? I thought we could go out under the willow like old times."

Beth shuffled, glanced over her shoulder, sighed. Was she relenting? Or planning an escape?

"You should go." Marsha poked her head around the corner. "You don't like what I'm making for dinner anyway. Go catch up."

"What's she making?" Tommy hoped if he kept things light, maybe Beth would agree to this plan.

"Quiche with spinach in it." Beth narrowed her eyes. "Did she know you were planning this?"

Tommy shrugged and turned to head outside again. "So, want to see what Dawn sent?"

"It's not fair that my mom's on your side, you know." Beth followed behind him.

He'd count it as a win despite her stomping steps. Moving aside several long branches, he ducked through a few more and into the secret world that was their childhood natural playhouse. Being under this weeping willow gave him a sense of coming home more than anything else so far.

"How long have you been planning this?" Beth sank onto the quilt he'd spread earlier, a branch clinging to her ruffly sleeve.

"Since you said you didn't trust me." He sat across the

blanket from her and opened the plastic bag. "Here's your sandwich."

She brushed away the leaves and then accepted the wrapped food. "Thanks."

"You're welcome." He started to take a bite, but noticed she seemed to be waiting.

"Prayer?" One of her dark eyebrows lifted.

"Right." Setting his sandwich down, he brushed his hands together. "I may be a little rusty. Do you want to say it?"

Those brows furrowed down, a look of concern replacing her earlier anger. "Why are you rusty?"

"Let's just say God and I ... well ..." He looked away from her gaze. "It's hard to understand why He let things happen the way they did."

"You mean your mom."

One sharp nod.

"Bow your head." She didn't wait more than a second before she started praying. "God, thank you for this food and this special place. Thank you for good memories. Help us to glorify You." She paused, as if wanting to say something else, but not sure she should. "In Jesus's name, Amen."

"Amen."

They ate in silence for a few minutes. The July breeze was hot, even under the tree. He stretched his legs out to see if that was any cooler.

"Remember the first summer we played under here?" He wadded up his sandwich wrapper and tossed it back in the bag.

Beth smirked. "I had caught the flu and watched a ton of movies, including *My Girl*."

"And my name just happened to be Thomas. Like the character." He laughed and then scowled. "Though I don't appreciate you comparing me to a sissy like him. I mean, I haven't died yet."

"You did go away for a long time, though." She traced the outline of the quilt pattern.

"Did you take a poetry class and fall in love with the professor like that girl character?"

"Vada. No. No poetry." She glanced up and tugged at a branch blowing close to her face. "And no falling in love."

"Never?"

She hesitated and then shook her head. Interesting.

Since that morning, he hadn't been able to shake the image of her holding up his mom's wedding gown. Added to the statement of Mrs. Peabody the day before, it triggered ideas he'd never had. And he wasn't sure what to do about it.

Nothing right now. Not when she was still mad at him for something he couldn't figure out.

"When I went away, I didn't mean for it to be for so long. I thought I'd go to school and come back." Tommy scooted a bit closer. "Then, I got that job offer and knew it would give me the experience to eventually start my own company."

"But you hardly ever visited or anything."

"I came back several times a year." He leaned forward, his elbows on his knees.

"I guess I didn't realize it was that often. You never came to see me when you were in town." She tugged her knees to her chest and rested her chin on them. "Didn't even look my way at your mom's funeral."

"Is that why you're so upset with me?"

A huge sigh filtered through her teeth. "A lot of it."

"So, there's more?" He'd had a feeling there was, but still had no idea what it could be.

"I—" She shook her head and looked away. "Don't worry about it. It doesn't matter."

"C'mon, Bethie. This is me you're talking to. Your very own Thomas J. Except I'm not allergic to bees. And I'm here now."

"How long are you staying?" She kept her face turned the other direction, but he could hear the wobble in her voice.

"I'm not sure yet. Playing with some options."

"You're not going back to Memphis?" Her head jerked back his way.

"That's one of the options, but I'm liking it less and less. For right now, my dad needs me. And you and Mama Marsha do too."

Beth's back straightened, not that it made her much taller. "We're doing okay."

"Except for those unpaid bills." He tapped her foot.

Her eyes narrowed and she got up on her knees. "Look, Tommy. I get that you have a vested interest in the shop because you're part owner. But what have you actually put into that store? Your mom and mine have put their hearts and souls into it for years now, making a place of community and craft and love and fun. You can't just waltz in here after all this time and assume you know better than we do."

He rose up on his own knees, putting him almost a head taller than she was. "And I assume you have all the answers?"

"I never said that. But I do have a plan. And it's a pretty good one too."

"Let's hear it."

She sank down a bit more, resting on her heels. "I'm going to make sure we win the Best Watermelon Spirit prize at the festival. The reward this year is pretty substantial since it's a big anniversary year. And, all the items I'm sewing will be for sale. And I'll have a bowl to collect names of people interested in classes. And Mom plans to have a table for clearance fabric and stuff."

"Good plan."

She opened her mouth as if to protest and then realized he agreed with her. "Yeah?"

"Yeah." He reached over and tugged on her ruffle that had blown up over her shoulder. "But what if you don't win?"

"I have to."

"Okay. But what if we start working on a few other things just as a contingency plan? I want to help, Beth."

"Why?"

His heart pricked knowing she still didn't understand. Maybe he didn't completely understand himself. "For my mom, for one. And for you and Mama Marsha for another. And because I want to help make up for all I've missed over the last seven years."

Her head turned away again. "I'm not sure it's completely possible."

"Will you let me try?" He scooted forward until his knees bumped into hers. "I miss our friendship."

She blinked a few times. "As long as you don't go off and stop talking to me again."

"I promise." He held up three fingers. "I will talk to you so much you'll wish I never came back."

A giggle burst from her, and it was the best sound he'd ever heard.

"So, now that we've agreed to be friends again, catch me up." He sat back and grinned. "I want to know everything I've missed. Even if it takes all night."

"There's no way I'm staying out here all night with you. The mosquitoes would eat us alive."

He swatted his leg where one had just landed. "Better talk fast then."

Chapter Six

Much as Beth was glad to have Tommy back in her life, she couldn't let herself be completely happy. After all, she hadn't admitted everything she was still upset over. Really, she needed to get over it, but it was hard. Because the feelings that spurred her on to that crashed hope over seven years ago still lingered in the back of her heart.

And might never leave. Unlike Tommy. She couldn't expect him to stick around forever, even if it felt possible when he walked through the door the morning after their picnic.

"Put me to work." He held out his hands as if expecting her to hand him a pair of scissors or a measuring tape.

"I thought you were going to enlarge my sign. Or update the website or something." She didn't even look up.

"That's the best place for me?"

"I definitely trust you with those things more than this." She motioned to the fabric she was cutting into pieces for a little girl's watermelon-themed dress.

"Are you saying I've forgotten everything my mom taught me?"

"Let's just say I remember how well you learned it the first time." She finally allowed her gaze to meet his.

His grin just about knocked the breath out of her. "Ouch, Bethie. You sure know how to wound a man."

"Go check in with Mom or something." She shooed him away.

The morning went quickly as she knocked out a few different sized girls' dresses, two more sets of coasters, and a bag. As well as helping customers. Though Mrs. Prinsky was her usual nitpicky self.

"Why is this print available in pink and green but not in blue?" She held up a floral cotton.

"That's the way the company decided to do it. I can look online and see if they make a blue or not, but I'm pretty sure we ordered a bolt of each of the fabrics available when that set first came out."

"No, no. Don't go to any trouble for me. I'll just keep looking and see if anything else will match close enough." The older lady moved her gnarled fingers over each bolt, tutting and clucking as they didn't meet her approval.

Beth stifled a sigh and glanced back at her unfinished work. So much for getting done before lunch. Still, she'd accomplished quite a bit.

"Morning, Ms. Beth." George, the delivery guy, breezed into the store, two big boxes on his dolly. "Where would you like these today?"

"Can you bring them over to this table?" She pointed toward the one nearest the front window. "Thanks so much."

"You bet." He waited while she signed his tablet and then left, whistling a tune.

Even though she itched to see if the packages held what she'd been anticipating, she couldn't leave Mrs. Prinsky completely alone. She'd have to wait a bit longer. But she hoped it was the set of fabrics with fairies and gardens and quaint little quotes all over it. Or the ones with the sewing machines and buttons.

"What's that?" Tommy appeared at her elbow.

"Oh!"

"Sorry. Didn't mean to startle you. Just curious what's in the boxes."

"New fabric. Are you going to make me feel guilty for ordering more when we have so much and ..." She glanced over her shoulder to see if Mrs. Prinsky was in hearing range. "... and not much money."

"Nope. Just had an idea, though. I've ramped up your social media pages and I bet it would be fun to go live on there while you unbox the fabric. Get people interested in seeing what's new in the store."

"Go live? Like where people would see me?" Beth stepped back.

"Sure. You could hold the bolts up with the prints visible, tell a little about the designs or what they might make with it. It would be a great way to grab some interest. Build your following."

"Why would anyone want to see me?" Her voice barely came out audibly.

He finally glanced her way, a frown wrinkling his forehead. "Hey. Sorry. I didn't mean to make you nervous. Just thinking marketing. I bet Mama Marsha could do it instead."

Beth swallowed and nodded, but her heart still raced. "I better go check and see if Mrs. Prinsky found what she needed."

"Who is that young man?" Mrs. Prinsky pointed at Tommy as Beth cut her fabric and rang up her purchase. "Is that Laura's son?"

"It is. He's back in town and trying to help out at the store." Amazingly enough, her voice sounded mostly normal.

"Well, isn't that nice? I bet his mama would be real proud."

"Yes, ma'am." Beth stacked the cut pieces neatly and tapped the amounts into her register. "Okay, you're right at twenty dollars today, Mrs. Prinsky."

"Thank you, dear. I'm doing a baby blanket for a new great-grand. Due in October, so I gotta get started now." She handed over the bills. "Someday, maybe I'll get to make one for you, Beth. Any marriage prospects on the horizon?"

Before she could stop it, Beth's gaze darted Tommy's direction.

And evidently, she didn't hide it well, either, because the older lady cackled. "Oh, I see how it is. Well, missy. Just keep me updated, eh?"

Beth swallowed and nodded, sure her cheeks were pinker than the fabric she'd just cut.

Time to go hide at her sewing machine again for a while.

TOMMY COUNTED ABOUT ten ladies who came in the shop during the day. Most seemed to be regulars. And while having customers who came back repeatedly was great, bringing in more would be better too. Because after a while, those ladies wouldn't need as much fabric due to the stash already at their houses.

If only he could convince Beth to do the live unboxing on social media. He didn't remember her being this shy. Maybe if her mom participated ...

Marsha readily agreed to help do a trial run on a video. "Beth?"

Beth poked her head around. "What's up?"

"Come help me, please."

"Oh, I was going to inventory those and get them unpacked later." Beth frowned as Marsha ran a box cutter down the tape to open the front box.

"Tommy had an idea to put some of the unboxing on social media. Said it might bring in some new customers." Marsha lifted a flap and peeked inside. "This is one you've been waiting for. Want to help?"

"Is it the fairies?"

Marsha smiled. "It is. You won't have to say anything. Just help me hold the bolts up to show them off. I think we're going to do it with the store in the background so the light coming through the windows won't cause a glare. Right, Tommy?"

"Yep." He moved to the window side of the table and held up his phone. "Ready when you are."

"Hi, I'm Marsha down here at The Missing Piece. We're so excited to show you a new shipment we got in today, and we couldn't wait for you to see this. It's a set of fabrics by Brad Harrison called Fairy Garden. Check these out."

Marsha's voice was friendly and calm. Beth stood slightly behind her looking awkward, a fake smile pasted on her face. Strange. She wasn't like that when talking to a real person in the store.

As Marsha lifted each bolt from the box and pulled the plastic off, Beth accepted the fabric from her, unfolded it to show off the pattern and then laid it carefully on the table, stacking them neatly to show how they all went together. And the longer the video went, the more relaxed she seemed. As if she'd forgotten he was recording it. Perfect.

"Come on down and check these out in person. I can't wait to see what all you make from these gorgeous prints." Marsha ended with a wave and a smile.

"That was great. Want to do the other box while we're in

the zone? Then, I can post one in a bit and one later. See if we can get some buzz going."

"What do you think, Beth?" Marsha touched her daughter's shoulder. "You up for it?"

"I guess. I mean, I was almost finished with those sewing projects."

"They'll still be there. Let's do this, and then you can grab lunch before you go back to that machine. You've been working too hard lately."

Marsha ripped into the next box. "The sewing machines!"

Beth's smile was natural as she reacted to her mom's glee. And Tommy couldn't take his eyes off her.

"You ready, Tommy?" Marsha waved.

He blinked. Right. He was supposed to be watching the fabric more than the girl holding it. "Almost. Okay, now."

As they went through the same routine they'd just established, Beth was much more relaxed showcasing each piece. She even offered her own wave at the end. There was the friend he knew and loved.

Loved?

Sure. He'd always loved her. But was it shifting to something more than just a sister-brother thing? No time to figure that out right now.

Clearing his throat, he clicked a few buttons to upload the videos to the cloud. "Okay. Let me go polish these up a bit and post them on the sites."

"We're not polished enough for you?" Marsha poked his arm. "Hold onto that thought for a minute. I need you both to help me with something else right now."

Beth met his glance, but she looked as confused as he was.

"What's up, Mama Marsha?"

She led them through the converted house. While the store took up the main section of the building, and the sewing room and kitchen were to the left, near the back were several former bedrooms that had been adapted into spaces used for classes or overflow. In the one where they'd stored his mom's stash, Mama Marsha had a quilt frame set up.

"It always takes two or three of us to get a quilt put on a frame, so I'm recruiting you two." She grabbed something from a table in the corner and brought it over.

"Mom's quilt." He touched it. "But it wasn't finished."

"It is now." She unfolded an edge and he could see a new ring where the missing corner had been. "I thought you'd like to have a hand in quilting it."

Tommy took a step back. "I've never quilted anything in my life."

"That's why Beth is going to help you. She can show you what to do."

Beth squeaked, but Marsha didn't wait to see if they agreed or not. Simply set about showing them how to attach one end of the fabric and batting layers to the far end and then roll them until tight enough so all the layers stretched evenly and without wrinkles.

"I don't have time to quilt anything right now. Why can't we use the quilting machine in the other room?" Beth propped a fist on her hip.

"Because I think Laura would prefer it done the old-fashioned way." Marsha smoothed a hand over the fabric. "And you can just work on it as you have time. I know you're getting ready for the festival next week. But it's here when you need a break from watermelons."

Tommy stood next to the frame long after the Nortons walked back out to the other part of the store. If he listened long enough, could he hear a message from his mother in this unfinished blanket? Is what Mama Marsha proposed exactly what his mom would've wanted?

Something told him it was.

Which meant he and Beth would have to find a way to improve their working together. After the festival. Though if they worked together better before, she might be less stressed about it.

New project—besides the quilt—convincing Beth to let him help. After he uploaded the videos.

Chapter Seven

It took him a bit, but Tommy worked on Beth until she grudgingly let him iron and even cut a few pieces out. The countdown to the festival was on, and her stress showed more each day. Her brown hair went from braids or mostly down styles to messy buns on top of her head. While she was always dressed nicely, the outfits didn't look quite as put together after a while. And one day, she even wore two different shoes.

Their relationship itself was awkward—and yet not—at the same time. In the banter and teasing, they slipped back into old habits as if no time had passed. But then one of them would mention something happening and the cold truth of all those missing years doused their friendly atmosphere.

"What are you working on now?" Tommy leaned against the sewing room door. He'd made sure she wasn't about to start sewing before asking his question this time. No need to add another puncture wound to her stress.

"A couple more coasters and bowl cozies."

"How many does that make?"

"I've sort of lost count." The words came out a bit mumbled around the few pins held between her teeth, but still recognizable.

"Seriously?"

She finally took her eyes off the seam she'd been pinning. "Yes. Why?"

"Come here."

Frowning, she didn't budge. Of course not.

He stepped over, plucked the project from her hand and set it on the table, then gently pried the pins from her mouth. Her eyes widened as his fingers grazed her lips, but then seemed to hide all emotion except frustration. Tugging her hands, he pulled her into the room where they'd stored items for the festival.

"Do you see all this?" He motioned to the various piles and basketfuls and racks of hanging garments.

"Yes."

"Where is it all going to go?"

"What?" She crossed her arms. "It's going to the festival tomorrow. You know that."

"How big is your booth? Didn't you say part of the booth is going to be clearance fabric too?"

Her lips twisted to one side while her mind obviously whirled in thought. "Yes. It's big enough to have three long tables and the hanging rack. I thought we could also squeeze in a blanket rack near the front."

"I don't think you're going to have room for all this."

"Well, I'll take a couple of totes to store extras under the tables."

"Weren't you the one telling me you didn't want too much inventory because if it didn't sell, you'd be out more money than you'd make?"

Her huff of exasperation stirred several hairs that had

escaped her messy updo to dangle across her forehead. "Do you always have to be right?"

"No." He reached over and tucked a strand behind her ear. "I'm just tired of seeing you run yourself ragged when you probably have enough done already. Take a breath and rest for a minute. The weekend will be busy enough without you being worn out before it even starts."

"I just need everything to be perfect." Her voice cracked.

On instinct, he tugged her over and tucked her into his side. "I know. But it already is. You've done an amazing job."

"Can I at least finish the two things I already cut out?" The words came out muffled where her nose was buried in his T-shirt.

He chuckled. "Yes. And then maybe you can show me some quilting basics."

She leaned back and shook her head. "I thought you told me to rest."

This time his laugh was even fuller. "True enough. Okay, it can wait."

"Good. Because this afternoon, I have to make sure everything is squared away for us to set the booth up first thing tomorrow morning."

"Let me know when you're leaving, and I'll go with you."

"Thanks, Tommy."

That was the easiest she'd accepted his help since he came back. Maybe he was making more progress with her than he thought.

She meandered back to her sewing and he checked his emails quickly. Working his website business every evening after putting in a full day here hadn't been ideal, but he was making it work. Still, if he wanted to do this long-term, he'd have to find a better solution.

His inbox was full of the normal junk. He deleted most of it, but one message caught his attention. A job offer.

Though he'd settled in nicely here, not to mention enjoyed the freedom of working for himself, he couldn't resist seeing what it was about. Little Rock. Good wages. His own office space and secretary.

Little Rock wasn't far. Maybe an hour. So, he'd still be close to Dad. Not to mention the Nortons. He glanced over his shoulder to where Beth worked away, her music playing not quite as loudly as the first day he'd come back.

An hour away.

He set the message aside for later and went to ring up a customer who'd finished making her choices. At least she'd just grabbed several jelly-rolls, thick stacks of precut fabrics that coordinated with each other. No cutting required on his part. He could handle this.

"You ready to walk over to city hall and get our final information?" Beth slid her sunglasses on.

"Sure. Should we let your mom know?"

"I told her."

He nodded and followed her out into the heat of early afternoon. August had come in with a vengeance. If it weren't peak time for watermelons, he'd wonder who in their right mind had set the festival for this time of year. Arkansas had much more pleasant seasons than the middle of summer.

Several areas were already cordoned off where bounce houses and food trucks would park that evening. Orange cones marked where each booth would appear once the business day was complete and the parking spots opened. Tomorrow, all of downtown would be a no-drive zone. Parking was available at various church lots and the elementary school on either end of Main Street.

The city hall was cooler than outside, but not by much.

The building was so old, it probably had little-to-no insulation compared to today's standards. But it was a historic landmark, and no one would dare suggest making updates or renovations.

"I'm here to confirm everything for The Missing Piece's booth." Beth smiled at the lady behind the counter.

"Sure thing, Beth. Let's see." Her finger ran down a list. "Right here. Yes. I have you in lot three-oh-seven. It's right in front of the bookstore. There wasn't anything closer to your shop left, unfortunately."

"That's no problem. We can cart things down. It's only a block." Beth accepted her paperwork and signed where the lady pointed. "And we're still a double-sized spot, right?"

"Um ..." There went the finger again, sliding across columns only she could interpret. "Yes, dear. That's what I have you down for."

"Perfect."

"You can set up tables and tents tonight after seven, but no products need to show up until after six tomorrow morning."

"I'm on it, Beatrice. Thanks for your help."

"You bet, sweetie. Got lots of cute things this year?"

"Tons." Tommy winked. "Including some fun little dresses that would look adorable on a great-granddaughter."

"Well, I have a couple of those now. I might need to come by." Beatrice beamed at him and then waved them off. "See you tomorrow."

"How did you know she had great-granddaughters?" Beth fanned herself with the paperwork as they headed back down the street.

"She brought dinner over for Dad and me the other night and chatted for a while. Showed us all the pictures."

"That was sweet."

"It was. I'd never had a sweet meatloaf before. And I think she sugared her green beans."

Beth wrinkled her nose. "That's not what I meant. And ew. I'm more a fan of bacon grease in green beans myself."

"And that's why we get along so well." He hip-bumped her. "What's going on over there?"

A stage was set up just past the courthouse, speakers lining the front.

"You know they always do the talent show. And the beauty pageant." Beth's voice dripped scorn as she mentioned the second part. What was that about?

"Right. For the Watermelon Queen."

"Yeah. Apparently, it's not only the sixtieth anniversary of the festival itself. It's the pageant's twenty-fifth anniversary. They're trying to get all the former queens to come back and do a reunion thing." Beth crossed her arms despite the heat.

"Beth! Tommy!" A voice from near the stage pulled his attention down to the crowd around it. A woman waved and squealed as he looked her way.

"This cannot be happening." Beth's mumble was almost indiscernible, but he heard it.

No time to figure out why she'd said it though. The woman dashed their direction and threw herself at both of them in a perfume-infused hug. "Hi, y'all! It's been forever."

Beth stiffened beside him and didn't even pretend to smile as the other woman beamed. A closer look, and he realized it was Paige Davidson, Beth's former best friend. And his prom date—mistake number fifty-seven or something from senior year.

"I can't believe we're all back here together again." Paige gushed more than the geyser he'd seen when his family took a vacation out west.

"Me, either." Beth's reply was just loud enough for him to hear, but it almost made him lose control and laugh. What had come between these two to estrange them? Had Paige been gone for seven years like he had? Or was it something else?

"I'm back because of the pageant. You know. All the former Watermelon Queens. I like to never found my crown." Paige talked with her hands, showcasing all her fingernails painted like tiny watermelon slices.

"Where had you stashed it?" He couldn't resist asking, though it would probably aggravate Beth.

"Oh, my goodness! You'll never believe!" Paige giggled. "My mama used it for the tree topper last Christmas."

That did it. The laugh burst free.

Beth huffed and said something about "nice to see you, but I've gotta get back" before stalking away. She'd never even looked Paige's direction. Tommy watched Beth halfway down the block before Paige touched his arm.

"She's still not forgiven me, huh?"

"Forgiven you? For what?"

"You seriously don't know?" Paige rocked back on her heels, no easy feat considering they had to be at least three inches high. "Really?"

"I'm lost. Why is Beth ticked at you?"

Paige shook her head. "Because you took me to prom."

Tommy blinked. "What?"

"You honestly don't know?" All of Paige's cheerful antics disappeared. Instead, a worried expression covered her face thicker than her makeup.

"I have no idea what you're talking about. I mean, I know I went to prom with you. But why should that upset Beth?"

Paige squeezed her eyes shut a second and then opened them. "Because she wanted you to ask her."

The words hit him like a gut punch. That couldn't be right. He and Beth were friends. Had always been friends. Nothing more.

"But you said she told you to ask me. When you asked if I had a date yet, you said Beth told you to see if I was going with anyone."

Pressing two fingers to her temple, Paige nibbled her lip for a second. "She was hoping you'd get the hint that since you didn't have a date and neither did she …"

No. "And instead I thought she meant I should ask you."

Paige nodded.

"But you knew what she was after. Why did you accept?"

Paige glanced away. "Because every girl in our class wanted a chance to date you, Tommy. We just figured you were off-limits. You were Beth's, even if you didn't know it yet. So, when you asked, I couldn't find it in me to resist. I tried to apologize to Beth after—"

"But she never forgave you."

The perfect curls cascading around Paige's face bounced like springs when she shook her head. "It wasn't even that great of a date, anyway."

Something between a laugh and a grunt burst from him. "Well, thanks a lot."

"You spent the whole night looking for Beth."

He had. And now things were clicking into place. This was why she was still upset with him even though she wouldn't admit it. This was what remained between the two of them and kept them from moving forward.

She'd wanted more than friendship all the way back in high school. But she said nothing.

And now that he was thinking of it more and more as a possibility, did she even feel the same way?

Chapter Eight

Beth laid out several placemats and coasters, cocked her head to the side, and rearranged them for the fifth time. Nothing looked like she imagined when she'd been sewing it all. It didn't help that yesterday afternoon's bad mood lingered.

How dare Paige act like them all being together again was a perfectly happy reunion? The backstabbing traitor. And Tommy, completely oblivious, laughing along with all her jokes.

That part of her life was like the selvage edge of fabric. It was necessary for the printer so the designer and colors could be listed, but no one wanted to use it or have anyone see it. Beth might've had to live through Paige stealing away her dream, but she didn't have to forgive her for it.

If Tommy was still more attracted to Paige than Beth, he could have her. And Beth would be fine. She'd been bracing her heart for this for years.

"I'm fine." Beth slapped down a few bowl cozies and spun, almost colliding with Tommy.

"You okay?" He braced her arms and leaned over to meet her eyes.

"Fine." Beth repeated with less vehemence, shrugging away from his grip. She hadn't seen him since storming away the day before. Couldn't face him until she got herself under control again.

"You're sure?"

"Yep. Just trying to get everything ready before the festival officially starts."

Six o'clock in the morning had come early, but at least it wasn't too hot. In dawn's dim light, she'd gotten ready and driven down to arrange things. The national anthem would play around nine, and then everything would be open. But judging was at ten, and some of the other booths had her second-guessing how hers would fare.

One catty-cornered from them also had potholders and coasters, not to mention a few girls' dresses. And a little farther down was a booth with all kinds of bowl cozies. Would their prices be better than hers? Or their products more attractive?

"Hey." Tommy gently turned her head back to their space. "Everything looks great. Don't worry about it anymore."

"I just don't think it's enough."

"Seriously, Beth? You painted seeds and added a green edge to your red canvas gazebo. I don't think there's anything else you could do to make this booth feel like the spirit of the Watermelon Festival."

The edges of her mouth turned up against her will. "I'm just trying to do Mama Laura proud. This was her baby. She loved all things watermelon."

"She would've adored this. Just like she loved you." He opened his mouth like he was about to say something else.

"Good morning!" Mom pulled a wagon down the sidewalk and waved, interrupting whatever he might've said.

Just as well.

"I've got clearance stuff."

"Perfect." Beth met her at the one empty table and started arranging remnants and pieces that hadn't sold as well this last year. Maybe thirty percent off would entice someone to take them home.

"Everything looks amazing, Beth. You did a great job. And I particularly like the fan with the mister attachment in the corner." Mom motioned around.

"That was probably my best idea for the whole thing. Though it did take a minute to figure out how to get it all set up and angled where it wouldn't make anything too damp."

"They're calling for a heat index of over a hundred. I don't think that little bit of water will make it to the tables." Tommy chuckled.

"True." Beth looked around again. "Linda and Maysie are set to help out too?"

"They'll open the store at the normal time today and work there all morning. Then, we can switch out and some of us can cool off in the air conditioning while they man the booth."

"Perfect." Linda and Maysie were two of their regular customers who also helped teach a class or two and picked up part-time shifts as needed. They were like extra grandmothers to Beth, and she trusted them as much as she did her own mom.

"Do you think I should move this rack of dresses over a few inches? I can't decide if it's hiding the edge of this table too much or not." Beth started for the display, but Tommy caught her hand and tugged her away.

"I think you've looked at all of this too much. What if we wander around and see what else is going on? Give you some space and then you can see it more clearly when we come back?"

"Great idea!" Mom chimed in before Beth could protest.

"In fact, judging isn't until ten. Why don't you go check out the talent show and get some snacks and stuff before coming back? It's only eight-thirty."

"I can't just abandon you." Beth tried to resist Tommy's pulling, but her sandals had no traction.

"Don't be silly. Go have fun before it gets too hot. People won't start arriving until closer to ten anyway. Or even later if they have to work."

And just like that, Beth was tugged past the other booths she'd been studying earlier and toward city hall. "I bet you think you're so smart, huh?"

"Only most of the time." Tommy's answer didn't have the usual playfulness she'd come to expect. Strange.

"Did you have a nice time catching up with Paige?" Jealousy spit the question out before she could snatch it back.

"It was ... enlightening." His hand hovered at the small of her back, guiding her through the growing crowd.

She was afraid to ask what that meant.

"Any idea when things are happening today? Isn't there a list of events and times somewhere?" Tommy skimmed the area around the stage. Was he looking for Paige?

"I think it's on the website. Hang on." She pulled her phone out and clicked until she found the schedule. "Here."

His fingers cradled her hand as she held the phone out for him to see, making the day seem even warmer than it already was. "Seed-spitting over near the gazebo. That'll end up with the parks and rec people mowing down watermelons next year."

"You think they'd learn."

"Melon-bailin' won't start until closer to ten. Over near the fire station. That's always fun."

"Remember the year Marvin Reed chucked his melon almost a hundred feet farther than the record?"

"Didn't they decide that was rigged?" Tommy glanced at her, eyebrows raised.

"I don't think so. Anything going on in the next little while besides the talent show after the national anthem?"

"Hmm." Tommy scrolled down the page. "Food trucks, booths and vendors, and the melon carving contest. What's that?"

"Something they started a few years back. It's pretty cool, actually. To me, they look even neater than carved pumpkins because of the pink showing through."

"We'll have to check it out."

A loud screech filled the morning air as the mayor took the microphone from the stand. Everyone grimaced while the speakers calmed down and Mayor Grimsby could get the attention he wanted. Time to start things up. After an ... interesting ... interpretation of the "Star Spangled Banner," everyone scattered toward various events.

"So, what first?" Beth stuck her phone back in her pocket and then realized Tommy still held her other hand. What was that about?

"Food trucks?"

"Did you not eat breakfast this morning?"

"I mean, not much. I'm a bachelor, remember?" He gave her a pitiful face, sadder than any puppy she'd ever seen.

"As if these trucks would have anything considered breakfast-worthy."

"I'm up for anything. It's a festival weekend. Who cares if we eat healthy or not?" He pointed to a booth where Dawn offered several items from her café. "What about there?"

"Watermelon smoothie?" Dawn smiled brightly as they stepped up to the table.

"What do you think, Beth? Want to try one?" Tommy pulled out his wallet.

"No, thanks. I'm good right now."

"I forgot you don't actually like watermelon." Tommy paused in handing money to Dawn. "Can you believe it? Living in this town and not liking the fruit its festival is named for."

"I've tried. It's just not my favorite." Beth wrinkled her nose.

Tommy accepted his smoothie and thanked Dawn before they headed down the row. Beth never ceased to be amazed by the different foods people made from watermelons this one weekend of the year. Salads, slushes and smoothies, popsicles, sorbet, breads and jellies, watermelon limeade, cupcakes, roll-ups, pickled rinds, and regular old slices. Not to mention the things flavored like the fruit.

It turned her stomach a bit.

"Sure you don't want a sip?" Tommy offered the straw her way.

"I'm sure. Thanks."

He smirked and finished the drink off. "Mmmm."

When she shoved his arm, he snatched her hand and wove it through the crook of his elbow instead, pulling her closer. This was new. And she couldn't bring herself to trust it.

They watched seed spitting for a while, but she could only handle that so long. Moving on, they meandered past the carved melons, each sitting in a cooler of ice to keep it from turning too soggy in the heat. The creations could've mesmerized her for much longer, but Tommy didn't want to miss the melon-bailin'.

On their way toward the fire station, they passed a bunch of the former queens, all dolled up and wearing their crowns. Paige caught Beth's eye, but didn't speak or anything. And Tommy never looked that way.

After an hour of watching watermelons catapult through the air and bust in random piles across the yard, and meandering much longer than Beth had intended, they headed back toward The Missing Piece's booth. Pinned to the front right corner, just above the dress stand Beth had worried about earlier, was a giant ribbon that said, "Best Watermelon Spirit."

Her hand flew to her mouth, but not fast enough to cover her squeak. She bounced on her toes, moisture welling behind her eyes. So many hours of work.

"You did it." Tommy drew her close and pressed a kiss to her temple.

A kiss?

But no time to analyze it now. The booth was buzzing more than the adrenaline rushing through her. Time to focus on what she was actually here for.

Mom beamed as she helped several customers choosing from the clearance table. A few others browsed through sewn items. And the bowl she'd put out to collect names of people interested in classes already held several pieces of paper.

A weight heavier than she'd realized lifted from her shoulders. The money from the prize, as well as the people wanting to take classes, would more than cover those missed bills. Not to mention promising more sales down the road to keep them from falling back into debt. Plus, she'd been able to honor Mama Laura in her own way.

Thank you, God!

One problem on its way to being solved. Then, to figure out the mystery of what was going on with Tommy.

Chapter Nine

Tommy couldn't concentrate. He was trying to update the class schedule on The Missing Piece's website, but giggles from the front of the store drew his attention again and again. Beth knelt near a little girl who told her something terribly fascinating—or at least it looked that way by the large arm movements.

"Well! I have just the thing." Beth stood and offered her hand to the child. "We actually have several different unicorn prints right back here. And I'm fairly certain at least three of them are pink, just like you want for your new curtains."

"Really?" The child glanced over her shoulder at her mom, a huge grin displaying a gap where her front teeth should be.

"Would I make something like that up?" Beth led her to where most of their children-themed prints were displayed.

The girl squealed as she reached out to touch a bolt. Beth looked over and caught his eye, a beaming smile on her face. And Tommy's heart skipped a beat. Beth blinked and looked away again, as if unsure what had just happened.

The feeling was mutual.

"How's it coming?" Marsha leaned next to him behind the counter.

He jerked his attention back to where it was supposed to be. "Pretty good. I added a form and an online payment option for your classes. People are more likely to sign up on a whim if they can pay right away instead of having to drive down to the store. And once someone's paid, she's more likely to come to the classes. Win-win."

"You've been a blessing from God, moving back when you did." Mama Marsha squeezed his arm. "Thanks for working so hard to make this place even better than it already was."

"You and Mom gave it a good start. I'm just polishing the edges." Tommy grinned around the tears that threatened. "Besides, that daughter of yours has helped more than I have."

"She's a treasure, for sure."

"I still think you need to do more social media posts than just the unboxings. Those went over great. But Sewing Tip Tuesday or some other little thing like that would be a huge draw. And posting pictures of people with their finished projects."

"Keep working. I'm mostly onboard. Now, we just need to get Beth to agree." Marsha glanced over where her daughter helped pick out fabric. "No one wants to see a fifty-something-year-old woman giving tips. Besides, Beth is much prettier than I am."

Tommy nodded before he could help himself.

Marsha gave his arm a swat. "I saw that."

"I didn't mean you were right ... I mean, about her being prettier ... I mean ..." He groaned. "Let me start over. Beth is gorgeous. You're right about that. But I think you're lovely too. And people will probably trust you more because of your years of experience."

"You almost worked your foot out of your mouth there,

bud." Marsha smirked, then leaned closer. "Have you told Beth you think she's gorgeous?"

He opened his mouth, though he had no idea what to say. Salvation came in the form of his phone ringing. He held up a finger and answered without even looking to see who called. "Thomas London."

Mama Marsha's expression said she'd probably revisit that conversation, but at least he'd have time to think of an answer before then.

"Thomas, this is Daniel Morris over at Morris Technical Industries in Little Rock. We sent you an email last week about a job possibility, and I wanted to follow up and chat with you about it."

Maybe he wasn't saved after all. This was another conversation he'd been putting off. "Right. Hi, Mr. Morris."

He motioned to Marsha that he needed to take this call outside and walked out into the August heat.

"Is this a bad time?"

"Honestly, sir, I'm not certain about moving to Little Rock right now."

"Hear me out for a minute." Morris's voice was friendly but firm. "Priestly has nothing but good things to say about you. He's been singing your praises and said you were moving back to Arkansas. The more he talked, the more we knew you were exactly what we were looking for."

Tommy leaned against the shaded side of the shop and closed his eyes. "Thank you. I've enjoyed working with Mr. Priestly for the last three years."

"How about this?" Morris continued before Tommy could object again. "Why don't you come down and spend the day with us? See the facilities, check out some of what Little Rock has to offer, talk numbers and possibilities. Just to see what you're turning down. Are you free one day later this week?"

If the numbers were still what they'd offered in their original email, it would be ridiculous to turn this opportunity down. Especially since he hadn't been able to bring in as many new clients of his own as he'd hoped. Besides, it would be just as easy to tell Mr. Morris *no* to his face as on the phone.

"I'm fairly flexible the rest of the week. What's a good day for you?" Tommy hit his fist lightly against the siding.

"Let's do Thursday."

Two days away. Tommy agreed and hung up, his heart constricting in his chest. This was a great job, but how on earth could he tell Beth? She was finally acting like she had before prom. Their friendship probably couldn't survive another falling out.

BETH FINISHED RINGING up Chrissy and her mom as Tommy came back in the store from his call. He looked conflicted. What could he have been talking about to leave him like that?

"Here are your new curtains, Chrissy. I can't wait to see pictures once you get them sewn."

"Thanks so much, Ms. Beth!" Chrissy bounced on her toes. "Mommy says even she can't mess up straight lines."

Beth laughed and waved them off. Tommy stepped behind her and settled back at his laptop. He didn't even offer a greeting, which was unusual after the last couple of weeks.

"What's up? About to get our website so fancy I'll never be able to update it myself?" She bumped his arm.

"You're smart enough to figure all this out, too, Bethie. Especially since it'll just need basic maintenance. Anything harder than that, you can just call me."

"And how much is having Thomas London design our

website going to cost us?" She offered the tease with the hopes he'd lighten back up. "I mean, surely your services aren't free."

His chocolate eyes finally shifted to meet her gaze and he shook his head. "Good thing I'm already on your staff, then."

The air was suddenly a bit stuffier than it had been. Had he brought some of the heat inside when he stepped back in? She moved back a couple paces and gripped the edge of the counter to keep from fanning herself.

"You about to a stopping point? We've rather neglected your mom's quilt."

"Sure. I can stop for a bit. If all else fails, I can finish this at home tonight."

"Working after hours?" Beth tutted. "Such dedication."

"Or I'm just boring." He hip-checked her as he fell into step.

"Boring is a such a relative term." She flipped the light switch and moved to the frame, running her fingers over the intricate piecework yet again. So many hours went into this, and she wanted to make it as perfect as possible for Mama Laura.

"So, where do we start?"

"This is quilting thread." She tossed a spool his way. "It's a bit stronger than normal thread so it can hold all the layers together. You want a piece not too long or too short. Too long and it gets tangled. Too short and you have to rethread a lot."

"Okay." He pulled some out and then glanced at her with a raised eyebrow. "Like this?"

"Good."

She helped him get his needle threaded and then the end knotted. "Okay. Now, we have to decide what pattern we want to use to quilt this."

"Pattern? I thought that was what Mom used for all the pieces?"

"Well, you use a different pattern for the stitches." She ran a finger around the edge of a circle. "We could follow the circles. That would be fairly simple. Or we could do straight lines, like an X through the middle of each loop. I've seen it done that way, and it looked very nice. Might be easier. But we'd need to use a ruler."

"This is much more complicated than I expected." Tommy shook his head.

"What do you think you'd prefer? You aren't going to notice it much because the background and thread are both white. So, it really doesn't matter as long as the stitches are close enough to keep the batting from bunching." She propped her hands on her hips, considering.

"You're asking me what would look better?" He snorted. "You know my taste is all in my mouth."

She giggled with him. "Okay. I vote for straight lines. I think that will keep us from having to cut the thread and start in a new place as often."

"Sounds good to me."

"Okay, watch me." Wiggling the needle a bit, she worked it through only the top layer and pulled until the knot went underneath and didn't pull out again. "That's how we start. You want to make sure it's secure and then we'll work through all three layers."

With difficulty, he tried three different times, but his thread pulled out each attempt. She moved into his space, grabbed the needle and worked it through. Then, she wrapped his hand around the thread and tugged.

"Not too hard. Just enough to get the knot to hide."

"All right." His voice was quiet. Almost breathy.

They were much closer than she realized, his front pressed to her back, their hands wound together. She started to move away, but his other arm trapped her. Slowly, she lifted her face and really looked at him—this boy who'd grown up as a best friend and almost-brother, but who she'd loved forever.

Were things changing between them or was she only seeing what she'd longed for?

"Oh, sorry!" A voice from the doorway pulled them apart.

Beth blinked a few times and drew a deep breath through her nostrils. Public place. Even if Tommy's feelings might finally be aligning with her own, this wasn't a great time for it to happen. Though when she turned and found Paige wearing a sheepish grin, she almost wished she hadn't stepped away from him.

Petty, yes. But revenge was sweeter served cold, right?

Chapter Ten

"Paige, fancy meeting you here." Tommy smiled as if nothing crazy had been happening a moment before. Maybe Beth had imagined everything she thought she felt.

"Just coming by before I head out of town again." Paige glanced between the two of them. "Though I wasn't expecting ... anyway—"

"Remind me where you're living now." Tommy straightened from where he'd leaned against the back of a stool.

Why did he care where Paige was living? Was he hoping to reconnect with her further?

"Tulsa, actually. Nothing fancy, but I like it." Paige glanced at Beth. "You probably won't believe me, but I'm glad I ran into both of you. I've really missed you over the years."

Beth pinched her lips together. Sure she did. Maybe she should've considered the consequences before coercing Tommy into taking her to prom.

"Anyway, my cell hasn't changed since high school. You know. If you ever want to reach out and catch up." Paige shifted from foot to foot, pushed her purse strap farther up her shoulder. "I'd love that."

Beth refused to meet her eyes. Maybe she'd missed Paige a bit, too, but enough to overlook what happened? A girl didn't treat her best friend that way.

"Guess I better scoot. Hoping to get back before the vet closes. I boarded my puppy while I was here this last week. My mom can't stand having a dog in the house."

"I'll walk you out." Tommy moved from Beth's side to Paige's, as if he'd just been waiting for an excuse.

So much for whatever Beth had thought was happening between them earlier. She could've sworn he was about to kiss her before they got interrupted, but that was ridiculous. Because he still looked at her as Bethie, his friend who played under the willow tree and under the quilt frames, hiding and seeking between the bolts of fabric. Nothing more.

"Is Beth finally getting her prom wish?" Paige tossed a lock of blonde hair over her shoulder as they paused in the shop's doorway.

"Prom wish?" Tommy lifted his brows. "I'd rather not go back and redo prom, if it's all the same to you."

"I meant about you seeing her as more than a friend." Paige half-heartedly smiled. "She's still pretty angry with me, but maybe you'll have better luck saving your relationship than I have."

"Maybe I can help save yours too."

Paige shook her head. "Don't worry about me. But you better not stay out here much longer or she won't talk to you at all when you go back in. She's pretty jealous right now."

"Jealous? Of what?"

"You seeing me off." Paige looked him right in the eye. "Beth is really special. I broke her trust all those years ago and lost my best friend. Don't make a similar mistake, Tommy. She's the best, and she's loved you forever."

Loved him?

These last few weeks, he'd been noticing her in different ways than ever before. Besides her being a full-grown woman instead of the eighteen-year-old girl he'd left behind. He'd seen her tenacity, her creativity, her pain tolerance, even a few insecurities she hadn't been able to hide. But love? For him?

Is that what was going on between them? And how did it mesh with the job interview he had in two days? Was he even worthy of her?

He wandered back to the room they'd been in. At first glance, it appeared empty, but as he turned to leave again, something caught his eye. What was it?

Feet.

They poked out from under the quilt frame, the rest of her petite body hidden in its shadows. He quietly pulled the door most of the way closed and then crawled under there with her. This newer frame wasn't deeper than a few quilt squares, so when he laid back, his legs hung out into the room with only his torso under the quilt. She glanced over just long enough he could tell her eyes were redder than before. Had he caused that?

"Remember when we did this as kids?" He folded his hands under his head and looked up. The fabric was thin enough you could see the colors of the quilt top where the light shone through. "We'd watch the women's needles poking in and out above us and pretend it was God making new constellations only we could see."

"That was a long time ago. Back when they used the big frame that took up almost a whole room."

"We were much smaller then too. Our feet wouldn't have stuck out so far."

She giggled and ran a hand over her face. "Is that how you found me?"

His tennis shoe nudged her flat. "What you get for wearing bright yellow shoes."

Shaking her head, she pushed up and moved out from under the frame. "We're never going to get this quilted if you just stay under there reminiscing."

"Right. At your service." He crawled out and stood beside her. "Now, we've got our knots in. What's next?"

"Next is the quilting. You have to make sure you get your needle through all three layers. Otherwise, it doesn't do any good. But you also need to keep your stitches small and fairly even. I penciled in the lines you can follow."

Her finger moved across the fabric, tracing the path he was to somehow convince his needle to take. The piece of metal felt tiny and slippery between his fingers, more used to computer keys than anything. But Mama Marsha seemed sure his mom would've wanted this blanket finished this way. And he wanted to do Mom proud.

"Watch me for a minute." Beth easily rocked her needle back and forth, one hand underneath while the other worked on top. Within seconds, she pulled it through, revealing three new stitches.

She made it look so easy, but he had a feeling it wouldn't go as smoothly for him. "Okay, here I go."

After he pulled his through, she leaned over and looked underneath. "Nope. You only got the top layer." In a heartbreaking move, she pulled his stitches out and rethreaded the needle. "Try again."

After several more attempts, he finally managed to do one

stitch through all three layers. One to her twenty-or-so. This would take forever.

"It's okay if you do it one stitch at a time until you get the hang of it. I've done this more than you have." Beth didn't even look at him as she worked her way across her line.

"Right." He settled onto the stool and got to work. One stitch after another. "Ouch!" He jerked his hand out from under the frame and stuck his finger in his mouth.

"It's good luck to prick yourself while quilting. Especially if you get some blood on the quilt."

"Seriously?" Holding his finger up, he glared at the little red spot.

"That's a Hawai'ian thing, I think. I read it somewhere." She grabbed his hand. "Let's see. Oh, please. That's nothing."

"Nothing? I jabbed a needle into my skin!"

Lifting her brows, she displayed the thumb she'd sewn through a few weeks before. Right. That had been much worse. But this still hurt.

Displaying the rest of her hand, she smiled. "Eventually, you'll build up callouses and your fingers won't feel the pricks as much. I haven't hand-quilted anything in a while, but in a few more days, my fingers will toughen up. See?"

Her fingertips looked much like his, full of tiny little pokes. But her skin was already tougher than his because of the various ways she'd built it up through the years, working with needles and scissors and who knew what else. He ran his thumb over her fingertips and heard her intake of breath.

Such lousy timing. His Little Rock trip loomed over him, stealing the joy that flooded him, knowing she felt that way. How had he not seen it before? But he had things to deal with before he could act on it.

Like the job interview. And his relationship with God. His mom would kill him if she knew he'd shunned God since her sickness and death. And Beth probably wouldn't be too happy either.

For that matter, God probably wasn't thrilled with him. Going to worship again the last few weeks made him realize he missed it more than he thought. Now, he needed to make things right with God before he could go any further. But he didn't want to ruin what seemed to be growing between Beth and him, either. How to make her understand?

Swallowing, he cleared his throat. "Sort of like what I've been doing with my spiritual life, huh?"

"What do you mean?" Her voice was barely above a whisper.

"Like you said, doing something over and over builds up a callous where you can't feel the pain anymore." He moved his hands away from hers to distance himself from temptation. "I wasn't the best at attending worship services when I lived in Memphis. When Mom got sick ... and passed away, I blamed God. Couldn't understand why He'd let it happen. Then, even when the grief wasn't as overwhelming, I didn't try to find my way back to Him."

Beth started to say something, but he shook his head. "I'd built up callouses. Every time I chose to do something else instead of putting God first, it was growing those tough spots where I couldn't see the pain I added to my life. And I need to work on that part of my life some more before I can ... before I can work on other parts of it."

It wasn't elegant. But maybe it would show her he wasn't pushing her away. He just needed time.

"Coming back home has been good for me. It's opened my eyes to some things I'd let build up or slack off over the last few years. And made me aware of a few other things, too, but I'm still a work in progress. Sort of like this quilt. I need to figure out what the final product will look like."

"Your mom would be so proud of you." Beth reached over and squeezed his hand. "And not just because you're learning how to quilt."

The corners of his mouth tilted up without his permission. But he didn't mind too much. Beth had always been able to make him smile.

"I have to take a trip in a few days. But I'll be back. Maybe we can talk more then?"

"You know I'm always up for talking to you."

"You weren't a few weeks ago." He nudged her. "Seems to me you basically avoided me for a while."

"Yeah, well. That was before I remembered how much I like having you around."

"The feeling's mutual." He pulled her tight to his side for a minute—any longer and he might be tempted to do other things they weren't ready for. But the next few days would give him time to make some decisions. And finish his soul-searching. "Now, how about we see if we can finish at least this much of this quilt before we leave tonight?"

"Sure your fingers are up for it?" She poked him in the side.

"Gotta build up those callouses somehow, right? The good ones, at least."

"Yes. Good callouses are always welcome."

And while he worked on hardening the skin of his fingers, he'd pray about how to shed the thick layers built over his heart. And that God would give him a clear answer on the job front. And the Beth front too.

Chapter Eleven

L ittle Rock was no Memphis. But it was a city offering a job, which would allow Tommy to bring in money while he built up his own personal clientele. Assuming he had time to work his own business as well as whatever Morris Technical Industries had in mind for him. What was he doing?

I don't know what to do, God. I need to be able to support myself, but nothing about this feels clear. The possibilities that come with this job are amazing. But it's not where I want to be. How do I make this decision?

He drummed his fingers on the steering wheel. Or was that the problem? Was he trying to do this all on his own instead of listening to what God might be saying?

"Stupid."

And now he was talking to himself.

The last few years, he'd been leaning on his own abilities, not stopping to think what God might want or expect. Especially after all those prayers to heal his mother were answered with a resounding *NO*. Why bother praying if he didn't get what he asked for?

I'm sorry, God. I know I haven't talked to you in a while. Or even really been a very good son. But I want to do better. And I need your help. I don't want to move to Little Rock ... because I think I'm in love with my best friend.

"Take next exit ..." His GPS interrupted that trainwreck of a prayer, and reminded him he was only a few turns from his destination.

He'd come this far. Might as well go through with the interview. Being here didn't mean he was accepting the position. Only that he agreed to listen to their offer.

Right.

Ten minutes later, he tugged at the sleeves of his button-down shirt and adjusted his laptop bag over his shoulder. A receptionist said it would only be a minute, that he was expected. But that second hand seemed to move slower in this office than in the real world.

"Thomas London? Daniel Morris." A smartly dressed man who looked to be in his late thirties strode toward him, hand outstretched. "So glad you could join us today. Come on back and we'll go over some details of what I'm thinking."

"Sure." Tommy forced a grin and followed the energetic man.

In a conference room, he took one chair while Morris claimed the seat across from him, behind a rather intimidating pile of paperwork.

Morris smiled. "Let's get right to it. When Priestly sent me your information, I was impressed to say the least. We're actually opening up a new position with our company that would be only for website design and maintenance for small businesses. I've seen your work. Everything is professional, runs smoothly, quick-load time, crisp images. Exactly what we want."

Morris passed him one part of the paper stack. "Here's what we'd offer as a salary. I realize a job like this isn't necessarily going to maintain a regular nine-to-five workday. People have emergencies at all hours when it comes to websites, for some reason. You'd have an office space here, of course, as well as a company computer. But don't feel obligated to only work here."

"You mean I could work from anywhere?" Tommy blinked, an idea forming.

"What are you thinking?" Morris leaned back and studied him.

"I guess Mr. Priestly told you I moved back to my hometown."

Morris nodded.

"After my mom passed away back in April, she left me a share in the quilt shop she ran with her best friend. I've been trying to help them get back on their feet. And found I really like living in a small town. Sassafras is only about an hour north."

"So, you're thinking working from there and maybe checking in here every now and then?" Morris's lips pulled to the side and his fingers tapped against his biceps. "I don't think it would be a problem. We might need to set up days for you to come check in so many times a month."

"That's very doable." Tommy pinched his lips to keep them from grinning too widely. "This might actually end up being rather perfect."

"I'm glad you think so. I was prepared to have to haggle a bit, but you've made it easy for me."

Tommy laughed. "I was trying to figure out how to turn

down such a good offer because I don't want to live in Little Rock."

Morris chuckled. "Sounds like we just need to work out some details and get you a start date."

"That would be great, sir. Thank you so much."

After hammering out expectations and requirements all morning, Morris treated Tommy to lunch and then gave him another hearty handshake. And it was like all the burdens that had weighed Tommy down on the drive over lifted.

Well, most of them.

Okay, God. I owe you a big thank you for that one. Now, can we talk about Beth? How do I make things all the way right with her? Or even better than right?

WHEN TOMMY HAD TOLD her he'd be gone for a day, Beth nodded and tried to accept it without asking questions. But now he was missing in action on Friday too. And the quilt shop seemed strange without him shooting her random smiles and funny faces across the room.

Try as she might to focus on work, her brain had other ideas. Speculations and worries crept in around the edges, painting pictures of where he might possibly be.

Was he moving away again?

Had he gone after Paige? They'd had a fairly long good-bye the other day when she came by.

"No." Her whisper was loud enough her mom gave her a strange look from across the room.

Beth shot her a tremulous smile and then went back to marking labels for the random remnant pieces that had piled up during festival prep. She should probably focus more on the task at hand—it required figuring yardage and original price and ten percent off—but her mind didn't want to listen. Instead, it delved back onto the dark path it had traveled a minute before.

Sure, he'd walked Paige out. But then he'd come back in and crawled under the quilt frame with her. And when he'd talked about callouses, it sounded like maybe … maybe he was beginning to see her in the same light she'd always seen him. Was it possible? After all this time?

Besides, Paige lived in Tulsa. That was several hours away. If he was only supposed to be gone for a day, surely he wouldn't drive that far and back again.

"But he's not back." Her finger jerked as she stuck it with a pin. Despite her own callouses, jabbing her skin that hard hurt.

"You okay over there?" Mom called.

"Fine. Just pricked myself. I'll just go grab a bandage."

She needed to quit talking to herself. Otherwise, she'd look insane. Or more insane than normal.

Wrapping the bandage around her finger immediately took her to when Tommy first reappeared. How gently he'd kissed her thumb.

Where was he today?

"There's an easy way to find out." She whipped her phone out and started to call him, but froze. "It's just Tommy. Call and ask."

But her throat closed up at the possibility he might be one of the places she most feared. Just as her screen was about to go black again, a social media app caught her eye. Could she snoop on him that way?

He hardly ever posted anything. Today was no exception. Nothing new since the watermelon festival—he'd posted a selfie of the two of them that day. They looked so happy. She needed to quit overreacting.

As she scrolled back up, his friends list made her pause. Or at least one friend in particular. Paige.

Thumb trembling, she clicked on her former best friend and went to her feed. Since they weren't actually connected, she couldn't see much. But one phrase jumped off the page and practically screamed at her.

In a relationship.

It didn't say who she was dating, though. Beth held her breath and swiped through Paige's photos. One of the very first ones showed her kissing a guy, his baseball cap hiding most of his face. Just like Tommy's had the first day he came back here.

She blinked against the moisture pooling in her eyes. Some Thomas J he was. At least in the movie, Thomas J had given Vada her first kiss. And a mood ring. What had Tommy London ever given Beth?

Just a broken heart.

She knew better than to let her hopes build up again. Why, oh why, had she started to believe her dreams might come true this time?

"What are you looking at with that angry expression?" Tommy's voice startled her.

How did he keep sneaking up on her?

She jammed her phone into her back pocket and crossed her arms. "What does it matter to you?"

His curious, friendly expression slipped into one of confusion. "Hello to you too. Missed you yesterday."

"Ha." What kind of game did he think he was playing?

"Beth, you're worrying me a little. Acting sort of strange." He took a few steps closer, but held his hands out as if approaching a wild animal.

"Acting is a good word." She slammed the kitchen drawer and slid further away. "You seem to be pretty good at it."

"What are you talking about? Did you hurt your finger

again?" He motioned toward her wrapped digit. "Because you can't blame it on me this time. I wasn't even here."

"No, you weren't here." She stiffened her bottom lip where it was trying to quiver. "How's Paige?"

His brow furrowed even more. "What? I haven't seen Paige since she came by here the other day. She was headed home, remember?"

"So the picture of you kissing her is photoshopped or something?"

"Picture?"

She jerked her phone back out and swiped to reveal what she'd seen. "Seriously? You can quit pretending now."

But his expression never changed. "I don't know why you think that's me, but it's not. I wasn't anywhere near Paige yesterday unless she was in Little Rock."

"But the hat ... and the hair ..." She glanced at the photo again. Was she wrong? Then, the rest of his words registered. "Little Rock?"

He pulled his own phone out and swiped a few times before showing her another picture of Paige—one where she could see all of the guy. And he looked nothing like Tommy. Her heart skittered and moisture welled behind her eyes.

Tommy rested a hand on her upper arm. "I drove down to Little Rock for a job interview."

And there went her peace again. "A job interview."

"It's perfect, really." Tommy grinned, pure excitement oozing from him. He kept talking, but the words droned in the background, unable to penetrate the buzzing in her head.

The bottom had dropped from under her. Sure, he wasn't in another relationship. But he wasn't staying here, either. Hadn't she known he wouldn't stay? Hadn't she warned herself not to get close to him again?

"Bethie?" He leaned down to be at her eye level. "Were you listening?"

"You're leaving again." How the words got around the giant lump in her throat she had no idea. "I am so stupid."

"Beth, you weren't listening. I'm not—"

"No. I'm tired of listening. I listened when you first came back, opened myself up to being friends again, even started to believe—" She blinked a few times, trying to keep the tears at bay. "No. No more. I can't do this anymore, Tommy. You're never going to be happy here and I'm never going to be happy anywhere else."

"Will you please stop and hear me out for a minute?" He stepped closer again, but she ducked around him.

"No. Move to Little Rock. Do me a favor and stay there."

"Beth!" Tommy started after her, but she was fast. The back door slammed before he could weave his way across the store.

"What was that about?" Mama Marsha rested a hand on his shoulder.

His hands fisted and he drew in a deep breath. "I was trying to tell her about my job, but she started off accusing me of being with Paige yesterday. And then, when I finally proved I wasn't Paige's boyfriend, she went crazy and wouldn't listen when I told her I wasn't moving."

"That girl." Marsha shook her head. "She's held on to that high school grudge for so long it's clouding her thinking. And when she didn't hear much from you except through Laura all those years, it didn't help. Her trust in you got shaky."

"But I thought I'd been building it back up. Proving she could trust me."

"Trust takes a long time to build up. And you broke hers seven years ago. That's a lot to make up for."

Seven years ago, when he didn't ask Beth to prom. But it wasn't like he could go back in time and redo that.

Or could he?

He turned to Mama Marsha. "I need a favor or two."

"What kind of favor?"

"Does Beth still have her prom dress?"

"Ye-es." Mama Marsha stretched the word out. "I hid it away just in case. Why?"

He finally let that grin take over his mouth. Time to go back to where everything went south.

Chapter Twelve

Beth waited until she saw Tommy's car leave before returning to the store. Somehow, she made it through the rest of the workday without completely breaking down. She even finished going through all the remnants, marking their clearance prices. But as soon as closing time came, she escaped, ready for nothing more than a good cry.

Two steps into her bedroom, she froze. On the back of her closet door, her prom dress hung in all its glory. What in the world? Why would anyone bring out such an awful reminder of one of the worst nights of her life?

She hadn't even worn the gown that year. Hadn't attended prom. Couldn't stand to see Tommy and Paige together.

A note was pinned the bodice. Carefully freeing it, she unfolded it to read the words.

"Put me on."

Have I fallen through the looking glass? If this was a joke, it wasn't funny. She jerked her door open and stopped short at the sight of her mom.

"I see you found it." Mom breezed in, lifting the hanger down and unzipping the dress. "Why aren't you changing?"

"Why should I?" Beth crossed her arms.

"Do you trust me?" Mom laid the gown on the bed and clasped both her arms. "Because I know you're going to want to be in that dress and ready in half an hour."

"What happens in half an hour?" Beth's curiosity was overcoming her anger and hurt.

"Bethie, just trust me." Mom pressed a kiss to her forehead. "Get the dress on, and I'll help with your hair."

Still not understanding, Beth slipped out of her blouse and capris and let the silky layers of baby pink taffeta slide over her head. The lacy white bodice fit just a bit snugger than when Mom first made this gown seven years before. But she could still breathe easily with it zipped, so that was something. And it wasn't too tight in the round neckline or the armholes.

Mom sat Beth down on a stool and curled her brown strands before pulling some of them back into a knot and letting the rest cascade around her face and neck. A few beaded bobby pins accented the simple but elegant 'do. A sparkly necklace and earrings, along with a pair of low slingback wedges, completed her princess look.

The doorbell rang as Beth pulled the final strap over her heel.

"Perfect timing." Mom smiled. "That's for you."

Heart fluttering, Beth clutched her stomach as she walked to the door. Who was on the other side? What was going on?

Peeking around the door as it creaked open, she gasped.

Tommy stood just off the porch, a giant sign next to him, all covered in gold stars.

"Will you be the star of my show at PROM?"

Even though she read the words, it didn't make sense.

Prom? They weren't in high school anymore. What was he talking about?

"I messed up seven years ago." Tommy took a step forward and held out a wrist corsage of light pink roses. "You see, I asked the wrong girl to go with me."

She blinked against the moisture threatening to run down her cheeks.

"I was ... well, rather blind to what was right in front of me. I hurt our friendship and broke your trust." Tommy slid the flowers over her hand. "And I'm hoping you'll let me make it up to you."

"But how?" She took in his white shirt with cuffs rolled to the elbows, grey trousers, and dress shoes. "Didn't we miss our chance?"

"Not if I have anything to say about it." He offered his elbow.

Could she do this, knowing he wasn't going to stick around? Knowing the future she'd hoped for would never be? And yet, how could she say no?

She slid her arm into the crook of his and stepped off the porch with him. Instead of leading her to his car, he headed toward her backyard. What?

As they rounded the corner of the house, her feet froze. From the willow tree and across to several others, thousands of tiny white lights glittered among the branches. It wasn't quite dusk, but the sun was low enough to let their sparkles shine. Below the lights, a table for two was set up. And music played from somewhere she couldn't see—a tune from their senior year.

"I believe you missed prom, Bethie. How about a redo?"

"You did all this?"

"Took me all afternoon."

Her hand slapped over her mouth. "Why?"

He urged her forward and helped her into one of the iron chairs. "Because I recently found out I wasn't as smart as I thought I was in high school."

"What?"

"When Paige asked if I had a date to prom, I thought she was hinting she wanted me to ask *her*. I didn't realize she was doing reconnaissance."

Beth didn't know what to say. This was all like a dream, and she was afraid to break the spell.

"How about some food? Dawn sent several things for us to try. She said you needed to eat something besides the same thing you always order." He motioned to the spread of goodies on the tabletop.

"As long as it's not watermelon." Beth giggled.

As they munched, Tommy leaned an elbow on the table and studied her.

"What?" She wiped her mouth, sure she'd dripped something.

"Can you listen to the rest of what I was trying to say this morning now?"

She ducked her head, reality bursting her fairy tale bubble. He was moving.

"I'm not moving."

That brought her gaze back up to him in a hurry. "But you said the job was perfect."

"I accepted the job offer." A corner of his lips turned up.

"I don't understand."

"It's perfect because it's a remote position. Since I'll be working through Morris Technical Industries, I'll have to drive down and check in with them a few times a month. But I can do the rest from here."

"You're staying?" Her heart felt like a ping-pong ball, bouncing back and forth between all the emotions.

"For as long as you want me." He stood and tugged her up, too. "Come here."

Stepping through the willow branches, he pulled her under the tree. With the sun setting, the twinkly lights shone brighter. Mixed in with those, fireflies danced in the evening air. And just when she thought things couldn't be more perfect, "My Girl" started playing.

Tommy spun her around and then twirled her back into his arms, while singing the words. A laugh burst from her, the happiness no longer contained. He was staying. And he'd done all this for her. Could it possibly mean what she hoped it did?

"I've dated several girls through the years." Tommy's mouth was right next to her ear as they swayed together. "But those relationships never lasted. And I could never figure out why. Until I came back home."

She leaned back to see his face. "Why didn't they last?"

"Because they weren't you, Bethie." He rested his forehead against hers. "I don't think I realized it at the time, but I compared them all to you. My life was like that quilt my mom made. It was beautiful, but missing a piece."

Afraid to ruin the moment, she stayed quiet, waiting.

"You're my missing piece." His words washed over her. "And I'm sorry I wasted so many years not realizing it. And even more sorry I lost your trust along the way."

"You're here now." She wrapped her arms around his neck. "That's helping a lot."

His chocolate eyes searched hers for a minute before he lowered his head a bit more. And a bit more. And then there was no distance at all, as his lips pressed against hers in the gentlest, sweetest kiss she could have ever imagined.

"I'm still working on removing those spiritual callouses. Will you be patient with me while I do it?" He pressed his cheek to hers, his beard hairs tickling her skin.

"Maybe I can help?"

"Maybe you can." He studied her face for a moment. "And in return, maybe I can help you."

She frowned. "With what?"

"Forgiving Paige."

Her back stiffened, her heart automatically rebelling.

"Hey." Tommy lifted a brow. "It was a mistake on all our parts. But it's in the past. And look at us now. We ended up here anyway, even if we took a bit longer than you wanted."

"I don't like it when you're right." She sighed. "And I know I needed to forgive both of you a long time ago."

"We'll work on it together. It's only fair, right?"

"Mmm." It was all the agreement she could muster. It was a problem to work on in the future, when she wasn't living out a dream so long delayed.

The song switched to something else, but she didn't pay attention. Her heart was too full. Her head buzzed.

"I think I figured something out." Tommy smiled and spun her out and back again.

"Oh?"

"Well, for one thing, I really like this Princess-y dress." His eyes sparkled under the lights as he gave her a teasing grin. "I'm glad it wasn't wasted after all."

She went to punch his arm, but he caught her hand and pressed a kiss to it. "What else?"

"I think our moms were hoping we'd get together all along."

Her brows dipped into a frown. "How do you figure?"

"The quilt."

"The quilt?"

"Made of pieces from me and you."

Burying her head in his collarbone, she shook with giggles. "The pattern makes sense too."

"What pattern?"

"It's called a double wedding ring quilt."

He froze. "Really?"

She nodded, laughter shaking her shoulders.

"Huh." He stole another quick kiss. "I mean, you did look good holding my mom's wedding dress a few weeks ago. I'd be okay with seeing you try that on."

"Hmm. Maybe we should work on your callouses for a while longer before we start making any plans about wedding dresses. We're still getting to know each other again. Still rebuilding."

Letting out a huge sigh, he rolled his eyes. "Fine. I guess that makes more sense."

She pressed a kiss to his cheek. "Thank you for my prom."

"Thank you for forgiving me. And trusting me tonight. And being patient with me while I realized what you really meant to my life."

"Your missing piece?"

He drew her in close. "Not missing anymore."

About the Author

Amy R Anguish grew up a preacher's kid, and in spite of having lived in seven different states that are all south of the Mason Dixon line, she is not a football fan. Currently, she resides in Tennessee with her husband, daughter, and son, and usually a bossy cat or two. Amy has an English degree from Freed-Hardeman University that she intends to use to glorify God, and she wants her stories to show that while Christians face real struggles, it can still work out for good.

Follow her at http://abitofanguish.weebly.com or http://www.facebook.com/amyanguishauthor

Or https://twitter.com/amy_r_anguish

Learn more about her books at https://www.pinterest.com/msguish/my-books/

And check out the YouTube channel she does with two other authors, Once Upon a Page (https://www.youtube.com/channel/UCEiu-jq-KE-VMIjbtmGLbJA)

A Sweet
DREAM COME TRUE

SARAH ANNE CROUCH

For Elizabeth, Lily, and Peter with all my love. Thanks for always sharing your ice cream.

Acknowledgments

If you are ever in Middle Tennessee, go get some ice cream at Janarty's. You won't regret it.

Thank you, Janelle and Marty, for all of your insight and delicious ice cream.

Thank you to Amy, Heather, and Regina. I'm honored to be included with you talented ladies.

Michael, thank you for your love and support.

Thank you to Linda, Shannon, Susan, and everyone at Scrivenings Press for all the work you do.

To you, dear reader, thank you for taking this journey with us. I pray you will be blessed by our stories.

And to the God who created all things, may my work always honor You.

Chapter One

Isaac Campbell was exhausted, and he'd never felt better. He stretched his arms and cracked his knuckles. A grin spread over his face as he surveyed the customers around him.

Three teenage girls huddled over their bowls, leaning in toward one another and chatting with animated expressions. A set of parents juggled cones and twin toddlers covered in a sticky mess. An older couple stood at the counter tasting samples.

Isaac inhaled a deep breath laced in sugar and cream and vanilla. *Oh, man.* His lifelong dream really was the best job in the world—getting to serve delicious ice cream and make people happy every day.

The door swung open to allow his best friend, Zeke Harvey, entrance. Isaac couldn't help smiling at Zeke's exaggerated wave as he stepped into line.

"Hey there, Zeke."

The Mr. Dream Ice Cream shop stayed busy most weekends through the spring and summer, but today was extra special. Last night had kicked off Bestwood, Tennessee's annual fall festival, Best Fest. Visitors came in from all over Middle Tennessee and even farther to admire the giant pumpkins, take a train ride, eat pulled pork barbecue, and listen to excellent country music.

Isaac turned his attention back to the register where Josh was backed up filling orders again. His smile fell a fraction of an inch, but he pushed a grin back in place when Josh handed the older couple their two cones and sent them down his way.

"Two double scoop waffle cones?"

"Yessir." The gentleman reached in his wallet and pulled out a credit card and a store loyalty punch card. "And I think this makes our tenth ice cream."

As he whipped out the hole punch, Isaac racked his brain. He'd seen this couple in the shop several times now and he should know their names. Sparks? Smart? No, Sharp.

"Wonderful, Mr. and Mrs. Sharp. That means your second cone is free." He reached for another loyalty card from the plastic container on the counter. "Here's a fresh card for the next time you come in. And be sure to leave a comment in the suggestion box."

Mrs. Sharp leaned over her husband's shoulder as he took back his credit card and signed his name on the tablet. "We love your ice cream, Isaac. We can't get enough of it."

"Well, I can't get enough of you, either."

The couple chuckled together before waving goodbye.

Two more double cones and a fudge sundae before Zeke made it to the counter. "This place is hopping!" He handed over his credit card.

With practiced automaticity, Isaac slid it through the reader and flipped the tablet over for Zeke to sign. "Not as busy as I'd like though. I took all of your suggestions to heart. We pushed hard on marketing leading up to this weekend.

And we gave out door prizes last night to open up the festival."

Zeke licked a stray drip of mint chip off his cone and gave a low groan. "Man, your ice cream is good."

Isaac's lips pulled into a satisfied grin. "Thanks."

"Well, it looks like you're going to have a great end to the season."

The downside of owning an ice cream business was the winter and early spring. Few wanted to buy a frozen dessert when temperatures dropped. Isaac knew, even before Zeke and the rest of the Chamber of Commerce told him, he needed to go out with a bang at the end of the season if he wanted to make it through his first year. Sales had been good, but Isaac worried it wouldn't be enough.

As Zeke left to find a seat at the bar against the back wall, Isaac mentally assessed all the customers in the small restaurant. Everyone looked satisfied. A few people had chosen to eat at the two tables on the patio, the Sharps and a mom with her kid. He spotted a mess that needed to be cleaned up. Maybe that would be a good job for Josh.

"Hey, Josh. How about you wipe down that middle table and clean up a little?" He turned to the young woman making waffle cones behind him. "Abby, could you take over scooping?"

"Sure thing, boss." Abby grabbed an aluminum scoop from the canister and stepped up with a smile. "What can I get for you today?"

As the man behind the plexiglass ordered his ice cream, Josh stood looking left and right.

"Here, buddy." Isaac stepped back to pick up a clean rag from the shelves. He handed Josh a spray bottle of cleaner.

Josh nodded and ambled away, walking right past the messy table.

"Over at the middle table, Josh."

Isaac shook his head. He'd trained the kid over two months ago. Why couldn't he get the hang of things? Josh came highly recommended by a friend and had wowed Isaac with his stellar interview. He'd told Isaac he was studying business at Middle Tennessee State and hoped to become an entrepreneur.

But that was the last time Josh had impressed Isaac. Since then, he'd needed constant hand-holding and assistance. Isaac knew he should have a heart-to-heart with his employee. He just hadn't worked up the nerve to do it yet.

The next customer he rang up ordered a triple. Lemon blueberry crunch, peanut butter cup, and mint chip. Not a combination he would've chosen, but such was the beauty of an ice cream shop. The customers got to pick whatever flavors thrilled their hearts. And they always left happy.

Isaac sighed and rolled his shoulders. He checked to see that Josh had finished wiping tables and noticed the mom and boy still sitting outside. He frowned. Had either of them ordered ice cream earlier?

The mom drank a swig of water from a plastic bottle then handed it to her son. She smiled at the boy and pointed to something across the street.

"Abby, did you see those two come in earlier? The lady and the kid outside? Did they buy something?"

"No, but maybe I missed them."

"Cover the register for me. I'll be right back."

Isaac patted Josh on the shoulder as he walked toward the middle of the shop. "Go help Abby, would you?" He smiled at the customers he passed. "How's everything tasting?"

Murmurs of delight answered his question.

Isaac's skin itched. He was embarrassed he even had to approach the woman sitting outside. And he was irritated with himself that he was acting like such a coward. But deeper than that was a fear his business would fail. Isaac needed this weekend to go well. He couldn't have people taking seats from his patrons.

"Excuse me, ma'am. I need these seats for my customers."

The woman looked up at him sharply. She had the most arresting blue eyes, and they practically sizzled with anger. He had to remind himself to breathe.

"It's ninety degrees outside. We can't sit for a few minutes in the shade?" She pointed to her son. "I have a small child here. He'll get overheated."

The boy squirmed.

"You're welcome to come inside and order a sundae for him." Isaac's heart raced. He never spoke to people this way. But his discomfort was worth it for the sake of the store.

"No, thanks." She grabbed her purse and her son's hand, then marched off in a huff, dragging the boy behind her.

Isaac covered his face with his hands and blew out a breath. That exchange had been excruciating, but it was over now. He smiled and waved at a family passing by before walking back in the store. Zeke was turned around in his seat at the bar, watching him with an amused smirk on his face.

"Remember that lady I was talking to you about? The single mom from my church who makes chocolate and candy?"

"Yeah." A sinking feeling grew in the pit of his stomach.

"That was her. Melanie Wilson."

"Of course it was."

Zeke hooted with laughter. "She can be a little fiery, huh?"

"That's putting it lightly." He'd gotten third degree burns from her glare. Isaac groaned as a realization dawned on him. "I've got to go talk to her now, don't I?"

Zeke shrugged. "Eventually, you probably should. You've gotta taste her chocolates. She could help you bring in serious traffic this winter."

Doesn't that just figure? The one time Isaac mustered up

enough courage to stick up for himself and make someone unhappy, it backfired on an epic scale. He should've known better. Confrontation went against his very nature and made him uncomfortable in his own skin.

Quitting his accounting job in Nashville and starting a business had been a big risk, but the smiles he saw every day and the peace he felt in his own heart made everything worth it. Isaac had stepped out in faith to trust in God and follow his dreams, and he'd been blessed more than he'd ever thought possible. But if he wanted his ice cream shop to last beyond the first year, Isaac needed to pull out all the stops. And it couldn't hurt to make nice with the chocolatier.

He shot a glance to the counter. Josh and Abby seemed to be handling things fine. Surely he could step out for a minute without the whole store blowing up.

He pulled a coupon from his pocket. Time to see if Melanie Wilson could be won over with a little free ice cream.

Chapter Two

M el Wilson couldn't take another minute at the
festival. The day was hot and her feet were
swollen. Every year, Best Fest took place during
the first weekend of autumn. And every year Mel hoped for
crisp, chilly weather to accompany the fall festivities. She was
usually disappointed. Tennessee autumn was never as cool as
she wished it would be.

This year, she'd spent all morning with her son, Braxton,
volunteering at the church booth, giving away cookies and
cotton candy. They spent the next few hours walking around
the entire Bestwood downtown strip.

"Mom, can we ride the train?"

A groan threatened to slip out, but Mel clamped her lips
shut.

Braxton looked up at her, his eyes alight with excitement.
"Please?"

How could she refuse?

"Okay, Brax." She couldn't quite keep the reluctance from
her voice. "We'll ride the train."

As she slipped two dollars to the conductor and climbed into a pint-sized bright yellow car, a smile crept over her face. Despite her discomfort and embarrassment at sitting on the tiny kid's ride, it made Braxton happy.

Six years ago, when she'd found out she was pregnant and that her baby's father had no intention of sticking around, Mel had been devastated. Only weeks before, she'd been accepted into a prestigious apprenticeship program overseas. She would've had the chance to learn how to make chocolate from a master in Europe.

The same day she told her parents about the baby, Mel tore up her acceptance letter and phoned the coordinator to tell her she wouldn't be coming.

Never once had Mel regretted that decision, or any of the sacrifices that followed. She'd do anything for Brax. She'd worked her way through college while her parents helped with childcare. When she finished her bachelor's degree, it was an easy transition into the position of administrative assistant in the admissions department at the university. Her job offered good benefits and the promise of a generous scholarship for Braxton once he was ready to go to college.

Mel took a deep breath as a breeze blew across her skin. The shade and the wind were pretty nice side benefits of the train ride. She snapped a photo of Braxton smiling out the window of their car and leaned over for a selfie with him.

They passed a giant haystack full of multicolored pumpkins where a family attempted to take pictures of a fussy toddler and her brothers.

"Look at that baby." Braxton pointed and laughed. "It looks just like a pumpkin."

"Shhh! Stop." Swatting his hand, Mel said a silent prayer that the baby's parents hadn't heard. "Don't point at people."

"I don't think the baby minds."

She narrowed her eyes in a playful scowl at his sassy tone. "No, but her parents might."

The couple in question was busy waving and making silly faces while their toddler sat with a grumpy scowl, being squeezed by her older brother. They all seemed too distracted to notice the little boy pointing and laughing at them.

The train drove by a small stage where a bluegrass trio of fiddle, banjo, and mandolin serenaded the crowd. A line of hungry customers wrapped around one of the barbecue food trucks, and smells of smoke and tangy sauce drifted their way.

"Are you hungry, Braxton?" Mel scanned the area for something that wasn't loaded with grease or sugar. Farther down the street were trucks selling funnel cakes and kettle corn. There were snow cone and frozen lemonade stands. And a cart with roasted spiced nuts. Every type of fair food imaginable seemed to be offered at the festival. But not a fruit or veggie in sight.

"More cotton candy?"

"You had enough to last you a lifetime this morning." Somehow he'd managed to swipe a handful of the sugary fluff every few minutes while they volunteered at the church building.

Braxton pouted but kept walking. "I'm not hungry then."

It was for the best. Now she could feed him something a tad healthier at home. They walked along Main Street, admiring the booths and shops.

Each storefront along the strip had decorated windows and awnings for the annual Best Dressed Best Fest Contest. Pumpkins, scarecrows, hay bales, and colorful leaves abounded all along the street. The grand prize winner would be announced the next day, but everyone knew the bookstore would win.

A giant scarecrow sat in a rocking chair in their window. It was surrounded by jack-o-lanterns and appeared to be reading *The Legend of Sleepy Hollow* to them. The owners had also strung pumpkin lights and leaf garlands all around the window and awning. Mel was sure they had even more decorations inside the store.

In spite of her tired body, the charm of the festival worked its way into Mel's spirit. She loved the quaint town of Bestwood and its people. They sure knew how to throw a good festival. Plus, it was the perfect place to raise a child. Bestwood had good schools, safe streets, and was close to Nashville, where she worked.

"Can we go to the firetruck?" Braxton tugged her hand and pointed down the street.

"Okay, but that's it and no more. I need to go home and take a nap."

"Excuse me." A tall man stood over her.

She shaded her eyes as she looked up at his face. It was the ice cream store owner who'd kicked her and Braxton off his patio earlier. Her pulse sped with anger and embarrassment. Was he here to further humiliate her?

"Can I help you?"

He rubbed the back of his neck and winced. "I'd like to apologize for earlier. For chasing you away."

Really? Why? She'd been irritated at the time, but she completely understood his reasons. Her heart rate slowed. Maybe he was a nice guy, after all. "It's fine. I mean, you needed those spots for paying customers. I get it."

"My name's Isaac, by the way." He held out a small card.

"I'm Mel Wilson." Taking the card, she turned it over. It read 'One Free Scoop' with the 'Mr. Dream Ice Cream' logo at the bottom.

"I'd like you guys to come back and have a free scoop of ice cream on me."

"Thanks!" Braxton grabbed the card from Mel's hand.

"Sure thing." Isaac smiled down at Braxton, and the sight thawed Mel's heart a little more.

"Yeah, okay. We'll stop by sometime."

"Great." He let out a breath, looking relieved. "I know a friend of yours, Zeke Harvey."

"Sure. Zeke goes to church with us."

"He mentioned that. And he said you make the best chocolates and candies."

Mel shrugged. "I like to make them. I don't know if they're the best or not."

"He said they're delicious and you even sell them for people's birthdays and special occasions."

That was true. Just last week she'd gotten an order for someone's anniversary. She'd be making chocolate covered strawberries. "I do, but only on an unofficial basis. And just for family and friends." And sometimes family of friends of friends.

"I'd love to talk to you about selling chocolates in the ice cream shop."

Mel furrowed her brow. "I don't know."

Isaac shoved his hands in his pockets. "Well, just come by the store and we can talk more about it later."

"We will. We love ice cream!" Braxton said.

"Oh, good. I love it, too, and I make the very best ice cream in town."

"Then we'll have to try it." Mel looked into his eyes—eyes the color of a dark roasted cacao bean.

"Great." A wide smile spread across his face.

"Okay, well, see you around." Mel waved and grabbed Braxton's hand. Heading in the direction of the firetruck, she walked a few paces before looking behind her. Isaac stood, still waving with one hand and shading his face with the other.

He sure was cute with his big grin and dark eyes. His hair was just long enough to curl around his ears and forehead. Yes, Isaac the ice cream man was very attractive, but he wasn't her type. He seemed ten times nicer than all of the other guys she'd ever had a crush on. A little too nice. He was good with Braxton, but was that enough to tip the scales in his favor?

And, speaking of Braxton, he was the main reason to stop thinking about how cute Isaac was. She could never date someone while he was so young. Just in the few minutes they'd been together, Braxton had been energized and excited by attention from the man. She couldn't risk getting romantically involved with someone like Isaac only to break up with him and break her son's heart in the process.

Nope, it was the single life for Mel. She'd made her bed and now had to lie in it, as her mom always said. Besides, she was only twenty-four. She had plenty of time for dating later, if she ever decided to give men a chance again.

She took a few pictures of Braxton sitting behind the wheel of the firetruck before pulling him into her arms. At five years old, he was getting too big to carry anymore. He'd be as tall as she was soon.

She didn't regret having Braxton. Not for a single second. But she did wish the timing had been different. What if she'd been able to have the same sweet little boy in a family with a father? Or after she'd had a chance to study abroad and follow her dreams? What could their lives have been like? There was no sense in thinking like that. She couldn't change the past and didn't want to, not if it meant losing her son. Mel grabbed his sweaty hand in hers.

"Let's go home, Brax."

"Okay, Mama. But can we get ice cream later?"

"Maybe another day. Mama needs to rest right now. You wore me out."

"I think I wore me out too."

Mel laughed. "Maybe we should both go home then."

"Okay, Mama."

They plodded along, her steps tired and heavy, his steps skippy and light. Mel wrapped her arm around Braxton and pulled him close to her side as they walked. His head rested against her waist, his platinum blonde hair a perfect match for her own.

Her slate of wrongdoings had been wiped clean, and was continually wiped clean, by God. She didn't need to dwell on the past, and it didn't do anybody any good. There was no sense in wishing she could date. And there was no sense in trying to revive her old dreams. She had new dreams and new goals, and her son was smack dab at the center of all of them.

Why would she ever wish for anything more?

Chapter Three

Isaac whisked a pot full of eggs, sugar, milk, and cream as he carefully watched his thermometer climb in number. One hundred seventy degrees seemed to be the sweet spot according to his research and months of trial and error. Once his base reached the right heat level, he moved it off the burner to a hot pad waiting nearby. He mixed in a small amount of peppermint extract—a little could go a long way— and left the pot to cool to room temperature.

"Do you usually make new batches of ice cream in the middle of the day?"

When Isaac glanced up, a pair of blue eyes stared back at him. "Mel Wilson." A grin spread across his face, unbidden. "I'm glad to see you."

The corner of her mouth lifted. It was almost a smile. She tilted her head toward the young boy tugging at her hand. "Braxton wouldn't let me rest until we came back for our free scoops."

Breaking free of his mother's grasp, Braxton practically plastered his face to the glass covering the ice cream display.

"So, do you always mix up new batches of ice cream all day long?" Mel asked again. "Seems time-consuming."

"It is, but I think you'll agree the effort is worth it."

"Can I have chocolate?"

Kinley, the other employee in the shop today, spoke up from behind the counter. "Would you like regular Triple Chocolate, Peanut Butter Cup, or Chocolate Avalanche?"

Braxton's eyes grew three sizes. "What's Chocolate Avalanche?"

After she expertly dipped a tasting spoon in the ice cream tub on her far left, Kinley handed it over to Braxton. "A chocolate base mixed with caramel, marshmallow, and fudge sauces, with brownie chunks and chocolate chips."

"Mmmm." Braxton turned to his mom, his face a picture of delight. "Can I get two scoops?"

"Let's stick with just one for today. We don't want to ruin your supper."

The boy let out a whine, but with one look from his mother, he turned his attention back to his tiny spoon and licking every last drip of ice cream off it.

With three nieces and a nephew, Isaac had seen some colossal tantrums. From what he could tell, Mel was doing a great job as a single mother with Braxton, although he knew it wasn't his place to comment on her parenting.

Kinley scooped a small cone for Braxton and turned to Mel with a smile. "What can I get for *you*?"

"What do you recommend?"

"The Chocolate Avalanche is always good, but my favorite flavor is coffee."

"Let's try that."

While Kinley dipped her scoop into the tub of coffee ice cream, Mel fished around in her purse. She handed the coupon card to Kinley in exchange for her cone.

Even though Isaac needed to start another batch of vanilla, he wanted to talk to Mel more. Something about her drew him in and made him think she could do wonders with his store. He couldn't put a finger on exactly why he wanted her help so badly. She certainly wasn't overly friendly.

Maybe it was Zeke's recommendation. Or maybe it was that he hadn't spent time around a beautiful woman in a long time.

Mel's whole face lit up as she tasted her ice cream. Something inside of him lit up, too, like a small spark igniting.

"This is amazing!"

He shrugged and smiled. "Thanks. I use fresh beans from the coffee shop down the street."

Now that he had Mel's approval on his ice cream making abilities, he just needed to convince her to sell him some chocolates.

THIS IS *the best ice cream I've ever tasted.* Mel took another bite, just to make sure. Yep. Still delicious.

"Brax, wanna give me a taste of yours? I'll trade you." She waved her cone to him and wiggled her eyebrows.

Her son frowned before pulling his cone tight to his chest and turning away. He could be a little stinker sometimes.

"Come on kid, let's find a seat." She led him toward a small table with two chairs in the corner of the restaurant and grabbed a fistful of napkins along the way.

They savored their desserts in silence for a few moments before Isaac stepped out from behind the counter. "How is everything?" His gaze focused on Braxton.

"Amazing. Like, so so good."

Just like the old saying, the way to Braxton's heart was through his stomach. Or his sweet tooth. One of those.

"Really. We both love our ice cream." Mel took another lick. "I can taste how fresh everything is—you were right."

"I'm glad you like it. We've had a good year so far. But I'm concerned about the winter. I'd love to find a way to bring in more customers through the cold months."

Mel had an inkling as to where this conversation was headed, and she wasn't sure how she felt about it.

"I've heard great things about your chocolates. Would you ever consider selling them in a store?"

Mel took a bite from her cone—mostly to stall for time—but man, was it delicious.

"Zeke just raves about how talented you are." Isaac inched closer as he talked.

"I've never produced them on a large scale before." Mel sighed. "People just hire me for parties or to make gifts."

"You wouldn't have to make many." Isaac waved to the ice cream display behind him. "I was just thinking about a small candy display. And maybe some hot cocoa balls or cookies. Nothing too fancy—" He stopped himself. "Unless you want fancy. We can do whatever you like."

What *did* she want?

Mel had dreamed for years of an opportunity like this one. Was she crazy to turn it down? Or was she crazy to actually consider it? She had a full-time job and a child keeping her busy. She didn't have spare time to build a small business on the side.

But this is what you've always wanted, a small voice echoed inside her head.

"I don't know ..." Her gaze drifted to Braxton blissfully licking stray drips from his cone and his wrist.

Was she a terrible mother for considering adding an extra

obligation to her life? Would following her passion mean shortchanging her son?

"What if we start small?" Isaac straightened.

Her heart screamed at her to say *yes*. "What do you mean?"

"How about we start with a trial run?" He raised an eyebrow, and a hint of excitement gleamed in his eyes. Could he tell her defenses were lowering? "Bring in some samples next week, and I'll see how I like them."

Mel bit her lip, hesitating. "Okay." Her inner self jumped for joy even as she glanced at her son again. He wasn't paying attention to their conversation. Instead, some squirrel burying a nut outside caught his eye.

A smile crept over her face. She was actually going to sell her chocolates in a real live store. "When would you like the samples?"

"Would Monday be okay? The shop will be closed, but I'll be here getting the ice cream ready."

"After I get off work Monday would be great."

"Um, could I get your number?"

Mel rattled off her number as Isaac typed on his phone. Wait. Were his cheeks pinker than before? But why? Was this about more than selling chocolates? Could he like her for more than his shop? And why did that possibility make her smile even more than her new business opportunity?

"Got it, thanks." Mel felt her phone buzz with Isaac's message but didn't look down. Braxton had created quite the mess while she'd been distracted. She'd add his information to her contacts list later.

As she stood up, Mel caught a scent of something clean and fresh. Maybe Isaac's soap or laundry detergent. Whatever it was sent butterflies through her stomach.

Nope. She would not have a romantic fling with the ice cream man. Bad, bad, bad idea.

With a speed and precision that came from years of practice, she wiped Braxton's face and fingers in two seconds flat. Grabbing her son's hand in hers, Mel scooped up the napkins and her purse, then tossed her trash in the can on the way out. "Have a great night. I'll see you on Monday."

Her phone pinged again with the text alert from earlier. Once she'd safely crossed the street to the parking lot, she peeked at the screen.

This is Isaac Campbell. I can't wait to see you again on Monday.

What did he mean? Was he happy with the anticipation of a business partnership and more customers in his shop during the slow season? Or was he looking forward to seeing *her*?

She turned briefly back to the ice cream store—just to glimpse Isaac's expression. His tall, broad frame nearly filled the whole doorway. A bright blue apron with the ice cream shop logo was tied around his waist. A lock of curly brown hair fell across his forehead. And his smile took over his whole face, from his curved full lips to his dreamy brown eyes. The image seared into her brain.

Mel blew out a breath and gripped Braxton's hand tighter. She could never have him, but that Isaac Campbell sure was handsome.

Chapter Four

"Can I help?" Braxton gazed up at her with wide blue eyes.

Mel bit her lip. He blinked quickly, unaware of how his long, dark eyelashes always melted her heart. She groaned. Every night, she'd been working a little bit on the chocolate samples for Isaac. After Braxton went to bed, she'd log a couple hours or so chipping away at the long list of treats she wanted to bring to the shop on Monday.

A cooled and crumbled cake sat in the fridge, as well as a tub of plain buttercream frosting, a batch of raspberry buttercream filling, and a dozen balls of peanut butter rolled and waiting on a sheet pan. Now, on Sunday afternoon, she was attempting to melt chocolate to cover the raspberry and peanut butter and warm a pot of heavy cream to mix with more chocolate to make truffles.

Mom would say you spoil him. Parenting Braxton was always a point of contention between Mel and her mother. Her mom accused her of being overly indulgent, while Mel thought she should cherish her little boy while he was still young. So what if she had a hard time saying 'no' to Brax? Didn't *all* mothers want to give in to their adorable sons?

"Sure thing, kiddo. Pull up a chair."

Braxton darted over to the kitchen table and dragged a chair to the counter, right next to her. Mel took a step to the side so she could move her elbows without whacking into the chair. And now she couldn't pull open the drawer where the measuring cups were stored.

"Hang on. Let me get some things real quick, and then you can hop right back up here." She lifted him under his arms and set him gently on the floor.

Mel's mom rarely let her assist in the kitchen when she was growing up, until it came time to wash the dishes. *And that's why I learned everything I know from Gramma Wilson.*

Her dad's mother had been the one to patiently train her in the art of candy making. Every major holiday found the two of them side by side in the kitchen, Mel standing on a chair in the years before she was tall enough to reach the counter. They measured and poured, checked thermometers, and stirred until Mel thought her arms would surely fall right off into the pot of syrupy candy.

Maybe allowing Braxton to help would be the perfect compromise. She'd get to pursue her dreams while having quality time with her son. And she just might pass on a love of cooking in the process.

After pulling out everything she might possibly need from the drawer, Mel scooted the chair into a better spot and motioned for Braxton to climb onto it.

"Okay. I'm making chocolate truffles right now. We need to warm the cream first." She swatted his hand away. "Don't put your hand over the burner. It's hot."

"Why don't you have a pot on the burner?"

"I was about to put it on before you interrupted me. We need to measure out the cream."

"Can I do it?"

Pouring and measuring seemed like good jobs for a little kid. "Okay. We need a third cup. So, this line right—"

Braxton splashed half the carton of cream into the cup.

"Too much, buddy. Let's pour some back."

He spilled even more cream all over the counter, but eventually, Braxton and Mel got the right amount in the measuring cup. Then Mel showed him how to stir, but when the time came to hand over the spoon and give him a turn, she just couldn't handle watching him narrowly miss sloshing the cream over the edge or scorching his skin. So she took the spoon back after about thirty seconds.

Braxton peered into the pan. "What's a truffle?"

"It's just a ball of chocolate. I'll roll it in sprinkles or cocoa powder or nuts."

"Blech. No nuts. I hate nuts."

"These aren't for you."

"Who are they for?"

"Isaac Campbell. The guy from the ice cream shop."

"You're making all these for Isaac?"

Mel laughed. "I'm sure he's not going to eat them all himself. They're for him to taste and maybe sell at his store."

Braxton nodded to her with an impressed expression on his face. "That's pretty cool, Mom."

A smile crept in, unbidden. "Yeah. I think so too. But we've got to see how these turn out." She eyed the pot. "It looks like it's about warm enough. We don't want it to boil, just simmer."

"What's a simmer?"

Mel sighed. So many questions. How did her grandmother ever get anything done in the kitchen all those years ago? She turned to look him in the eye. "Simmer means we want the cream to have little fizzy bubbles, but not big boiling bubbles."

"Like those?"

Drat! Mel whipped the pot off the burner while holding out an arm to keep Braxton away from the hot stove. "Maybe it'll still be okay. It only boiled a couple bubbles."

"What's next?" Braxton rubbed his hands together.

"We're going to pour this over the chocolate, but not until—"

Braxton grabbed the plastic pot handle before she could stop him. "I can pour." He eagerly splashed the cream over the chocolate.

Immediately, Mel knew the whole recipe was ruined. She'd been making truffles as long as she could remember. A quick stir of the chocolate would confirm her suspicions. The cream was too hot and the ganache would never set. What she had on her hands was a big bowl of messy, oily goo. She might as well throw it all out and start from scratch.

A sudden flash of anger bubbled to the surface.

"Braxton! What were you thinking?" Mel held her head in her hands. She turned on her son. "You've ruined it, and now I have to start over."

Brax's lower lip stuck out. "Do we have more chocolate?" His voice came out in a whisper.

"Yes, but this stuff is expensive. I'm not using store brand chocolate chips here, kid." She sighed. "Go play in your room. I need to clean up this mess."

As she watched Braxton sulk off down the hall, Mel knew she should go after him and apologize. She'd never yelled at him like that. Not since he was two years old and destroyed an entire bottle of liquid foundation. The huge tears in his eyes had cut her to the core, and she'd promised herself she'd never lose her temper with her son again. But here she was feeling guilty and still fuming at the same time.

Mel surveyed the kitchen. Spilled cream and chocolate shavings covered the countertop. The fridge was full of half-finished confections. Yelling at Braxton hadn't released any of the pressure building inside of her. She wanted so badly to impress Isaac, but was it worth all this stress?

After wiping down the counter, Mel chopped another eight ounces of chocolate and set it aside. She'd make that into truffles later. Now she needed to make amends with her son.

"Knock, knock." Mel gave Brax's door a gentle push. He sat on the floor surrounded by a pile of Legos. She joined him, hugging her knees to her chest. "Listen, B. I'm sorry about yelling at you like that. I was upset about the chocolate, but I think I'm actually a lot more worried that *I'm* going to mess up. I took it out on you, and that was wrong. Can you forgive me?"

One of the very best parts of being Braxton's mom was the hugs. He wrapped his arms around her, and some of Mel's tension melted away.

"Sure, Mom."

"Thank you, buddy. Do you mind if I finish the rest of the chocolates by myself?"

He shrugged and began piecing blocks together.

"How about you and I make some popcorn after I finish these truffles? I'll let you dump in the salt." That was a generous offer. He always poured in way too much salt and then insisted the popcorn tasted better that way.

"Yeah, okay." He smiled a little this time and even made eye contact before returning to the structure he was building.

An hour and a half later, Mel had dozens of little chocolate truffles, peanut butter balls, and raspberry cream chocolates lined up like soldiers on parchment paper on the counter. One by one, she selected the prettiest specimens and placed them gently into paper boxes to present to Isaac the next day.

"Want to scoop?" Mel called Braxton into the kitchen. The chair scraped the floor as she pulled it back to its place at the counter.

Braxton measured with a tablespoon and managed to get nearly every kernel in the microwaveable bowl.

"Watch your head, B." Carefully, Mel placed the bowl inside as Braxton ducked out of the way of the microwave door.

"Can I press the buttons?"

"Sure thing." She pointed to the number three before he jammed his finger into the button.

They watched together as the corn popped. Mel still enjoyed seeing the fluffy white popcorn explode in the microwave as an adult, but she loved watching Brax's face even more. His wonder and excitement made everything in life more magical.

Mentally, Mel ran through a to-do list in her head as she sat next to her son, bowl in hand. They had evening worship services at the church that night. Afterward, she'd need to get Braxton fed and ready for school the next day. She needed to pack a lunch and double-check she hadn't ordered a school lunch for Monday. Braxton got reduced lunch fees—one benefit of being a single parent with a single income—but he didn't always like what was being served at school.

Then, finally, Mel could finish making the cake pops she'd started the day before. She wasn't going to attempt anything cute or fancy. Just white cake and buttercream frosting dipped in white chocolate. If she decided to get a little crazy, she might add some sprinkles.

Just thinking about all the work still left to do exhausted her. Maybe some moms could handle working a full-time job while pursuing a passion and raising kids. But not Mel. Today made that fact abundantly clear.

Mel loved making candy. She loved the memories it brought back of Gramma Wilson. She loved the smell and taste of delicious chocolate. She loved making people happy with her sweet treats.

But she loved Braxton even more. And nothing was worth sacrificing their relationship.

Maybe she'd still have time to sell some chocolates at the ice cream shop every once in a while—when she wasn't so busy. But this couldn't become a weekly occurrence.

So Mel would finish making these chocolates. She'd take them to Isaac. And then she'd let him know she couldn't be his business partner.

Chapter Five

All day long, Isaac had looked forward to seeing Mel again. When his feet hit the floor in the morning, he'd remembered it was Monday and Mel was coming to the shop. He hummed a tune as he brushed his teeth. His step had a significant bounce as he walked from his car to unlock the shop door. And he tapped his toes as he stirred a sweet cream base on the stove.

He was thankful there weren't other people around to witness his happy mood and ask what caused such ridiculous behavior.

It was just excitement about the potential business partnership. The weight of worry that rested on his shoulders could be lifted by Mel agreeing to sell her chocolates at the shop. He could go into the winter months without fear of the future.

But if he was being honest, there was more to his peppy attitude than the promise of chocolates. The memory of those blue eyes, snapping with laughter—or even anger—lingered in his mind. The way Mel cared for her son, like it was the most natural thing in the world, had affected him more than he'd realized at the time. Mel Wilson had worked her way into his psyche, and there was no getting around it. He had a crush.

Could a grown man have a crush? Whatever he called it, Isaac knew he needed to either face the music and ask her out on a date or get the woman out of his system.

What time does she get off work, anyway?

Isaac checked the clock. It was nearly five o'clock in the evening. Surely she'd be coming soon. He'd long since finished making all the ice cream he'd need for the next day. Too much more and he'd risk having leftovers. Isaac prided himself on serving the freshest ice cream in town. No one else made small batch bases the way he did, and everyone could taste the difference.

After he'd stocked the freezer, Isaac washed all the dishes and cleaned the store.

Then he took inventory and checked the books on his computer.

I guess I could wipe the counters down. Again.

Finally, at five thirty, Mel walked toward the front door with a cardboard box in her hands.

"Hey, there!" Isaac stepped around the counter, a little too quickly. Did she notice how over-eager he was? He unlocked the door for her, then wiped his sweaty palms on his jeans. "Can I carry something for you?"

"I've got it, thanks." Mel set the box on the largest table, right in the middle of the store. She gave a slight smile, but something kept her from giving him a full-on grin. The happiness didn't quite reach her eyes.

One by one, Mel pulled out smaller white boxes and placed them in a row in front of Isaac. Each was sealed with a teal and pink sticker.

"Very impressive." Isaac picked up the nearest box and slid

his finger under the lid, breaking the seal. "Wow." Inside were four chocolate truffles, one with chocolate sprinkles, one with colored raw sugar, the third one with cocoa powder, and the last one covered in chopped nuts.

He stared at the box a moment before raising his gaze to Mel. "May I?" The chocolates looked too good to eat, but when she nodded her assent, he picked up the truffle dipped in nuts and took a bite. "Oh, man." He groaned around the chocolate in his mouth. "Mel, these are amazing."

A spark lit in her eyes. "Thanks. Here, try these." She pushed another box toward him. Inside were four more balls, each half-covered with chocolate.

"Are these buckeyes?"

"I've always called them peanut butter balls."

He sampled the closest one to him. "Yep, these taste just like the ones my mom always makes at Christmas."

"I assume that's a good thing." Her mouth lifted on one side.

"It's a great thing." He put another in his mouth and closed his eyes. "Mm." His eyes popped open. "I need something to drink. You want anything?"

"Oh, um."

Isaac hopped up and jogged to the fridge at the back of the store. He always kept a stock of drinks and snacks separate from his inventory so he and his employees could eat something other than ice cream all day. "Coke or water? Or I could make coffee or tea if you want."

"Water would be fine."

He grabbed a soda for himself and water for her. Mel seemed to have gotten a lot shyer since the last time they spoke. Compared to the way she'd acted at their first encounter, she was positively demure. Was she just nervous about showing off her chocolates? Maybe if he made a greater effort to tell her how much he liked them, she'd warm up a bit.

"What's next?" He pulled the next box toward himself and lifted the lid. "More truffles?"

"These are filled with raspberry cream."

He took a bite and shook his head. "Incredible." He slid the chocolates toward Mel. "Here, have some. I don't like being the only one eating."

She popped the whole truffle in her mouth without reacting to the delicious flavor. She swallowed, took a drink of water, then spoke. "I've got one more box. These are always a big hit with kids."

Inside was a row of cake balls—white with multicolored sprinkles. Isaac took one and handed another to Mel. "Cheers." He tapped her cake ball with his. "Mm. Very sweet, but delicious." The cake was moist, and the sprinkles added a fun touch. He could see himself selling out of a dozen of these in a day.

Isaac swallowed a mouthful of soda before wiping his mouth. He didn't usually eat so much sugar in one sitting, and he was beginning to feel the effects in his stomach, but tasting Mel's chocolates had been worth the extra calories.

"I've eaten a lot of sweets, as you might guess." Isaac swept his arm behind him, indicating the ice cream freezer. If the fact he had an ice cream shop didn't clue her in, surely the pudge around his gut showed how much he liked dessert. "But you've blown me away, Mel. I'd love to work with you. We can start whenever you're able."

"Right—"

He barely registered that Mel had said something before he continued. "I mean, I don't know about licensing. If you've been selling chocolates out of your home, do you already have all the paperwork in order to sell food?"

"Isaac, I can't." She placed her hands on the table.

"Sorry?" Did she mean she couldn't file the paperwork? Or that she couldn't work with him?

"I can't be your partner."

The expression on her face was so sad that Isaac wanted to reach around and give her a hug. Hadn't she been almost as excited as he was about selling her chocolates in his shop? From the way Zeke talked about her, and from the quality of the food he'd just sampled, she was obviously serious about her craft. And the way her eyes lit up when Isaac raved about the truffles made him think she also enjoyed sharing her gift with others.

So why was she backing out? And why did she look so devastated?

"I don't understand. Why can't you?"

She shook her head. "I thought I could do it all—work full-time, be a good mom, and start a small business. But this was too much." She waved over the half-empty boxes in front of them. "I can't handle a regular large order like this."

"What if we kept it smaller? I don't need this much variety every time."

Mel shrugged. "I could do special events and maybe just one or two types of chocolate."

"There, see? We can make it work." He smiled.

"No," she said. "You need a business partner who can bring in enough business to last you through the winter. And I can't commit to that much."

She was right. He should cut his losses and search for someone else to help him. But he didn't want anyone else. He wanted Mel. She was talented, she already had a local presence, and she wasn't so established that he couldn't afford to buy her chocolates. Plus, he just liked the woman.

"Would you at least consider working with me for the Main

Street Trick-or-Treat event? We could pick just a couple chocolates and make it something simple."

Sucking in her cheeks, Mel seemed to think his suggestion over for a moment before replying. "I'm sorry, Isaac. It's a wonderful opportunity, but I have to say no."

She was resolved. It was obvious every effort he made to convince her would fall on deaf ears. The set of her jaw and the flash in her bright blue eyes told him he might as well not try.

"Please let me know if you change your mind." Isaac stood as Mel pushed back her chair. He rested a hand on her arm. "I'd love another chance to eat those delicious truffles."

Smiling, she pushed a lock of blonde hair behind her ear. "You'll be the first to know."

Isaac started to pack the boxes away for her, but she stopped him with a hand on his. "Those are for you to keep. I have loads of extras at home."

"Thanks." He'd be lucky if the confections lasted the night.

As Mel pulled her purse back on her shoulder and turned to leave, Isaac's heart twinged. If he didn't say something now, he might not get another chance. What if she never came back to the shop?

"Mel." He took a deep breath. Asking a girl out on a date was nerve-racking no matter how old he got. "I hate to be too forward, but since we aren't working together, maybe it would be okay."

She waited while Isaac gathered his courage.

"Would you like to go to dinner sometime? With me?"

Her eyebrows shot up. So maybe he'd been imagining the chemistry between them. But the way she'd been smiling at him tonight had led him to believe she might feel the same way.

"Oh, wow. Um."

Isaac's first impression of Mel was that she was direct and

even a bit brash. Yet today, both when she first arrived and now, she seemed at a loss for words.

"I can't. It's just ..." She tugged at the purse strap on her shoulder. "I have to be really careful about who I date. If Braxton got attached and something happened ..." She winced. "You seem like a great guy. I just don't really date. At all."

What a loss. Such a beautiful and smart woman deserved a guy who told her so every day. But maybe she was right.

Had he jumped into this infatuation with Mel too quickly? Every single decision she made was through the lens of being a mom. She wouldn't work with him or date him—or anyone for that matter—all because of a kid. Maybe he'd taken the responsibilities of parenthood too lightly. Was he ready to be a father figure? He'd never even considered the possibility.

"I understand. You take your job as Braxton's mom very seriously, and I respect that."

Isaac waved as Mel walked down the sidewalk toward the nearby downtown parking lot. Sighing, he flicked off the shop lights. His feet plodded as he locked the doors. Isaac wasn't looking forward to returning to square one on his business plan for this winter. Mel was his best shot, and now she'd officially rejected him.

On multiple levels.

At least he had some chocolate to keep him company.

Chapter Six

"Morning, boss."

"Morning, Abby." Isaac attempted his usual happy expression at his employee. *Does my face typically look like this? How do I normally smile?* His muscle memory must have been good enough, because Abby grinned back before hanging her coat and purse in the utility closet.

It was barely still morning—the store didn't open until eleven most days. Most people wouldn't eat ice cream for breakfast, and the later hours allowed him to keep the store open in the evenings. Plus, he had the added benefit of fitting more easily into the lifestyle of a college student with his night owl routine. College students equaled cheap and energetic employees. Well, most of the time.

"Who's on the schedule for today?" Abby tied an apron around her waist as she joined him behind the counter.

"You and Josh."

Abby winced. "Sorry. I was hoping for Claire or Ella."

You and me both.

"I think Claire has a morning class on Tuesdays and

258

Thursdays this semester. She and Ella are working tomorrow. I'll try to get you two together soon. You're welcome to take a look at my calendar later." Arranging work schedules was one of his least favorite parts of the job. But he didn't have a manager or enough money to pay one. If Abby was willing to do the task for free, he'd gladly let her.

They worked together in silence, setting out each flavor of ice cream. Today was mint chocolate chip, peanut butter cup, blackberry cobbler, mocha, vanilla bean, and triple chocolate. Abby fired up the waffle cone maker and set to work making some fresh cones from the batter Isaac had prepared earlier that morning.

If only all his employees were like Abby. She never needed reminders to restock toppings or wipe down tables. Abby even made helpful suggestions, like posting a list of opening and closing duties, as well as a list of tasks to perform when the store was empty.

But they weren't all like Abby. In fact, Josh was about as far removed from her as anyone could get. It was eleven thirty when he finally showed up to work.

"Hey, man. What's up?" Perhaps he should've been more direct. What Isaac meant was *Why in the world are you so late?*

"Hey." Josh barely nodded in Isaac's direction before sauntering up to the counter.

"Forget something?" Isaac waved his apron at Josh with what he hoped was a friendly expression.

"Right." Josh pivoted and returned to the closet, grabbing an apron.

"It's eleven thirty, Josh. You were supposed to be here an hour ago." Abby gave Josh a look that meant business, her hand on her hip, her lips pursed.

Thank You, God, for Abby.

Josh had the good sense to appear penitent. "I'm sorry. I missed my alarm and overslept."

"Next time, call or text to let someone know." Abby swiveled back to the sink. "Go sweep up the floors, and then wash your hands."

Once Josh was out of earshot, Abby whispered to Isaac. "I overstepped, I know. I'm sorry. I was just so mad at him."

"It's okay, Abby. Although I'm pretty sure the floors are clean already."

"I know." Her lips lifted in a wry smile. "But Josh doesn't know that, and he *hates* sweeping."

Isaac couldn't help but chuckle to himself.

Business picked up quickly after that. A group of moms and toddlers came in for their biweekly post-playdate ice cream. They always met up for a picnic at the playground and stopped by for a treat after.

Later, a couple of college students stopped in to buy a cone and work on a project. Several kids came by after school let out. That night, they'd get a few families wanting after dinner snacks. And teenagers on dates or just hanging out would dominate the shop after eight in the evening.

When they hit a late afternoon lull, Isaac checked his suggestion box. He'd been pushing people to fill out slips of paper and put them in with flavor ideas or ways they'd like to make the shop better. Now he dumped the contents of the box on an empty table.

His thinking had been that reading the suggestions could help knock him out of his funk. Ever since the night before, when Mel had turned him down as a business partner and as a date, he'd been stewing. Mel had clearly told him her rejection had nothing to do with him and everything to do with her son and their season in life. But he couldn't help thinking if she were a little more into him, she would've had a harder time telling him no.

'Great job! Love the ice cream!'

'Keep up the good work!'

'So glad to have you in town!'

A smile took over his face. While they weren't exactly suggestions, the nice comments sure cheered him up.

'Peppermint'

'Salted Caramel'

'Cake Batter'

'Something with lots of nuts'

Several ice cream flavors were written on the slips, some he'd already tried and some new ones. He counted five suggestions for a pumpkin flavor, in some form or fashion. Pumpkin wasn't his favorite, and he tried to only serve ice cream he loved, but maybe he could make an exception for the upcoming Trick-or-Treat event. He could advertise it as a special flavor to bring in customers.

The next flavor took him by surprise. 'Fruity Cereal.' Isaac remembered reading a recipe for a cereal-flavored ice cream when he was researching last year. He'd saved everything in a file on his computer. That could be something to start with. Maybe as early as this evening.

He kept reading. 'I wish you had different waffle cones. The ones you serve now are too chewy and overpriced.'

Isaac frowned. He liked their waffle cones. They were made fresh throughout the day and gave the store a delicious, sugary scent.

"Abby, Josh?" For once, Josh actually looked up and paid attention when Isaac spoke to him. "Do you guys like the waffle cones?"

"Like? More like love." One of Abby's eyebrows shot up.

"Those things are delicious. And I'm saying that even though they're a huge pain to make sometimes."

"You think they're a pain?"

Abby's cheeks turned pink. "No, I mean, they can be. At least, they were early on when I was still getting the hang of using the waffle cone maker and the little shaper tool."

"What about you, Josh?"

He shrugged. "I've never tried them."

"What?" Abby swung around to face Josh.

"Do you usually eat the ice cream from a bowl?" Isaac knew some people preferred the bowls for the convenience and to save themselves a potential mess.

"Yeah. I guess I don't eat that much ice cream."

"Like, at all? Or just while you're working?" Abby still wore an incredulous expression.

"I like ice cream fine. I just prefer other desserts, okay?"

"Okay, okay." Isaac held up his hands. "That's perfectly fine, Josh."

To everyone's relief, the bell on the front door clanged and they all had to get back to business. Isaac swept the comment cards into a pile and carried them to the back. He'd read the rest later. He started to return the suggestion box to its spot, but he hesitated. *Do I really want people's honest opinions?*

The negative comment about the waffle cones still stung a little. He should be able to let it go—the comment wasn't personal in any way—but he hated that someone didn't like the food in his shop.

Maybe I'll make up for the bad comments by trying some of the new flavor suggestions. That way, he'd be able to please more customers and focus his energy on something productive. He'd start by picking up some canned pumpkin and fruity cereal on the way home tonight. It was time to start experimenting.

Chapter Seven

"Helloooo," Mel called into her parents' living room, poking her head around the entryway. "Mom? Braxton?"

"Back here."

Following the sound of her mother's voice, Mel ventured down the hallway to the guest room. "Hello?" She rapped on the door before pushing it open. Braxton sat with her mother in the middle of a pile of pictures. "What are you guys doing?"

"Getting carried away, I think." Mom chuckled as she stood and dusted off her pants. "Braxton was asking questions about you as a kid on the way home from school. So I pulled out some albums, one thing led to another, and now we're surrounded by old photos I'd forgotten I had."

Mel set her purse on the bed before kneeling beside Braxton. "What've you got there?"

He held up a picture of her as a little girl with her older brother and sister. There was a ten-year age gap between Mel and her sister, and her siblings had towered over her when she was a child. Mel was still the shortest of the three, but only by a couple inches. "Wow. Did you know Aunt Macy used to have braces?"

"Is that those things on her teeth?"

"Yeah. You think she got her beautiful smile for free?" Mel nudged Braxton with her elbow.

"No, she did not." Mom coughed. "It was a very expensive smile, actually."

Another picture caught Mel's eye. "Look at this one, Mom."

"Who is that?"

Mel bit her lip. She hated that Braxton didn't already know the woman in the picture. "That's Gramma Wilson."

"Right. She died when I was a baby."

"She did." Mel pulled Braxton close to her side and took a deep breath. She blinked back the sting in her eyes. "We'd better help Nana clean this up, buddy." She turned to her mom. "We'll pick up and then get out of your hair."

"Why don't you stay for dinner tonight?" Mom gave Braxton a significant look. "I thought I could make burgers."

Mel shrugged. She didn't have any dinner plans and would've needed to stop at the store for groceries. It would be nice to hang out with her parents and catch up. They saw each other almost every day but hadn't had time to really talk in a while. Plus, it was Friday night and Braxton didn't have school in the morning. "If you're sure it wouldn't be too much trouble."

"Not at all." Mom grinned. "I'll just go chop some potatoes while you two finish picking up those photos."

Mel didn't really care to organize the mess, and she knew Braxton wouldn't be able to help figure out which photos belonged to which year. So they pulled them all into a neat stack which they stored in a box under the guest bed.

"Is this where Nana got the box from?"

A Sweet Dream Come True

"Yep. Can I go watch a show?"

"All right. But just one episode, and then you need to help set the table."

Mel found her mother sliding a pan of diced potatoes into the oven. "How can I help?"

"You could pull out the condiments for me." Dusting off her hands, Mom headed toward the pantry to pull out a can of beans and some spices. Once the beans were heating on the stove, she got the ground beef and a jar of pesto from the fridge. "Think potatoes and beans will be enough for sides? I can make some pasta salad if you think Braxton will still be hungry."

Braxton had been eating a ton these days—probably going through a growth spurt—but pasta salad wasn't high on his list of favorite foods. "Oh, I think that'll be plenty."

Mom always added pesto and liquid smoke to her burgers, and—in Mel's humble opinion—they were the best burgers in the world. With condiments and all the fixings lined up and ready to go, Mel leaned against the counter. "How was your day?"

"Good, thanks." Her mom smiled at her before returning her gaze to the meat. "Braxton is getting so big. He was telling me all about a science experiment they did at school today. And we read his sight words."

"Thank you." Mel preferred to do homework with her son, but Braxton liked to get it over and done with right after school. When Mel tried to make him work on spelling or sight words after he'd already switched his brain to play mode, he balked and made the entire experience miserable for everyone.

If Mom took care of the homework, Mel could just play with him while sneaking in questions about his progress at school. It wasn't a perfect system, but it worked.

"Weren't you talking to that ice cream shop man about selling your goodies there?"

Mel had told her all about Isaac's offer before Monday and hadn't bothered to fill her in on her decision. "It's not going to happen."

Mom turned with a look of shock on her face as she washed her hands at the sink. "What? Why? Did he not like your chocolates?"

"Oh, he loved them." Mel almost laughed, remembering how over-the-top Isaac's reactions had been while he'd sampled the truffles. "It was my decision not to sell them at the shop."

"But why? Selling chocolates has been your dream for ages." Mom dried her hands but never broke eye contact.

Mel squirmed under her gaze. She hated to confess how she'd lost her temper with Brax. She wanted her parents to think she had everything together so they wouldn't worry about her. But her mom wouldn't let this go.

"I just can't handle all of it. The full-time job and the parenting and the chocolates. It's too much."

Her mom kept staring, and Mel was compelled to continue. "The afternoon before my meeting with Isaac, I was trying to finish everything up. I was making truffles and cake balls and chocolate covered raspberry cream, and peanut butter balls. Braxton wanted to help, so I let him, but he's five and he got overeager and ruined a batch of ganache. And I yelled at him." Mel lowered her gaze to the floor. Guilt still ate at her.

"I get it, Mel. I never could work with other people in the kitchen, especially when you were little. I had no confidence in my cooking when I was a young mom and I needed every ounce of concentration just to keep the dinner from burning."

"What?" Mel couldn't conceal her shock. "You're a great cook."

Mom waved her off. "That's very sweet of you, but we're not talking about me." She tapped her finger on her chin. "Did you really need to make all those different kinds of chocolate?

You usually just make one or two for people. Maybe three if it's a big event. Not *four* all at once."

"I wanted Isaac to have lots of options."

"Okay, but what if you just made one type of chocolate at a time for the shop? Wouldn't that be easier to handle?"

She knew her mom had a point, but they were missing the bigger problem. "Okay, but when would I find time to do all this? Isaac needs someone to make food for him to sell every week. He's wanting someone to help keep the store afloat during the winter season." She blew out a breath. "I can't handle that kind of pressure."

Her mom sighed and turned back around to the stove, flipping the burgers one by one, then adding a slice of cheese to the top. When she was finished, she gazed at Mel. "I think you *can* handle it. You've handled raising Braxton and selling chocolates for a while now."

"Sure, but it's just family and friends. I'm not even registered with the state. I'd need to get licensed or whatever." She waved her hands in the air. "I'm not even sure what that would entail."

Mom frowned. "So are you operating an illegal business?"

"I don't *have* a business, Mom. I'm just doing a favor for our friends, and they pay me for it. I don't even set prices."

Mom held up her hands in a defensive posture. "Okay, okay."

"If I wanted to do this for real, I'd need a business name and a social media presence ..." She trailed off. "It's just too much."

"Hello, hello," Mel's dad called out as he walked into the kitchen from the garage.

"Hi, Daddy."

"You staying for supper tonight?" Dad wrapped Mel in a hug. The scent of his cologne comforted her like it always had.

"Mom's making burgers, so ..." Mel grinned up at him.

"Ah, *that's* what smells so good." Dad released her and gave Mom a kiss on the head. "Now, where's my grandson?"

Mel let the subject of chocolates drop until after dinner. Just like she'd thought, the burgers were delicious, and Braxton ate even more than she did. And they all had generous portions of Mom's brownies afterward.

As she and Braxton were packing up to leave, Mel remembered something. "Hey, Mom. Could you and Dad watch Braxton the first Friday of October? I think it's the seventh? There's a recruiting event at work I have to go to."

Just as Dad was saying, "Sure, honey," Mom said, "I'm sorry."

Dad turned to Mom with a curious expression.

"Remember? We have that fundraising dinner at church."

"Well, we don't *both* have to be there."

"Yes, we do, sweetheart." If a tone of voice could be both exasperated and patient at once, Mom had nailed it. To be fair, Mel's dad was always forgetting important dates and events. "I'm going to be in the kitchen, and you're helping with the auction."

"Could Braxton come with you?" Mel hated to beg, but she was desperate. "I'm sure he'd love to help."

Dad looked up with a hopeful expression.

"I'm sorry," Mom said. "We're both going to be very busy that night. Could you ask one of your friends?"

"Yes, of course." Mel shouldn't have pushed back as much as she did. Her parents deserved a weekend to themselves without having to babysit. The problem was, she didn't have a ton of friends outside of work. She racked her brain for who to ask. Maybe someone at church.

After her parents and close friends, the next people she'd told about her pregnancy had been the church. She'd never forget the fear of standing in front of her entire congregation and confessing her sin. She was having a child out of wedlock. Her mom and dad and best friends had warned her that her boyfriend wasn't worth her time, but she'd gone and gotten pregnant with his baby before finding out they'd been right all along.

But even greater than her fear and shame at standing up in front of that crowd was the intense relief when her church family had embraced her. It took some people longer than others to forgive, but one by one they'd wrapped her in their arms and given their support.

"And Mel? About the job, I think you'll be great at whatever you choose to do."

Mel had worked hard to get to where she was today. She'd built a life for her son and herself. A life she was proud of, surrounded by friends and family.

"Thanks, Mom." Mel knew Mom only questioned her decisions because she wanted the best for her daughter. She'd just have to understand that Mel made the choices she did because she wanted the best for her son.

Chapter Eight

"Well, look who finally decided to show up."

Isaac twisted his lips in chagrin as he greeted Zeke outside the church building. Zeke had been after him for months to visit his congregation in Bestwood.

"You know, I have a church home in Nashville, and they like me to show up every once in a while."

Zeke threw his arm around Isaac's shoulders. "Well, they can spare you for a Sunday here and there. You're a business owner in Bestwood, and it's important you build some relationships here."

"I'm here now, aren't I?"

"Yes, and you came on a great Sunday. Our minister just got home from visiting his son in Georgia. You're going to love his preaching."

This church building was even bigger than the one where he usually worshiped. Bestwood only had a handful of churches, while Nashville had hundreds. So this congregation had a lot more people than he was used to seeing on a Sunday morning. Despite its size, everyone was very welcoming. Isaac recognized a few of his regular customers, and they all wanted to say *hello*. Zeke nearly slipped away, but Isaac caught up to him and his wife before they headed into the auditorium.

"Hi, Jayla." Isaac gave Zeke's wife a hug.

"Hey there. I'm so happy you could come this morning." Jayla smiled as she pointed toward the left side of the auditorium. "We usually sit over there, if you'd like to join us."

"Lead the way."

Isaac couldn't help but remember Zeke had been the one to tell him about Mel and her amazing chocolates. He'd talked up how involved she was with their church and how much everyone loved her. Isaac craned his neck as he searched the crowded room for some sign of her.

Just as the first song started, he saw her toward the back, between Braxton and a middle-aged couple who must be her parents. He breathed a sigh of relief. For whatever reason, he felt better knowing where Mel was.

Isaac found himself swept up in the worship songs, ignoring how terrible his voice must sound in comparison to Jayla's soulful alto and Zeke's powerful bass. He just closed his eyes and sang from his heart.

When the sermon began, Isaac opened the bulletin he'd grabbed out in the lobby. The message today was from Joshua chapter three. The preacher, Tim Brubaker, had printed an outline with fill-in-the-blank spots for people to follow along, but Isaac set it aside and listened with his eyes glued to the front.

Zeke was right. Mr. Brubaker was an excellent speaker. He spoke about how the Israelites came upon the Jordan River just before entering the land they'd been promised. Isaac had read the passage before, but what he'd never realized was that in the early spring, the river was swollen with runoff water from melted snow.

It would have been incredibly dangerous to cross with animals and small children. And the Israelites waited on the banks of the Jordan for three days, watching the water rushing past, wondering how God would bring them through.

Mr. Brubaker broke the passage down into three parts: seek God, sanctify yourself, and step out in faith. Although part of him wanted to groan at the forced alliteration, Isaac enjoyed how the sermon flowed. They ended with a reading from Psalm 114:3-7, a song written about that very time when God turned back the Jordan River.

At the end of the service, Isaac looked to his friends, a huge smile on his face. "What a sermon! I'm so glad I came today."

Zeke clapped him on the shoulder. "Do you have lunch plans? We're heading over to Jayla's parents' house. You're welcome to join us."

"Can't—I've got some work to do before I open the shop. But thanks for the invitation." His gaze roamed the auditorium. Where had Mel gone? She wasn't in the same spot as before.

"Looking for someone?" Jayla watched him with a bemused expression.

"Oh—" Isaac could feel his face warming.

Zeke laughed. "Mel Wilson maybe?"

Her face lit with excitement, Jayla squealed. "Really?"

"No, no." Isaac waved his hands at her. "Mel already turned me down. She said she can't date anyone because of Braxton."

"So she's not going to date anyone ever?" Zeke cocked an eyebrow. "That seems pretty unreasonable."

"I don't want to argue with her about her dating policies. I just wanted to say *hello*." At his friends' doubtful expressions, Isaac conceded. "And maybe I'm hoping she'll change her mind once she gets to know me." Although he still hadn't fully accepted the fact that a relationship with Mel meant one with Braxton as well, he couldn't get the woman out of his head.

Jayla squeezed his arm. "I'm sure she will."

"Well, go talk to her." Zeke pointed toward the back section of seats. "I'll see you later."

Isaac followed Zeke's finger and found Mel exactly where she'd been sitting earlier. She must've been blocked by people standing around her. But now, with almost everyone headed outside, Isaac could see her clearly.

He wasn't sure what to say. Everything in his head sounded dumb, but he walked toward her anyway.

All through Tim's sermon, Mel felt like he was preaching directly to her. She'd never zeroed in on this passage from Joshua 3. It was like a smaller version of the parting of the Red Sea in Exodus and the precursor to the great march around Jericho, so she'd basically ignored it.

But the way Tim talked about the Israelites crossing the Jordan River, it sounded like one of the most important moments in their history. And he made clear that the message of the miracle very much applied to Christians today.

They should follow God first, cleanse themselves of sin, and then step out in faith. Mel felt she was doing a decent job of following after God and of keeping sin out of her life. She wasn't perfect, but when she did make mistakes, she confessed and prayed for forgiveness.

It was just the stepping out in faith she had such a problem with.

A *big* problem.

"Can I go play?" Braxton stood in front of her, bouncing on his toes.

Following his gaze, Mel saw some of the boys he usually played with in the back of the auditorium. "No running and stay off the stage."

He was already gone, walking about as fast as one could without actually running.

"Mind if we squeeze past?" Mom patted her knee before stepping out into the aisle.

As Dad moved past her, Mel turned her knees to the side.

"See you at lunch today?" Dad asked.

"Yes, as soon as I can drag Brax away."

"You might beat us there." Dad gestured to Mom already talking to a group of her friends in the aisle. He waved before finding his own friends to greet.

Crayons and coloring books from Braxton's busy bag were still strewn across the pew, and Mel bent to retrieve them. Her thoughts returned to the sermon topic.

What do You want from me, God?

For years, she'd had a passion for candy and chocolate. She'd scratched the itch by making treats for potlucks and special occasions, then by whipping up larger and larger orders for friends and family. And then they started paying her for it and referring her to their friends. And now the offer from Isaac.

Are You asking me to work with Isaac?

"Good to see you, this morning, Melanie."

Mel rose to greet Mrs. Barton. The woman had taught about fifty years' worth of fourth grade Bible classes and was one of the few people who refused to call Mel by her nickname.

"You, too, Mrs. Barton. Have a nice morning."

Back in her seat, Mel wondered what to do with her questions for God.

It all seemed so trivial. Compared to conquering the Promised Land, making chocolate wasn't earth-shattering. She wasn't going to change anyone's life with a peanut butter ball.

Why would God be calling her to chocolate? Was she crazy for even thinking that might be a possibility?

God, could You help me out here? I'm floundering, and I need wisdom from You. Could You make it painfully obvious? Could You send a sign and just whack me over the head with it?

Mel closed her eyes and lowered her forehead to her hands.

Please, God, show me what You want me to do.

"Great sermon, huh?"

Mel's gaze shot up. Isaac stood directly in front of her. He didn't even attend this church. And now, right when she'd been asking God for guidance and wisdom, he'd appeared before her. How had he known how the sermon had affected her? Or was he going through the same issues too?

She closed her mouth and attempted to regain composure.

"It was ..." She struggled to find the right words. "I think God may be trying to tell me something."

"Oh?" Isaac sat in the chair next to her. He took up a little more than his fair share of space, so Mel shifted in her seat. His presence flustered her in more ways than one.

"Is it crazy to think that one way to follow after God and step out in faith is to make chocolates for people?" Saying it out loud made the whole idea sound ludicrous.

"You know how I feel. I'd love for you to sell your chocolates at Mr. Dream."

"But I'm not saving the world. It's just a few truffles."

"Your business could make a lot of people happy. And it might be the thing that saves my ice cream shop."

Saving an ice cream shop versus saving the world. It still seemed like small potatoes, but Mel knew Isaac cared deeply about his business. And she'd tasted his ice cream for herself. The man had a gift.

"Okay." Mel stood up. "I'll make chocolates for you."

A wide grin spread across Isaac's face.

"But only for Main Street Trick-or-Treat. As a friend, and not as a business partner."

The smile on his face didn't diminish one bit. "Sounds good, friend."

Mel found herself smiling too. It was time to test the waters.

Chapter Nine

To celebrate learning fifty sight words and all the exhausting work that had been for everyone involved, Mel took Braxton out for ice cream. They'd come to Mr. Dream almost once a week to celebrate one thing or another since their first visit.

When Mel told Isaac Brax's good news, he added extra toppings.

"No charge on the sprinkles, those are F-R-E-E."

Braxton paused for a moment, his brows furrowed in concentration. "Free!" He turned to Mel, a grin on his face.

"That's right, B." To Isaac she added, "Thank you. You didn't have to do that."

"I know." He gave her one of those irresistible grins, and her stomach flipped.

What was that? Ever since he'd asked her out on a date, Mel saw Isaac in a completely different light. When he smiled at her or did something kind—and he did both of those things basically all the time—there were butterflies. *Was I too quick to turn him down?*

Mel's gaze drifted toward Brax, and she registered the total adoration he showed toward Isaac. If she were in a relationship with the man, how would her son look at him then? And what about when they broke up?

If there was a way to skip the dating and the drama and go straight to marriage, Mel would do it. She wanted Braxton to have a dad. And she desperately wanted some help around the house. And maybe she was a little lonely.

But Isaac—and pretty much any other man in America—expected some courtship to occur before marriage. He hadn't even asked her to be in a relationship, just dinner.

"And what'll it be for you, Mel?"

Jolted back to reality, Mel scanned the flavor options. "I'll have a double scoop of the cinnamon."

"Do you want to try it first?"

"I trust you." It was true. Everything Isaac made was amazing, and she was positive the cinnamon would be too.

When Isaac handed her the cone, she licked around the perimeter, making sure no ice cream escaped.

"What do you think?"

Mel sighed. "Wonderful. Just like I knew it would be." She took another lick. "Is this a new flavor?"

He nodded. "I've been trying out some new recipes based on the suggestions I got."

"It turned out great." She swiped her card through the reader and signed the tablet. Then she grabbed several napkins —Braxton always needed about a dozen—and followed Braxton to their usual table. Stopping, she turned to Isaac with a sudden thought. "Have you ever thought about adding cinnamon to your chocolate base?"

Isaac cocked his head. "Go on."

"Well, if you made the chocolate a little darker and added spice, I think you could get some great flavor complexity."

"I like it." He patted his pockets until he found what he was searching for. Pulling out his phone, he tapped on the screen. "Cinnamon, dark chocolate," he muttered. Then he glanced up at Mel. "Thanks. I've added that to my list of flavors to try."

Mel looked around, noticing no one else was behind the counter with Isaac. He didn't usually operate the cash register and scoop ice cream by himself.

"Are you working alone tonight?"

He twisted his lips into one of the most displeased expressions Mel had ever seen him wear. "I'm not supposed to. But Josh called in sick and I couldn't find anyone to come in at the last minute." His smile returned, but only partially. "It's okay. The store is slow tonight, and Claire will be in early tomorrow. I had some time to get prepped for tomorrow, although not as much as I'd like ..." He trailed off, his gaze resting on the electric burners he always used for making the ice cream bases.

"Sorry for keeping you talking. I'm sure you're anxious to get back to work."

"No, Mel," He leaned across the counter and rested his hand on hers. "I always enjoy talking to you."

"Thanks, well—" She held up her ice cream cone. "This ice cream isn't going to eat itself."

A peal of laughter rang out from where Braxton sat. "Ice cream eating itself." He choked out those few words before descending into giggles again.

Mel shrugged at Isaac before sitting next to her son. When Braxton finally settled down, they talked about school and the upcoming Halloween parade.

"What do you want to be this year?"

"The same thing I'm going to be when I grow up." He took a bite of ice cream way too big for his little mouth.

"You're going to get brain freeze eating like that. You want to dress up as a mail carrier?" That's what he'd told her to write on the chalkboard she'd used for his first day of school pictures.

"No." He said this as if she was an idiot for not realizing he'd changed his mind. "I'm going to be a superhero."

"Okay." *Do I tell him that's impossible?* No, if he could change from mailman to superhero overnight, he could always change again just as quickly. "Which superhero?"

"I don't know what my name will be yet. I haven't gotten my superpowers."

Of course.

"But I'd like to have superspeed. And be able to fly."

"Well, yeah, that would be pretty awesome." She wouldn't mind having those superpowers either, come to think of it. "But what do you want your costume to be? We need to come up with something you can wear to school for the parade."

He frowned. "Maybe just blue. With a cape."

Could she find a generic blue superhero costume on the internet? She knew the grocery store wouldn't sell something like that.

"Oh, and a mask."

"No masks at school." Thank goodness. She didn't need this costume getting any more complicated.

"Okay, but a lightning bolt or something on the cape to show I'm fast."

"I'll do my best, Brax." Where in the world would she find the time to make a costume?

"What did you want to be when you were my age?"

Mel looked up from digging around in her purse for her planner. Sometimes Braxton showed real empathy for someone so young. "I wanted to sell chocolates at a chocolate shop. Mel's Chocolate Shop."

"Well, you make chocolates now. Are you going to sell them at a shop?"

"Maybe someday." She sighed. "I always thought I'd go off to study chocolate-making under a real professional, but that didn't happen."

"Why didn't you?"

Mel wished she could take back her words. Why had she told him all that? She could've just said she wanted to make chocolates and left it at that.

How could she possibly answer his question without blaming everything on him? If he hadn't been born, she *would* have gone to Europe. She might even have that chocolate shop right now.

"Well, I changed my mind."

"Why?"

What was with this kid? Always so inquisitive. Normally she didn't mind so much, but she didn't care for the interrogation right now.

"I needed different things when I got older."

"Why?"

Good grief. She couldn't bring herself to lie to Braxton, but he was making it awfully hard for her.

"I decided to get a job somewhere that paid enough for me to be a good mommy. That's my most important job right now—being your mom."

Her answers seemed to satisfy him. But she knew deep down this conversation wasn't over forever. How would she answer him someday when he asked why she gave up on her dreams?

"How's EVERYTHING TASTING?" Isaac knew they'd long finished their cones, but he wanted an excuse to spend more time with Mel and Braxton while they were in the shop.

"So good." Braxton looked up with a grin. "I love the chocolate."

"Are you still missing a tooth?" On the bottom right, there was a gaping hole where a tooth had once been.

Braxton's smile grew even wider. "You knew that. I showed you at church last week."

Isaac smacked his head in pretend frustration. "Of course. You haven't had time to grow it back yet."

After the excellent worship service the first time he visited Zeke's church, he'd found himself wanting to come back nearly every week. Zeke had been right to insist he visit. If Isaac wanted to be a member of the Bestwood community, he should get to know the other Christians in town. He'd even entertained thoughts of finding a house in Bestwood. But first he needed to make sure Mr. Dream Ice Cream survived the winter.

"I'm going to be a superhero for Halloween."

"Awesome. Which one?"

Mel glanced up from the planner open on the table. "A blue one with a cape and a lightning bolt."

"To show I'm fast," Braxton posed in a running stance, one tiny fist at his face, the other by his side.

"I'm just trying to pencil in some time to work on the costume, so I don't forget."

As an accountant, Isaac had worked with some very organized people. But scheduling time to make a costume was on a level of its own.

Mel sucked in a breath.

"What's wrong?" Isaac and Braxton both turned their gazes to her.

"I forgot about the recruiting event on the seventh."

Even though Isaac wanted to make fun of her for being shocked about an event that hadn't happened yet, Mel looked too upset for him to attempt humor.

"I don't have a babysitter for Brax." She lowered her head to her hands. "Mom and Dad have a fundraiser at church, and half my friends will be there too. The other half work with me."

"I could watch him." He'd spoken before even thinking about it. But watching Braxton's face light up solidified his decision. What kid wouldn't want to spend a whole night at an ice cream shop? Without the added pressure of a romance with Mel, a night with Braxton could actually be fun.

"Are you sure?" Mel's expression wasn't quite as excited as her son's.

"Totally." From the look in her eyes, Isaac figured she might be weighing the facts in her mind. They'd only known each other a few weeks, but she was desperate.

"Won't you need to be working?"

"He can hang out here at the shop with me, and I'll make sure someone is keeping an eye on him at all times." He remembered something then. "And Zeke can vouch for me."

A wave of relief passed over her face. She nodded slowly, still visibly thinking over his offer. Then a sparkle flashed in her eyes. "Don't you need to save the tables for paying customers?"

He grimaced. "I see what you did there. Would you like another apology for tossing you out during Best Fest?"

When she smiled, his heart skipped a beat. "No, no. Babysitting will suffice."

Whipping his head back and forth between the two of them, Braxton studied their expressions. "So I can stay with Isaac?"

Mel threw up her hands. "Yes, you can stay with the ice cream man in his amazing ice cream shop while Mommy goes to work at her not-at-all-fun event. But don't say I never let you do anything fun."

Braxton squeezed his mom in a hug. "Thank you! Thank you! Thank you!"

Now if only Isaac could make both Braxton *and* Mel excited to hang out with him, then he'd be set.

Chapter Ten

"If you have any questions or need anything, please text me. Seriously. Anything at all. I'll come back as soon as I can. It shouldn't be any later than eight." Mel took a baby step back. "Thank you so much for doing this. Really."

Isaac could barely keep from laughing, she was so nervous about leaving Braxton. But she didn't need to worry because he and Brax would have a great time.

"He's going to be fine, Mel. Abby is here," He gestured to where she stood behind him. "She's my most responsible employee. And Braxton is going to help me try out a new recipe."

Mel's eyebrows shot up. "I don't know—"

"Just go." He finally gave in to the urge to laugh at her. "You're going to be late."

At that, Mel's lips pinched together. She checked the bright yellow clock on the wall. "Thank you again." She called out to Braxton, "Love you, buddy. See you soon!"

When the bell above the door clanged, Isaac turned around with a grin. "Now the fun begins."

He shimmied to the pop music playing in the store, turning up the volume as he passed the speaker. Only a couple customers were in, so he didn't mind scaring them a bit with his dance moves.

"Braxton, I'm going to need you to help me out tonight."

The kid's eyes lit up as he rose from the table. "What are we doing?"

"I've got a new flavor I'm working on. How do you feel about fruity cereal?"

Braxton practically glowed. He nodded his head, a giant smile spread across his face.

They washed hands, then Isaac pulled a giant apron over Braxton's head and cinched it as best he could around the tiny waist.

"Come join me at the counter, good sir." Isaac pulled a barstool from across the room toward the counter. He set Braxton on top of the tall chair, then set up his workstation across from him.

"So first we're going to make something called cereal milk." Isaac pulled out the cream and a large liquid measuring bowl. "You know how after you eat a bowl of cereal, the milk gets sweeter at the end?"

"I like to drink it out of the bowl."

"Me too." He was growing fond of this kid. "So we're going to let the cereal soak in some cream so it gets all that delicious fruity flavor soaked in. Then we'll strain it out and use what's left to make the ice cream. At the very end, we'll mix in more cereal that's nice and crunchy."

Isaac let Braxton pour the cereal into the cream.

"Maybe a little more." Once they were both satisfied with the ratio of cereal to cream, he set the bowl aside. "And now we wait."

The bell rang out as a large family walked in.

"Do you have some homework to work on, buddy?"

"No."

"What grade are you in?"

"Kindergarten."

Right, so not much homework then.

"Well, you're in luck because I brought something for you to look at."

He helped Braxton get down and pulled the barstool out of the flow of traffic. Abby seemed to be fine without him for now. Earlier that afternoon, he'd pulled a small table to the back of the store where Braxton could sit and Isaac could see him from behind the counter. Now Braxton settled into the chair, and Isaac drew something out of a backpack.

"What is it?"

"Comic books. Superhero comic books, to be exact."

"Cool." He reached for the top book, tracing his finger along the first page.

"Now, you won't be able to read all the words, but they have a lot of pictures."

Braxton wasn't really listening at that point, so Isaac left him in the capable hands of Superman.

Isaac served three families and a young couple before he had the chance to check on Braxton again. "How's it going?"

"Good." Braxton looked up. "Can we eat the ice cream now?"

The ice cream. He'd totally forgotten to check on it.

Back at the counter, the cream and cereal combination had turned into a gooey mess. "We might've put in too much cereal."

"Is it ruined?"

"My favorite ice cream experts Ben and Jerry always say, 'There's no such thing as an *unredeemingly* bad batch of homemade ice cream.'"

Braxton stared back at him.

"That means it's not ruined. You and I can still eat it, although we won't be able to sell it to anyone." He hadn't actually planned to sell customers an ice cream a five-year-old had helped him make. Tonight was just about experimentation. And he was learning a lot from this particular batch of ice cream. "Let's get a strainer and see how much of it we can squeeze out."

But the gloopy cream didn't want to cooperate. They tried straining, but only tiny drips came out, even when Isaac pushed on it with the back of a spoon. Finally, he pulled out a cheesecloth, filled it with the cereal cream and twisted the ends, dripping about a quarter cup of milk into the waiting bowl each time. Then he scraped the leftover mealy mess into a trash bag before dumping another glob of cream onto the cloth.

The end result wasn't quite what he'd hoped for. Despite their best efforts to strain the liquid, pieces of soggy cereal sat in the bowl. It was all much too thick and a weird shade of yellow.

The despondent look on Braxton's face matched his own disappointment. "It looks disgusting."

"Well, let's try it out and see what happens."

The rest of the evening, between waiting on customers, he and Braxton finished the ice cream base. But it looked like it was going to have a very strange texture. "Tomorrow, I'll mix this up and then you and your mom can come pick up a pint."

"So we don't get to eat it now?"

"No, it has to get cold."

Braxton's face turned a bright shade of pink, and his lower lip stuck out. "But I thought we were going to eat it tonight. I worked so hard on it."

He'd never seen this side of Braxton before. While Isaac wanted to correct him about who exactly had worked so hard on the ice cream, he attempted a distraction instead.

"How about you eat a bowl of one of the flavors we have out?"

Braxton nodded and ambled toward the ice cream counter, ignoring the family waiting in line. "They all look bad."

Isaac chuckled nervously, smiling at the paying customers. "You're upset right now, and I understand. But try this chocolate and you'll forget all about that other stuff."

Braxton accepted the bowl from Isaac. He dipped his spoon in the creamy treat. Isaac watched with bated breath and … there it was. A tiny smile. Ice cream man for the win.

"When you're done with your ice cream, you can help me come up with a name for our new flavor."

As Braxton ate his dessert a wave of customers came in. Isaac barely noticed time passing before Mel showed up.

"Sorry I'm late."

The clock read eight-thirty, but it felt much earlier. "No problem. We've been having a blast."

"Have you?"

"Mom! Isaac let me make some ice cream. And I came up with a name. Cereal Crunch." He showed her the picture he'd drawn for a display card. "And Isaac let me read some of his comic books. And we like all the same superheroes!"

It was true. They'd had a long discussion about the merits of super strength, super speed, and the ability to fly. "Braxton has good taste." He gave Mel a sheepish smile. Although he still wasn't sure about his disciplinary skills, he was proud of the fact that he'd kept the kid alive. And they'd discovered some shared interests along the way.

She met his gaze with a strange expression on her face.

MEL COULDN'T BELIEVE how quickly Isaac and Braxton had clicked. Sure, they'd seen each other several times at church and here at the ice cream shop, but only for a few minutes at a time. After one evening together, they were bonding over shared interests and cooking together.

What if you asked him out?

The thought flew into her head unbidden, but her pulse raced as she considered it. Isaac was a good man. Much better than anyone she'd dated in the past. Of course, she hadn't gone on a date in six years, so maybe her taste had changed. He loved Jesus, he made her smile, and he cared about her son.

Mel didn't pay attention to another word Braxton or Isaac said as she helped pack her son's things. They didn't seem to mind much, their conversation still all about comic books and superheroes as far as she could gather.

"So I'll see you tomorrow?" Isaac asked.

The question drew her back to the present. "Sorry. What's tomorrow?"

"The ice cream will be ready tomorrow." He rounded the counter, giving Braxton a wink and a high-five.

"We have to get the ice cream tomorrow, Mom. Pleeeeease."

"Yes, okay. Sure."

Satisfied with her answer, Braxton waved to Isaac and Abby and stood to leave.

Mel signaled for her son to wait, then turned to Isaac. He smiled down at her, and those familiar butterflies returned.

"So, about that dinner." She hadn't actually thought through what she was going to say, or even convinced herself it was a good idea.

But Isaac's whole face lit up. "Name the night, and I'll be there."

Her body hummed in response.

Could he really leave the shop so easily? Perhaps he was more eager for this date than she'd realized. "Let me talk to my parents and see when they're free to babysit. I'll text you."

He nodded quickly. "Yes. Okay. Great."

Mel laughed. He was so excited. But she was too.

A date with a decent man. What a thought. She grinned all the way back to the car and all the way home.

Chapter Eleven

"Just tell me which shirt you like best." Isaac frowned at his phone screen.

His sister Faith rolled her eyes. The video chat hit a lag and for a second her face froze in a hilarious pose. "You go on your first date in over a year. Two years, maybe. And you expect me not to ask any questions? What kind of big sister do you think I am?"

"The kind who loves me and will help me pick out an outfit."

"What's her name? Where did you meet her? Where are you taking her?"

With a sigh, Isaac plopped down on his bed. He'd known Faith would give him the third degree, but he was desperate. Everything had to be perfect tonight. "Her name is Mel, we met at the shop, and I'm taking her to dinner at an Italian restaurant."

"And you're okay to leave the ice cream store for a whole night?"

"I've got my best employees there. And I'll drop by after dinner to close up."

"What is she like?"

A smile spread across his face—he couldn't help it. "She's great. Strong-willed, but very passionate. Smart, talented." He added the next part warily. "A good mom."

Faith's eyebrows shot up. "She has kids?"

"One kid, a son. He's five years old and really cute." He enjoyed getting to know Braxton almost as much as he did Mel.

"And you're okay with the possibility of being a stepdad?"

His stomach turned at that word. "Stepdad'" sounded so strange. It wasn't a new revelation, but Isaac hadn't actually thought about being called a stepdad.

"I think so." No need to fill her in on all his insecurities about becoming a parent. "Now, can you please help me out?"

She nodded, her lips pursed. "The green shirt. Wear it with some nice jeans and dress shoes."

"Thank you, Faith." Isaac jumped up and grabbed the clothes off his bed.

"You better tell me all about it afterwards."

Not a chance. "Bye, talk to you later."

The hour slipped by too quickly as Isaac showered and changed. In no time at all he was at Mel's apartment. He'd been so grateful she hadn't backed out of the date, and so eager to plan every last detail, he hadn't had much of a chance to feel nervous.

But as he stood on Mel's doorstep, the nerves set in. *I really like Mel.* The thought terrified him. *What if she doesn't like me as much? What if I totally mess this up?*

"Hi there." Mel opened the door, and Isaac couldn't think of anything but how gorgeous she looked. She wore a navy dress with a scarf and a brown sweater. When she turned her head, her earrings sparkled and her lip gloss shimmered.

He almost didn't have the presence of mind to answer. "Hi, Mel. You look amazing."

Her smile nearly bowled him over. *You'd better not mess this up.*

During the car ride to the restaurant, Isaac distracted himself by asking lots of questions about Mel and her job. She confessed she was considering applying for a promotion at work.

"That's exciting." When she didn't respond, he glanced her way. "Right?"

"Yes. It's just ... more responsibility can also mean more stress. But it might be the right move for us."

"Us?"

"Braxton and me."

It hit him again, how little he understood about being a parent. Mel made it all seem so effortless. Did he have what it took to be a father figure to Braxton? It would require a lot more than ice cream and a love of superheroes. Mel was probably right to have doubts about him, but Isaac couldn't resist the attraction he felt for her.

"How about you?" Mel asked. "How's Mr. Dream?"

"Good. It's just ..." He winced. Should he mention the difficulty he'd had with Josh the day before? "I can't seem to figure Josh out. It's like he doesn't even like working at the shop."

"Maybe he doesn't."

He risked a glance to make sure she was serious. Who wouldn't like working in an ice cream store?

"Every time I see Josh, he's either daydreaming or being lectured by the other staff. I think you should let him go."

"Hmm." Isaac didn't care to continue this particular conversation, so he asked about her family. "You mentioned you have a brother and a sister."

Mel smiled.

From then on, they talked freely, sharing about their siblings, and laughing about stories from when they were young. Isaac admitted his sister had helped him pick his outfit.

"What do you think?" He gestured to the button-up shirt and jeans they'd settled on.

"Very nice."

He didn't have time for more than a glance, but Isaac liked the look Mel sent his way. Something about her had changed. A wall had come down. He didn't know what he'd done right, but he hoped he could keep winning Mel's heart.

The restaurant he'd picked wasn't too fancy, but the hole-in-the-wall Italian food was perfection.

Thank goodness Mel agreed. "Oh, I love this place."

Score one for the best date ever.

The dining area wasn't crowded—only four other tables were occupied. They followed the server to a booth in the back where a vase of roses sat on the table and candles flickered beside it.

If possible, Mel looked even more beautiful in candlelight.

After placing their orders, Isaac turned the conversation to their mutual passion—food.

"When did you first fall in love with cooking?"

Mel told him about her grandmother and their time in the kitchen. "Candy and chocolate became our *thing*. I was the youngest grandkid, so I got more one-on-one time with her, I think. Even though I didn't have as many years with her as my siblings and cousins."

"When did she pass away?"

"Five years ago, when Braxton was only a few months old." Mel fiddled with her silverware in a rolled-up napkin on the table. "She really helped me through a difficult time." Mel leaned back and blew out a breath, her countenance changing as she gave Isaac a small smile. "How about you? When did you fall in love with ice cream?"

"My mom and I used to make homemade vanilla ice cream every summer. We'd bring it to church potlucks or family barbecues. When I got older, I started experimenting with flavors." He patted his belly. "As you can see, I've tasted a lot of ice cream in my time."

Mel shrugged, her mouth twisted in amusement.

"I haven't always wanted to own an ice cream shop. For a while, I really thought I'd be satisfied with accounting. But one day, I wasn't. And then all I could think about was getting out and starting my own business. And ice cream was something I was already passionate about. I prayed and prayed over every step of my decision," He swept his arms out. "And I believe I'm where God led me."

The waitress came with their food, and Isaac led them in a prayer. He debated whether to reach for Mel's hand, but nerves won out and he merely bowed his head. Then they focused on savoring their delicious pasta for a while.

Isaac broke the silence. "Listen. About chocolate and ice cream. I wanted to show you something."

He'd been brainstorming ways to help Mel with her dream of becoming a chocolatier. After an extensive amount of internet research, he'd come up with a business plan of sorts.

He pulled out his phone and opened the web browser where he'd saved a few pages. "I found out Tennessee passed a couple laws that make it easier for home-based cooks to sell their food."

"I know, it's called cottage food." She dabbed her mouth with her napkin. "I've been doing my own research."

"Good. So you might know you don't have to get a license or have your home inspected. But you aren't allowed to sell wholesale to Mr. Dream Ice Cream."

She nodded, her lips tight.

"I was thinking what we can do is have a pop-up shop in the store. Your chocolates and candies can have their own display case. I could charge you a fee, kind of like a farmer's market would. And then you get all the profits from your chocolates. And I get the benefit of extra customers as well as the fee. We can discuss what you think would be fair."

"And this is just for the Trick-or-Treat on Main Street?"

"Well, I'll admit I'm still holding out hope that you'll keep working with me."

She scrolled through his phone screen, not looking up.

"And I did some more research." Now this was the part he was actually excited about. "I found a bunch of different website names that aren't claimed yet. There's Mel's Candy and Chocolate, Mel's Chocolate Shop, and my favorite— Chocolate Mel."

"Do you usually discuss business plans on a first date?"

"What?" Isaac realized now that Mel wasn't nearly as excited as he was, and she hadn't been for a while.

"This is all too much, Isaac. I didn't ask you to do this." Mel shook her head. She'd been looking forward to this date, and now she felt like she'd been duped into a sales pitch.

"I know, I just—"

"Can we please talk about something else?"

"I don't understand." His expression was hurt, and Mel hated that she was the reason. "Isn't this your dream? We were just talking about—"

"Yes, but it's just a *dream*. It's not real life. I can't start a chocolate business." Why couldn't he think rationally for one minute? "I have a son and a good job with a steady paycheck. I can't give it all up just to pretend I'm a chocolatier."

"You're not pretending, Mel. You have a real gift—the world needs your gifts. What if it all goes to waste while you sit at that job?"

"Excuse me?" Her mouth dropped open.

"I'm sorry." Isaac rubbed the back of his neck and took a breath. "Maybe I'm projecting ... and I'm not saying you have to leave your job. But I still think you need to take this more seriously. Starting a chocolate business could be a real blessing for everyone, you included. I think you need to trust that God can make this dream a reality."

"Isaac, just stop." The chilliness in her voice surprised her. "I don't have the luxury of leaving my job I hate. I have to be a grownup and accept the consequences of my actions."

"Okay. I'm sorry." His head drooped.

Mel twirled her fork in her pasta. There was no way she could finish her meal. When the waitress came by, they both asked for to-go boxes. Isaac gave her a hopeful, questioning look when the waitress offered a dessert menu, but Mel shook her head.

"We'll just take the check, thanks," she said.

The drive home was uncomfortably quiet. She wished desperately that she'd driven herself.

"Can you forgive me?" Isaac stood next to her on her doorstep.

His pained expression hurt her, but Mel felt just as betrayed. She'd been ambushed as soon as she let her guard down.

"Yes, of course. I know you were just trying to help."

Isaac reinflated a little.

"But I don't think dating each other is a good idea."

Nodding, he took a step back.

"Good night, Isaac." It took every ounce of energy she had to unlock the door.

"Good night, Mel."

Even though she'd just rejected his advances—again—she saw that he watched faithfully, only returning to his car once she'd gotten inside.

Mel collapsed on the couch, head in her hands. What a disaster.

Chapter Twelve

"High Hopes for Mr. Dream Ice Cream Store Melted"

Isaac reread the headline, hoping he'd misunderstood. Nope. The reviewer hated him and his store. Just when he thought he couldn't get any more miserable.

He'd moped around his house and the store since his date with Mel, reliving every agonizing detail. If only he could go back and change what he'd said. He'd been too eager and too excited about her future as a chocolatier. But there wouldn't be a future for a chocolate business or a relationship. He'd effectively killed all hope of a second date.

And now this. Isaac read through the article with increasing dread. When he got to the words "Cereal Crunch," he let out a groan. He raced to the freezer to double-check. He'd had a large container of the ice cream he made with Braxton. A pint of it had gone home with the Wilsons, but the rest of it stayed in the freezer. And he couldn't find it anywhere.

"Jo-o-o-osh?"

The young man looked up from the table he was wiping.

"Did you put that Cereal Crunch flavor out the other day?"

He squinted, thinking. "Yeah, the yellow one with little flecks?"

"That's the one." Isaac sat in the nearest chair. "Apparently a reviewer came from the Bestwood Journal."

Josh shrugged. "I don't remember anyone coming from a paper."

"Well, she probably didn't announce herself. But she tasted every flavor we had."

"Oh." Josh's eyes grew wide. "I remember her. I thought she was really weird asking to taste everything."

Like a moth to a flame, Isaac's eyes returned to the article on his phone screen. Someone had been rude to her too. She wrote about the irritable service and the lackluster flavors. But before he could crawl in a hole in the floor and wallow in misery, the door opened.

With a smile pasted on his face, Isaac called out. "Welcome to Mr. Dream Ice Cream!"

Zeke walked in slowly, wincing and holding up his phone. "Did you see today's paper?"

Shoulders slumping, Isaac returned to his previous despondent posture, covering his face with his hands. "They saw the need to share it on every possible outlet. I don't think there's a human in Middle Tennessee who hasn't seen the article."

"It wasn't that bad."

He looked up over his hands just enough to glare at his friend.

Zeke pulled out a credit card. "Let me buy you some ice cream. It'll make you feel better."

Obediently, Isaac scooped Zeke's favorite—mint chocolate chip—and his own—triple chocolate—into two paper cups. He pushed aside Zeke's card and walked to the other side of the counter.

"Josh, I think the trash needs taking out."

The young man nodded, bagging up the half-full cans without complaint. He forgot to put in the new bags, but Isaac could do that later. At least Josh was out of sight for the next few minutes.

Business had slowed to a trickle, and on this particular Tuesday, Isaac and Zeke were the only people in the restaurant. They sat at a table against the wall, Isaac positioning himself where he could watch the front door. He let out a long sigh as he slid into the seat.

They took a couple bites. The chocolate did soothe some of Isaac's aches, but only a little.

"What are you thinking?" Zeke asked in kind tones, but Isaac squirmed.

"I'm thinking I should've stayed in accounting."

Zeke barked a laugh. "Don't be ridiculous." He waved his spoon. "Have you tasted this stuff?"

"Yes, but so has the Bestwood Journal, and they don't like it too much."

"Now, that's not exactly true." Zeke slid his phone out of his pocket, typed on the screen, and swiped a couple times. "Here it is. She said she loved the chocolate and vanilla.

"But she found the pumpkin spice and cinnamon latte to be less than exciting. And the cereal crunch—"

"Don't worry about that one." Zeke grimaced and shook his head.

"The cereal crunch was one of the suggestion box flavors. Someone wanted it enough to write it down for me, so I had to give it a try."

"Is that why you've been serving so many new flavors lately? Because of the suggestion box?"

"Yes, but I shouldn't have done so many so quickly. What was I thinking putting all those varieties out?" Isaac felt a wave of anxiety grow. He ate another large spoonful, letting the chocolate calm his nerves. "I hadn't perfected the fall flavors, and that Cereal Crunch was never supposed to see the light of day."

"What happened?"

"Josh."

Zeke raised an eyebrow.

Isaac sighed. "I'm mostly to blame for not just taking it straight home, but Josh pulled the Cereal Crunch from the freezer without me realizing." He gave a single, mirthless laugh. "It figures the one time that guy shows some initiative, it turns out terrible."

"So is Josh the one who was so rude to her?"

"Must be." None of his other employees were ever rude to a customer. They were usually all smiles all day long. "Unless it was me."

Zeke gave him a hard look. "It wasn't you." He swept his spoon around the rim of his cup and ate the last morsel. "So what are you going to do now?"

"Besides updating my resume?"

"Yes, since I'm not letting you leave Bestwood."

"I've got to fire Josh." Just saying it out loud gave him hives. If he was being honest with himself, he didn't even like the guy, but the thought of upsetting someone else and putting himself in such an awkward position made his skin itch.

"Why do you look like you're about to be sick?"

"The whole reason I got into this business, why I love it so much, is because I want to make people happy. How can I fire someone? That doesn't make anyone happy."

Zeke leaned back in his seat.

"I know," Isaac said. "I have to fire him because he's making

303

the customers unhappy. And no one will come to the store if we keep getting bad reviews."

"You're telling me your whole mission in life is to make everyone happy?"

"No." Isaac tilted his head. "I mean, I wouldn't put it that way. But, yeah, I do want to make people happy. Isn't that what everyone wants?"

"No, man."

Isaac could tell Zeke wanted to laugh at him, the way his lips twitched up at the corners. But his friend furrowed his brows and took a deep breath. "You can't make everyone happy. Don't you know that?"

"Sure." Isaac waved his hands. Everyone knew that. He didn't literally want to make *everyone* happy all the time. But if he could, wouldn't that be nice?

"Isaac. You can't live your life that way. You'll go crazy."

Blowing out a breath, Isaac looked through the window. A burst of sunlight broke through the cloudy sky. He was going a little crazy. All year long, this tension had built up inside him.

He couldn't make Mel happy—his attempts to help had only driven her away. He couldn't make his customers happy with all the flavors they wanted. And he couldn't keep his employees happy, not all of them at least. Why was Josh always so miserable working at an ice cream shop? What was wrong with this place that it couldn't keep him happy?

He glanced around at the store with its cheerful yellow and blue chairs, clean white tables, and bright photographs on the wall. A deep breath, and Isaac could smell vanilla and chocolate with a hint of cinnamon. There was nothing wrong with this place. The problem must be with Josh.

"I like to make people happy." Isaac shrugged. "What's so wrong with that?"

"Nothing. That's the way God made you," Zeke said. "But you're working for the wrong people."

"What do you mean?"

"You remember that verse from Colossians? Whatever you do, work as if working for the Lord."

"I've been doing that," Isaac scoffed. "I've been working my tail off."

"But who are you working for? Are you trying to make everyone else happy? Or are you trying to please God?"

Isaac couldn't say anything. His spoon scraped the bottom of the cup. Empty. Not even a smidgen of chocolate to distract him.

Had he been working for the Lord? Or had he been trying to prove something to himself?

"I stepped out in faith to quit my job and open this shop. Every square inch of this place has been covered in prayer. And every step of the way, I asked God for help and guidance." He swiveled in his seat, glancing at the empty shop, the freezers in the back, and around the room again.

The sugar maple trees out front glowed a brilliant red. The oak across the street was nearly half brown, and he knew the poplars and dogwoods down the way would be yellow and purple in a couple of weeks. Fall had come to Bestwood, which meant winter would arrive soon.

Instead of the icy fingers of dread which usually wrapped around his gut when he thought of the passage of time, calm settled over him. *God is in control.* The Creator of fall and winter, of mankind and trees, was in control.

"I didn't even realize I'd stopped praying so much. I think I've lost sight of the bigger picture."

Zeke sighed and pushed back from the table. "I believe with my whole heart—and all my taste buds and my stomach—

that you are meant to be here, running this ice cream shop. But maybe you need to pray that you're in it for the right reasons."

Isaac nodded, and his gaze returned from the floor to his friend's kind face. "Thanks for stopping by, Zeke. You've given me a lot to think about. I appreciate it."

Standing, Zeke slapped him on the back. "Anytime." He picked up his empty cup and tossed it in the trash. "Seriously, I'm planning to keep coming for ice cream this winter, so you'd better be expecting me."

A breeze from outside blew a couple of leaves in through the door as Zeke stepped out. Instead of sweeping them out to the sidewalk, Isaac picked them up and placed them on the counter. It was high time he decorated for the season. The brightly colored leaves were a nice touch, but he needed more. And he knew just who to call for help.

Chapter Thirteen

According to Pinterest, Mel should be able to whip up a picture-perfect Halloween costume for Braxton using materials she could find around her home. But the internet was no help when it came to remembering exactly where she'd stored her leftover fabric from the last time she attempted a sewing project.

"Hang on, Mom. Let me see if it's in the closet."

"Are you sure you don't want me to run home and grab some of my fabric?" her mother asked.

"I'm sure. It's around here somewhere."

Mel had accepted her mother's help on the Halloween costume somewhat reluctantly. But having an expert nearby was probably a good idea. The fact that she didn't even know where to find her supplies wasn't a great start.

This year, Braxton wanted to dress up like a superhero, so he'd need a cape. She'd purchased blue sweatpants and a blue sweatshirt from the store the week before—because it wasn't the eighties, and they didn't have matching sweatsuits in every color like the people in magazines who "threw together" "easy costumes" in a "few minutes."

Mel sighed as she surveyed the contents of her closet. The things she did for that kid. Here he was playing with Legos in his room, while she tackled yet another project just so he'd be happy with his costume.

The box of fabric sat on the back corner of a shelf behind a stack of notebooks, so Mel grabbed the stepstool from the laundry room and popped it out on her closet floor. She pushed the notebooks aside, but one fell off the shelf, tumbling through the air.

"Is everything all right?" Mom called out.

"Yes, but can you help me with this box?"

Mel scooted the clear plastic box closer to her and hefted it onto her shoulder, passing it awkwardly down to her mom. While Mom set the box on the bed, Mel picked up the fallen notebook.

The cover was a simple purple plastic, but she immediately recognized it. She'd used the same inexpensive spiral-bound notebooks for her prayer journals since high school. Only in recent years, she'd grown a little too busy for daily journaling. Mel always made sure to pray, but she didn't have as much quiet time at night as she used to.

I should journal more, now that Braxton is older. I really could make space for it.

"What's that?" Mom stood behind her shoulder.

"One of my old prayer journals." Mel flipped to the front page, curious as to what year she'd happened to knock off the shelf and which past self was contained on these college-ruled sheets of paper.

The date showed the notebook was from about six years ago. She'd been anxious about college courses and a friend who'd been in a car accident. On the next page, she'd petitioned for help and patience in waiting to hear the results of her chocolate-making apprenticeship.

Don't worry, you're going to get into the program and immediately back out, never to travel to Europe, or anywhere else, ever again.

The words of her past self taunted her. She winced, remembering how naive and hopeful she'd been, all while making terrible life choices with her boyfriend.

"It's from right before I got pregnant with Braxton." She flipped to another page and skimmed the words there. "I can't believe I actually thought I could change Brian's mind and bring him back to Christ."

Mom sat on the bed and patted the space beside her.

"I should've listened to you and Dad." Mel joined her mother on the bed. "I was stupid."

"Don't be hard on yourself. None of us expected him to be so heartless."

Mel had thought their love for each other would work through all obstacles. In the end, Brian loved himself and his freedom more than anyone else. Young Mel was confused about how Brian felt about her and his plans for their future, but he'd made his wishes abundantly clear once Mel got pregnant. And Mel finally found the courage to cut ties with him once the life of her son was on the line.

"I'm worried about how to tell Braxton the truth about his father someday." Mel knew how to contact Brian and kept tabs on him through social media for when that day came. "But for now, I'm grateful to have that man out of our lives."

"Me too." Mom rubbed her back.

"Look at this." Mel flipped through until she found the page she was looking for. "It's the day I found out I was going to have Braxton."

A simple prayer was written there. *God, I don't know*

what's going to happen, but I know You're going to take care of me.

"God did take care of you."

Mel nodded at her mom's words. "Better than I could've imagined." When had she stopped trusting God?

She turned through the pages, each bringing a new petition, a new way for Mel to see how God had provided.

In hindsight, the plans she'd thought were so big were tiny in comparison to what God had done with her life. He made her into a mother. She'd grown and changed into a different person. A better and stronger person.

"Look. The day Braxton was born." There weren't many entries after that one. She'd been so sleep-deprived in those first few days, most of her prayers were whispered or wept in the wee hours of the morning.

But that first day when she rested beside her sleeping boy in the hospital, she'd written a full page about his sweet little face and the tiny grunts and puffs of air that came from his lips. She'd been overcome with love for the boy she'd borne. And she knew that morning God could turn her sins and past mistakes into joy.

"What a wonderful day that was."

"Mooooom!" Braxton yelled from the next room.

Mel started to stand, but her mom gently pushed her back down. "I'll see what he needs. You stay here." She shut the door behind her.

Sitting back against her pillow, Mel was soon deep in thought. God had taken care of her through her hardest days. Here was proof in her hands.

Did her goals and dreams come from God? Isaac seemed to think so. He lived out his dream in the ice cream shop every day. And if he was right, that meant Mel's desire to start a chocolate and candy business could be from God.

She remembered the sermon she'd heard weeks ago. When the Israelites came to the Jordan River, they'd stepped out in faith. Their trust in God allowed Him to work miracles.

Am I keeping God from working in my life by not trusting Him?

Ever since Braxton came along, her mission in life had been to support him and raise him in a loving home. She wanted to give him everything he needed and never allow him to suffer because his biological father was an irresponsible fool.

But God had proven over and over again that He could take care of the two of them. What if she stepped out in faith like the Israelites? What if God proved to her again how much He could provide? What if her cup overflowed?

Mel slid to the floor. "God? I'm so sorry I haven't been trusting You. I've worked so hard to provide for Braxton that I forgot about the One who is taking care of me."

Tangling her fingers through the carpet fibers, she took a breath. "Do You want me to do this? To follow my dreams?"

Mel had never been one to wait quietly, but she made herself sit in the silence and discomfort. She briefly wondered if her mom would come in to find her crouched on the floor, but she pushed the thought away. She cleared her mind.

What was she afraid of?

"Okay, God. I'm going to do it." A smile tugged at her lips. "I'm going to trust You."

Chapter Fourteen

" I wasn't sure you'd come." The knot of anxiety in his gut loosened as Isaac saw Mel and Braxton walk into the shop Monday morning. He'd reached out, not knowing how she would respond. But Main Street Trick-or-Treat was Tuesday, and he desperately needed assistance.

"You texted that you needed help." Mel smiled as she held up a large box. Braxton carried a sack of something as well.

"I know, but after the other night ... " Isaac grimaced. "I'm really sorry for what I said."

Mel set her box down on a table in the back of the store. "You've told me. About twenty times now."

"But I am. I need you to know—"

Mel placed her hand on his arm and silenced him with a look. "I forgive you, Isaac." She took a breath. "Can you forgive me?"

"Of course. For what?"

"I don't know if you've noticed, but I've got a bit of a temper." She slid her hand down, locking her fingers with his.

"I overreacted when you only wanted to help. And you were right." Mel squeezed his hand before letting go.

His skin tingled where her fingers had touched.

"I decided on a name. For my chocolate business." Mel pulled a small box from the bag on the table. It was a package of truffles with a sticker on the outside. She'd printed 'Mel's Chocolate Shop' in large letters at the top. On the back was a label with all the ingredients and her address and everything.

"This looks so official."

"I've checked and double-checked every requirement. These chocolates are very official. And ..." She winced, looking up at the ceiling before resting her gaze on him again. "I signed up for a domestic kitchen training course through the university."

Isaac pinched his lips to keep from gasping, but he couldn't help the smile on his face.

"It's going to be incredibly boring, but it will help me on the path to becoming licensed to sell commercially."

"I'm really proud of you, Mel. Can I say that?" He didn't want to sound presumptuous. They weren't in any sort of a relationship, though Mel's behavior made him question whether that door really was closed forever. "Listen, I did something I think will make *you* proud."

She raised her eyebrows.

"I fired Josh."

"You set Josh on fire?" Braxton stood beside him with his mouth opened in a shocked expression.

"No, buddy." Isaac set his hands on the boy's shoulders, laughing. "I told him he can't work here anymore."

"He can't work at the ice cream shop?" Braxton had the appropriate reaction—devastation. But Josh hadn't felt the same.

"Do you know what? He was actually happy. Turns out,

neither one of us wanted him here." Isaac turned to Mel. "Josh never wanted to work in food service—he's actually considering accounting now."

"Go figure." Mel laughed. "Well, I'm glad you finally took care of that."

She glanced around the store. "So what do we need to do to get ready for Main Street Trick-or-Treat? That's why we're here, right?"

Isaac loved the bright colors that filled Mr. Dream Ice Cream Shop, but the place felt like perpetual summer. If he wanted to keep up with the other main street businesses, he needed some autumn flair, and fast. "We've got the chocolates, thanks to you."

"We can open a box and take a picture for your social media accounts. I just made two different kinds—dark chocolate truffles with black and orange sprinkles and orange and white pumpkin spice cake balls. Nice and simple."

It didn't sound simple to him, but Mel had made it all work, and she seemed pleased. She wasn't nearly as stressed as the last few times they'd spoken.

"So the next step is to decorate the shop. I don't want anything spooky or gaudy."

Mel surveyed the space, her gaze lingering on the front windows. "Let's just take our cues from God and decorate with nature."

"I love it."

For the next half hour, they worked on collecting fallen leaves outside.

"I like this one." Braxton held up a bright red leaf for Isaac to see.

"Nice. What do you think about mine?" Isaac fanned out his collection like a hand of cards.

"Great job, Dad—I mean—" Braxton stopped himself, his cheeks flushed red. "Sorry. I meant to say Isaac."

"I don't mind, buddy." To his own surprise, Isaac actually meant it. Rather than feeling anxious, hearing Braxton call him Dad made him proud. He felt like he'd earned Braxton's respect and affection, even if it had been an accident. Maybe being someone's Dad could actually be pretty great.

The rest of the evening, Braxton made several leaf rubbings using crayons and paper. Isaac made a quick run to the craft store for fake leaves to scatter on the tables and counters. Mel filled vases with goldenrod and dried flower stalks they'd found behind the shop. By dinnertime, they were all satisfied with the effect.

"I won't win any awards, but no one can say we didn't try." Isaac looked to Mel for approval.

"I think it looks nice." Mel rested her head against his shoulder as they admired their work. "Tomorrow night will be perfect."

MAIN STREET TRICK-OR-TREAT wasn't perfect—Isaac ran out of Halloween candy at one point and had to run to the store, Claire accidentally spilled a whole jar of sprinkles on the floor, and one of the customers clogged the toilet—but in Isaac's opinion, it was as close as could be.

When he totaled their earnings at the end of the night, he let out a sigh of relief. "I think we're going to make it." Even with the negative review in the Bestwood Journal, his clientele kept coming. And they'd shown up in a big way tonight.

Mel bit her lip and looked at him expectantly. Braxton was helping Claire and Abby sweep up the shop, and Mel stood beside Isaac at his computer.

"I'm going to be able to stay open." He grinned at Mel and found a matching smile on her face.

"And I'll be here to help you." She squeezed his hand.

A knot formed in his throat. Being close to her made him long for her even more. "Mel, I need you to know I still like you very much."

"I like you too."

"No, I mean—"

"I know what you mean, Isaac." She smiled and reached for him. Her hands rested on his cheeks. "And I feel the same way."

Before he could speak or even take a breath, her lips were on his. He closed his eyes in satisfaction.

How had he managed to get the ice cream shop *and* the girl? He'd been blessed more than he could have possibly imagined. He pulled Mel into a hug and said a prayer of thanks to the God who'd made all his dreams come true.

About the Author

Sarah Anne Crouch lives in Arkansas with her husband, three children, and thousands of books. She always wanted to be an author, but spent some time as a teacher, earned a degree in library science, and makes feeble attempts to corral her small children as a stay-at-home mom. Sarah loves reading books, recipes, piano music, and emails from readers.

Sugar

AND SPICE

Heather Greer

To those who have let mistakes of the past steal the sweetness of the present.

"For I will be merciful to their iniquities, And I will remember their sins no more." ∼ Hebrews 8:12

Acknowledgments

Heather Greer would like to thank Amy, Regina, and Sarah for making this process so much fun. We should do it again sometime!

Thanks to our readers. Without you, the stories we write wouldn't have life. And the team at Scrivenings Press because without you, the stories wouldn't shine like they do.

And special thanks to Shelly for her insight into German towns and creativity in coming up with New Kuchenbrünn, even if I can't say it.

Chapter One

"Have you seen the announcement?"

Emeline Becker started at the unexpected interruption of silence, accidentally banging her head on the underside of her desk in the process. She groaned, glaring first at the pen she'd been trying to retrieve, still on the floor, and then at her best friend.

How had Kelly managed to sneak up on her? The tinkling bells on the front door of Sugar and Spice Bakery usually got her attention, even in her office.

"That depends on what you're talking about."

"Oh." Kelly baited Emmie, unfazed by her mood. "So you haven't heard about the Gingerbread Festival."

Emmie winced as her fingers found a tender spot on her head. "Did they finally decide to scrap the gingerbread and host a sugar cookie festival instead? Did my best friend, the festival coordinator, finally take my suggestion to the rest of the committee?"

Hands braced against her hips, Kelly smirked. "Yes, Emmie. New Kuchenbrünn, Missouri, the American namesake of the gingerbread capital of the world, has decided to eighty-six the gingerbread in favor of sugar cookies on the one hundred fiftieth anniversary of the festival."

"I don't see a problem." Emmie shrugged. "Ginger is perfect for redheads, but it does not belong in my kitchen."

Kelly plopped down into the chair across from Emmie. "Your great-grandma would roll over in her grave hearing you talk like that. The Sugar and Spice Bakery has been a prominent feature in the festival since she opened the place. And the only reason you don't like gingerbread is because of the Unfortunate Incident of Festival 133."

"Do we have to call it that?"

One brow rose impossibly high. "Would you rather I call it, 'the day my best friend puked gingerbread all over the boy she was crushing on'?"

Emmie huffed. "First of all, it was not all over him. It was on his shoes. Second, I'm still surprised no one else has gotten sick in that stupid gingerbread eating contest. And third, he wasn't my crush. He was my sister's boyfriend."

"Who you were trying to impress by winning the trophy."

Emmie toyed with a pen on her desk. "I was thirteen. Fine. I had a teenage crush on him, but he was sixteen and dating Karen. It didn't matter anyway. He was nothing but a jerk in the end, breaking her heart when he left after high school."

Kelly's sigh put Emmie further on edge.

"Give it up, Emmie. You say it's all about your sister, but we both know your heart took a little damage in that move too. Still, I think fifteen years has exceeded the statute of limitations on heartbreaking crimes."

Kelly placed a hand on top of hers, stilling the furious beat she tapped without realizing it against her desktop. A feeling close to betrayal snuck in. Kelly knew how much teenage Emmie had admired Ryker Lehmann. When Emmie found out he left without even a good-bye to her, Kelly was there.

It didn't matter that he'd been Karen's boyfriend. In the year before he left, it seemed she and Ryker hung out almost as much as he did with Karen, since he often waited at the house for Karen to get out of after-school clubs or off work. She'd thought they were friends. At the very least, she deserved a good-bye. She'd gotten nothing.

The subject needed to change.

"It doesn't matter. You came here with big news, and all we've done is talk about the horrors of my past and the one person I'd rather not talk about again. What happened with the festival?"

Kelly bit her lip. The expression made Emmie's insides tense. Guilty? Nervous? Sheepish? Yes, definitely sheepish. What was going on with her today?

"Out with it. Whatever it is, you know it will be worse if you try to hide it now."

Kelly fidgeted. Emmie pinned her with a look.

"Fine. The Gingerbread Festival Committee wants to do more to boost tourism year-round, and they think the festival is the place to start. They want to professionally photograph and video the events, and they also want to develop a coffee table book to promote all our town has to offer throughout the year."

"So?" Emmie frowned. "I think the additional advertising sounds great, as long as I don't have to commit to gingerbread, forsaking all others for the additional eleven months of the year. I don't see the problem."

"Neither did I." Kelly's smile seemed tense. "Until a few minutes ago. The committee already chose the photographer. He'll be here at Sugar and Spice tomorrow to begin. Everyone thinks it's perfect they've managed to get a local guy to return to his hometown for the festival."

The blood drained from Emmie's face. "No. You're kidding me, right?"

Kelly shook her head. Emmie stared at her friend, as if a glare could change the outcome.

"The festival hired Ryker as the photographer?"

Kelly gave a slight nod. "Ryker Lehmann, successful professional photographer and hometown darling, returns home to promote the festival he loved as a child."

"And you couldn't stop them?"

"What was I supposed to do? I don't have that kind of power."

"Come on, Kelly. You're the mayor's personal assistant by day, and the festival committee coordinator by night. Personally appointed to the task by your illustrious boss. If anyone could derail their plans, it would be you."

"Not this time." Kelly shook her head. "The idea reached him before I did. He thinks it's a wonderful plan, and there was nothing I could do to stop it."

"Did you even try?"

Kelly's tight-jawed stare convicted Emmie. Of course, she'd tried. It was only her spiraling emotions that prompted the question.

"Sorry. That was uncalled for." Emmie rubbed her temples. "This is not happening. First, my bakery is taken over by the only cookie I truly hate. And now, you're telling me the one man I'd hoped never to see again will be in my bakery tomorrow morning?"

"Eight o'clock sharp." Kelly reached across the desk and laid a hand on Emmie's arm. "But it's not going to be so bad, is it? That was a lifetime ago. You've grown up, matured. You can handle this."

"How mature is it for me to hope he's gotten fat and wrinkly and gone bald in the last fifteen years?"

"Emmie. You've got to forgive and get past this."

"I know. I know. I have to put on my big girl panties and deal. With the gingerbread and with Ryker Lehmann."

Kelly laughed. "That's the spirit."

RYKER WIPED STEAM from the bathroom mirror and stared at his reflection. The man who looked back at him wasn't the same boy who left New Kuchenbrünn after high school. His face wasn't as thin as it'd been at eighteen, but it wasn't near heavy.

The five o'clock shadow covering his cheeks was rough against his palm. Should he plan extra time to shave in the morning? No. The stubble stayed. Without it, he'd been told he looked like a kid again. And while he didn't thrill at the idea of getting older, he didn't want to look like the boy who went away to college and never returned.

That wasn't really fair either. He'd come home the first couple of Christmases to see his parents. But when they'd retired, they found a renter for their home and moved to Sevierville, Tennessee like they'd always dreamed. Two hours from his place in Asheville, North Carolina. The perfect distance for autonomy and regular visits, though it took away all reasons to return to his hometown.

When he got an itch for the feel of New Kuchenbrünn, he'd make a trip to nearby Helen. Their Oktoberfest and Christmas Markets always did the trick. Well, almost. Even after all these years, he still hadn't found gingerbread quite like what Sugar and Spice Bakery offered.

Tomorrow, he'd taste it again for the first time in years. Not to mention the opportunity it would give him to reconnect with the people who'd been like a second family to him.

"That's what this is really about." He hoped no one was in the adjoining room to hear him mutter to himself.

Frustrated, Ryker flipped the light switch off and stepped into the bedroom portion of his hotel room. Was it still called a hotel room when it was at an inn? He didn't know and wasn't sure he cared. But he needed a distraction to get his mind off seeing the Becker family tomorrow. A warm welcome wasn't guaranteed after the way he left, but that hadn't been his fault. They couldn't hold the silence against him.

He grabbed his laptop and stretched out on the bed. A little research would benefit him in dealing with local businesses. He could accomplish more in less time and wrap up his work when the festival ended.

Starting with the festival pages outlining all the events taking place in the next two weeks, Ryker made notes about possible photo opportunities and which ones would be better captured using video. Before long, he made his way to the individual shop websites.

His finger paused over the touchpad, the cursor hovering over the link to Sugar and Spice Bakery. It felt a little like spying, but the shop was his first stop the next morning. And he did like to be prepared. He clicked the link. A history of the nearly sixty-year-old business filled his screen along, with photos of the bakery's interior and some of its specialty items. Not bad images, but he could provide them with better.

The menu page could stand a good overhaul. It was easy to see someone cared, but they didn't have the know-how he possessed. He clicked the next page and froze. When had the Becker family sold the bakery?

The caption under the photo of the woman listed her as baker and owner. He looked at the woman again.

Photogenic for sure. Pretty in a cute way, without even trying. Long, straight dishwater-blond hair pulled back into a no-nonsense ponytail. High cheekbones and the stronger line of her jaw gave angles to her otherwise round face without sacrificing the softness. Her smile was perfect, showing off one dimple on the left side. A light in her sky-blue eyes proved her smile wasn't for the camera alone. They were beautiful and also vaguely familiar.

Ryker scrolled past the picture. Emeline Becker. His eyes flew to the photo again. This was Emmie? Karen's little sister? Fifteen years had changed her more than it had him. While he'd filled out some as he went from his late teens to his thirties, his features had already matured by the time he graduated.

When he left New Kuchenbrünn, Emmie was fifteen, if that. She'd gone from a little kid to a cute teen who had the attention of all the boys in her class. Still, she'd kept a little preteen awkwardness around the edges and was completely oblivious to the attention she received. He'd noticed the change then, but now? The little kid and awkward preteen were evicted, leaving a confident, beautiful woman in their place.

He skimmed the rest of the page. No mention of Karen or Emmie's parents except in paragraphs talking about the history of the restaurant. It seemed Emmie had taken the reins roughly six years after he left. What happened to the rest of the family?

One last look at Emmie with her bright blue eyes and single-dimpled smile, and Ryker shut down his laptop. A yawn and a glance at his watch confirmed the need to get some sleep. Before he knew it, the time would come for his trip to Sugar and Spice. And his chance to find out why Emmie seemed to be on her own.

Chapter Two

Emmie bit back a yelp as the hot metal baking sheet connected with her thumb instead of the potholder. She dropped the offending pan of gingerbread men on the stainless-steel table and moved to the sink. While the room temperature water cascaded over the burn, cooling it, her irritation at allowing herself to be distracted continued to sizzle.

Every noise stole her attention from the task at hand, and Emmie ended up watching the clock tick away the minutes. She needed to focus on her job, rather than the impending doom coming her way in the form of Ryker Lehmann. Could this restless, nervous energy bursting from every pore of her body be harnessed for good rather than evil? If she failed, she'd never get all the gingerbread men done in time to deliver them to the senior center for their pre-festival gingerbread decorating practice session.

She examined the red blister forming on her skin. "I've got to get my head in the game. He'll get here when he gets here. No amount of agonizing is going to change anything. If it did, he wouldn't even show up, and I'd live in Sugar Cookie, South Dakota where I'd never bake gingerbread again."

"Can I quote you on that?"

Emmie winced as she smacked her injured thumb on the faucet, increasing her discomfort and rerouting the water all over her sink and apron. She jerked around to face Ryker. In that moment, her hopes were dashed.

Time had treated him well. While subtle lines creased his forehead and he had filled out with adulthood, he'd definitely not inherited the pudge many men began developing in their thirties. His build, though not as slight, was still as athletic as she remembered. His hair was the color of chestnuts under the lighting in her bakery kitchen. There wasn't even a hint of salt and pepper or receding hairlines.

In fact, the longer length on the sides might have looked unkempt on others, but paired with the heavy stubble covering his cheeks, the look gave him an easygoing, inviting appearance with just a hint of his artistic nature. The spark of laughter in his rich brown eyes was enough to snap Emmie out of her silent assessment and add starch to her stance.

"No. You may not." Good. Impatience with his humor laced her voice, leaving no room for his jokes. This was business only. It had to be that way. Her shoulders straightened into an impervious line of defense. "Haven't you heard of knocking? Even in a small town, announcing yourself is generally accepted as a polite practice."

He had the nerve to shrug as he brushed a loose strand of hair away from his eyes. "I did. Maybe you didn't hear it while you were busy soliloquizing about gingerbread men."

She bristled when he met her stare with one of his own. Though his held less animosity than hers must show, he didn't back down. One brow raised, his head tilted toward his shoulder. Emmie fought the urge to close her eyes and sigh. The look was one she knew well, and it didn't bode well for her.

"Why didn't you want me to show up? We used to be friends."

A snort escaped before she could stop it. "Really? Is that what we were? I seem to remember you being at my house quite frequently, but it wasn't to hang out with me. When did we become friends?"

He tucked his bottom lip into his teeth. The laughter that lit his eyes faded. Swallowing hard, she refused to squirm under his scrutiny. It wasn't really a lie. Maybe a half-truth. Back then she'd considered them friends, but looking back with the clarity of adulthood, she saw it for what it was. There was no friendship. His gaze continued to unnerve her. Ridiculous. She'd done nothing wrong.

"Fine." He hooked his thumbs on the pockets of his dark blue jeans. "We weren't friends exactly. Back then you were a little young to be part of my friend circle. But we were friendly enough, considering the age difference. So, why wish me away now?"

She narrowed her eyes. "Don't pretend you're innocent and clueless. It doesn't work for you." Motioning to the counter where her abandoned pan of gingerbread men cooled, Emmie brought them back to the present. "Look. I have a job to do, and I know you do too. How about we set this other junk aside and get our jobs done? Deal?"

"Whatever you say. I'm still not sure what all of this is about, but fine. I'm here to document the Gingerbread Festival and the town, not make friends. Why don't I start by getting some pictures of your shop and then of you making the gingerbread, if you're not already done?"

"Fine."

RYKER LIFTED the camera and framed the storefront in the lens before snapping the picture. He blew out his frustration. The tension would drain his creative ability if he didn't get it under control. He closed his eyes and sucked in a deep breath, holding it for five counts before slowly exhaling.

Why on earth was she so tied up in knots because of him? She'd been a kid the last time he saw her. He'd barely moved past childhood himself. There'd been his relationship with Karen, but she couldn't hold that against him. It had faded into nothingness the way most high school relationships had a way of doing. They hurt, they learned, and they moved on. There was no way that could be the reason she'd erected this huge wall between them.

Whatever the cause, there was more than enough heat in her voice and in the way she looked at him to prove he wasn't overthinking the situation. Despite what she'd pushed him into saying, he'd always considered them on friendly terms at least. Yeah, she was a bit younger, and in those days, it made a difference. Fifteen and eighteen seemed light years apart. Still, he'd enjoyed her being around. Where Karen was serious and quiet, Emmie had always been fun and up to any challenge he threw at her.

Now it seemed she was flipping the script, and the challenge issued was to find the problem between them and fix it before the festival ended, sending him back to Asheville. He'd never been one to run from a challenge, and this one tugged at him harder than most in recent years.

"That's it, then. Project Win Over Emmie has officially begun," he announced to the empty sidewalk.

He placed the lens cap on his camera. It was time to get some shots of Emmie in her element. He yanked the bakery door open. An initial weight to it gave way as Emmie came stumbling out the door, eyes wide and balancing a bakery box in one hand.

Too late, Ryker reached to steady her. The unexpected help with opening the door had thrown her completely off balance, and she couldn't recover in time. Ryker grimaced as she fell to the pavement with a cry of surprise. The box she tried so hard to save flew into the street, ejecting gingerbread men like crashing fighter pilots as it sailed toward its doom.

"Nooo." Emmie's cry brought his attention back to her.

Arms and face scratched from contact with the rough concrete, Emmie knelt on the ground looking at the gingerbread devastation in front of her. A tear made its way down her cheek, prompting Ryker to action.

"Here. Let me help you up."

He reached out, offering his hand to support and lift her as she stood. Instead of taking it, Emmie turned toward him. Her jaw was tight as she swiped the moisture from her reddening cheek.

"I think you've helped enough. Don't you? Did you even look before jerking the door open?"

Ryker opened his mouth, but his mind failed to shape an adequate reply. It was unnecessary anyway.

"I worked all morning on those cookies." Emmie continued railing at him. "And the assisted living center is now patiently waiting for four dozen gingerbread men that aren't going to arrive anywhere near on time. And I have other orders waiting. Believe it or not, running a successful bakery isn't all sugar and sprinkles, Mr. Lehmann. Now, if you'll excuse me. I have to clean up the gingerbread carnage and get back to the kitchen."

Shocked, Ryker watched as Emmie picked up the destroyed gingerbread men from the street and stormed inside her bakery without another word. She didn't even pause long enough to glare at him one last time.

Ryker brushed the hair out of his eyes as he looked at the now closed door. Maybe Project Win Over Emmie wasn't going to be as easy as he thought.

Chapter Three

Ryker cracked open the kitchen door and peeked around the frame. Scooping ingredients from containers and dumping them without mercy into a large metal bowl, Emmie telegraphed her ire without words. A slight squeak as the door shifted alerted her to his presence in her domain. She did nothing to disguise her glare when she saw him standing there.

"I thought we were done."

Her tone left no doubt that his opinion didn't matter. For Emmie, their dealings for the day were complete. Ryker licked his lips. He had zero desire to rile her any more than she already was, but he couldn't leave things as they were.

"I'm so sorry," he said quietly. "I had no idea you were on the other side of the door. Can I run and get your mom or Karen to help you?"

She speared him with a scowl. "Karen married after college and moved to Indiana with her husband. Mom and I ran the bakery for a while, but after Dad passed away six years ago, she moved in with Karen and Robert. As far as the bakery goes, I'm it."

"I'm sorry, Emmie. I didn't know."

"It's fine."

"How can I help you?"

A disbelieving snort served as her immediate answer. Ryker grit his teeth. Though he'd never been given to anger, Emmie's dismissal grated on his nerves. Deep breath. One. Two. Three. By the time he reached five, Ryker trusted his voice to remain cordial.

"I mean it, Emmie. I know I set you back, and I want to help fix the mess. So, tell me what to do."

Ryker winced as her eyebrows rose impossibly high. Maybe his wording wasn't the best. It left too many openings for less than pleasant suggestions, none of which would lead to fixing the jam he'd created for Emmie.

"Please."

The drop in Emmie's shoulders contradicted the slight rise to her chin. He'd seen that look before when they were teenagers, usually leveled at her sister, who managed to get under her skin like no one else could. She would accept his help while simultaneously testing him. If he failed her again, it would not go well. How many times had he saved Karen from the same fate with his uncanny ability to smooth things over with Emmie? Hopefully, he still had the knack for it.

"Fine." The word was accompanied by a twist to her mouth. Emmie pointed her ingredient-smeared spatula toward a rack on the wall displaying a variety of aprons. "Wash your hands and grab an apron and cap."

Emmie returned to her measuring and stirring. After washing his hands, Ryker reached for a plain, dark red apron revealing one with a different pattern hidden beneath it. He glanced at the selection of hats hanging from pegs further down and spied the one he wanted. Perfect. Donning the apron and cap, he crossed to stand opposite Emmie.

"Ready to work, boss. What should I do?"

Emmie glanced up at him, to her bowl, and immediately back up to him. The dramatic roll of her blue eyes didn't hide their twinkle any more than the pursing of her glossed lips convinced him she didn't want to laugh.

He straightened the green elf hat, ringing the bells attached to each point of its red trim. "What?" He brushed his hands down the apron, patterned to look like an elf suit. "I'm ready to work. Your wish is my command, Santa."

While he preened, she managed to cross her arms over her chest and school her features into a bland expression. "You think you're cute, don't you?"

"Of course. Don't you?" He gave her his most innocent smile and a wink.

EMMIE TURNED AWAY. She wasn't about to let Ryker Lehmann see the rose she knew would accompany the heat in her cheeks. Oh, the nerve of him. It was more than just the day's disaster. She couldn't help it that her brain and mouth threatened to commit treason by shouting 'yes' to his rhetorical question. Those weren't the only treacherous parts of her. With his smile crinkling the corners of his eyes right before one dropped into that flirtatious wink, her tummy rebelled with an excited flip.

She opened the door to her commercial refrigerator. At least the blast of cool air would drain the fire from her face. Rummaging around, pretending to look for ingredients she didn't need, gave her time to give herself a stern pep talk. She was not a child anymore, or even a lovesick teenager. She was a grown woman, an independent small business owner. Mature adult women didn't get giggly over the antics of boys.

Shutting the refrigerator, Emmie retrieved a box of parchment paper from a nearby shelf before returning to her workspace. She held it out to Ryker without allowing herself to look directly at him.

"Here. Get six baking sheets from the rack over by the dishwasher and prep them with a sheet of parchment paper. We'll roll out the dough on this table. So, the pans can go on the one next to it."

Ryker moved to do her bidding without a word, allowing her to return to the dough she was mixing. The rustle of the parchment paper as he started lining the sheets drew her attention, and she allowed herself a side-eye glance in his direction. The precision he exhibited in completing the menial task made her smile. Each piece was perfectly placed on the metal baking sheets.

Job completed, Ryker retrieved his camera from a nearby counter and began snapping pictures. Emmie happily ignored him as she completed the dough and turned it out onto the lightly floured surface she'd prepared on the tabletop.

"What's with the paper?" He asked as he continued to snap pictures.

"I'm not sure I know what you mean." She rolled out the dough carefully keeping uniform thickness.

"I didn't do a lot of baking growing up, but I seem to remember Mom using shortening or some type of spray on her pans. Why are you using paper? One would think paper in an oven would be dangerous."

She looked up from her task to another snap of his camera. He glanced at the LCD panel to check the photo and nodded.

"That's a great one. You look so thoughtful."

She frowned. "Did you ask to get a shot, or do you really want to know?"

"I'd like an answer. I just know better than to waste a great photo opportunity."

"In that case," she began as she held up the box like a commercial spokesperson. "I could use spray or shortening, but I prefer the parchment paper. It's non-stick and makes for easier clean up. Plus, it can help extend the life of my pans."

She placed the box on the counter and held out a gingerbread man cookie cutter for him. "As to why it doesn't burn, I don't really have an answer. I just know it works."

"Good enough." He placed his camera back on the counter and took the cutter from her before circling the table to stand beside her.

With his shoulder brushing hers, Emmie realized she hadn't thought through this part of the process. Her control over her heart and mind was already strained. If she wasn't careful, it would crumble like the gingerbread men in the trash.

She stepped away and scooped a second ball of dough from the mixing bowl. Moving around the table, she prepped another spot and began rolling out the new dough. "How about you work on that one while I get the next one ready?"

"Works for me." Ryker shrugged without looking up from his task. "You roll 'em. I'll cut 'em."

An hour later, Emmie and Ryker placed the freshly baked and cooled cookies into a white bakery box. Later than she originally planned, but not as much as she would have been without Ryker's help, Emmie traded her apron for her coat and purse before scooping up the cookies.

"Thanks for the help." She headed out of the kitchen toward the front door. "I've got to get these delivered. I'll see you later."

Ryker hurried to shed his apron and retrieve his own coat. "I'm coming with you."

She paused. "That's not necessary."

"It most definitely is necessary." He moved past her and opened the front door, holding it to let her pass.

"Listen," she began matter-of-factly. "I appreciate the offer, but you've done more than enough to make up for destroying my first batch of cookies. Your penance is complete, and you are absolved of all responsibility."

Ryker shook his head, causing a strand of hair to fall forward over his eyes. He brushed it back before answering. "It's not always about you, you know. I'm the photographer hired to record this festival and hopefully get the attendance up for the town. This is an activity in preparation for the festival, and I need to photograph it."

Oh. Well, that made his accompanying her so much more appealing. He was doing what he had to do. And here she'd thought they'd had a decent time working together. At least there wasn't a chance she'd have to deal with any more of those pesky butterflies in her stomach.

"Suit yourself. I'll meet you there."

Emmie didn't give him a chance to respond before twisting the key in the door to lock it and striding down the sidewalk to her delivery van.

Chapter Four

Ryker gathered his equipment from the passenger seat of his rental car. Despite the distractions, he'd actually accomplished quite a few goals the previous day. He'd only stayed at the nursing home long enough to grab some shots of their decorating practice session before giving in to the unexpected chill directed at him from Emmie.

He'd hoped to secure some goodwill from her through their cookie baking, but obviously it was an error in judgment. Telling himself it was pointless anyway, since he was there for a job and nothing more, he'd packed up and managed to check the Christmas tree farm, Santa's village, and New Kuchenbrünn First Baptist's live nativity planning committee's workday off his list of must have shots.

He locked the car door and turned, narrowly missing someone walking past. The woman looked at him for a moment before recognition settled in her eyes.

"Hi. It's Kelly. Isn't it?" Ryker was surprised the name came so readily. Kelly had been a friend of Emmie's back when they were all in school. She'd been around some when he'd hung out at Karen's house or when Emmie tagged along with them to various events, but Kelly wasn't a constant figure in those memories.

"Ryker Lehmann." Kelly smiled and extended her hand. "I'm surprised you recognized me. We didn't exactly travel in the same circles in school."

Ryker shook her hand, finding it easy to offer a friendly smile in return. "I'm kind of surprised myself. Maybe being back in New Kuchenbrünn has jogged my memories."

Kelly's smirk revealed her doubt. "Or maybe your roller coaster ride of a day with Emmie yesterday shook loose the memories."

A groan escaped as they walked toward the town's community center. "So, I was right. She was upset with me yesterday at the nursing home."

"You could say that." Kelly's apologetic smile was more like a grimace as she shrugged.

"And if I did, what would be the reason?" Her raised brow had him backtracking. "I mean, I know I messed up her order, but I stayed and helped her fix it. And I thought we were having fun working together by the time we packed up the cookies. Then, well, I'm not sure what happened. She said I didn't need to accompany her to the nursing home. I told her it was my job to photograph the festival. Then the wall came up and the temperature dropped."

Kelly's sigh made him feel denser than his great-aunt Harriett's Christmas fruitcake. When she shook her head and walked away from him, he adjusted the strap of his camera bag on his shoulder and sped up to stay in step with her.

"I take it I should know what I did?"

"Yes, Ryker. You should know what you did." She paused to look at him with disbelief before resuming her path to the Community Center. "Didn't you learn anything last time?"

The words were barely audible.

"Last time? What are you talking about?"

She trapped her bottom lip between her teeth with a wince. Those final words weren't meant for him, then. Ryker had to take a step back as she stopped without warning.

"I shouldn't have said anything. Forget I did. Okay?"

"I can't do that."

"Why not? You're only here through the festival. Then, you're gone just like before. Do your job. Leave it alone."

He should. But he couldn't. "Emmie and I used to be friends. I can't leave with things like they are between us."

Kelly harrumphed. "It didn't stop you the first time."

"Right there." He pointed at her. "That's the third time you've brought up the past. What huge sin did I commit when I left for school? I didn't even see Emmie before I left."

"Hmm."

Without looking back, Kelly walked up the steps of the Community Center and through the door. Ryker knew he should follow. Even if they couldn't continue their conversation, he had a job to do. The center was the hub of the festival events. Behind the scenes set-up photographs were a no-brainer. But his feet refused to take the steps.

Would Emmie be inside? More than likely. As much as he wanted to see her, he needed to sort through his conversation with Kelly before he had any hope of smoothing things over with Emmie. The town's tree lighting this evening would be soon enough. Until then, he needed some time to think and pray about his next step.

EMMIE'S SMILE faded as Kelly approached. Panic and apology showed in her friend's wide eyes and tight smile. Emmie glanced over Kelly's shoulder and saw nothing amiss. What had she done?

"I'm so sorry, Emmie. He came out of nowhere, and I didn't know what to say. And I think I may have said too much. I didn't mean to. It slipped out, and I'm sorry."

Emmie stared at her friend as a sick feeling took up residence in her stomach. "What did you do?"

"I ran into Ryker outside."

Emmie's eyes slid shut. A quick inhale of breath made her head spin momentarily. Kelly's hand coming to rest on her arm was meant to calm. But Emmie needed answers.

"Tell me."

"He wanted to know why you were angry with him yesterday. I didn't want to say anything. It slipped into the conversation on accident. He was so clueless. Acted like he had no idea why you'd be hurt, even though he treated you like nothing before. It kind of frustrated me, and I spoke without thinking. And I'm so sorry."

"You didn't."

Little lines edged Kelly's eyes as her grimace caused a squint.

"You told him I was hurt over the way he left back then?"

Her suspicions were confirmed with Kelly's slow nod. Emmie's hand flew to cover her mouth, whether in disbelief or sudden nausea, she couldn't decide. If he knew she was upset over his leaving, it wouldn't be too hard for him to connect the dots and realize she'd been crazy about him.

"I'm sorry, Emmie," Kelly said. "But maybe this is a good thing. You two can talk about everything, forgive, and move on."

As much as she might want to shake her friend senseless, Emmie understood the way Ryker could frustrate the words out of a person. As for forgiveness, she wasn't sure she was ready for that. But they could find ways to make this work. They were both professionals.

She gave her friend a reassuring smile. "It's fine. All I have to do is figure out a way to do damage control and keep Ryker at a distance for the next two weeks. Piece of cake."

Maybe it would be more like constructing a gingerbread house complete with a wrap- around cookie porch and a turret. Still, she could do this. There was no other choice.

Chapter Five

" Se you at the tree lighting," Ryker called to the owner of Märchen, the town's fairytale themed book shop, as he exited the store.

He readied the camera around his neck as he headed up the street to the giant Frasier fir rising from the town square. The annual event would happen later that evening, but Ryker wanted a few daylight shots for variety.

He breathed in the spicy, woodsy scent, made sharper by the chill in the air. His finger hovered over the shutter release button as he moved around the tree and Emmie came into the viewfinder. Standing at the top of a stepstool, she stretched to reach a limb a sliver away from being too high. Her gaze settled on the branch where she carefully hung an ornament. Wonder and tradition and serenity were reflected in her expression.

The shot was as beautiful as the woman in it. Focusing the camera and capturing the image did little to restore the breath she'd stolen from him, but the photograph would be a perfect memory, even if it didn't end up in the promotional book.

The crunch of snow under his boots alerted her to his

presence. Her hand dropped from the ornament while the wonder in her expression was replaced by wariness. With her eyes trained on him, her boot slipped from its place. Her yelp, as her shin scraped down the edges of the steps, shattered the silence.

Ryker was at her side in seconds, grasping her arm to help her regain her balance and avoid landing seat first in the light covering of snow. Her face pinched with pain as she spun around and plopped onto the top step of the stool. An attempt to rub the discomfort from her shin ended with a quick jerk back as soon as her hand came to rest on the injured area.

Gingerly, Emmie worked the blue jeans above her shin to check the damage. The lack of bleeding was a plus. Seeing discoloration already beginning, Ryker knew she was in for a sizable bruise by the next morning.

"Ouch." He winced at the sight.

Emmie stared at him as if she'd forgotten his presence. Without acknowledging him any further, she returned her attention to her leg.

"I'm so sorry, Emmie. I didn't mean to startle you. I came around the tree and saw you hanging that ornament. Your expression and the image were perfect. I never dreamed I'd surprise you."

"It's fine," she muttered, pain lacing each word. "Accidents happen."

Ryker did his best to hide his smile at the announcement. Her glower informed him of his failure.

"I'm not laughing at you," he said.

"Really?"

"I'm not. But to show you how sorry I am, why don't you let me help you over to The Kringle Cup. You can rest your leg and enjoy a cup of the best hot chocolate New Kuchenbrünn has to offer. At least, I assume it's still the best."

"Did you take leave of your senses while you were away? Of course, The Kringle Cup's cocoa is as wonderful as it's always been." Her sharp words were dulled by her incredulous grin.

She'd agreed with the sentiment, but not the suggestion to join him. Apparently, she was as uncomfortable with him as he felt around her. But he could help change that. His talk with Kelly ended with soul-searching and a theory as to what went wrong in their friendship. But if she wouldn't spend time with him, he couldn't prove he'd left her feeling like a third wheel or try to convince her that nothing was further from the truth.

"My treat. What do you say?"

She sighed. "Fine."

The patronizing tone grated. He ignored it. At least, she'd agreed. There was hope.

Emmie let her weight rest on her good leg as she carefully tested the injured one. It was barely audible, but Ryker caught her small groan as she took a step forward. There was no way she wouldn't be sore for a few days.

"Should I grab the stepstool?"

Emmie shook her head. "Throughout the day, business owners place their shop ornaments on the top half of the tree. Tonight's decorating and lighting is reserved for the people. Each family hangs an ornament featuring their names on the lower branches."

"I remember. It always made the tree feel like it belonged to everyone." He watched as she took another slow step. "Do you need help? You can rest your weight on my arm if you'd like."

"I'm fine." She pushed the words through clenched teeth.

There was no way she was fine, but he knew he should leave well enough alone. Forcing her to accept his help would only alienate her more. Instead, he shortened his steps to match her painful gait and held the door for her to enter the coffee shop ahead of him. Once she was seated at the closest table by the window, he quickened his pace to the counter and placed their order.

"I've always found it strange," Emmie began as she accepted the cup from him, "this place is called the Kringle Cup."

He took the seat across from her and sipped his cocoa. "Why?"

"I know they're using the name Kringle like Kris Kringle, but a Kringle is a Danish pastry. It was brought to Copenhagen through German bakers who replaced Danish ones during a strike."

"Hmm." Ryker nodded while he tried to formulate a response. What did one say to bits of random trivia thrown into daily conversation?

Emmie's attention shifted to the tree in the square as she sipped her cocoa. Maybe she didn't need a response. He followed her gaze.

The town's tree was unlike any he'd seen, though it took moving away to realize how unusual it was. There was more to its uniqueness than the way the town participated in the decorating, but that was a special way to give everyone ownership of it.

While other towns filled their trees with bright colors, sparkling decorations, and twinkling lights, New Kuchenbrünn took a different approach. A variety of resin gingerbread ornaments hung from all but the lowest branches waiting for the families to add their own. Some were simply decorated, others more ornate in their icing designs.

Twinkle lights were replaced with weather- and fire-safe plastic candles. The only pops of color were from fake red berries, cinnamon sticks, and bright slices of orange. The effect was simple, yet memorable.

Ryker couldn't see it, but he knew the town park boasted another tree where berries, real orange slices, and seed-covered pinecones provided a buffet for local birds. He'd started the tradition as a service project for his church's kids' club when he was in middle school. Knowing his town still went the extra mile to provide for nature during the winter months brought a sense of satisfaction.

He nodded toward the tree laden with gingerbread ornaments. "I'm surprised you enjoy the tree considering your hatred of gingerbread."

"How do you know I do? Maybe I only put up with the tree's decoration because it's expected."

He laughed. "I saw your face. Full of wonder. You don't fake that because someone tells you to."

Emmie shrugged. "Fine. I like the tree. Just because I don't want to eat gingerbread or bake it 24/7 doesn't mean I don't find the ornaments aesthetically pleasing. I think it gives our town tree a sort of rustic charm. It keeps the fairy tale of New Kuchenbrünn alive. I wouldn't change that for anything."

Turning to look out at the tree, Emmie's expression turned wistful. The dreamy expression and the way the afternoon sun made her light brown hair shine like rose gold, picking up every highlight, had Ryker's finger itching to capture the image on film as he had at the tree. Good sense overrode desire, reminding him that his impulse was the reason they were sitting in the coffee shop to begin with.

"How's your shin feeling?"

"Fine," she answered quietly.

At least this time the word wasn't spoken through clenched teeth or shot at him like a bullet. It even came with a reassuring smile. How could two people with so much to say sit across from each other searching for what came next?

"Are you going to the tree lighting tonight?"

Ryker lifted the camera from where it hung around his neck. "It's kind of a job requirement. Not that I'd think about missing it since I'm in town."

She nodded understanding, but the downward turn to her lips left Ryker wondering how he'd disappointed her. The frown fled as she drained the contents of her cup and stood from the table with only the slightest wince.

"Thank you for the cocoa, but I've got to get back to the bakery. I've left my part-time girl, Ann, there by herself longer than I planned. The morning rush might be over, but there's still plenty of work to be done. I'll see you at the tree lighting."

"See you then." Ryker barely got the reply uttered before she threw her cup in the nearby trashcan and left for Sugar and Spice. Though it started poorly and ended with an unanswered question, the time sandwiched in the middle gave him hope. There was still a chance he could win over the beautiful Emmie Becker.

Chapter Six

E mmie scanned the growing crowd. As she gripped it, the resin ornament nestled in her pocket felt cold against her skin.

"Where is he?" She muttered the question under her breath.

Ryker was the event photographer. He had a reputation to protect. There was no way he wouldn't have arrived before the first attendees.

She continued to search, and Kelly came into her line of sight. As she approached, Emmie recognized the conclusions Kelly had jumped to in her wide-eyed stare. If her eyebrows arched any higher, they'd be in her hairline. Jerking her head to the left, Emmie attempted to ignore her friend.

She was certain that with one glance Kelly knew what, or rather who, Emmie was looking for and had already judged why. But it wasn't what Kelly thought. The desire to find Ryker came solely from the need to give him the ornament. He was a hometown boy. Participation in the tree lighting was a given, though he'd probably not planned for it.

Emmie's search for him had nothing to do with the frustrating way her pulse sped up when he stood near her. Or the way the citrusy and warmly spicy cologne he wore caused an involuntary deep inhale of the inviting scent. And it especially wasn't caused by their latest conversation tugging warm memories of their past friendship from the back of her mental closet.

No. It definitely had nothing to do with any of those things. Ryker was still the man who'd broken her sister's heart and left town without so much as a good-bye to Emmie. Those memories would return to the dark recesses of her mind where they belonged. Of course, it didn't have to happen right away. As long as she kept her wits about her, a little indulgence couldn't hurt.

Kelly stepped up next to her and pointed past the tree. "I think what you're looking for is over there."

Ignoring the smug tone, Emmie followed the direction of her finger. Ryker stood on the top step of the small ladder she'd used earlier that afternoon, using it to gain a different vantage point to capture his images. He snapped a picture before resting the camera against his chest so he could wave at her.

Emmie returned the gesture until Kelly's elbow connecting with her ribs sent a jolt through her middle. Ryker descended the stepstool and made his way through the crowd.

"Oh, and he's coming over," Kelly cooed in a singsong tone.

"You need to stop," Emmie hissed.

"I don't know what you're talking about," Kelly argued. "Oh, look over there. The hot chocolate and cider stands are opening. I'll be back in a minute."

Squashing the urge to stomp her feet and screech in frustration, Emmie contented herself with balling her hands into fists in her pockets and sucking in a quick breath. As the cold air pelted her lungs with icy darts, Emmie realized her mistake. A coughing fit seized her, doubling her over.

"Are you all right?" Ryker's smooth, deep voice blanketed her with warmth but did nothing to stop her hacking.

With her mouth still nestled in the sleeve of her puffy, pea-green coat to cover her cough like a demented vampire, Emmie nodded. The fit-induced tears were freezing on her cheeks. Great. She must look a mess.

"Are you sure? Can I get you a drink or something?"

Clearing her throat one last time, she dropped her arm from her face. "Really. I'm fine."

His lopsided grin creased his cheek with laugh lines. "It's good to know some things haven't changed."

"What do you mean?"

His eyes held a teasing glint. "Let's just say, I'm pleased to see your middle name still fits as perfectly as it always has."

Realizing what he meant, she bristled. As images of burning herself, picking up cookies from the sidewalk, and slipping from the stepstool flitted through her mind, her injured feelings fled. He was correct, and she couldn't deny it. She could, however, play back.

"I don't know what you're talking about. Emeline Grace fits me to a *T*. I have always exhibited oodles of grace. But my unique way of showing it doesn't alienate others."

Ryker's head tipped to the right as he regarded her with a nod. "Sure. I see it. Your grace wants to make others feel better about themselves. That's why I ended up with puke on my shoes after the gingerbread eating contest that one year."

Heat crept into her cheeks as she groaned. "Can we please talk about something else?"

His rich laughter drew the attention of several people milling around. If it weren't at her expense, the sound would fit around her like her favorite sweatshirt, warm and comforting. Instead, it left her wishing she could melt away like the witch in *The Wizard of Oz*.

"You'll have to excuse him," she explained to the onlookers. "He has a strange sense of humor and a huge lack of self-control."

A few curious stares continued, but most resumed their focus on family and the tree. Emmie crossed her arms and tapped her foot. Ryker got the picture. Standing stiff and tall, he cleared his throat.

"I'm so sorry."

When she continued staring at him, he raised his hands in surrender.

"Really. I'm sorry. What would you like to talk about?"

Was he offering a do-over? He batted thick lashes over his brown puppy dog eyes.

"Anything at all," he said. "And I promise I'll be good."

Emmie snorted. "I seriously doubt that. But ..."

A tapping from the microphone near the tree cut her off. Convinced it was working, Kelly smiled at the gathered crowd. A flash lit beside Emmie, as Ryker snapped a picture.

"Thank you all for coming," Kelly began. "Tonight we kick off the one hundred fiftieth anniversary of the New Kuchenbrünn Gingerbread Festival. With two weeks of old-fashioned family fun planned, there's something for everyone. And it wraps up with our annual Gingerbread Ball and awards ceremony, where we will crown this year's Gingerbread Queen."

She looked out over the crowd, beaming at them. "Schedules for the events have been posted in every shop window for your convenience. But before we get to games and contests, we have a tree to light. Our mayor would like to say a few words as we begin. Please welcome Mayor Gretchen Schulze."

Ryker took a few more pictures as the mayor once again invited visitors to join in all the festival events and extolled the virtues of both town and festival. The crowd shifted around her in anticipation of hanging the family ornaments. As Ryker was jostled, the space between him and Emmie disappeared. The nearness of his chest against the back of her shoulder created a flurry inside her.

Cold seeped through her coat as she shifted away from him. How could he still have the ability to send a snowstorm swirling inside her? He broke Karen's heart. That fact should be front and center in her mind. And he left without saying good-bye. The thought enabled her to push Ryker firmly back into the friend zone.

"And now, I ask each family of our fine town to place their ornament on this year's tree," the mayor announced from the platform beside the tall fir. Everyone waited as she moved to the tree and draped the red ribbon of her family ornament over one of the branches.

As the crowd surged around her, Emmie kept her place and turned to Ryker. She pulled the heart shaped gingerbread ornament from her pocket and held it out to him.

"I thought you might need this."

He glanced at the ornament before looking back up at her. "Is this ...?"

"Yes, it's your family's original ornament. Kelly found it stored with some of the town's decorations. I was supposed to give it to you at the bakery, but ..." Emmie shrugged.

His care in taking it from her was sweet, as if it was made of delicate crystal instead of hard resin. He brushed fingers over his family name, written across the front in white paint script mimicking icing.

"Thank you."

His grateful smile sent her previously stilled flurries swirling again. Focusing on his smile was not helping her. She looked up and regretted her decision immediately. The warmth and tenderness emanating from his brown eyes would melt her defenses completely. She jerked her gaze toward the tree.

"Looks like the crowd is clearing out a bit. Maybe we should go hang these before the countdown starts." It was a reasonable suggestion. She wasn't running in the slightest. There was no reason to flee. She and Ryker could be friends, nothing more, nothing less.

Together they wove their way through the crowd. Placing their ornaments on free branches, they moved back into the throng as the countdown began.

"Three ... Two ... One!"

The crowd cheered in unison as Mayor Schulze pressed the button, and the tree lit up with hundreds of flickering candles. The melody of "O Tannenbaum" rose through the air as every town resident joined in the song. Even with the cold chapping her cheeks, nothing brought more warmth to Emmie's spirit.

Was Ryker feeling the same way? She looked away from the tree to find an empty spot next to her. Confused, she searched until she saw him off to the side of the crowd, his camera around his neck and a small video camera panning everyone, capturing the magic of the moment for others.

He was still snapping pictures when the crowd started to disperse for the evening. She considered joining him, but morning would come early. If she wanted to get all her baking completed for Sugar and Spice and still be at the community center in time for her gingerbread decorating tutorial, sleep was a must.

He lowered his camera when she came into view, and she

smiled and waved. As she turned to leave, disappointment flickered across his face. Had Ryker hoped she'd stay? And if they were only ever going to be friends, why did the thought leave her with a smile?

Chapter Seven

The sweetly spicy scents of cinnamon and ginger invited Ryker to come in and savor the moment as he opened the door to Sugar and Spice Bakery. Happy to accept, he stepped inside. With an hour to go until it opened, the front of the bakery was empty. But the sound of Brenda Lee singing "Rocking Around the Christmas Tree" guided him to the kitchen.

Ryker bit back a chuckle when he slipped through the kitchen door to find Emmie dressed in apron and cap, dusted with flour, and dancing around the kitchen before sliding a filled cookie sheet into the oven. Spinning back in his direction, she froze. Pink painted her creamy cheeks, making her even more adorable.

"You really should keep the front door locked, if you're not open." Try as he might, Ryker couldn't keep the mirth from his voice.

Looking less than amused, she pulled her phone from the speakers and swiped the music away. "Maybe the other people in town know how to read the bakery's hours and respect them enough not to drop in early."

"Maybe those people aren't thinking about how you've got to carry a cartful of gingerbread down to the community center today. I thought I might be able to help. Am I forgiven?"

Emmie licked her pale, glossy lips and huffed. "I suppose. Kelly says I need to work on having a forgiving attitude and stop holding grudges. I guess she's right. I mean, for a Christian, forgiveness is part of the package, right?"

"Sure," Ryker agreed. "But I'm curious. What did Kelly do that begs for a forgive and forget attitude?"

"Not Kelly," she started before catching herself. Her smile was tight as she snatched a spatula from the table and began transferring cookies from a pan to a cooling rack.

Truth hit. Kelly was right. He'd hurt her. Good thing she'd given him a heads-up. After she scooped another cookie onto the cooling rack, he stilled her movement by placing his hands over hers. For a split second, he thought she'd shut him out completely. Then, she looked up at him.

"I'm so sorry, Emmie. I should have said good-bye when I left. If I'd known how badly it would make you feel, I would have."

"It doesn't matter."

The pain in her eyes told a different story. He couldn't begin to guess why his leaving hurt her so much, but it did. And he needed to make it right.

"It does. We were friends, and I shouldn't have let anything keep me from telling you good-bye. Even if it made things more difficult for me."

Emmie straightened and sucked in a deep breath. Her jaw was tight as hope of forgiveness fell away from her eyes, leaving a glare in its place.

"More difficult for you?" Her words were laced with

venom. "You broke my sister's heart, and what you were worried about is how difficult it was for you?"

Ryker tried to keep up with her train of thought, but it made no sense. "I think you may be confused."

Her palm smacked down on the table. "I'm confused? No. I'm perfectly clear. You broke my sister's heart and moved away without a backwards glance for any of us. Those years you returned to visit your parents, you made it clear. Not once did you stop by or grace us with anything more than a nod in passing. We no longer existed to you."

"I couldn't." As Ryker said the words, a sense of understanding came. She didn't know the truth. Whether Karen lied or Emmie assumed, she didn't have the whole story. "I can explain, if you'll only listen."

He hadn't meant to sound like an impatient parent speaking down to a young child. But the fire in Emmie's eyes told him he'd managed to nail the unwanted tone with perfection. The buzz of the timer saved him from getting burned. Emmie jammed her hands into her oven mitts and pulled the finished pan from the oven before turning back to the table. She barely spared him a glance as she set the pan down.

"I think I've heard enough."

"Emmie," he begged. "Please. I think there's been a misunderstanding. Let me explain."

This time she didn't look up. "I've heard enough. Please, just go."

Leaving was the last thing Ryker wanted to do. He finally had clarity on everything that went wrong between them, and she wouldn't give him a chance to make things right. He stood in indecision, but Emmie refused to acknowledge him.

Disappointment clogged his throat as he turned to go.

Chapter Eight

Emmie didn't look away from her gingerbread as she felt Ryker pause at the kitchen door.

"When you're ready to hear what I have to say, you know where to find me."

The words, spoken quietly and without judgment, brought the sting of tears to her eyes. Emmie bit her lip while attempting to hold them in until she felt him leave. There wasn't anything he could say to make the situation right. And as easily as Ryker Lehman could still make her legs turn to Christmas cranberry sauce with his perfect smile, Emmie needed to remember that.

"You can do this," she whispered, rearranging the gingerbread on the rack.

"Do what?"

Emmie started, nearly crushing the cookie in her hand as Kelly's voice came from the doorway. She had to get a louder bell for her front door. When did people replace announcing themselves with scaring friends witless?

"You and Ryker!" she chided. "You're getting a giant jingle

bell necklace in your stocking this year. Maybe then you'll stop sneaking up on me."

"Speaking of Ryker, I saw him on my way in."

If Kelly was waiting for her to respond, she'd have better luck waiting up for Santa. Dealing with, thinking of, and talking about Ryker were off her to-do list for the day. She gave a noncommittal shrug and began boxing up the cooled cookies.

Kelly picked up one of the gingerbread men and looked at it thoughtfully before biting its head off.

"Hey! Those are for the decorating class!"

With an impish smile and challenge in her eyes, Kelly took another bite. "I think you'll have plenty. And it proves my best friend still has a voice. That means the storm cloud I saw hanging over Ryker probably developed in this very room. What happened?"

"I don't want to talk about it." Her tone left no room for argument. She glanced at the clock on the wall. "I need to load up before Ann arrives to open the store for me while I get everything over to the community center."

Kelly's lips twisted in the way Emmie knew meant they would revisit the conversation. But she let it drop for now, giving Emmie enough time to figure out what she wanted to share and what she should keep to herself.

"Then grab your coat, and let's get going," Kelly conceded. "My car is out front. Do you want me to load cookies or icing and sprinkles?"

"Cookies, please." Emmie slipped into her coat and grabbed the plastic bin she'd already filled with bags of icing for everyone to enjoy.

RYKER TRIED to stay unobtrusive as Emmie led the gingerbread decorating class. With a slideshow of professionally decorated cookies in a variety of shapes projected on the plain, white wall behind her, she talked about how each pattern was made. She spouted tips and tricks designed to help each participant create a cookie to wow the judges.

"Now, it's your turn," Emmie explained. "Remember, we've got plenty of icing. If you're not sure about something, practice it first. Since I'm one of the judges, I've got to scoot for the next hour while you decorate. If you have any issues or need any help, Gingerbread Festival Elf Kelly will be around."

Tutorial and contest instructions given, Emmie paused to speak with Kelly. When they looked Ryker's way, he quickly shifted his gaze to the room of contestants and began collecting the shots he needed. With camera poised and ready, he scanned the room, ending as innocently as possible in the area he'd seen Emmie and Kelly.

A sliver of light disappeared as the side door to the center closed behind Emmie. Kelly, however, was headed in his direction. He let his camera rest on his chest as he mentally prepped himself for what he assumed would be an onslaught from Emmie's best friend. If he were smart, he'd duck out much like Emmie had done and avoid a possible public spectacle.

But he couldn't spend the next few days avoiding people. He belonged in New Kuchenbrünn as much as the next guy, even if he was leaving after the festival.

"Kelly." He acknowledged her with a nod.

"Seeing how my best friend is refusing to fill in the blanks for me," she jumped into the conversation he dreaded without preamble, "how about you tell me what happened this morning."

Ryker breathed in deep. The comforting scent of

gingerbread and sweet icing filling the air stood in contrast to the knot of discomfort taking residence in his stomach. He fiddled with his camera strap as a list of possible excuses crossed his mind. Dismissing them, he opted for the truth. It was best, though rarely easy.

"Please don't put me in this position," he requested. "If Emmie doesn't want it talked about, should I really be the one to lay it all out?"

Kelly nodded. "I can respect that. Tell me one thing, and I'll leave you alone. Did you do something to upset her?"

"I didn't mean to if I did." Stubble scratched his palm as he rubbed his hand over his chin with a sigh. Unintended emotional injury seemed to fill their reunion, but understanding the issue didn't seem to help rectify it. "I still don't want to get into details, but I'll say this, I'm pretty sure a misunderstanding is adding fuel to a fire that should never have been lit."

"You two are impossible." Kelly gave a cheesy grin. "Just explain it to her and get this out of the way."

It sounded so easy. Just explain it. If only. Ryker hoped his silence simultaneously conveyed his agreement with her recommendation and the impossibility of taking it.

Kelly's look of superiority at her brilliant suggestion faded to one of confusion before her eyes widened with realization. "Oh."

"Yeah."

"Um, well." Kelly's mouth twisted as she bit the inside of her cheek. "I guess I should let you get back to work." She glanced around the room. "Besides, I told Emmie I'd make sure no one had any problems doing their decorating."

What a mess. If only Emmie would give him a chance to explain, he felt certain it would wrap up Project Win Over

Emmie with a bow on top. They might even come out of this visit friends. Or more than friends?

Ryker shook his head, dislodging the idea, before lifting his camera to capture more of the gingerbread decorating contest. After the festival, he was leaving New Kuchenbrünn. It didn't matter that Emmie's presence raised his heart rate every time she stepped into his space. He might win her over, but neither was in a place to give or take more than friendship.

Chapter Nine

Emmie tossed the free end of her scarf over her shoulder. More than the softness of the yarn against her neck, she craved the warmth it brought as she and Kelly walked down the sidewalk toward First Baptist's live nativity.

"The planning committee was pleased with the number of entrants we had in the gingerbread decorating contest." Kelly rubbed her hands up and down her arms. "Thanks for being one of the judges again this year."

"I'm always up for judging the decorations. Just don't ask me to judge the baking contest."

Kelly chuckled. "Or enter the gingerbread eating contest?"

"Ugh." Emmie stuck out her tongue in a fake gag. "Never. I repeat, never again, will I participate in that monstrosity of a contest."

Looping her arm through Emmie's, Kelly nudged her with her shoulder as they walked. "I promise I would never ask you to."

"Good. We can remain friends," Emmie said with a nod. "I'd hate to have to remove your photo from my fridge."

Kelly bit her bottom lip so quickly, Emmie almost missed it. "Speaking of photos."

"I'd rather we didn't." Emmie motioned toward a camel tethered to a nearby post. "Look at that. They added a camel this year."

"Emmie."

"But be careful. Camels spit."

A cloud puffed from Kelly's lips with her sigh. "Have it your way."

They continued past the sheep and donkeys, secured far enough from the camel to keep nervous animals from disrupting the peace of the nativity. While children oohed and aahed at the animals, Emmie and Kelly chose to pause in front of the first of several yard signs, each offering a verse of prophecy highlighting Jesus' birth.

As they moved down the path, the scriptures changed to set the stage for the nativity. The angel's announcement to Mary and Joseph gave way to Mary's praise song before moving to scriptures declaring the census and the young couple's travel to Bethlehem.

"Do not be afraid!" An angel clad in white with a sparkling gold halo cried out as they neared. "I bring you good tidings of great joy which will be to all people."

As he finished his announcement, a dozen angels gathered behind him praised in unison. "Glory to God in the highest, And on earth peace, goodwill toward men!"

The thought warmed Emmie from the inside.

"I've always loved that part," she said quietly to Kelly as they neared the stable. "Peace on earth and goodwill to men."

They stood in silence before the stable. Above it, suspended from a slender pole, a giant star lit up the dark sky. Separate strings of twinkling lights illuminated a path from the star's base to the top of the simple wooden structure.

Sitting serenely on a bale of hay, Mary cuddled her newborn with Joseph standing behind her. His hand rested on her shoulder. Emmie could imagine the strength and comfort the mother of Jesus would have experienced in that single act. A donkey stood behind the holy family, nestled in the back corner of the shed. Shepherds bowed beside the manger while a single sheep lay in front of it. Wise men draped in purple and gold robes stood inside the far edge of the stable, their elaborate gifts held reverently in their hands.

Hidden speakers allowed the strains of "God with Us" by All Sons and Daughters to replace angel song, growing louder as Emmie and Kelly reluctantly moved away from the manger scene. The path winding toward the church's fellowship hall was lined with scriptures clarifying man's need for forgiveness and God's provision of the way.

With the music pouring over her, Emmie considered words from Isaiah declaring her sin as scarlet but promising Jesus' life and death meant God could make them white as the snow glistening in the starlight under her feet. Farther down the path, 1 John assured her of God's forgiveness when she confessed the sins she carried.

Emmie moved to the final sign. "For I will be merciful toward their iniquities, and I will remember their sins no more." Her eyes closed and she breathed the truth of the verse from Hebrews into her heart. As if forgiveness and eternal life were not enough, God chose never to hold her sins against her. When she failed over and over at the simplest acts of obedience, God wouldn't add it to her previous infractions and declare her over the limit of forgiveness.

"Thank you, Father," she whispered her praise before she and Kelly joined other guests in the fellowship hall.

Kelly set a cup of cocoa on the table. "Here you go. Hot

cocoa. Sprinkle of cinnamon. Dollop of whipped cream. Just the way you like it."

"And for you." Emmie nudged a holly-edged paper plate of sweets toward the empty seat Kelly would occupy.

Kelly plopped down and licked her lips. "Yum. You know I can't resist good fudge."

Emmie laughed as Kelly popped a bite size piece of the creamy confection into her mouth. "Fudge. Or puppy chow because there's nothing better than crunchy, chocolaty, peanut butter goodness. Or sugar cookies. You can't say no to the classics. Or, really, anything with sugar in it."

"There's nothing wrong with perfect little sweet things in our lives."

Though the comment was flippant, Emmie couldn't argue it contained a truth that moved well beyond sweet calories that inched up bathroom scales. The night's display was proof enough.

"You're right," she conceded. "Especially on nights like tonight, when I'm reminded so clearly of God's love for me. God with us for the sole purpose of giving us forgiveness is the definition of sweet perfection, even if it's not a little thing."

Emmie lifted her cup of cocoa to her lips and took a tentative sip. Rich, creamy, and hot enough to scald. She'd have to take it slow. Movement outside a nearby window drew her attention. She fought to keep a huff at bay when she realized the distraction was Ryker trying to get the best possible shots of the scenes outside.

Tonight wasn't about Ryker. She returned her focus to Kelly, who'd followed her gaze. Emmie blew a cooling breath across the top of her cocoa. It was enough to bring Kelly's attention back to the table.

"You know," Kelly began hesitantly, "forgiveness isn't just about us and God."

Emmie flashed her a warning look.

"I know you don't want to hear it." Kelly managed a weak smile begging lenience. "And I respect that. I really do. But it's time, Emmie. You've got to deal with this." Her hand was warm as she laid it on top of Emmie's. "Seriously. You almost had me convinced you'd moved past everything. But with Ryker back, I can see the truth. You haven't forgiven him."

Emmie raised her hands to her side and frowned. "Sure, I have. Just because I'm protecting myself from getting hurt doesn't mean I've not forgiven."

The tilt of Kelly's head and the pity she saw in her eyes were too much. Emmie stared at her cup. She knew Kelly wanted her to look up. That was why their table was a pocket of silence in a room filled with Christmas cheer. Well, she would have to deal with disappointment.

"That's not true," Kelly stated, her voice full of compassion. "It could be, but in this case it's not. You and I both know it. Ryker isn't some repeat offender you keep getting duped by and need to proceed cautiously with. You're not working to rebuild trust after having forgiven him. You're holding a grudge, plain and simple. He hurt Karen. He hurt you. And you have held onto it for fifteen years."

Emmie blinked against the sudden threat of tears. "No. I've forgiven him. I did it right after he left."

"You may have said the words. But forgiveness isn't often a once and done kind of thing. You never surrendered your want for whatever you believe justice would be in this scenario. You kept his wrong right there beside you, tucked away for the day he returned. Now he's back, and you've pulled the hurt out and piled new ones on top of it. It's a grudge. And this wall of hurts you're erecting doesn't just stand between you and Ryker. It could also come between you and God."

"But he hurt Karen. He hurt me. Don't you think that matters? I'm the victim here, not Ryker."

As Kelly moved the empty cup from Emmie's hands and took them in her own, Emmie chanced a glance at her friend. A small, sad smile graced her lips.

"You were the victim, but the event is over and done," Kelly explained. "When it happened, God wanted to heal the hurt and grow something good in your life from the experience. He wanted you to have victory over the pain. By holding on to this grudge, by not forgiving, you've allowed your hurt to keep you prisoner all these years. Aren't you ready to deal with this and let God change you from victim to victorious?"

Was it true? Had she allowed this hurt to hold her back from all God wanted for her? Emmie stared past Kelly, out the window. The glow from the stable's star beckoned, inviting her to the manger.

"Do you mind if we talk later?" She slipped back into the wool coat she'd draped across the back of her chair.

"Sure." Kelly nodded. "I'll talk to you later."

"I'm not ignoring you. I promise. There's something I feel like I need to do."

Chapter Ten

Emmie stood outside the stable drinking in the nativity scene. Peace filled the atmosphere. But she knew for baby Jesus, the peace would not last long, at least not in the literal sense. His parents would doubt him, his friends would disappoint him, the people would misunderstand what he stood for, and those who claimed to know God best would seek to steal his life.

Why did Jesus submit Himself to that? For the creation God loved so much. To offer them forgiveness and salvage the relationship, even from his place on the cross.

"Father God. What have I done?" The prayer flowed from her lips in a whisper only she could hear. "I've refused to give up this hurt for so long. Why? It never did anything good for me. But You wanted to, and in refusing to forgive I wouldn't let You. Help me let go."

"Are you okay?" The familiar male voice was filled with concern.

Emmie rubbed gloved hands over her cheeks to remove

tears she hadn't noticed until Ryker broke into her prayer. She managed something resembling a smile and nodded.

Uncertainty filled his eyes. His lips parted, but he closed them again without saying anything. Who could blame him for his hesitance? Her own stubbornness caused it.

"I'll leave you alone then." Ryker turned toward the fellowship hall.

"Ryker?" Emmie forced herself to speak despite the tightness in her chest.

He turned back to her. Even with the shadows cast in their direction from the star lighting the manger scene, both confusion and yearning were evident in Ryker's expression. He remained silent, appraising her with a stirring look she'd seen so often in the past. If she could clearly see them, his brown eyes would be begging permission to enter the deep places of her soul. Even after all she'd done to hold her hurts against him, he was still there waiting to be a friend.

"Can we go someplace and talk?"

"I'd like that." The faintest of smiles accompanied his quiet answer. "How about the Kringle Cup? I'll pack up my gear and meet you there."

She shook her head. "How about Sugar and Spice? I know the owner, and I think I can get her to let us in, even after hours."

Too cliché to be funny, her comment made Ryker chuckle anyway. "I'll meet you there."

WITH MOST OF the businesses in the area locked up for the evening, Ryker had no problems finding a place to park in front of Sugar and Spice. Though not as brightly lit as it usually was, a soft glow emanated from the window of the little bakery.

Emmie, however, was nowhere to be seen. Ryker stepped inside, unsure whether he should call out or not. The quiet tinkling of the bells Emmie placed on the door never seemed to alert her of anyone's presence in the shop if she was in the back.

"Thanks for coming, Ryker."

Ryker sucked in a breath at the unexpected voice coming from his left and turned toward it. When he didn't see her through the window, he'd assumed Emmie was in the kitchen. He'd forgotten about the little nook with only a couple of tables sitting out of view of the rest of the shop, where she waited for him.

"Of course I came."

He took the empty chair across from her and pointed to the steaming cup sitting on the table in front of it. "Is this for me?"

"Hot cocoa. My mom's old recipe. I wasn't sure if you still liked it, but I didn't think either of us needed a coffee-sized dose of caffeine at this hour."

Just as the cup reached his lips, Ryker paused to inhale the rich scent before taking a sip. Nothing beat homemade hot cocoa, but Emmie must have had a case of nerves to whip up a batch while he was packing up and driving over. He didn't think he'd been far behind her.

"This is perfect. Thank you."

Emmie's lips twisted to the side. Her shoulders rose with a deep breath. She mindlessly turned her cup on the table. "I guess you're wondering why I asked you here?"

He lifted one shoulder and took another drink before answering. "I figure you'll tell me eventually."

Fidgeting in her chair, Emmie looked everywhere but at him. Her discomfort was palpable. Despite the frustration of their recent encounters, Ryker wanted to bring her some measure of peace.

"It's okay, Emmie. It's just you and me. We can sit here as long as you like."

She met his gaze and swallowed. "I'm ready."

With a silent nod, he waited. She didn't speak, but there was an expectant look on her face. Ryker frowned. Was he supposed to understand it? What was he missing?

"Ready for what?" He hated asking, but if there was another way to find out, he was clueless.

"I'm ready to hear your side of what happened when you left. To me, it's simple. You broke my sister's heart and left without even a good-bye to me. I was fifteen, Ryker. I know you were Karen's boyfriend, but I'd thought we were pretty close friends. You treated me like I didn't even matter, and it hurt." Her voice intensified with each sentence until she suddenly stopped speaking. Her eyes slid shut as she took a deep, slow breath.

Sensing she wasn't through, Ryker stayed quiet.

The pain she'd carried was evident when she looked at him again. Ryker suppressed a groan. All this time, and she'd held onto hurt he'd never intended. The thought caused a tightness in his chest. How many times had he returned to New Kuchenbrünn those first few years? How easy would it have been to seek her out and ease her hurt?

He opened his mouth to apologize.

A raised hand cut him off. Emmie had more to say.

"Honestly, it still hurts. But apparently, God wants to use this Christmas and your return for the festival to start lessening that for me. I'm choosing to forgive and let go. The first step is allowing you to tell me whatever it is you wanted to say last time we spoke."

Ryker squashed the desire to argue there was no reason he needed her forgiveness. But did he? Hadn't God just shown him her pain and how he could have eased it before it got to this point? He focused on that in an effort to keep his motivation for sharing his side of the story in the right place.

"I'm not sure what Karen told you about us."

"She didn't," Emmie said. "She went to her room after you left and shut the door in my face. I sat in my room and listened to her cry. I'd never heard her so upset. I tried to ask her about it. All she said was it was over and we weren't going to talk about it again."

Ryker smiled. "That sounds like Karen. Large and in charge. And I understand how it looks, but I didn't break up with her. I was going away for school, and she was, too, but to a different state than I was. I told her we could make it work, but she refused. She wanted normal college experiences with someone by her side, not hours away. Three years of dating were over, just like that."

"But then, why didn't you say good-bye?"

Emmie's confused pout was heartbreaking and adorable at the same time. Karen aside, Ryker sensed this was the real crux of the matter. Without Karen filling in the blanks for her, Emmie had nothing but his absence to color her perception of the events.

"I wanted to. Your family was family to me. And you're right. You may have started off Karen's little sister, but by the time I left for school, I didn't see it that way. You were my friend."

"Then, why didn't you?"

"Karen didn't want me around," he explained. "She told me not to come by and not to call. No chances for me to plead my case one last time. She wanted a clean break, and I gave it to her."

Wanting to give her a moment to digest this new information, Ryker gathered their empty cups and tossed them in the garbage can then sat back down. Everything he'd said was true, but there was more to say.

"I'm not blaming Karen."

"Really? It kind of sounds like it." Though her tone wasn't angry, there was an edge to it that raised his hackles.

Lord, help me keep my cool here. There's already been too many misunderstandings and disagreements.

He ran a hand through his hair as he considered his answer. "What I've shared is all true, but it doesn't absolve me of my responsibility. You and I were friends—in some ways we had more in common than me and Karen. I didn't have to let her decide whether I could say good-bye or not. I was angry, hurt. And I was a dumb kid who should've known better. Will you forgive me?"

Tears flowed down Emmie's cheeks. How long had she waited to hear those words from him? This evening had given her a lot to deal with. Ryker took her hands in his as he stood. Moving around the small table, he gently tugged her to her feet before letting go of her hands to slip his arms around her.

As her forehead rested against his chest, Ryker held her, an arm around her waist and the other stroking her long, soft hair. Seeing the hurt his earlier leaving caused, Ryker determined when he left this time, he'd make sure he said good-bye. Why did the thought of leaving start a pain in his chest, where Emmie's head rested?

He'd come to do a job. Like any other job, he would complete it and go back home. Only, his return to his hometown left his current place of residence feeling like a poor imposter.

Continuing to cradle Emmie in his arms, Ryker looked up in silent prayer. *Lord, when will these feelings pass?* They had to over time. New Kuchenbrünn's draw on him would fade. He and Emmie would part friends, maybe even stay in touch. Life would return to normal.

Emmie's muffled voice cut into his musings, but he couldn't tell what she'd said. He loosened his hold, and she stepped from his arms. He fought the urge to pull her back against him, knowing they had more to talk about.

"I missed what you said."

A tempting rose shade filled her cheeks as she sat back down. "You don't need my forgiveness."

"Yes, I do. I let my youthful pride keep me from saying good-bye, and I hurt a friend I cared very much about. Will you forgive me?"

"I'd like to bargain with you and say I'll forgive you, if you forgive me. But that's not how forgiveness works, is it? So, yes, I forgive you."

"Thank you."

She licked her lips. "But I also need to ask your forgiveness. I've held onto the pain of you leaving for far too long. I let bitterness take root in my heart, and I didn't even realize I was doing it. I can't imagine what I've missed tending the poisonous plant. And I held things against you that you didn't even do. Can you forgive me?"

"Yes." He didn't hesitate. "Now, how should we celebrate this new beginning? How about some gingerbread?"

His attempt to lighten the mood worked wonderfully. Emmie glared at him from across the table, but there was laughter hiding in her eyes.

"I don't think so," she flatly answered. "Besides, I have a long day tomorrow. I need to get home and get some sleep."

He stood and helped her into her coat. A comforting scent of vanilla caught his attention. It figured a baker would lean toward the warm fragrance. Spicy would work too, but not for

Emmie. Her dislike of gingerbread would probably keep her from that path.

"Was it only the Unfortunate Incident that made you dislike gingerbread?"

If she was surprised by his question, she didn't show it. She didn't even pause as she locked the bakery door behind them.

"I never really liked it before then. I just didn't loathe it."

Ryker stared at her in confusion. "If you didn't like it, why did you join the gingerbread eating contest?"

"I overheard you and Tommy talking about how he won the year before." Emmie's cheeks practically glowed. "You kept going on about how awesome the contest and his win was."

Her eyes widened as she looked at him with a silent "there you have it." He knew she expected him to understand, but he didn't. Whatever was so clear to her was completely lost on him.

"So?"

She shook her head at him and walked to her car. Opening the door, she started to get in but paused. Ryker hadn't moved, and he hadn't figured out the meaning to her cryptic message. He silently pleaded for pity. She must have understood, because she smiled.

"Someone winning the competition got your attention. You were impressed. Karen's boyfriend or not, you had all of my thirteen-year-old attention, and I wanted nothing more than to have yours." She paused to let her admission sink in. "I guess I got it. Just not the way I'd hoped."

Without waiting for a response, Emmie ducked into her car and started it up. Ryker watched as she pulled away. This whole night was full of the unexpected. When they began their conversation, he'd assumed the revelation of their misunderstanding would be the biggest surprise of the night.

But Emmie had just casually admitted to having a crush on

him. At least he was pretty sure that's what she meant. Of course, she admitted to having one seventeen years ago. That didn't mean she felt the same way now. She hadn't even indicated she'd still nursed the crush two years later when he left, just that she'd been hurt by his silence.

Like a strange phantom pain, the feel of her in his arms plagued him, and he ached to have her there again. With their friendship moving back onto solid ground, would she be open to exploring something deeper?

Ryker shoved the thought from his mind. It didn't matter if she were open. He was here for a job. It wouldn't be fair to start something he couldn't finish.

Project Win Over Emmie was a success. They were finally able to put the past behind them and start moving toward the close friendship they'd had before. That's what was important. If he reminded himself enough, maybe his heart would believe it.

Chapter Eleven

K elly's mouth dropped open. "You told Ryker about
your crush? What happened? Did he take you in his
arms and kiss you silly?"

Emmie fumbled her spatula and dropped it on the floor.
"What?"

Scooping it up from the tile, she smacked her elbow on the
counter. She rubbed the sore spot before tossing the
contaminated spatula in the sink.

"No. Of course not. Have you lost your mind? Ryker
kissing me?" The words squeaked past her lips. She cleared her
throat. "Why on earth would he do something like that?" A
frantic shake of her head accompanied the rambling questions.

Snatching a new spatula from a drawer, Emmie returned to
her dough. The thought of Ryker kissing her threatened to
weaken her knees. Instead, she concentrated the buzz of energy
surging through her into mixing her ingredients with more
focus and vigor than necessary, before forcing herself to slow
down. No sense in risking flat, crisp cookies.

Kelly plopped down on a stool across from Emmie's

workspace. "Oh, I don't know. Maybe because when the super-cute boy finds himself attracted to the beautiful and surprisingly available girl in all the movies, they share an unexpected kiss, melting even the coldest of hearts."

Emmie snorted. "Yeah, well, this isn't the movies, and I'm definitely not the leading lady type."

"I notice you didn't say anything about the leading man in our story."

It would be better to acknowledge the truth. Kelly had been able to see through her since they were kids.

"I'll admit it. The man still has it, maybe even more so now than when he left." Emmie tried to sound as disinterested as possible. Not an easy task. "And finding out I'd been holding things against him when they weren't his fault? I'm glad I didn't know when he arrived. It's the only thing that kept me from falling completely."

"Did you trip again?" Ryker's voice entered the kitchen right as he appeared.

Emmie shot a frantic look at Kelly. How much had he heard? Kelly shrugged.

"You may be an amazing baker, but you're the most accident-prone woman I've ever met."

Good. He was clueless and would remain so if she had anything to say about it.

Kelly's chuckle sounded forced. "Yep. That's our girl. Always getting tripped up."

Emmie narrowed her eyes and pursed her lips at Kelly, unamused by the double meaning in her words. Her discomfort brought a real chuckle from Kelly.

"It's been fun." Kelly hopped off her seat. "But I have to get back to work. The Gingerbread Festival doesn't coordinate itself."

The pleasure Kelly took in setting her up and then leaving

was written all over her face. Emmie squelched the urge to fling cookie dough at her in answer to the hasty retreat. One day, their roles would be reversed, and Emmie would enjoy every minute of discomfort Kelly faced.

"I hope I didn't run her off." Ryker took Kelly's vacated stool.

If only he knew. "No. I don't think so. Tonight is the Cookies for Kids event. Since it's the town's fundraiser to supply families in need with everything from food to presents for Christmas, Kelly takes the responsibility seriously."

"It's a worthy cause."

"Yes, it is," Emmie agreed. "It's also why I was here before dawn preparing a day's worth of cookies and pastries needed for the bakery, and why I'm now up to my armpits in gingerbread cookie dough, yet again."

Ryker cringed. "Ew. Not sure I'd put that description in any of the promotional materials."

"True." Emmie giggled. "It's not very appetizing, but then again, neither is gingerbread."

"Only to you."

Warmth filled her cheeks. They weren't going to revisit that conversation. She'd embarrassed herself enough, admitting her teenage crush. Discussing it would only increase her chances of slipping up and letting Ryker know his return had reignited the flame.

"Did you need something?" Unintended impatience laced her tone. She pointed her spatula at the camera hanging around his neck like an oversized pendant. "I mean, are you here to get photos for the promo materials?"

He shook his head as he ran a hand through his hair. "Not really. I'll get photos of the people decorating their plates of cookies at the event tonight. I'll probably get some shots of the donations they give. And I'll need some of the firefighters and cops, when they use the funds to shop for and deliver items to the families. It's a great event."

"It shows the heart of our little town." Emmie pulled a pan of gingerbread from the oven and set it aside to cool. "And every family ends up with a dozen cookies to take home and a dozen to share with others during our caroling event for their donations."

"Does anyone help you with the baking?"

"Not really, but I don't mind. It's my contribution to the fundraiser."

He waggled a finger in her direction. "But it does keep you from enjoying some of the other festival offerings. I didn't see you at the scavenger hunt yesterday, or the gingerbread relay races yesterday afternoon."

Emmie hoped her lazy shrug hid the flurries swirling inside her—he'd been looking for her. Head down, she busied herself with cutting more gingerbread men from dough rolled out on the table. If she kept her attention on her work, Ryker might miss his effect on her.

"I was swamped all day, but I dutifully handed out gingerbread man lollipops every time someone came into the bakery for the scavenger hunt. Believe it or not, my bakery's daily needs do not take a vacation when the festival begins."

"Hmmm." He frowned at her. "I never thought about it, but you must not get to enjoy much of the festival with all that baking."

"The first few days of the festival, I'm pretty busy." She paused long enough to slide another batch of cookies in the oven. "I get to enjoy the tree lighting and the nativity as an attendee. Even though I'm there, the gingerbread decorating contest is more work than pleasure."

Ryker's look of disappointment was sweet, spreading more warmth through her than her ovens. Did her festival days sound that bad? The volunteer hours did take a lot of her time, but she enjoyed giving back to the town she loved, even if it was in the shape of gingerbread men. And she did get to have fun too.

"But after the Cookies for Kids event, I'm back to my regular bakery schedule. Even though I don't have an outdoor booth or keep later hours, the customer flow is pretty steady during the Christkindlesmarkt days."

Ryker shifted on the stool and fidgeted with his camera strap. "Would you want to walk with me during the caroling tonight?"

"I don't usually go caroling."

Resignation flashed in his eyes so quickly Emmie almost missed it. Was he asking as a friend? Or was there something more to his request? No. That couldn't be it.

The timer beeped behind her. Emmie turned to shut it off and remove the last pan of cookies from the oven. She didn't realize her mistake until too late.

"Owww!" she cried as she let the hot metal pan drop back onto the oven rack. She shook her burned hand, glaring at the unused oven mitts on the counter.

"Emmie!" Ryker jumped from the stool and stood in front of her in seconds. "Are you okay?"

Blinking back tears, she looked at the injured digits. Already, her fingertips were starting to blister.

"I'm fine," she muttered through clenched teeth. She hurried to the sink and turned on the cool water, shoving her hand under the tepid flow. Noise behind her drew her attention. Turning, she saw Ryker placing the pan of cookies on a hot mat to cool. After tossing the oven mitts on the counter, he turned the oven off.

"How long should I wait before I move the cookies to a cooling rack?"

Emmie swiped a tear from her cheek with her free hand. "I usually wait a minute or two, but go ahead and get them transferred. Thank you."

Focusing her attention on the water pouring over her hand helped keep the tears at bay. If she were alone, she wouldn't have thought twice about letting them flow. But movement at the counter behind her reminded her she was not by herself. She sucked in a shaky breath.

She stiffened as Ryker's hands cupped her shoulders. When had he come close? The man was like a ninja, always moving into her space with surprising stealth. The gentle rub up and down her arms undid her. Tears flowed freely down her cheeks.

Taking care to avoid moving her hand from the water, he turned her to face him. Emmie always thought brown eyes a dull, cool color, but Ryker's were warm, brimming with concern.

"Do we need to go to the urgent care clinic?" His voice was soft and serious.

Emmie pulled her hand from the water. Examining it, she found a majority of the injured area was angry red. Blisters forming on a couple of the fingertips would create issues for her in the coming days. Though worse than she'd experienced before, she'd treated plenty of mild second degree burns through the years.

She shook her head, thrusting her throbbing hand back under the flow of water. "No. It's nothing I can't take care of here."

"Are you sure?"

A new lump formed in her throat. She nodded. Why now, when she was so busy? How would she get everything done one-handed? Failing in her festival duties was not an option.

Disappointment and frustration welled up until more tears released the pressure.

Ryker's arms slipped from her shoulders to rest across her back, pulling her in against his chest. For the second time in as many days, Ryker embraced her. And for the second time, Emmie allowed herself to soak in the comfort he offered.

The throbbing in her hand subsided along with her tears. Regret pulsed through Emmie as she stepped out of his arms.

"I...I need to, uh, I need to get back to work." She shut off the faucet.

"No," Ryker countered. "You need to take care of your hand. Bandage it or whatever you need to do to it. I'll be right back. Don't touch those cookies. Understand?"

Leaving no time to argue, he headed out the door. Emmie planted herself on a stool and rested her hand, palm up, on her thigh. Better to let it air dry. She glanced at the cookies cooling on racks on every counter space, ready for packaging.

"Don't touch those cookies," she whined in poor mimicry of Ryker. She lifted her chin. "It's my bakery. I'll do as I please."

Pain shot up her hand as she tried to bend her fingers. Opening them again eased the sharpness, but a throb remained.

"And what I want to do right now is wait for Ryker to get back."

Chapter Twelve

R yker held the door for Kelly. Finding her was easy. With the Cookies for Kids event taking place at the community center, he knew she'd be there. After he explained the situation, she'd dropped everything to follow him back to Sugar and Spice.

"Girl, why am I not surprised?" She asked as she stepped into the kitchen before Ryker had made it halfway across the front room of bakery. Her voice carried through the door swinging shut behind her. "It's one predicament after another with you. Do we need to bubble wrap you?"

Calling in reinforcements could have landed him in a world of trouble, but the relaxed smile on Emmie's face when he entered the kitchen assured him the decision was right, whether she decided to put up a fuss or not.

"Ryker shouldn't have asked you to come."

And there was the fuss.

"Give me a little bit, and I'll be perfectly fine." Emmie held up her hand. "It's a burn. I've had them before."

Hip slack and resting against the counter, Kelly folded her

arms across her chest and nodded to the cookie-laden kitchen. "Fine. Pack up the cookies."

Emmie glared and picked up a delivery box with her uninjured hand. "See?"

"Sure," Kelly answered. "Now, how about you fill the box with cookies. One good hand can't hold the box and pack it at the same time."

A sly smile twisted Emmie's lips. Setting the box on the counter, she held the lid open with the forearm of her injured hand and used her good one to pick up cookies. It was a passable solution, until she had to reach far enough for a cookie that her arm slipped from the box lid. In her haste to reopen it, she inadvertently squeezed her good hand, crushing the cookie she held.

A low growl of frustration rumbled as she deposited the broken cookie in the waste basket. Emmie marched to the nearby stool and plopped down on it.

"Fine. You win, even though I could do it. I just don't have time to go so slow."

Without so much as an I-told-you-so, Kelly packed the box, sealing it with a Sugar and Spice logo sticker. As she retrieved the next empty box, Ryker found himself under Kelly's scrutiny.

"Make yourself useful," she directed. "Wash your hands and put on gloves. Two dozen cookies to a box."

It was not a request. Ryker washed up, put on the vinyl gloves, and reached for a box. After several minutes of silent filling, he left his assigned station. Kelly and Emmie tracked his movements across the room.

"I'm sorry, but we're packing cookies, not prepping for war. Let's liven things up."

As he turned on the radio, the bouncy sounds of Michael Bublé singing "Christmas (Baby Please Come Home)" filled the room.

Singing along, he grabbed Emmie's good hand, pulling her from where she perched on the stool. Carefully avoiding her injured fingers, he slid his hand around her waist pulling her close before dancing her around the work area in time to the music. His exaggerated movements and enthusiastic singing drew not only a smile but laughter as well.

He deposited her back on her seat and shuffle-stepped his way back to the counter, then picked up an empty box. With the container as his new partner, he did a quick spin, holding it high, before resuming his work. Pleasure zinged through him as Emmie giggled and Kelly shook her head, grinning from ear to ear. Ryker even noticed a little bouncing and swaying going on as she packed her box.

With the silence dispelled, it didn't take long for chatter, singing, and laughter to take its place. How long had it been since he'd enjoyed himself like this? The thought caught Ryker short. He ducked his head as he continued placing cookies in his box.

It wasn't like his life in North Carolina was horrible. He had a good church family to worship with and friends, though he tended to be the odd man out. While the rest of his friends were getting married and starting families, he suffered through dates he knew within the first five minutes were going nowhere. Hanging out with the gang left him feeling like a third wheel. Recently he'd started taking on more work as an excuse to bow out of their gatherings.

Admitting it cost him nothing but pride. Still, Ryker couldn't deny life in New Kuchenbrünn fit. People waved or stopped him to chat every time he walked down the street. From the time he arrived, he'd slipped into his old life effortlessly.

Reconnecting with Emmie was definitely another plus.

She'd gone from being his girlfriend's little sister to being his friend. He enjoyed spending time with her. And since they'd cleared up the misunderstandings about the past, nothing stood in the way of growing their friendship.

Emmie's laughter interrupted his thoughts. He glanced up from the box he was working on. The song had switched to "The Twelve Days of Christmas," and Kelly was giving her performance a dramatic flair. Five golden rings took on an operatic quality as she thrust her hand high in the air and bellowed out the words.

Joy sparkled in Emmie's blue eyes. Air rushed from his lungs when she turned her gaze on him. Gorgeous. Sitting in her kitchen, letting herself enjoy the moment, she looked completely relaxed. It was the Emmie he remembered from before he'd messed things up so badly. And if he had any say in it, this Emmie would be here to stay.

"Looks like you're having fun," he commented before his dazed stare could make the situation awkward. "Maybe going to get Kelly wasn't such a bad idea after all?"

She crossed her eyes and stuck out her tongue at him. "Whatever, Mr. Smartypants. I can admit when I'm wrong."

"Maybe," Kelly interrupted as she closed the lid on the last box, "next year you can bypass the injury but still ask for help with this kind of thing. You take on too much."

"Everyone else is just as busy as me. I couldn't ask them to help."

Kelly huffed. "We can spare a few minutes to help you pack up the gingerbread we're all going to use. You can count on me."

"Me too," Ryker offered.

Both women frowned at him.

"I'm not sure how much help you'll be in North Carolina," Emmie said matter-of- factly. "And I doubt the town will need to hire a photographer for next year's festival."

Did he detect a note of disappointment in her voice? Or did he only hope it was there, matching the one lodged firmly in his chest?

"I guess I got caught up in the moment," he admitted. "But enough of that. You two hold the doors, and I'll get these boxes loaded into the delivery van."

Though Emmie and Kelly talked back and forth to each other while they held the doors for him, Ryker kept to himself as he carried box after box to the waiting vehicle. While he hadn't thought it through before offering to help at next year's event, even Emmie's correction didn't erase the idea.

Maybe it was time to start coming back to New Kuchenbrünn for the festival each year. The town might not hire him, but he could take time off. He could even photograph the festival pro bono to give the town a pictorial record of each year's event.

"Thank you both for your help." Emmie interrupted his internal planning session. "You may be right about getting volunteers each year. I don't think I've ever gotten all the cookies done and loaded this quickly."

"I'm driving." Kelly snatched the keys from Emmie and turned to Ryker. "You want a ride?"

He shook his head. "No, thank you."

"Suit yourself." She hopped into the driver's seat and shut the door.

Ryker waved as the van pulled away from the curb. He'd need to swing by the center later to capture the Cookies for Kids event. But first things first, he needed a walk to clear his mind.

As much as he wanted to tell Emmie he'd be back each year to help, something kept him from speaking the commitment into existence. Returning would keep him connected to the town.

He and Emmie might even end up closer friends than ever. The thought failed to bring optimism with it.

Friendship wasn't the only thing Ryker wanted growing between him and Emmie. And a once-a-year return wasn't enough to build a relationship on. But what was he supposed to do about it?

Chapter Thirteen

The tinkling of the bells on her door caused Emmie to pause in stocking the bakery display case. She smiled and glanced toward the entrance.

"Hey, girl." Kelly waved. "Did you get rested up last night?"

Emmie shrugged and continued placing the variety of sweets behind the glass. "I guess. I almost caved and went caroling, since you and Ryker helped me get my festival chores done early. But I needed a little breather."

"I understand. How's the hand, by the way?"

Holding it up for Kelly's inspection, Emmie gingerly flexed her fingers. "Definitely sore, but I'll make it. Without special orders or festival demands added to my daily baking, it's slow going but doable. How was caroling?"

"We had a good crowd. Everyone had fun." Kelly snatched a chocolate chip muffin from the tray and lifted it to her lips before lowering it again. "Except for maybe one person. He seemed kind of lost, like he was waiting for something ... or someone."

Emmie wouldn't take the bait. It would only feed Kelly's delusions. Nothing was happening between her and Ryker. So what if her teenage crush had been stoked until it was full-blown adult attraction? The fact that he was Ryker Lehmann only made him more desirable, but that didn't matter. He was leaving in a few days, and she wouldn't put her heart in harm's way this time.

"Be that way, then." Kelly shrugged. "I don't have a pony in this race. Doesn't matter to me at all that his mopey self will be at the main stage by the town tree for the Gingerbread Eating, Hot Cocoa, and Ugly Gingerbread Sweater Contests this afternoon. Or that he'll take photos of all the Little Miss Gingerbread contestants right after that."

"You're very informed for someone who says it doesn't matter," Emmie countered.

"I'm the festival coordinator. It's my job to know what's going on."

"Speaking of your all-important position, shouldn't you be out mingling with the festival goers and cheering on the contestants or something, instead of badgering me about my personal life?"

Kelly laughed. "Have it your way. I'll leave you to your sweets, for now. But I'll be back, and you'd better be ready to take my stellar advice."

"Whatever." Emmie shook her head.

As Kelly left, Emmie headed to the kitchen for her last tray of cookies and pastries for the display. Before the door could swing shut behind her, bells chiming signaled Kelly's return. Emmie grabbed the tray and started for the front of the bakery. Kelly's interference wasn't needed.

"While I appreciate your diligence," Emmie began as she pushed open the door and entered the room, "I refuse to abandon my bakery to go chasing after Ryker like some lovesick teenager. You might as well give up."

"Really? Because he wouldn't be opposed to it."

Emmie's head snapped up at the distinctly masculine voice.

"Ryker." His name came out a breathless whisper as heat flooded her cheeks.

Could this day get more embarrassing?

As the swinging door slammed against her backside, she lurched forward. Despite her quick reaction to balance the tray, several cookies and pastries fell to the floor.

Apparently, it could. Refusing to meet his gaze until her face no longer felt like the surface of the sun, Emmie glared at the mess.

Obviously, Murphy's Law had it in for her. There could be no other explanation.

"Here," Ryker said as he took the tray from her hand. "Let me help."

He placed the baked goods on the counter before squeezing past her into the kitchen. Emmie's shoulders sagged as she stepped around the mess to finish filling the display case. She could sweep up after the mindless task calmed her emotions.

Movement behind her alerted her to Ryker's return, but her attention remained on her task. Not even the swish of broom bristles collecting her wasted hard work into the dustpan gave her pause. Though, really, she should thank him. The situation wasn't his fault, and it definitely wasn't his to clean up.

"Thank you," she managed quietly.

Tray empty, she started past him for the kitchen. A gentle hand to her wrist stopped her retreat. She stared at the tray she held.

"I'm sorry." His thumb stroked the inside of her wrist. "I didn't mean to startle you. Or embarrass you. Or ruin your hard work."

"I know."

"I meant it, though." He gently tugged. "I wouldn't be opposed to you chasing after me. How did you put it? Like a lovesick teenager."

Her gaze flew to his, searching for signs he was making fun of her. Instead of humor, yearning tempted from the brown depths of his eyes. He was serious.

The realization should have made her giddy. Teenage Emmie dreamed of this day. Even now, she couldn't deny the attraction was there. And it was deeper than the physical. As they reconnected, they'd managed to clear out the past and find the friendship she thought would never be found again. Still.

"I can't," she began. "I can't do this right now."

She fled into the kitchen. The tangle of thoughts and emotions swirling inside her demanded she sit down and sort them out. She couldn't with Ryker there. Not even Kelly could help with this one.

"Go to the Gingerbread Ball with me on Saturday." Ryker interrupted the storm inside her from the doorway.

"I don't know if ..."

"Please. You don't have to answer now." He moved in front of her and waited until she looked at him. "Just promise me you'll think about it."

That she could do. "Fine. I'll consider it."

His smile was immediate. And bright enough to power a small country for a month. Emmie shook her head as she fought to keep her own grin under control. It wouldn't do to give him the idea that she would answer in his favor when she hadn't determined she would. But his smiles had always been able to coax out one of her own.

"I'll get out of here and let you think about it." Ryker headed back out the door.

Whether she wanted to or not, Emmie would be thinking

about the entire conversation. And it wouldn't stop until the festival ended and Ryker returned home. Maybe not even then.

Chapter Fourteen

"What do you mean, you're not going?"

Emmie glared at her friend. "Can you say it a little bit louder? I'm not sure they heard you over in Illinois."

"You're only being dramatic to avoid the issue." Kelly waved a hand toward the crowd. "Take a look. Nobody noticed. I could stand on the main stage and shout, 'Emmie isn't going to the Gingerbread Ball,' and everyone would simply go about their business."

A quick glance at the people milling around the Christkindlesmarkt booths and those shuffling through the crowd, all less than attentive to the mock outrage in Kelly's voice, cooled Emmie's irritation. Not even the owner of the jewelry booth Emmie and Kelly were perusing paid them any attention. But their disinterest didn't change her mind about the dance.

"You're right." She considered a gingerbread charm bracelet as a possible gift for her mother. "No one cares whether I go to the ball or not. So, you shouldn't either."

Kelly held up a finger. "*Au contraire*, my friend. I didn't say no one cares. I said everyone is in their own little shopping world in the square. Picking out table runners and potholders, ornaments and earrings, all adorned with happy gingerbread men. I, however, care whether you go to the ball tomorrow, and I know at least one other person has very strong feelings on the matter."

"I should never have told you. I know how you get." Emmie turned her attention to the owner of the stall. "I'll take this one please."

She handed the bracelet and a twenty to the woman, who moved over to her register to wrap up the gift. When she returned with Emmie's change and the little plastic bag holding the bracelet, Emmie moved on to the next stall, leaving Kelly no choice but to follow.

"Really?" Kelly cocked her head to the side and pursed her lips. "You think you could have kept something like that from me? Not a chance."

Emmie shrugged. "Maybe not. But it doesn't change anything. I'm not getting into a relationship with someone who will leave in three days' time."

"Who's asking you to?"

"You are." Emmie huffed. "With all this talk about going to the ball. How Ryker will be disappointed if I don't go with him."

"It's a date, Emmie." Kelly rolled her eyes. "Not a proposal. We're not even talking about agreeing to a relationship."

"But..."

"But nothing. You like him, and you have since we were kids. This week has made it perfectly clear those feelings are not going away."

"And last time he left, it devastated me. We were friends

then. What do you think it's going to do this time when he leaves?"

"You know it's different now."

"Whatever. It doesn't matter. I'm still not going."

"Please think about it."

"Fine." With her best friend and Ryker pushing for the same thing, Emmie could get a job as a professional thinker, if there was such a thing.

"I WONDERED if I'd find you here."

Ryker's voice broke through the modicum of peace Emmie had enjoyed since Kelly left to perform her festival coordinator duties. In the silence following her departure, Emmie had moved to a bench by the town tree. Nothing was better than sipping hot cocoa while admiring the sparkling beauty, even if it was covered in gingerbread cookie decorations.

"It's my favorite place during the festival."

"I remember." He took a seat next to her on the bench. "I always favored the gazebo at the park. Less traffic."

Emmie chuckled. "That's because you had someone to share it with. You miss some of the magic when you visit it alone."

"You might be right. I never thought about it. I guess I like the way the town goes all out decorating it, even when it's only used to stage the various contests."

The citrusy scent of his cologne mingled with the cold air and the chocolaty steam from her drink, wrapping a sense of serenity around her shoulders as she breathed them in. Closing her eyes, she welcomed the feeling. Peace fled as the urge to inch closer to the man beside her conjured an image in her mind of them snuggled together in the gazebo he loved so much.

Dispelling the image by opening her eyes, Emmie focused on the tree in front of her and edged a bit farther away from Ryker as inconspicuously as possible.

"I like sitting here during Christkindlesmarkt days of the festival." She attempted corralling her wayward thoughts. "The contests are over, leaving the area closest to the tree fairly empty, but I'm still close enough to watch everyone mingle at the shopping booths."

"It's a great vantage point for a big picture shot of the market," Ryker pointed to an identical bench across from them. "I got a few shots from the other side of the tree before I noticed you sitting here by yourself. I didn't want to disturb you, but once I saw you, I had to come say hi."

"How's it going? Photographing the festival, I mean."

He toyed with the camera in his hands before letting the strap around his neck take the weight. "It's great. I've gotten a lot of really great photos and videos. The town has been great. Very welcoming. So, yeah, it's been great."

"Great?" She cocked her head as she looked at him and squinted. "Your words are toeing the party line, but your tone seems to be arguing against it. What's going on?"

"Nothing, really. I mean, it's all gone smoothly." He glanced her way with a sly smile. "Well, almost all of it's been drama-free. There was this one business, a bakery, that gave me a bit of trouble. The owner was a real piece of work, but I think I'm winning her over. At least, we seem to have put the past behind us so we can be friends again."

With a laugh, Emmie shoved his shoulder. "You make it sound like I was being difficult."

A shrug and innocent smile provided his only response.

"I wasn't difficult, I was ..." She paused to choose the right word. "Okay, I might have been a little difficult. But as you said, that's all in the past, where it belongs. So what's really bothering you?"

He motioned at the expanse of town and people spread out in front of them. "It's all this, I guess."

"I don't follow."

"When I first left for school and then decided to pursue my photography dreams in the Asheville area, I missed New Kuchenbrünn something awful. My parents' move put them closer to me and allowed me to put my hometown out of my mind for the most part."

He stood and meandered to the town tree. When he didn't turn back to her or continue, Emmie joined him. Silence settled around them in contrast to the hubbub of the outdoor market taking place down the street.

Tentatively, he lifted his family ornament off the branch it dangled from and held it in his open palm. He brushed his other hand over the lacquered surface where the Lehmann name was written in white script.

"Coming back," he continued, "didn't feel like a big deal. It was a job like any other. But it's not. New Kuchenbrünn is still home. The people. The traditions. All of it."

"Nostalgia," Emmie suggested. "Memories are powerful."

Ryker shook his head and placed the ornament back on the tree. "Maybe. But I think there's more to it. I've been praying about it, and I feel like maybe God is moving me back this way."

"Really? Can you do that?"

"My parents rented out the house when they moved, instead of selling. The family that's been living there is growing out of it. I could rent it in a few months."

"That's a big decision." Emmie placed a hand on his arm. "I

407

mean, I understand following God's leading. But why would He want you back here?"

"I don't know." He shrugged. "Maybe it has something to do with reconnecting with a certain friend I've ignored for way too long."

A flutter in her middle brought heat to Emmie's cheeks that she didn't want Ryker to see. She scooted to another section of the tree, close enough to converse but angled just enough to keep her cheeks hidden, and fiddled with the ornaments hanging from the branches.

"Pray about it." Emmie tried sounding like he hadn't just loosed a hurricane of emotions inside her. "It has to be God's best for you, without any others factoring in. And until He makes your path clear, don't let the wait keep you from enjoying the rest of the Gingerbread Festival."

Ryker eyed her as if he wanted to say more. She'd sidestepped his mention of renewing their friendship, the hint in his voice that it could be more. All Emmie could offer was an uncomfortable smile, willing him to let it go.

"You're right."

His smirk was too reminiscent of the teasing from childhood. Unease knotted in Emmie's stomach. He was waiting for her to answer his question. Well, he was just going to have to wait. Age had taught her a thing or two. There was no way she was going to march straight into whatever he had planned.

"I do need to leave the festival on a high note. So, what about it? Will you go to the Gingerbread Ball with me?"

Emmie groaned. Of course, he would use this as an opportunity to reiterate his invitation.

"You did promise to consider it." He childishly waggled his eyebrows.

A smile at his antics couldn't be helped, but she had her

reasons for declining. What those were, she couldn't remember as she stared into his puppy dog eyes. But she knew they were valid.

"I don't know."

He took her hands in his. "Please. You missed all the fun of the contests."

"Those are not fun."

"They are for most people." He shrugged. "I can see why you wouldn't think so. But other than handing out the trophies to the winners and naming the Gingerbread Queen, the cursed cookie won't be anywhere in sight. So, you're safe to accompany me. Though we will need to get there early so I can get some pictures."

"I can't go early. I have to close up the bakery."

"You can meet me there."

"I'm a horrible dancer." She was grasping at straws. Truth-filled straws, but it signaled her weakening defenses.

"I don't care. Step on my feet all you want."

"Are you sure about that?"

Still holding her hands in his, he drew her a breath closer, waiting until she looked him in the eyes. "Positive."

"Yes." She hoped she didn't sound as breathless as she felt. "I'll go with you."

Chapter Fifteen

Stunning. It was the only way Ryker could describe Emmie as she walked into the main room of the community center. He lifted his camera and adjusted the zoom. The lighting shimmered across her knee-length navy skirt as each movement left the material swirling around her shapely legs. The fitted lace bodice was perfectly matched in color, with snug sleeves falling right below her elbows.

As a professional photographer, Ryker had seen lace dresses that left little to the imagination. Though Emmie's scalloped neckline had the same see-through effect as the sleeves, it was wide and high, lying modestly at the base of her collar bone, and it was lined below the edge with the same blue material used in the skirt.

She'd forgone her usual ponytail in favor of what he could only describe as a fancy bun resting low against the nape of her neck. A few wavy tendrils of her dishwater blonde hair framed her face, drawing attention to her eyes, which now scanned the room looking for him.

Setting his camera on a small table beside the stage, Ryker

made his way to his date. If Emmie's appearance hadn't already caused a smile, thinking of her as his date would have.

"You look amazing." He took her hand.

"Thank you. You don't look half bad yourself."

He held out a hand to her. "Would you like to dance?"

One corner of her lip tucked between her teeth. She glanced in the direction of the dance floor before attempting a tight smile. "Could we get something to drink first? Maybe talk or something?"

"Sure." Ryker chuckled and nodded toward the tables scattered along the outside edge of the dance floor on one side of the room. "Find a seat somewhere. I'll grab a couple cups of punch and meet you there."

From her vantage point at an otherwise empty table halfway down the length of the room, Emmie watched Ryker retrieve their drinks from the refreshment table. Amazing. He'd nearly rendered her speechless with his compliment.

You don't look half bad was the first thing that came to mind, and if her heels wouldn't puncture the skin, she'd kick herself for returning his compliment with one so flippant. Not only did Ryker not look bad, he was as gorgeous as she'd ever seen him. His pewter gray suit fit as if tailored especially for him, and the midnight blue of his tie against his cobalt blue shirt provided a perfect contrast with his deep brown eyes.

Ryker made it to her without mishap, more than likely a feat she couldn't have accomplished. Too many people lingered in the space around the dance floor. Bobbing and weaving through would have resulted in them or her wearing the drinks.

"Thank you." Emmie took the cup he offered.

"I think the whole town, visitors included, must be here

tonight." Ryker watched couples on the dance floor moving to the upbeat tempo of the current song.

Emmie sipped her punch. "They usually do, I think. Most of the time, I don't attend. So, I'm not the one to judge this year's turnout against previous ones."

"Why do you skip the ball?"

"No one's asked me before. Besides, I don't really enjoy ..."

"Oooh," Kelly cooed as she swept up to the table. "Look at you two in matching colors. Aren't you cute? But why are you sitting around? All the fun is out on the dance floor."

A quick glance at her dress and Ryker's suit confirmed their unintentional twin status. Leave it to Kelly to pick up on it and think their coordination was intended. Like Emmie had ever done that with anyone but her. And only one time, in fifth grade.

Emmie tilted her head toward Ryker while giving her attention to Kelly. "I was telling Ryker I don't really dance very much."

"Sure you do." Kelly smiled sweetly. "I've been in your kitchen enough to know you're always dancing. You dance while you're mixing up stuff, and even when you're doing dishes."

"That's different. Me, alone, doesn't count as dancing."

"If you enjoy it," Ryker said, "why don't you do it more? Or in public?"

Kelly would be making this up to her for a long time. Emmie hoped the unamused look she shot her warned Kelly of her impending doom.

"I don't go out and dance," Emmie said, turning to Ryker, "because I'm not any good at it. I don't know any real dance moves, and I'm not great at anything requiring coordination on even the smallest level."

"How about a slow song? Those don't take much

coordination." Ryker shrugged as he spoke. "If all else fails, you can resort to the generic swaying back and forth to the music that, let's be honest, most people do anyway. You're not alone. Most people don't know real dance moves, no matter what those weekly romance TV movies my mom watches say."

"I'd still step on your toes. Maybe even break a couple. I excel at klutziness."

"I'm fine with that."

Kelly's gaze went from Emmie to Ryker and back again. A triumphant smile told Emmie she'd lost this battle.

"Great." Kelly turned. "I'll go tell the deejay we need a few more slow songs mixed in."

Any hope of saving Ryker's feet from the punishment of dancing with Emmie was dashed as Kelly rushed to the front of the crowded room to speak with the deejay. As soon as the current selection ended, he replaced it with a slower ballad.

Ryker stood beside the table, hand extended in invitation. "May I have this dance?"

Chapter Sixteen

At Ryker's wince, Emmie quickly moved her foot from his. Only dancing the slow songs didn't keep her toe-stomping tally from rising rapidly into double digits. It didn't help that after Kelly's talk with him, the deejay consistently made every third song a slow one. Ryker took full advantage, though Emmie didn't understand why.

He couldn't be so desperate to dance with her as to place himself in such a precarious situation. Yet, every time the lights lowered, he led her to the floor once more. Not one time did he complain, but Emmie saw the discomfort each time her foot connected with his.

"I'm so sorry," she whispered.

"No need." He gave a small shake of his head. "I knew what I was getting into. Besides, I'm made of stronger stuff than that."

The lights brightened as the song ended. Ryker's hand left the small of her back, taking the warmth it gave with it. Dancing with him all evening was better than she could've ever imagined. Well, except for stepping on his toes. Maybe he should have worn steel-toed boots.

Emmie bit back the urge to find Kelly and demand she tell the deejay to only play slow songs for the rest of the night. Instead, she followed Ryker to their table to watch other couples flood the dance floor for a livelier number. They knew the countdown to the ball's end had begun.

The ball officially wrapped up the Gingerbread Festival for another year. No matter how homesick Ryker said he was, his home was now in North Carolina. Tomorrow he'd be gone, and all Emmie would be left with were the memories of their time together. And maybe even a bit of a broken heart. Again.

Kelly stepped to the microphone as the newest set of songs ended. "It's time, ladies and gentlemen."

A buzz worked its way through the room as people made their way to their seats. The presenting of prizes for all the contests and the crowning of the Gingerbread Queen always preceded the final few songs of the ball.

"Will you please excuse me for a few minutes?" Ryker asked. "I need to get some shots of the awards and coronation."

Emmie nodded before he retrieved his camera from safekeeping. He deposited the bag on their table and moved to the front of the room. As Kelly read each contest category and winner, Emmie applauded with the rest of the crowd. Maybe she needed to rethink her lack of attendance at the ball. Celebrating the fun and accomplishment of her friends was a perfect way to wind up the festivities.

Someone passing by jostled the table, knocking Ryker's camera bag to the floor. The contents slipped from various compartments. At least there weren't any lenses in there, or other expensive items that could break.

Emmie stacked all the business cards together and placed them in a small pocket inside the bag. A handful of receipts took up residence in the next section. Emmie paused. A plane ticket to Switzerland waited, along with a photo shoot itinerary, for its return to the bag.

Switzerland. A photographer would need to excel at his profession to be hired to do a shoot in a foreign country. More than likely, he'd also be in high demand.

Ryker was that kind of photographer. And she'd been toying with the idea of him returning to New Kuchenbrünn, of them moving forward in a relationship. But a man with his passion and skill for photography could never be happy settling down. It would feel like, well, settling. Wouldn't it?

"And now," Kelly's voice intruded on her musings, "for the announcement of this year's Gingerbread Queen. The decision was unanimous, chosen by the planning committee for her tireless dedication to making the festival events a success year after year. Without her contribution, many of the activities we enjoy wouldn't take place. Let's welcome to the stage, our Gingerbread Queen, Emeline Becker!"

Emmie stared at her friend. What? There's no way the committee named her Gingerbread Queen. She didn't even like gingerbread. Shouldn't it be a requirement?

From the stage, Kelly beckoned her forward with a 'what are you waiting for' look. Others in the audience turned to Emmie with applause and smiles. She rose and made her way to the stage. Ryker winked as she neared, before lifting his camera to get photos of her approach.

On stage, Kelly handed Emmie a bouquet of roses and turned her to face the audience before placing the tiara on her head. Cheers went up from the crowd. Kelly's hand on her back propelled her toward the microphone.

"Go on." Kelly prompted quietly. "Say a few words."

"I'm stunned." It was the first thing that came to mind. "And I'm honored. Thank you."

Emmie adjusted the bouquet in her hands and looked at her friends and neighbors scattered throughout the building. No, she might not like gingerbread, but she loved these people, kneaded so thoroughly into the recipe of her life.

"But as nice as it is being named the Gingerbread Queen," she continued, "the real honor is being able to give back to the people who've been such a big part of my life. God's blessed my family's bakery through the years, and I'm grateful to be able to pass those blessings on in my small way each Gingerbread Festival."

No matter how much she despised gingerbread and complained about baking it nonstop each festival, Emmie realized the truth of her words. The festival and gingerbread were part of her heritage, and she didn't ever want to lose that.

Ryker set his camera aside as she stepped down from the stage and drew her into a tight hug. The strength of his arms around her felt as much like home as New Kuchenbrünn and the Gingerbread Festival. The desire to melt into his embrace was strong, but Switzerland chased it away. Ryker was a home that would never be. She stiffened.

"Congratulations." His breath tickled her ear. "You deserve it."

As quickly as it began, the hug ended. Ryker pulled away, appraising her with a frown. He'd felt the difference. The questions in his eyes would have to remain unanswered. Emmie wasn't ready to deal with his leaving—her loss—at the moment.

"Thank you." She placed a hand on his arm. "I'm not feeling well. I think I'm going to call it a night."

His frown deepened. "I need to get photos of the Gingerbread Queen. Do you feel up to it?"

"No." It was the truth. Emmie only needed to escape, to get some air. "Can we do it tomorrow?"

"Sure. Let me put my camera away, and I'll drive you home."

"No, you stay here. Get those incredible shots the town is waiting for. I can drive myself home. Really. I'll be fine."

Emmie waited only until Ryker's slight nod of acceptance before she went to find Kelly and make her excuses to leave. Though Kelly wasn't happy about it, Emmie couldn't do anything else. Stopping on her way to the exit to accept congratulations from a few of her friends and neighbors, she could feel Ryker watching her. She refused to look back.

With only a few more well-wishers in her path, she inched her way to the door and out into the cool night air. Swallowing a gulp of it sent prickles through her lungs, but at least she didn't feel quite as numb.

Knowing there was only one place that would help her clear her mind, Emmie raced like Cinderella from the ball toward her safe place. The Sugar and Spice kitchen waited to embrace her with familiar warmth as she unlocked the door and let her tears fall.

Chapter Seventeen

"Let me guess." Kelly's voice echoed through the kitchen door before it swung open. "Chocolate chip cookies?"

Emmie shot her friend an impatient look before continuing to scoop the dough onto cookie trays. "What are you doing here?"

"I came to ask you the same thing." Kelly grabbed two mugs and set them on the counter beside Emmie's workspace. After filling them with milk, she plopped down on the stool next to the racks of already cooling cookies. "I went by your house, because I thought you didn't feel well. When you weren't there, I figured you'd come here."

Emmie drummed her fingers on the counter. "You act like it's a big secret that I bake when I'm upset."

"No. But it does beg the question. What's got you baking?" She scooped a cookie off the rack and took a bite. "Good, as always. But back to the point. I know you were surprised with the whole Gingerbread Queen announcement, but it wouldn't have driven you to bake. So, what's up?"

"He wants to come back." Emmie slid another pan into the oven and set the timer.

"Ryker?" Kelly's cookie dropped to the counter. "That's a good thing. Isn't it?"

Emmie pulled a stool opposite Kelly's perch and drew the second mug closer. Knocking her knee on the table leg as she sat, Emmie groaned and rubbed her knee. Kelly grabbed paper towels to sop up the milk that sloshed over the rim of Emmie's mug with the jostle.

"Thanks."

Kelly shrugged. "Now tell me why Ryker coming back isn't a good thing."

"He hinted that I'm a reason why he's considering it."

The teeny-bopper squeal and clapping from Kelly left no doubt she thought it was an amazing reason. Emmie knew better.

"Ryker cannot uproot his life for a chance that we might have something,"

"And why not?"

Emmie rolled her eyes. "Because the man has a career. He's a successful photographer."

"So?"

Emmie finished off her cookie and drained her mug while formulating the most reasonable answer. Only irrefutable logic would ever shake Kelly from her romantic ideal.

"I found a ticket to Switzerland in his bag." She gathered the empty mugs and put them in the dishwasher. "That's the kind of successful Ryker is. He's travel-the-world kind of good."

"Are you afraid he won't want to come back?"

Emmie started packing cooled cookies into containers. "He shouldn't. And I don't want to be the reason he gives all that up. Photography has always been his dream, and it's a lot bigger than chronicling festivals in the small town where he grew up."

"But he can be based anywhere, right?" Kelly sighed. "I mean, he can fly wherever he needs to go and then come back."

"You can't tell me Ryker would have the same job opportunities come his way if he worked from the middle of nowhere, Missouri." Emmie stacked full containers. She would make them tomorrow's special deal. "He needs to be in the city where people can notice him, connect with him."

"Shouldn't that be his choice?"

"Not when he's not thinking clearly."

"Can you honestly tell me, if Ryker chose to move here, you wouldn't want that?"

Emmie looked her friend in the eye. "I. Don't. Want. Ryker. Here."

An uncomfortable clearing of a throat behind her made Emmie's heart drop to her toes. Kelly's face went white. Emmie turned. Ryker stood in the doorway, his brown eyes pools of disappointment.

"I guess it's better I found out now, before I actually made my plans."

The door swung shut with Ryker's retreat.

"What are you waiting for?" Kelly jerked her head toward the door. "Go after the man."

"This isn't a movie. Chasing after the guy doesn't always result in a happy ending." Emmie straightened her shoulders and shook her head. "No. It's better this way."

Kelly's hands splayed in front of her. "Whatever. It's your choice. I'll leave you to it."

Pure stubbornness held Emmie in place as Kelly followed Ryker's exit. Her friend's disappointment hung heavy in the air. It might take time, but Kelly would come to see this was for the best. Until then, Emmie knew her friend would support her, whether she believed in her decision or not.

They were best friends. That's what they did for each

other. It was a good thing too. She would need her friend. While Emmie had to believe letting Ryker go was best, letting the man she fell for all over again walk out of her life forever shredded her heart. And there wasn't enough chocolate chip cookie dough in the world to heal this hurt.

"Wait up!"

Ryker ignored Kelly and increased his stride. Maybe she would get the hint. The hand grasping his wrist a few seconds later dispelled that hope. Unwilling to either pull her along or rudely shake her off, Ryker stopped.

"What do you want, Kelly?"

She held up a finger as she panted for breath. The wait chafed like sandpaper against his already raw nerves. Against every lesson his mother ever taught him about being polite, Ryker wanted to walk away. Kelly took in a final deep breath.

"She didn't mean it. You know that, right?"

Ryker shoved the hair out of his eyes. "No. I don't know that. And neither do you. Leave this one alone, Kelly."

"But Emmie ..."

"Is an adult, fully capable of finding me herself if there's been a misunderstanding." Ryker made a show of looking around. "I don't see her. So I'm going to assume. She. Doesn't. Want. Me. Here. Now, if you'll excuse me."

"You still have to get the Gingerbread Queen photographs done. You'll have to see her."

The smugness in her voice threatened to push Ryker past his limits. Instead of letting it goad him, he forced a hollow smile. "I'll deal with that when the time comes. I've given you the specs for the shoot's set up. Evening is best. Let Emmie know to be there in her ball gown and tiara at six. If she's not there, it's not on me."

"That's all there is to it?"

"Yes, Kelly. That's all there is to it. Text me if something changes. Good night."

Ryker strode away before Kelly could comment. It pushed the boundaries of politeness, but pressure was building inside. And like an overfilled jelly doughnut ready to explode its contents on the first unsuspecting person to take a bite, any further probing from Kelly would result in an unwelcome mess rather than the sweet treat of reconciliation she hoped for.

Great. He'd been spending too much time with Emmie. Now he was thinking in baking metaphors. There had to be a way to purge them from his mind, along with the woman who inspired them. But was that what he really wanted?

Nearing the town's Christmas tree, and without any indication of Kelly following to renew their conversation, Ryker dropped onto one of the benches flanking the evergreen. While the festival was officially over, the lights of the tree would remain lit through Christmas and only go off on December thirty-first, right before the clock ushered in a new year for the town.

"Some things never change." He spoke quietly, though no one was around to hear.

It took a few years of being away before Ryker understood the part each tradition played in sealing New Kuchenbrünn as home in his heart. The first Christmas away, he'd sought out other town festivals and holiday celebrations, especially those of German heritage. They'd helped soothe the ache for home, but none were able to heal it completely. He never understood why.

Coming back, the reason was clear. While those other

towns held elements of the home he loved, they didn't share the same traditions. There wasn't a town tree filled with gingerbread ornaments carrying the names of each family that filled his childhood memories. There wasn't a festival celebrating the spicy cookie with an outrageous array of fun and games.

None of those other places had Emmie Becker. Though, until he came back to town, his image of her was shrouded in the fog of memory. It had taken less than a second in her presence to blow away the mist and reveal the woman she'd become. Now, he desired more than their renewed friendship.

And she wanted nothing to do with him.

"What did I do?"

He stared at the tree, sparkling against the night sky as if it could extol the wisdom he sought. It couldn't. But Ryker knew where to find it.

"God." He raised his eyes and sighed. "I don't know what to do. I felt like You were calling me back to New Kuchenbrünn, bringing me home."

He rose and found his family ornament on the tree. After too many years' hiatuses, the gingerbread man was back where it belonged, nestled in the branches next to Emmie's, where it had hung through all those Christmases from his childhood.

"But that isn't what Emmie wants. Is it Lord? She's made it clear she doesn't want me to return, and I have no idea why or how to fix it. But if Emmie wants me to leave, was I wrong about moving here after all?"

Ryker brushed his hands over several branch tips, causing the gingerbread men on them to dance and sway in a bouncy rhythm. He smiled as the memories tucked away in the branches flowed from their movement, a town full of families and events that made New Kuchenbrünn home even after he'd been gone for fifteen years.

His path appeared. God's answer came with startling clarity. There was only one thing left to do. Things had to be made right with Emmie, and it had to happen before he boarded his plane to leave.

Chapter Eighteen

" I 'm here." Emmie stalked up to the gazebo. "And I'm cold. Let's get this over with."

Ryker's mouth bent in an unamused frown. "I don't think you appreciate it yet, but you will. Go stand over by that row of bushes."

The blank stare she gave as she followed his directions told Ryker all he needed to know. Emmie's guard was up, and she would do anything to be finished with him and get on with her day.

"Ready?"

Emmie nodded. Ryker flipped a switch in the post of the gazebo. The bushes beside and across from Emmie lit up with hundreds of twinkling white lights leading to the two small, light-draped evergreen trees flanking the gazebo steps. A glistening white star perched on the top of each one. The arched entries around the structure were framed to match.

A gasp escaped Emmie's lips. The scene was almost as breathtaking as she was, but Ryker wasn't about to admit that. Not with softness easing into her expression.

"Now," he said with a smile lifting his tone, "you appreciate it. I can see it all over your face."

"It's gorgeous. Peaceful and magical and inspiring, all rolled into one."

And if Emmie wasn't putting her walls back up, it was already working its magic. He wouldn't push his luck though. Ready-for-battle Emmie could re-emerge at any moment.

"And perfect for the photoshoot." He stood beside her. "I need you to stand in the gazebo next to the table of gingerbread. Keep your coat on until I get set up. Then we'll switch it out for your tiara."

Emmie complied. Within minutes, Ryker managed to capture beautiful images. One more would check every requested shot off his list.

"Last shot," he announced. "I need you to hold the plate of cookies and take a bite out of one."

"Not going to happen."

"But you're the Gingerbread Queen."

"You know I hate the stuff. Haven't had any since, well, a long time ago."

He grinned. A glare was the reward for his insolence. It didn't curb his good humor at all.

"Since the incident? Ever think maybe your dislike should have more to do with the fact that you gorged yourself on cookies, and not gingerbread itself? It's like you have a vendetta against them for what they did."

"Nope." Emmie shook her head. "I think I just don't like them."

Ryker lifted his chin. "It's been nearly twenty years. I can't believe you haven't tried another gingerbread, even once. It's time to give up the grudge."

"Nope."

"Please." He let the camera hang from its strap so he could

steeple his hands. "For me? I need this shot. The quicker I get it, the quicker we can warm up."

Emmie eyed the plate of cookies with a grimace. Ryker fought his smile this time. The battle would be lost if she saw him grin. He waited patiently for her to comply.

"One little bite," he encouraged.

"Fine." She snatched one from the plate. "But you'd better get the shot on the first try."

"Then, move slowly. It's not going to feel natural, but do it anyway. I won't miss the shot that way."

"If I'd known accepting the Gingerbread Queen title meant eating the stuff, I would have renounced the throne." With one last glare directed at him, Emmie forced a smile as she raised her nemesis to her mouth.

Ryker took a flurry of photos knowing there would be a few good ones. Finally, she took the requested bite. At the slight rise of her brows, Ryker couldn't help commenting.

"Not as bad as you thought?"

She chewed. Took another bite. He could see her mind working.

"I'd forgotten how the sweet scent gives way to the mildly sweet spiciness when you take a bite. It's unique and traditional at the same time." She placed the remaining cookie on the plate. "Gingerbread is nostalgia baked into a cookie. While I appreciate the sentiment more than ever, I'm still not sure it will ever be a personal favorite."

He joined her on the far side of the gazebo where he stored his camera in its case and grabbed her coat from the bench next to it. Holding it out, he waited for her to slip her arms inside before taking a seat.

"Come sit by me." He slipped on a pair of gloves.

Emmie buttoned her coat. "It's cold out here."

"We need to talk."

"There's nothing to talk about." The cautious ease that permeated the photo shoot fled. Emmie lifted her chin. "Besides, it's freezing."

"I come prepared." He lifted a canteen. "Salted caramel hot chocolate to warm you. Please?"

"Fine."

He retrieved two disposable travel cups from his bag and rejoined her on the bench. Though the need to talk hounded him, Ryker kept his demeanor carefree as he poured the piping hot liquid into the cups. If anything could tempt Emmie to relax enough to converse with him about the future, it would be her favorite holiday drink.

"There's still nothing to discuss." She pursed her lips.

He added lids to the cups and passed one to her. She wrapped her hands around the warm cup before bringing it close to her face. The escaping steam drew a sigh from Emmie. If only the cocoa could chase away the cold currently permeating their relationship.

Ryker reached into a duffle sitting with the rest of his equipment and pulled out a small quilt. The temperature had to affect Emmie more. She was wearing a formal gown, after all. He draped the quilt over her legs before retrieving a second for himself.

"Better?"

Emmie shrugged.

If he waited for her to become chatty, they'd be here all night. Ryker's lips twisted to the side. The Gingerbread Queen was a stubborn one. He might as well dive in.

"I'm moving to New Kuchenbrünn,"

Emmie choked on her sip of cocoa. After a few sputtering coughs, she cleared her throat. "I know you heard me last night."

"That's why I'm giving you warning."

"It's not going to work."

His brows dipped low as he frowned. "I don't follow."

"You can't move back here, hoping I'll change my mind."

"Emmie." He waited for her to look at him. "I'm not coming back here for you, though I would like us to be friends if possible."

"Really?" All her doubt poured into that single word until it was filled to overflowing.

"I'm not going to lie. Hearing you say that last night cut deep. Made me question whether I was heading in the right direction."

"What changed?"

"God. He reminded me that He wasn't asking me to move to win you." He clasped his hands and rested his arms on his knees. "There's a whole town here that I love, that I've missed through the years. He's being gracious enough to bring me home."

"What about Switzerland?"

He leaned against the back of the bench. "Switzerland?"

A sigh seeped out of her. "I saw the ticket in your case. I know you have a job in Switzerland."

"My moving here doesn't change my ability to go to Switzerland."

"But you'll miss future possibilities if you aren't in the city."

Ryker shook his head. "If I do, then they aren't the right opportunities for me."

Emmie slipped the blanket further under her legs. The way she tucked her bottom lip between her teeth was enough to keep him quiet. She was processing. When the silence continued, Ryker chose to gently prod her forward.

"What is this really about, Emmie?"

She picked at a loose thread on the blanket. "Regret. It's easy to say they're just the wrong opportunities when you still have plenty knocking on your door. But when it gets hard—when people want a photographer they don't have to chase to the middle of nowhere—what happens then?"

The twinkling lights made the tears pooling in her eyes sparkle. It would have been beautiful if it wasn't so sad. If only he knew the right words to ease her hurt.

"You leave." Her voice was a whisper. "You broke my heart once when this town wasn't enough. When I wasn't enough. Even if all we ever are is friends, I can't face another heartbreak when you decide you want more again."

Lord, help me get this right. Ryker nodded toward the plate of cookies on the table. "It's amazing what we can miss when we're stuck in what happened in the past."

"Ryker," she said in a hushed tone, "you know that isn't all this is about."

"I know." He took her hand in his as if touch could convey how much her words affected him. "And I'm sorry. I never meant to hurt you, but that is the past. I wish I could promise I'll never leave again. I can't. But I will make one promise. I will not leave you again without a proper good-bye. I will not break your heart like that again."

It wasn't good enough. The sad smile shaping Emmie's lips rooted that thought in his mind. At this point, he might as well go all in.

"I know I said I wasn't coming back for you." He stood and faced her. "But you have to know that, whether you're my reason for returning or not, it doesn't change the fact that I most definitely want you in my life. And if I ever do have to leave again, I'd want you by my side when I did."

HER MOUTH OPENED, but nothing came out. What could follow an announcement like that? Ryker paced in front of her. Still, she had no response other than shock. It wasn't a marriage proposal, but it was more than an "I think I'd like to see you again."

"I don't know if you're there yet." Ryker captured her attention again. "Maybe you meant exactly what you said last night. Or maybe that was your hurt talking, a way to protect yourself from a repeat of the past. But I know we've both felt this attraction between us. Is there any way we can forget the past and give our future a chance?"

Emmie closed her eyes and breathed deep, clearing her throat when the cold hit her lungs. She'd dreamed of a future for them when she was a teen. Even since his return, she'd toyed with the idea every time their interactions turned flirtatious. Now it was happening, and she couldn't immediately say yes.

Fear worked its tendrils around her heart. He admitted the hurt he unknowingly caused. Forgiveness was one thing. Could she give more? What they felt for each other now was already deeper than her teen attraction. And it promised something more real and better than the best fairy tale. If she lost that, would it shatter her heart completely?

Emmie could walk away. But hope planted a thought and kept her rooted. She might feel a deeper pain if it ended, but what if she didn't give them a chance? She could be giving up a beautiful gift from God. She might miss the sweetest love, built on a foundation of friendship.

"I'd like that," she answered quietly.

His smile was slow in coming as he realized what she said. "Really?"

She nodded. "It's funny. I never thought anything good could come out of the Gingerbread Festival."

"The Gingerbread Festival has always been a winner in my book. But this year, it outdid itself." Ryker took her hands and pulled her up from the bench. "It brought me here and reminded me where my home is. And I think I've even fallen in love," he grinned, "with gingerbread."

"Seriously?" Emmie's laugh rang out around them. Ryker pulled her close.

"But I know," he whispered before silencing her laughter with a tender kiss, "I've fallen in love with you."

About the Author

Heather Greer is a preacher's kid and pastor's wife who loves using her passion for reading and writing to encourage others in their faith. She has been a finalist for the Selah awards twice. In addition to all things book related, Heather loves baking. Christmas baking is her favorite, and each year, she makes dozens of treats to pass on to her family and friends in southern Illinois. And while it isn't her favorite, she's even been known to add gingerbread people to her cookie trays.

More Novella Collections from Scrivenings Press

Sharktooth Island

Trouble in Pleasant Valley

Book Three

A fabled island that no one dares to tame.

This collection contains four novellas:

Book 1 - Out of the Storm (1830) by Susan Page Davis

Laura Bryant sails with her father and his three-man crew on his small coastal trading schooner. After a short stay in Jamaica, where she meets Alex Dryden, an officer on another ship, the Bryants set out for their home in New England.

In a storm, they are blown off course east of Savannah, Georgia, to a foreboding island. Captain Bryant tells his daughter he's heard tales of that isle. It's impossible to land on, though it looks green and inviting from a distance. It has no harbor but is surrounded by dangerous rocks and cliffs.

Pirates outrun the storm and decide to bury a cache of treasure on this island and return for it later. On board is Alex, whom the cutthroats captured in Jamaica and forced to work for them. Alex risks his own life to escape the pirates and tries to help Laura and Captain Bryant outwit them. Beneath the deadly struggle, romance blossoms for Laura.

Book 2 - *A Passage of Chance* (1893) by Linda Fulkerson

Orphaned at a young age, Melody Lampert longs to escape the loveless home of the grandmother who begrudgingly raised her. Stripped of her inheritance due to her grandmother's resentments, Melody discovers her name remains on the deed of one property—an obscure island off the Georgia coast that she shares with her cousin. But when he learns the island may contain a hidden pirate treasure, he's determined to cheat her out of her share.

Ship's mechanic Padric Murphy made a vow to his dying father— break the curse that has plagued their family for generations. To do so, he must return what was taken from Sharktooth Island decades earlier—a pair of rare gold pieces. His opportunity to right the wrong arrives when his new employer sets sail to explore the island.

After a series of unexplainable mishaps occur, endangering Padric and his boss's beautiful cousin Melody, he fears his chance of breaking the curse may be ruined. But is the island's greed thwarting his plans? Or the greed of someone else?

Book 3 - *Island Mayhem* (1937) by Elena Hill

Louise Krause stopped piloting to pursue nursing, but when money got too tight she was forced to give up her dreams and start ferrying around a playboy who managed to excel during the Great Depression. When a routine aerial tour turns south, Louise is unable to save the plane.

After crash landing, the cocky pilot is stranded. She longs to escape the uninhabited island, but her makeshift raft sinks, and she and her companions are in even worse trouble. Can Louise learn to trust the others in order to survive, or will the island's curse and potential sabotage lead to her demise?

Book 4 - *After the Storm* (*present day*) by Deborah Sprinkle

Mercedes Baxter inherited two passions from her father—a love for Sharktooth Island, a spit of land in the middle of the ocean left to her in his will, and a dedication to the study of the flora and fauna on and around its rocky landscape.

For the last five years, since graduating from college, Mercy led a peaceful, simple life on the island with only her cat, Hawkeye, for company. Through grant money she obtained from a conservancy in Savannah, she could live on her island while studying and writing about the plants and animals there. Life was perfect.

But when a hurricane hits the island, Mercy's life changes for good. Her high school sweetheart, Liam Stewart, shows up to help her with repairs, and ignites the flame that has never quite died away. And if that's not enough, while assessing the damage to the island, they make a discovery that puts both their lives in danger.

∾

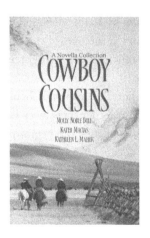

Cowboy Cousins

Saddle Up ... for the fastest reading ride of your life as three cowboys become cattlemen.

This novella collection includes:

Lucy and the Lawman by Molly Noble Bull: While on a business trip to Colorado in 1890, Sheriff Caleb Caldwell stops to inform Miss Lucy Gordan and her widowed mother of property they inherited in Texas, land coveted by a rich and powerful man—willing to do anything to get his hands on what is rightfully theirs, and Caleb feels obligated to protect them. However, he cannot reveal his attraction for Lucy. To do so would mean disaster for all of them.

The Meddlesome Maverick by Kathleen L. Maher: A new job as a bronco buster on a Lincoln, Nebraska ranch offers Boyd Hastings a fresh start. Cured of romance after a kiss-and-tell flirt falsely accused him, he must flee his hometown and cousins who have been like brothers. Banjo picking for a music show would lure him to the big city, but an opinionated tomboy with a heart of gold makes grand plans for him. Can he trust a meddlesome maverick to steer him true, or will she lead him into a briar patch of trouble?

A Panhandle Sunrise by Kathi Macias: Thirty-one year old Jake Matthews, newly appointed foreman of the Double Bar-J Ranch, is deeply attracted to the ranch owner's daughter, Anabelle, but he can't work up the nerve to approach her father, Jasper Floyd, and ask for permission to court her. But when tall, handsome, longtime Jasper-family friend, Clint Jordan, gets hired on, it seems Clint doesn't have the same insecurities and begins pursuing Anabelle immediately. Jake now accepts that his dreams of a life with Anabelle are hopeless—until a near life-and-death situation changes everything.

≈

Candy Cane Wishes and Saltwater Dreams

A collection of Christmas beach romances
by five multi-published authors.

***Mistletoe Make-believe* by Amy Anguish** – Charlie Hill's family thinks his daughter Hailey needs a mom–to the point they won't get off his back until he finds her one. Desperate to be free from their nagging, he asks a stranger to pretend she's his girlfriend during the holidays. When romance author Samantha Arwine takes a working vacation to St. Simon's Island over Christmas, she never dreamed she'd be involved in a real-life romance. Are the sparks between her and Charlie real? Or is her imagination over-acting ... again?

***A Hatteras Surprise* by Hope Toler Dougherty** –Ginny Stowe spent years tending a childhood hurt that dictated her college study and work. Can time with an island visitor with ties to her past heal lingering wounds and lead her toward a happy Christmas ... and more? Ben Daniels intends to hire a new branch manager for a Hatteras Island bank, then hurry back to his promotion and Christmas in Charlotte. Spending time with a beautiful local, however, might force him to adjust his sails.

***A Pennie for Your Thoughts* by Linda Fulkerson** –When the Lakeshore Homeowner's Association threatens to condemn the cabin Pennie Vaughn inherited from her foster mother, her only hope of funding the needed repairs lies in winning a travel blog contest. Trouble is, Pennie never goes anywhere. Should she use the all-expenses paid Hawaiian vacation offered to her by her ex-fiancé? The trip that would have been their honeymoon?

***Mr. Sandman* by Regina Rudd Merrick** – Events manager Taylor Fordham's happily-ever-after was snatched from her, and she's saying no to romance and Christmas. When she meets two new friends—the cute new chef at Pilot Oaks and a contributor on a sci-fi fan fiction website who enjoys debate—her resolve begins to waver. Just when she thinks she can loosen her grip on thoughts of love, a crisis pulls her back. There's no way she's going to risk her heart again.

***Coastal Christmas* by Shannon Taylor Vannatter** – Lark Pendleton is banking on a high-society wedding to make her grandparent's inn at Surfside Beach, Texas the venue to attract buyers. Tasked with sprucing up the inn, she hires Jace Wilder, whose heart she once broke. When the bride and groom turn out to be Lark's high school nemesis and ex-boyfriend, she and Jace embark on a pretend romance to save the wedding. But when real feelings emerge, can they overcome past hurts?

∾

Stay up-to-date on your favorite books and authors with our free e-newsletters.

ScriveningsPress.com

CPSIA information can be obtained
at www.ICGtesting.com
Printed in the USA
LVHW020101090922
727829LV00002B/4